A CHAMPAGNE
Christmas

JENNIE LUCAS
CAROLE MORTIMER
CATHERINE SPENCER

D0767707

MILLS &
BOON

Mills & Boon, an imprint of Harlequin (UK) Limited, Eton House, 18-24 Paradise Road, Richmond, Surrey TW9 1SR

A CHAMPAGNE CHRISTMAS
© Harlequin Enterprises II B.V./S.à.r.l 2013

The Christmas Love-Child © Jennie Lucas 2009
The Christmas Night Miracle © Carole Mortimer 2006
The Italian Billionaire's Christmas Miracle
© Catherine Spencer 2007

ISBN: 978 0 263 91041 4

010-1113

Harlequin (UK) policy is to use papers that are natural, renewable and recyclable products and made from wood grown in sustainable forests. The logging and manufacturing processes conform to the legal environmental regulations of the country of origin.

Printed and bound in Spain
by Blackprint CPI, Barcelona

THE CHRISTMAS LOVE-CHILD

JENNIE LUCAS

Jennie Lucas grew up dreaming about faraway lands. At fifteen, hungry for experience beyond the borders of her small Idaho City, she went to a Connecticut boarding school on scholarship. She took her first solo trip to Europe at sixteen, then put off college and travelled around the US, supporting herself with jobs as diverse as petrol-station cashier and newspaper advertising assistant. At twenty-two she met the man who would be her husband. After their marriage she graduated from Kent State with a degree in English. Seven years after she started writing she got the magical call from London that turned her into a published author.

Since then life has been hectic, with a new writing career, a sexy husband and two small children, but she's having a wonderful (albeit sleepless) time. She loves immersing herself in dramatic, glamorous, passionate stories. Maybe she can't physically travel to Morocco or Spain right now, but for a few hours a day, while her children are sleeping, she can be there in her books. Jennie loves to hear from her readers. You can visit her website at www.jennielucas.com, or drop her a note at jennie@jennielucas.com.

CHAPTER ONE

JUST when Grace Cannon thought her day couldn't get any worse, she came up from the Tube carrying £1,000 worth of lingerie for her boss's fiancée and got splashed in the face by a passing Rolls-Royce.

Mid-December in London was frosty in the violet twilight. The rain had turned to sleet, but the sidewalks in Knightsbridge were still packed with shoppers. The icy spray of gutter water hit Grace's body like a slap. She stumbled and fell down, her hip hitting the pavement as the shopping bag tumbled into the street. She cried out, holding up her hands to protect her face from the endless crush of feet pushing forward.

"Get back. Get back, damn you."

A tall, dark stranger pushed apart the crowds with his broad arms, giving Grace space to breathe. He towered over her on the sidewalk, black-haired and broad-shouldered in an expensive black cashmere coat.

He turned to face her.

Electric gray eyes stood out sharply against his olive-hued skin. Every inch of him whispered money and power, from his Italian shoes to the muscular shape beneath his black coat and gray pin-striped suit. His lush masculine beauty was like none she'd ever seen before. He had chiseled cheekbones, a strong jawline and a Roman profile. Her gaze fell unwillingly to his mouth, to the sensual lips that curved as he looked down at her.

A bright halo of sunlit clouds silhouetted his black hair as he extended his hand.

"Come."

Dazzled, Grace reached up and placed her hand in his far-larger one. As the handsome stranger pulled her to her feet, she felt a current run through her body more startling than the icy water that had splashed her.

"Thank you," she whispered.

Then she recognized him and literally lost her breath. *Prince Maksim Rostov.*

Her throat closed.

She looked again. There could be no mistake.

Prince Maksim Rostov was the man who had saved her.

The lavishly wealthy prince was the most famous Russian billionaire in a city that was full of them. He was so ruthless in his business and personal life he made Grace's boss look like a saint in comparison. For the past two months, since the prince had broken up with his famous fiancée, he'd been photographed with a new woman every night.

Prince Maksim Rostov. Her boss's main rival. His worst enemy.

And that had been *before* last month, when Alan had stolen both the man's fiancée and his merger!

"Forgive me." The prince's cool gray eyes looked

down at her gravely, searing through her like a laser. "It was my car that splashed you. My driver should have been more careful."

"That's…all right," Grace managed to say, utterly conscious of his larger hand still closed over her own. A few minutes before, she'd been icy cold. But her body was rapidly thawing.

Warming.

Boiling.

She tried to pull away. She shouldn't let him touch her. She shouldn't even let him *talk* to her. She was two blocks away from the Knightsbridge town house she shared with her boss. If Alan ever found out that his most trusted secretary had been speaking in private with Prince Maksim, he'd never forgive her. And Grace desperately needed Alan in a good mood, tonight of all nights!

But even knowing this, she found herself unable to pull her hand from the prince's grasp. He was like a rugged, brutal, smooth old-style movie star. Like Rudolph Valentino from the 1920s, seducing women ruthlessly in a savage world of blood and sand. Like a dark angel, sent to lure innocent, helpless virgins to their destruction!

His grip tightened over hers, sending little sizzling currents up her arm, warming her beneath her wet coat.

"I will take you home."

Her teeth chattered. "I…" She shook her head. "No. It's really not necessary."

Prince Maksim pulled her close. He stroked the length of her arm, languorously brushing excess water from her coat sleeve. Feeling his hand move over her clothed body, she suddenly felt so hot she might as well have been lying naked on a California beach. Her skin burned where he touched, as if whipped by a fierce Santa Ana wind.

"I insist."

Beads of sweat formed between her breasts. "No, really," she managed. "I live close. It won't take me long to walk."

He looked down at her, a smile tracing his cruel, sensual mouth. "But I want to take you."

And still he held her hand. Her mouth went dry. Even Alan, the boss she'd loved with hopeless yearning for two years, had never sparked a response like this— never caused her nerve endings to jumble with such an intensity of feeling. Even before he'd taken a new fiancée and asked Grace to buy his Christmas gift...

The lingerie!

Grace gasped, twisting her head to the right and left.

With a little cry, she saw the Leighton bag get nailed by a swerving black cab in the road, causing the embossed lavender box inside it to tumble into the bumper-to-bumper traffic. "Oh, no!"

Ripping away from the prince's grasp, Grace pushed through the tourists to the edge of the sidewalk, looking both ways on the street and preparing to duck between the cars, double-decker buses and black cabs.

But Prince Maksim blocked her with one strong arm in front of her chest.

"Are you suicidal?" His English was perfect, with an accent she couldn't quite place. A little bit British, a bit American, with a slight inflection of something more exotic. He glanced out at the busy road. "You'd risk your life for that blue box?"

"That box," she snapped, "is my boss's Christmas gift for his new fiancée. Silk Leighton lingerie. I can't go back without it!"

"Your boss isn't worth dying for."

"My boss is Alan Barrington!"

Glaring at him, Grace waited for a reaction when he realized she worked for his enemy, his rival in the gas and oil industry, who'd not only just stolen his merger with Exemplary Oil PLC but had stolen his fiancée, the beautiful, tempestuous Lady Francesca in the bargain!

Prince Maksim's handsome face was utterly impassive. She had no idea what he was thinking. A marked difference from Alan, Grace thought. Her flirtatious boss's thoughts were always instantly expressed, either by flippant words or the expression on his good-looking face.

But the image of her boss's toothy smile dissipated instantly from her mind as the dark Russian prince reached out his hand to lift her chin, forcing her eyes to meet his. "Your boss is truly not worthy of your sacrifice."

She licked her lips nervously. "Aren't you w-wishing you'd let me run into traffic now, Your Highness?"

Prince Maksim arrogantly smiled down at her.

"As tempting as it is to cause him staffing problems, I'm afraid I cannot allow you to cover the street with your blood." He gently stroked her hair from her face. "Call me old-fashioned."

He knew she worked for his enemy, so why was he still being courteous? Why wasn't he calling her names or wishing her to the devil? Although, he would have an easy time luring any woman anywhere, she thought. Even to the depths of hell itself.

Frightened by all the new sensations running through her at his touch, she pulled back. "I'll take my chances with the traffic."

"You'll get new lingerie."

"New lingerie?" Safely out of his reach, she regained her equilibrium enough to give an incredulous, scornful laugh. "Right! New lingerie. Maybe in your world Leighton clothes are disposable as baby wipes, but—"

"I will pay for it." He gave her a level look from his steel-gray eyes. "Of course."

If it had been any other person on the planet, she would have accepted gratefully. But not this man. She couldn't accept the help of her boss's worst enemy.

Could she?

As if in slow motion, she saw a red double-decker bus crush the lavender-blue box into a big greasy puddle in the middle of the street.

Alan would be furious if she went home tonight with the expensive charge on his credit card but no lingerie. Alan was completely unforgiving of others' mistakes when they caused him problems. For years he'd hated Prince Maksim, the rival who'd beaten him over and over again. With Cali-West Energy Corporation's stock prices falling, the stockholders had begun to call for Alan's replacement as CEO.

That was before Alan met Lady Francesca Danvers at a charity ball six weeks ago. Their whirlwind romance had gained him the support of her father, the Earl of Hainesworth, who was chair of Exemplary's board of trustees. The deal had changed from a merger of British and Russian energy giants to a British-American one. For weeks now Alan had gleefully recounted to Grace how he'd finally beaten his rival.

Grace hadn't particularly enjoyed his gloating, since it inevitably involved details of how Alan was luring the beautiful, feisty, redheaded Lady Francesca into his bed.

What if Alan was so furious about the ruined lingerie, he demanded Grace pay the bill? What if instead of giving her the advance she so desperately needed, he docked her pay?

She swore under her breath.

"Do not refuse my help, Miss Cannon," Prince Maksim said evenly. "That would be stubborn and foolish."

"Well, Stubborn and Foolish are my middle names!" Grace snapped, furious at herself.

She could have stayed in L.A. and made sure her mother's mortgage was paid each month—but no. She'd been too stubbornly and foolishly infatuated with her boss. *Pathetic,* she thought in disgust. There surely had to be some kind of self-help program for women like her, pathetically in love with a boss who believed her to have no feelings—like an animatronic robot!

"Stubborn and Foolish, Miss Cannon?" Maksim's lips curved. "Clearly American baby-name trends have changed over the years."

"My middle name is actually Diana." Narrowing her eyes, she looked up at Prince Maksim. "But you already know that, don't you? How do you already know my last name?"

"You told me you work for Barrington." He lifted a

dark eyebrow. "Don't you think I know the name of his most trusted secretary?"

Prince Maksim Rostov knew her name.

The fact made her feel warm all over. Made her feel…important.

Until a new, chilling suspicion went down her spine.

He knew her name.

He knew she worked for Alan.

And she was supposed to believe they'd just randomly met on the street two blocks from her home?

Grace was distracted and was nearly knocked over by two heavy tourists decked in cameras, Harrods bags and Santa hats, but she steadied herself to glare at him. "So you'll understand why, as his most trusted secretary, I can't accept any favors from you."

Prince Maksim gave her an easy smile.

"Barrington has nothing to do with this. Replacing the lingerie is repaying a personal debt to you." His smile spread into a carelessly wicked grin that she felt down to her toes. "I can hardly remain indebted to my enemy."

She swallowed, hardly able to collect her thoughts beneath the intensity of his gaze. "I wouldn't say I'm exactly your enemy…"

"Then there is no problem."

"But…"

He enfolded her hand back in his own. The warmth of his naked palm against hers was more erotic than she'd ever thought holding a hand could be. After so many years of useless pining over her boss, this was the most physically intimate she'd been with any man since…since…

Since that brief moment after the Halloween party

when Alan had drunkenly taken her in his arms and given her a big wet kiss before he'd collapsed in a drunken stupor on the office couch.

That sad event had been her first—and only—kiss. In school she'd been too focused on her studies to date anyone. After her father had died and she'd dropped out of college, she'd been too grief-stricken. Then she'd been too busy as a temp in downtown L.A., working to take care of her heartbroken mother and younger brothers.

Grace had become a twenty-five-year-old virgin.

A freak of nature.

And a million miles away from Prince Maksim Rostov's league!

But his car had splashed her, she argued with herself. He'd caused her to drop the lingerie. Wouldn't it be fair to allow him to replace it, when the alternative could mean her ruin?

Tempted, she licked her lips nervously. The sensation of his hand against her own caused a swirling in the tender center of her palm that sent awareness prickling up to the flesh of her ear, tightening her nipples and making her breasts feel strangely heavy. She felt his gaze trace her lips. Her cheeks went hot and her mouth went dry. Every breath she took, every rise and fall of her lungs, became more shallow.

"It is cold," he said. "My car is waiting."

"But, but Leighton clothes are expensive," she stammered, floundering. "They're so expensive they make Hermès and Louis Vuitton look like a bargain-basement fire sale."

He lifted his dark eyebrows.

"I think I can handle the expense," he said dryly. Signaling with one hand, he put the other against the small of her back, guiding her gently toward the curb of a side street where she saw a black Rolls-Royce limousine.

She felt his hand on her back and shook all over. It was that touch which finally forced her surrender.

Looking back at him, she whispered, "Alan must never know."

His lips trembled on the brink of a smile. "Agreed."

The shock waves from his hand on her lower back continued to sizzle up her arms and down her legs as she breathed, "Thank you."

"Thank you." His eyes gleamed down at her. "I always enjoy the company of a beautiful woman."

It broke the spell. She started to laugh, snorting through her nose before she covered it with a cough.

Her...beautiful? That was a good joke! She knew she wasn't anything special. And at the moment, wearing no makeup, with a damp old coat over her second-hand skirt suit and her hair tucked back in a soaked blond ponytail, she looked like a half-drowned refugee from an office in a swamp!

So why had a handsome prince dropped out of the sky to help her? Just because his driver had splashed her with water from the street? Did he have that much honor and generosity of Christmas spirit?

Or was it something else?

The dark suspicion returned to her. When she was younger, she'd believed the best of people. But since she'd started working for Alan, she'd seen how devious people could be. Both in business and in love.

Was Prince Maksim hoping to use her against Alan to take back his merger and his marriage?

"I hope you know," she said evenly, "that doing me this favor won't make me discuss Alan or the merger."

He just gave her a darkly assessing smile. "Do you think I need your assistance?"

"Don't you?" she said uncertainly.

They reached the Rolls-Royce limousine purring next to the curb. With a dismissive shake of his head to the driver, the prince opened her door himself.

"Get in."

Standing on the edge of the sidewalk, against the ebb and flow of Christmas shoppers, Grace looked at the open door of the car and hesitated. She wondered suddenly if she was doing a foolish thing, making a deal with the devil.

When she didn't move, he said mockingly, "Surely you're not afraid of me, Miss Cannon?"

Biting her lower lip, she glanced up at his handsome face. She *was* afraid of him. Afraid of his wealth, his power and well-known ruthlessness.

But even more than that, she was afraid of the sensual reaction that overwhelmed her body every time he touched her. Every time he even *looked* at her.

She shook her head uneasily. "No," she lied. "I'm not afraid of you at all."

He held the door wider. "Then get in."

Flurries of sleet swirled around Grace in a sudden gust of wind. Wet tendrils of blond hair whipped against her cheek, sticking to her skin. But she didn't feel the chill. His gray eyes seared through hers, sapping her will.

And she made her choice—which was really no choice at all. She climbed into the back seat of his Rolls-Royce.

He closed the door behind her.

Once released from his basilisk gaze, alone in the back seat, Grace was as suddenly shocked as if she'd just woken up sleepwalking in Buckingham Palace. What was she doing here? It wasn't a dream. She was really in Prince Maksim's limo. She was consorting with the enemy.

But he's not my *enemy,* she thought in confusion as she watched his dark shadow walk around to the other side. *He's Alan's enemy. And what do people say? The enemy of my friend is my enemy? Or is it that the enemy of my enemy is my friend?*

The door opened, and the most handsome, ruthless man in London climbed in beside her with a dark glance that made her feel hot and sweaty all over.

"Why are you being so nice to me?" she asked.

"Am I being nice?"

"If it's to get secrets about my boss—"

"It's Christmas. The season of joy." Festive lights from the nearby shops glinted off his wolflike teeth as he gave her a sharp smile. "And I'm going to give you joy." He turned to his chauffeur. *"Davai."*

The shadowy Rolls-Royce swept away from the curb. And just like that, Prince Maksim Rostov took her away from the drudgery and crowds and cold, and swept Grace up into his lavish world.

CHAPTER TWO

MAKSIM glanced down at the girl's lovely, dazzled blue eyes as his chauffeur drove east through the crowded traffic on Knightsbridge Road towards Mayfair. She'd called him "nice." He repeated the word in his mind as if he were trying to comprehend it.

Nice?

Prince Maksim Ivanovich Rostov had not become powerful by being nice.

His great-grandfather had been nice during his Paris exile, spending money as if he were still Grand Duke with his own fiefdom in St. Petersburg, giving largesse freely to every hard-luck story that walked into his pied-à-terre.

His grandfather had been nice, spending what little remained of the Rostov fortune down to the last penny in London as he waited impatiently for the Russian people to kick out the Soviets and beg him to return.

His father had been nice, hopelessly trying to support his young, sweet American wife by taking increasingly humiliating jobs until he'd finally followed his father's lead of suicide-by-vodka, leaving his gentle wife, eleven-year-old son and baby daughter to fend for themselves in her native Philadelphia.

But Maksim…

He was not nice.

He was selfish. He was ruthless. He took what he wanted. It was how he'd built a billion-dollar fortune out of nothing.

And now…he wanted Grace Cannon.

For the past hour, he'd been waiting for her. His chauffeur had driven back and forth on Brompton Road, waiting to catch the girl as she came up from the Knightsbridge Tube stop on the way home to her basement flat in Barrington's town house.

This young American secretary was the key to everything.

She would help him finally crush Barrington. The man had been a thorn in his side for far too long, and now he'd finally crossed the line by taking both the deal—and the woman—that rightfully belonged to Maksim.

Barrington thought he'd saved himself from ruin by taking Francesca as his fiancée. He'd soon find it was his last mistake. He would get neither the bride nor the merger.

Maksim would destroy him. As he deserved.

And Grace Cannon would help him. Whether she wanted to or not.

Maksim turned to her with a smile. Unfolding a soft cashmere blanket, he draped it over her shivering body.

"Thank you," she said, her teeth still chattering.

"It's my pleasure."

"You're not what I expected," she whispered,

pressing the blanket against her cheek. "You're not like everyone says."

"What do they say?" He carelessly placed his arm on the leather seat behind her. She was still shivering. He moved closer. Even though she was now covered with a blanket, her shivering only increased when he touched her.

"They say…you're a…ruthless playboy," she said haltingly. "That you spend half your time conquering business rivals…and the other half making conquests of women."

He laughed. "They are right." He moved closer, looking down into her face. "That is exactly who I am."

His thigh brushed against hers, and she nearly jumped out of her skin. She scooted away from him as if he'd burned her.

She was skittish. Very skittish.

There were only three possible explanations.

One—she was afraid of him. He dismissed that idea out of hand. She wouldn't have agreed to get in his car if she'd been truly afraid.

Two—she had no experience with men. He dismissed that idea, as well. A twenty-five-year-old virgin? Almost impossible in this day and age. Particularly since she not only worked for Alan Barrington, she lived in his house. He surely had seduced her many times over.

That left only the third possibility. She was ripe for Maksim's conquest.

He slowly looked her over. She wasn't a girl that any man would immediately notice. Compared to fiery bird-of-paradise Francesca, who had bright-red hair, sharp red nails and a vicious red mouth, Grace Cannon was a

drab sparrow, pale and frumpy with barely a word to say
for herself.

And yet…

Now that Maksim really looked at her, he saw that
the girl wasn't nearly as plain as he'd first thought. Her
ill-fitting coat and wet ponytail had made her seem so,
but now he realized his mistake.

The fact that she wore no makeup only revealed the
perfection of her creamy skin. Her eyelashes and
eyebrows were so light as to be invisible, but that proved
the glorious pale gold of her hair came from nature, not
a salon. She wore no lipstick and her teeth hadn't been
bleached to blinding movie-star whiteness, and yet her
tremulous smile was warmer and lovelier than any he'd
seen. She wasn't stick thin as the strange fashion for
women dictated, but her ample curves only made her
more lushly desirable.

He suddenly realized the dowdy secretary was a beauty.

A *secret* beauty, disguising herself away from the
world. Beneath the unattractive clothing and the frumpy,
frizzy hairstyle, her loveliness shone bright as the sun.

She hid her beauty. Why?

"What's wrong?" She frowned up at him suddenly,
furrowing her brow in alarm.

Had she guessed his plan? "What, *solnishka mayo?*"

"You're staring at me."

"You're beautiful," he said simply. "Like sunshine
in winter."

She blushed, biting her tender pink lip as she looked
away. Clutching the luxurious cashmere like a security
blanket against her wet, threadbare coat, she scooted

further away from him on the car's leather seat. With a swallowed sigh, she stared out through the window at the passing Christmas lights beneath the thickly falling sleet. "Don't be ridiculous. I know I'm not pretty."

She didn't know, he realized. She had no idea. She wasn't purposefully hiding her beauty. *She didn't know.*

"You are beautiful, Grace," he said quietly.

At the use of her first name, she gave him a sudden fierce, sharp glance. "Don't waste your flattery on me, Your Highness."

He gave her an easy smile. "Call me Maksim. What makes you think it's flattery?"

"You might be London's most famous playboy, but I'm not that gullible. A few false compliments won't make me blurt out details about the merger with Exemplary Oil. Alan has Lord Hainesworth's support now. You won't be able to win."

So she was intuitive, as well as lovely. He was growing more intrigued by the moment. "I wasn't lying."

"I'm not a total fool. I know I'm not beautiful. There's only one reason you'd say I am."

"And that is?"

"You want me to betray Alan." She lifted her chin. "I won't. I'd die first."

"Loyalty," he said, staring at her with even greater interest. The girl felt something for her boss beyond what he'd expected. Was it possible she was in love with Alan Barrington?

A pity if the little secretary believed herself in love with him, Maksim thought. He'd just been starting to respect her.

Would money be enough to convince Grace to turn on her lover? Or would Maksim have to seduce her away from him?

Seducing a woman who was in love with another man would be an interesting challenge, he thought. And poetic justice.

But Maksim's interest in Grace was no longer just about revenge. It was no longer just about rivalry or honor.

He suddenly wanted to peel away the deceptive layers of the little secretary's plain clothing. To see her true beauty. To see her naked in his bed. To feel her lush curves against his body and see her bright, unadorned face breathless in the soft pink light of dawn.

Beneath his gaze, her pale cheeks went slowly red, like the blood-colored sun burning through the thick morning mist on the wide snowy fields of his Dartmoor estate. He watched as she nervously licked her full, pink, heart-shaped lips. Her white, even teeth nibbled at her lower lip, followed by a small dart of her tongue to moisten each corner of her mouth.

He felt himself go hard watching her.

He prayed she'd refuse his honest offer of money. Then he could just take her. Without conscience. Without remorse.

"The Leighton boutique is on Bond Street," she stammered, caught in his gaze.

He gave a predatory smile. "My driver knows the way."

"Of course he does. You date so many women, I bet you go there a lot." She turned away, blinking fast as she stared out the window. Beneath her breath, she added wistfully, "It must be nice to never worry about money."

A sudden memory went through Maksim of the bone-chilling winter when he'd turned fourteen. There'd been no heat in their tiny apartment; his mother had been laid off from her temp job. Three-year-old Dariya had been shivering and crying, and their desperate mother had taken her to a shelter to get warm. Wanting to help, he'd cut school to sell newspapers on the street in Philadelphia. Freezing rain soaked through everything. It had taken three days afterward for Maksim's coat to dry—three days of winter so cold it left his skin the color of ash. Three days of a wet, icy wind that seeped beneath his clothes and left him shaking till his teeth chattered.

Three days of hiding the wet coat from his mother, knowing that she would insist on giving him her own, that she'd go without a coat herself as she trudged the distance between employment agencies, desperate to find a job, any job.

Those three days had taught him the most valuable lesson of his life.

Money made the difference between a good life and no life at all.

Money fixed anything. Money fixed everything.

And you didn't get it by being nice.

"What a fairy-tale life," the girl whispered, staring out the window at all the well-dressed shoppers on Bond Street, the expensive cars, the festive decorations and lights of Christmas. "A perfect fairy-tale life."

Looking at her wistful beauty, Maksim suddenly had the strong desire to tell this naive girl the truth about his ruthless soul.

But he didn't. She'd learn it soon enough.

She'd learn it the hard way.

Grace Cannon would tell Maksim what he needed to know. He would try to buy the information. If that didn't work, he'd seduce it from her.

Or maybe, he thought suddenly as he looked down at her, he would seduce her anyway.

He would show this little secretary a kind of romance she'd never seen before. Luxury on a grand scale. He would be lavish. He would kiss her senseless. And like every woman before her, she would fall.

He would make her talk.

He would take her body.

Then…he would drop her.

A man didn't get rich—or win—by being nice.

CHAPTER THREE

ELEGANT shops always made Grace uncomfortable, and the Leighton boutique was the snootiest shop on Bond Street.

She could feel herself tensing up the moment she walked through the door, past grim-jawed security guards in suits like FBI agents. They gave her a hard stare, and she had the sudden feeling they were waiting for her to make one false step so they could take her down as a warning to other broke secretaries who might try to venture inside this rarefied, exclusive world.

Grace swallowed, looking around the elegant primrose-colored boutique. Buying the lingerie the first time had just about killed her. Buying it on behalf of the man she loved, as a gift for another woman—in such a teensy, tiny size, to boot—was just another painful reminder of the fact that Alan had chosen Lady Francesca Danvers over her. The moment Alan had met the beautiful, wealthy aristocrat, he'd forgotten all about the drunken kiss he'd given Grace the previous night.

It had been Grace's very first kiss. But for him it had been instantly forgettable.

"Back again, I see," the snooty salesgirl sniffed. She looked dismissively from Grace's worn, wet coat to her scuffed-up boots. "Here to do more Christmas shopping for your boss?"

"I, um, yes." She swallowed. "I need more lingerie. The same exact one. I lost—"

But as she spoke, the salesgirl's eyes moved over her shoulder as someone new entered the shop.

Grace didn't need to look around to know it was Maksim. She knew from the immediate electricity in the room. She knew from the thousand watts that lit up the salesgirl's face as she nearly knocked Grace over in her haste to cross the marble floor. Reaching toward him. Wanting him like every woman in London.

Every woman except *her,* Grace told herself. He was dangerous and handsome and powerful, and he was her enemy. She didn't want him. She *didn't*.

"Your Highness! Such a pleasure to see you again," the brunette cried. "We have plenty of new stock—I'd love to show it to you!"

It was painfully obvious to Grace what the salesgirl would really love to show Maksim. For no good reason she felt herself get tight and tense all over. She turned away, used to feeling invisible. In her job, on the street, living alone in a foreign country…invisible. Alone.

Then she felt a strong masculine hand on her shoulder.

"You will start by getting my beautiful friend a replacement of the lingerie she bought," Maksim said to the salesgirl. He looked down at Grace. "Then—you will get her anything else she desires in the store."

"Yes, of course, Your Highness," the salesgirl gasped, her mouth a round *O* as she looked at Grace with new respect.

His steel-gray eyes and the touch of his hand caused a flash of heat to spread through her body.

"I splashed you with my car," he said. "It was an unforgivable rudeness. The least I can do is buy you new clothes. A new coat."

Grace stared at him, warmth cascading all over her. A moment before, she'd felt so invisible and cold, but with one touch he made her feel alive. With one word he'd made her feel she had value in the world.

"Anything you want, Grace," he said softly, stroking her cheek. "Anything at all. It will be my deepest honor to provide."

A shudder of longing went through her. Her face turned involuntarily toward his touch, and his hand cupped her cheek. She tried to pull away from him, but her feet weren't working properly. Neither was the rest of her.

Except for her breasts which started to ache, sending sizzles of longing down to her deepest core.

And at that moment Grace started to realize how dangerous the dark prince truly was.

She licked her lips. "Thank you, but I couldn't possibly accept."

His hand traced lightly down her neck to her shoulder, to her coat. "Why do you hide in these clothes, Grace? Why are you afraid to show the world your beauty?"

He really thought she was pretty? It hadn't just been

flattery? Her mind was spinning a million directions at once, and as long as he kept touching her she couldn't think straight. "I—"

"This would look lovely on you."

He touched a lovely pink nightgown displayed on a white headless mannequin. The silk and lace were the blush color of a spring rose, and while the low-cut neckline was covered in lace, the rest of the fabric went elegantly to the floor.

Grace, who normally slept in T-shirts and flannel pants, couldn't imagine sleeping in anything so sybaritic and luxurious.

Against her will, her eyes traced the shape of Maksim's muscular fingers against the delicate silk. She had the sudden image of what it might feel like to be in that nightgown with his hands on her. To be touched and caressed and stroked through the silk by his strong, powerful touch.

Grace fiercely shook the evocative image out of her mind.

What was wrong with her? She was growing as headless as the mannequin! No man had ever seen her in nightwear. Not even in her flannel pajamas. And it was likely to remain so!

"I'm not in the habit of letting strangers buy me nightgowns," she said, pulling her hand away from him and forcibly turning her back on the lovely pink silk.

"No lingerie, then," he said, sounding amused. "In that case, a coat. This one?"

"A coat?" She turned around, tempted. In spite of the cashmere blanket and warmth of his car, she was still shivering from the melted sleet and slush seeping through her old camel-colored coat. Having never owned a proper coat in California, she'd bought this one at a charity shop in London. It had seemed serviceable enough, and the price had been right. But it didn't hold up very well to rain, and was terribly ugly in the bargain, though Grace tried not to care.

"My car splashed your coat. It's ruined," he pointed out. "Surely even your overheightened sense of honor would allow me to replace it as a matter of course."

He touched a truly beautiful ankle-length black shearling coat with a wide collar. It was a dazzling sight, fit for a princess. She'd admired the coat when she'd first come into the shop a few hours ago. But she'd only admired it from a distance—she hadn't been nearly brave enough to actually touch it. Particularly after her eye had fallen on the price tag. Ten thousand pounds. In dollars, that equaled—

A new car.

She closed her eyes, suppressing her desire.

"And you must have this, as well." He pointed at an exquisite silk cocktail dress. "The color matches your eyes."

She looked at it hungrily. The dress was beautiful—something out of the fashion magazines she saw on newsstands. She reached out to touch the silk, then at the last moment hesitated and took the price tag instead. Four thousand pounds.

What was she thinking? She couldn't allow her boss's rival to buy her even a cocktail, let alone a cocktail dress!

Clothes like these were for glamorous, beautiful heiresses like Lady Francesca. Not for broke, plain girls like her. She'd bought her boots at a discount warehouse. Her shirt had cost less than ten dollars at Wal-Mart, and she'd bought her skirt suit used at a consignment shop in Los Angeles. For the past five years, since her father had died, she'd scrimped everywhere she could to help her family.

A lump rose in her throat. But it still hadn't been enough. She never should have left her mother alone....

"Let me do this small thing for you," Maksim said decisively. "You cannot refuse me this pleasure."

And she almost couldn't. She almost didn't want to refuse him *any* pleasure.

But she couldn't accept. She didn't trust him. And as much as she wanted these beautiful luxuries, she knew they weren't for her. Nothing in the Leighton boutique related to real life!

"And just where do you think I would wear that dress?" she retorted, raising her chin so he wouldn't know how tempted her weak soul had been. "To the grocery store? The post office?"

His lips curved into a smile. "I can think of a few places you could wear it. And not wear it."

Immediately a shiver of longing went through her body at his sensual smile. Why was he acting like this, wooing her as if she were a desirable, demanding woman?

There could be only one reason the ruthless billion-aire prince would have any interest in her: he wanted to use her to get back the things Alan had stolen.

The merger.

The bride.

Grace resolutely turned away. From him, from the black coat, from the extravagant teal cocktail dress and the lavish, hedonistic life they represented. She wouldn't sell herself, or sell out Alan.

"No," she said, forcing down the hunger in her soul for everything she knew she'd never have. "I'll allow you to replace the lingerie. No more."

He shrugged. "It's just money, Grace."

Just money. The words made her want to laugh. Easy enough to say just money when you had plenty of it. Just money had made Grace drop out of college when her father died five years ago. Just money had made her mother worry about bills ever since, with three teenaged sons who ate out the refrigerator daily. And just money was about to make her family lose the only home they'd ever known.

"What is it?" Maksim's steel-gray eyes were intent on hers, mesmerizing her will with the whispered promise of all her lost dreams. "Tell me what you want. Anything you desire, Grace. Say the word, and it is yours."

"A couple of mortgage payments," she said under her breath.

"What?"

"I…I…it's nothing." She couldn't possibly ask Alan's enemy for a loan. She could only guess what the cost could be. She'd have to stab Alan in the back. She wouldn't do that, not for any price.

Alan will advance me the money, she told herself desperately. *He will!*

With a deep intake of breath, she turned away from

Maksim to speak directly to the salesgirl. "Just the white silk-and-lace babydoll, please. Size extra small."

"I have it here, miss," the brunette said respectfully. Grace watched as the girl folded the lingerie carefully, then wrapped it in tissue paper. She placed it in a glossy primrose-hued box embossed with the Leighton crest, then tied it with a white silk ribbon.

"Only one woman in a hundred would have turned down my offer," the Russian prince said quietly from behind her. "One in a thousand."

She looked back at him with a trembling attempt at a smile. "You are my boss's rival. I feel enough of a traitor allowing you to replace the lingerie. Accepting a gift from you would not be appropriate."

"No one would ever know about it."

"I would know. And so would you."

"Ah." He looked down at her, his dark eyes intent. "A woman of honor."

She felt uncomfortable, unsure of what response to make. The way he looked at her didn't help. It just made her jumpy in her own skin. After feeling invisible for so long, being so suddenly *seen* by a man like Maksim made her dizzy.

It was like spending years in the darkness and then abruptly being hit by a blaze of sun. It sizzled her all over. She felt blinded by the intensity of his heat.

From the corner of her eye, she saw the salesgirl hold out the bag with a bright smile. "Merry Christmas, miss. Please come again soon."

"Allow me." Maksim took the bag, carrying it for her.

A prince *and* a gentleman?

It shocked her. If she'd been shopping with Alan, he would have made her carry everything. He liked to keep his hands free. After all, he always joked, didn't women love to carry shopping bags? But then, Alan was her boss.

Maksim was…her enemy?

He was different from any man she'd ever known before. Dangerous. Because he was so handsome? Ruthless. Because he was a billionaire? And gallant. Because he was a prince?

Whatever it was, he was just like the Leighton clothes. Not for Grace. Nothing to do with real life. And yet she couldn't look away, and a part of her couldn't stop wondering what it would be like to be his woman.

As they climbed into his waiting Rolls-Royce, she felt the strength of his hand beneath her arm as he helped her in. Felt his touch up and down her body. And she trembled in her wet coat for reasons that had nothing to do with cold.

"Is it strange for you to buy lingerie for your ex-girlfriend?" she murmured as the car pulled away from the curb.

He shrugged, looked away. "She may someday be my girlfriend again."

"But she's engaged to Alan."

She saw the twitch in his jaw. "And two months ago she was with me."

"You can't possibly think—"

"I don't wish to speak of her." He took both her hands in his own. "I wish to speak only of you." He looked down at her and the edges of his lips turned up. "You need warming up."

"I…do?" she breathed.

"Join me for dinner tonight."

He was asking her out on a date? She tried not to tremble. Failed. "I couldn't possibly."

His dark eyebrows lowered. "Why?"

"I'm not hungry, for one." As if on cue, her stomach gave an audible growl and she blushed. She'd worked through lunch writing engagement announcements for Alan's friends and family, while her boss met Francesca for a celebratory lunch at her father's estate outside the city. "If Alan found out…"

"He won't."

"Splurging on dinner is not in my budget."

"I will of course be pleased to—"

"No."

He sighed, clearly exasperated. "You make it impossible to pamper you."

"I don't want you to pamper me." Her stomach growled again, and she bit her lip. "But…perhaps a small snack wouldn't hurt. As long as we go Dutch." *And as long as Alan never finds out.* "There's a tea shop by Harrods, close to our house."

He raised his eyebrows. "'Our' house?" he asked innocently. "You have a roommate?"

She felt a blush go across her cheeks. "I share a house with Alan."

He gave her a knowing glance. "I see."

"We're not lovers, if that's what you think!" But she could see he didn't believe her. She felt her cheeks turn redder still. "I have my own three-room flat in his basement. As his executive secretary, he needs me to always be available. With London rents as expensive as they are, I'm happy to have a place to stay."

"How very convenient for you both," he murmured silkily.

"You don't understand," she stammered. "It's all fair and aboveboard. He deducts the cost of the rent from my salary each month!"

He suddenly laughed. "Does he really? So you're available to him around the clock, running his personal errands on your own time…and he still makes you pay money to live in his basement?" He shook his head. "I can see why he inspires such loyalty."

"Oh, forget it," she said in a huff, sitting back against the seat and staring stonily out at passing Hyde Park. "If you're going to insult Alan, you can forget the tea and just take me home."

"I didn't insult him."

"You did!"

"I'm just surprised at your loyalty. You deserve more."

She stared at him. She deserved more? It was an entirely new thought. She'd spent three years in low-paying temp jobs in downtown L.A. before she'd been hired by Cali-West. She'd been instantly smitten by the powerful, blond, handsome CEO who looked like a young Hugh Grant. She'd thought herself very lucky.

But the darkly handsome Russian prince thought she deserved…more?

"Are we close to the tea shop?" Maksim asked. She saw the driver waiting for directions, glancing at her in the rearview mirror.

She pointed grumpily. "Right there. Just past the light."

The white-haired lady who owned the patisserie appeared flustered by Maksim's broad-shouldered form appearing in the doorway of her dainty shop. He seemed massively masculine, out of place against the faded flowery wallpaper. She immediately seated them at the best table, tucked in a corner window overlooking the crowds and festive windows of Harrods across the street. When the Frenchwoman asked for their order, Grace waited for Maksim to order first, as Alan would have done.

Instead, he looked at her questioningly, reaching across the small table to take her hand. "What do you recommend, Grace?"

"I...um." She glanced down at her hand wrapped in his far larger one. She could barely think with him touching her. "The...er..." She pulled her hand away under pretense of picking up the gently tattered menu that she'd long ago learned by heart. "The English breakfast tea is good. The pastries are excellent, and so are the sandwiches." She looked up at Madame Charbon, handing back her menu. "I'll have my usual."

The woman nodded.

Maksim handed her his menu. "I'll have the same."

"Oui, monsieur."

As the Frenchwoman departed, Grace looked at him in surprise. "You don't even know what you just ordered!"

He shrugged. "You know this restaurant. I trust you."

He trusted her. She tried not to feel flattered. "Want to know what you're having?"

"I like surprises."

Normally Grace didn't, but she was starting to. She

took a deep breath. "I'm sorry I was so upset in the car. I guess you really weren't insulting Alan."

"He is lucky to have you."

She stared down at the tiny table. The truth was it was sometimes grating how small her paycheck was. And never more so than now. She'd been his junior secretary for eighteen months before she was promoted to executive assistant six months ago. But in spite of her additional responsibilities, he'd never given her a raise commensurate with her new position. He'd always managed to put her off with an excuse and a smile.

Then he'd decided to pursue a long-shot merger with Exemplary Oil PLC and he'd abruptly moved them to London in early October. In L.A. Grace had had fewer expenses. She'd been able to live at home and help her family. Now that she lived in London and paid Alan rent, she was barely able to send her mother a hundred dollars a month.

This led to one inescapable conclusion: the looming foreclosure of her family's home was entirely Grace's fault.

As Madame Charbon arrived with the steaming mugs of hot chocolate and croissants, Grace tried to push the depressing thoughts away. They just made her feel more powerless and scared and…angry.

Alan will help me. He will, she repeated to herself.

"What are you thinking about, *solnishka mayo?*" Maksim asked, leaning forward as he looked at her keenly.

She gulped down some hot chocolate, scalding her tongue. "Nothing. Um. I was just wondering if you've ever ridden the Trans-Siberian Railroad."

His dark eyebrows rose. "An odd question."

"You're Russian, aren't you?" She smiled wistfully. "I used to dream about that train when I was a little girl, a train that crosses seven time zones and nearly six thousand miles, going all the way from Moscow to the Pacific Ocean."

"Sorry to disappoint you," he said dryly. "I live in Moscow only a few months a year. When I travel or visit the northern oil fields I go by jet."

"Of course you do," she said with a sigh. "So where do you live when you're not in Russia? London?"

"I have many houses around the world. Six or seven. I live in whichever one is convenient."

She stared at him. "Six or seven? You're not even sure how many?"

He shrugged. "I have as many as I need. I sell them when I'm bored." He licked the thick whipped cream off the top of the mug with his wide tongue, causing her to stare in spite of herself. He took a sip of hot chocolate, then a bite of the croissant. "This is delicious."

"I'm glad you like it. Alan hates hot chocolate."

Maksim's eyes suddenly sliced through hers. "You're in love with him, aren't you?"

She felt sucker punched.

"What?" she whispered. "Who?"

"You're his loyal slave. You live in his house. You spend your free hours running his errands. It's plain you're not doing it for the money, since you have none. There's only one explanation. You love him."

Grace opened up her mouth to deny it, but suddenly she was so tired of lying. Tired of holding everything inside, of keeping it together, of having no one to confide in and no one she could rely upon. She took a deep breath.

"Yes. I love him." Sinking her head into her hands, she whispered, "It's hopeless."

"I know." She looked up, saw surprising warmth and sympathy in his handsome face. "I'm usually on the other side of it. Old or young, secretaries imagine themselves in love with me and drop like flies from my office. It's painful. It causes disruption. I hate it."

"Me, too." She gave a little laugh that ended with a sob—or was it a sob that ended with a laugh? She tried her best at a laissez-faire shrug. "And now he's engaged to someone who's beautiful, wealthy and so, well…"

"Vicious?" His eyes met hers. "Cruel and mean?"

With a gulp, she nodded. "I'm surprised to hear you say that. Didn't you love her?"

He changed the subject. "You don't have to endure it, Grace. Come work for me instead."

It was a good thing she'd already finished her hot chocolate or it would have snorted out her nose. Her eyes flew open, and she saw he wasn't joking. He was deadly serious.

Her throat closed.

"Work for you?" she gasped.

"I could use another secretary. Leave Barrington. Work for a man who will pay you well and take you far." He smiled. "The fact that you're in love with someone else is actually in your favor."

She swallowed. "Even though it's the man who stole your girlfriend?"

He took another drink of the hot chocolate.

"Delicious," he murmured, then looked up at her. "I need a secretary I can trust, Grace. A smart woman who knows the meaning of loyalty. You wouldn't regret changing your allegiance. I swear to you."

For an instant she was tempted. What would it be like to work for this handsome prince, instead of Alan?

Maksim was handsome, dangerous and ruthless. But he was also a man she would be free to fight, free to leave, free to speak her mind with, because she did not love him!

"I would pay you double whatever Barrington's paying you."

Double?

She licked her lips. "Would you consider paying me in advance?"

He didn't even hesitate. "Yes."

She took a deep breath, tempted beyond measure. This could save her mother's house. Save everything.

"And the catch?"

"You would help me win the merger."

"And Francesca?"

He shrugged, then held out his hand. "Do we have a deal?"

Grace closed her eyes, remembering all the times Alan had teased her, flirted with her. He'd told her more than once that he never wanted her to leave him. "I just couldn't survive without you, Gracie," he'd said with his charming movie-star grin. And it had made her so happy! She'd hugged his words to her heart, hoping that he might be starting to see her as more than just a secretary!

Then Lady Francesca Danvers had offered him money and power in such a perfectly beautiful package.

But no matter how Alan had treated her, Grace couldn't betray him.

Stubborn and foolish, she thought sourly, but she shook her head. "Thanks for asking, but my answer is no."

Taking back his hand, he nodded. "I understand."

But he didn't seem disappointed. On the contrary, he seemed to savor her refusal like a cat licking a bowl of cream.

Finishing the last crumbs of her croissant, Grace left some coins on the table and rose regretfully from her chair. She held out her hand.

"Thank you for a very pleasant afternoon, Prince Maksim."

He looked at her, and for a moment she was lost in his gaze, swirling in the endless shades of gray.

"No. I thank you, Grace." He took her hand in his own. A sizzling warmth spread through her body from their intertwined fingers. Then, still holding her hand, he kissed each of her fingers, and she shivered.

"Da svedanya, solnishka mayo. I'll never forget the way you looked in the street, with the last rays of winter twilight in your pale-blond hair. Like an angel. Like the sun." He turned her hand over and kissed her palm. An erotic charge arced through her, making her nipples tight and her breasts heavy. Her whole body was suddenly tense, waiting, waiting…

Looking up into her face, he murmured, "Until we meet again."

He released her, and Grace walked out of the tea

shop in a daze. As she slogged through the crowds outside Harrods, gripping her Leighton bag as if her life depended on it, she could still feel that sensual kiss against her palm.

With one brief touch of his lips, he'd branded her. In the dark winter night lit up by Christmas lights and shop windows, she looked down at her right hand, expecting to see the burn of his lips emblazoned on her skin for all the world to see.

But her skin was bare.

She knew she'd never see him again. Probably a good thing.

Definitely a good thing.

And yet…

When Alan yelled at her for not magically foreseeing his wishes in advance…when a check bounced in her bank account…when she was forced to watch the man she loved get married to another woman…when she felt helpless, hopeless, invisible…

She could treasure this one magical afternoon when she'd spent the day with a handsome prince who'd been kind to her. Who'd treated her like a princess.

As she walked home, the sleet softened to snow in the dark stillness of winter, leaving scattered, twisted flurries of flakes.

She'd loved Alan Barrington in hopeless silence for two years. But he'd never affected her like Maksim Rostov had. He'd never made her tremble and shake and feel hot all over. Maksim had changed her in a way she couldn't understand.

But whatever he'd made her feel didn't matter now.

With a sigh that created a puff of white smoke in the frozen air, Grace climbed slowly up the front steps of the three-story town house she shared with her boss.

The fairy tale was over.

CHAPTER FOUR

ALAN was waiting for her at the door with twinkling blue eyes. He was so boyishly handsome, he could almost be called pretty. Beaming with excitement, he dragged her into his reception room.

"You got home just in time, Gracie! I have a present for you!"

He placed a plane ticket into her hands. She stared down at it, and the sparkling white lights of his elegantly decorated Christmas tree seemed to whirl around her in the front room of his Knightsbridge town house.

"Merry Christmas," he purred.

Sucking in her breath, she looked up at him. And to think she'd wondered in her darker moments if he intentionally used her own feelings against her, taking advantage of her crush to avoid having to properly pay her. But with this gift, there could be no doubt that he truly cared for her...otherwise, why would he have done this?

"Thank you," she whispered. "I wanted so much to go home for Christmas. But I didn't have enough to—"

"I know, Gracie," he said with a big smile.

"Thank you, Alan," she said, feeling as if she was going to cry. "This means so much to me."

"On Christmas Eve, as soon as the deal is finished, you'll fly off to enjoy the sun and surf." He sighed. "I don't know how I'll survive while you're gone."

She took a deep breath. "Alan, I have a really big favor to ask you—"

"Oh, no." He groaned. "Not the raise again. Does it always have to be about money? I'm the CEO of Cali-West and you're my righthand woman." He gave her a wink. "Isn't that glory enough for you?"

His righthand woman, but not the woman in his arms. Grace managed a weak smile. "You said we could talk about maybe a raise or bonus at the end of the year, and I'm really desperate, Alan, because—"

"Sorry, kiddo." He held up his hand. "That'll have to wait a bit longer. I'm late for my date with Francesca."

"But Alan—"

"We'll talk about it tomorrow. I really promise this time." He took her hand, and she felt nothing like the painful zing she'd experienced with Maksim. Alan's hand was just warm and soft. "In the meantime, there's something I need you to do for me. A teensy, small favor." He flashed her a big white grin. "Help me get married."

"Wh-what?"

"Francesca's having trouble setting the wedding date. So I thought—why bother with a wedding at all? Why not just elope? That's where you come in." He gave her a bright smile. "Christmas Eve I want to elope. Scotland. Honeymoon in Barbados. I need you to make the arrangements."

Alan didn't realize what he was asking of her. How could he? To him, Halloween night had been just a kiss. To her, it had been the culmination of two years of fantasies. Which was probably why the kiss hadn't felt nearly as intense as she'd imagined it would. Not even as intense as the way Prince Maksim's lips had felt against her palm an hour before.

Trying to push the memory of the dark Russian prince from her mind, she took a deep breath. "Are you sure eloping is a good idea? The bride might prefer to choose when—"

"It's perfect," he said, frowning.

"All right," she sighed. She suddenly realized she was still clutching the Leighton bag in her hands. "Here's your gift."

"Thanks." Taking his coat from the hall closet, he slung the bag over his shoulder. He stopped at the door with a wink. "I'll need this tonight to close the deal. I'll be getting her something better for Christmas. In the meantime, start working on the elopement plans, will you?"

After Grace locked the door behind him, she turned back with a lump in her throat.

She'd thought buying gifts for his fiancée was bad. Planning their quickie wedding would be a thousand times worse.

It hurt more than she'd expected.

Because she'd spent the afternoon with Prince Maksim, she realized. Because for the first time in years she'd felt the full attention of a man's eyes on her, the consideration of his touch and regard, and it had brought something to life inside her. Something that wanted to be seen. Something that wanted to be touched. It had felt so good. She'd felt…

Alive.

Now she just felt numb.

Grace went downstairs to her basement apartment. Closing the door quietly behind her, she changed out of her damp clothes. She put on an old sweatshirt and flannel pajama pants. She heated some leftover takeaway Thai food in her microwave. She sat down heavily on the couch. She turned on the old television. She placed a fork, the food and a diet soda on the coffee table. She got out her laptop to start making elopement arrangements for Christmas Eve, just two weeks away.

But instead of opening her laptop or watching TV, she wrapped herself in the quilt her mother had made her as a child. She sat on the couch and stared blankly at the wall.

He was really going to marry Lady Francesca Danvers. The vicious, skinny, gorgeous heiress who always got away with her bad behavior because she was so beautiful that men put up with it. Men would put up with anything to be with a girl like that.

While Grace was such a pushover she couldn't even make Alan listen to her beg him for an advance. Not even though her family's security depended on it.

Tears fell softly onto the frayed fabric of the quilt. Why hadn't she found out until that morning that her father's life insurance money was gone? Why hadn't she known her mother had been keeping their financial difficulties secret? And why couldn't she stop loving a man who so plainly saw her as nothing but a secretary?

She jumped when she heard a loud knock at her front door.

Fiercely wiping her eyes, she wrapped her mother's quilt over her shoulders and rose from the couch. Alan had likely forgotten his key again and wanted to go up through her apartment. Her nervous heart beat faster. This time she would make him listen. *I need an advance,* she practiced in her mind. *Please, Alan, I need $10,000 right away or my family will lose their home.*

She opened the door into the dark, snowy night. "Alan, I need—"

Her words ended in a gasp.

The tall, dark-haired man who looked down at her with a gleam in his eye was definitely *not* her boss.

Prince Maksim leaned against the edge of the door, looking dangerous and oh, so seductive in a tuxedo beneath a black coat. Her heart pounded in a whole new way.

"What are you doing here?" she breathed.

"I forgot something," he said, looking down at her tear-stained face.

"What?"

She caught a sudden brief blur of icy moonlight above as she felt his hands, his warmth, wrapping around her. Saw the colors of her quilt blur around her as he cupped her face.

"This," he said simply.

And he kissed her.

The touch of Maksim's mouth on hers was gentle at first. He pulled her close. She felt his hands brush through her hair before they moved slowly down her back. Her breasts pressed against his hard chest. He held her more tightly, deepening the embrace. His lips caressed hers, leading her, teaching her, making her sizzle all the way to her toes. He forced her lips wide, penetrating her mouth, teasing and licking her with the tip of his tongue. Her whole body became tight with longing, and her core poured with heat.

It was the kiss she'd always dreamed of. The whole world seemed to whirl and shudder around her like a tornado as she was swept up in his fierce embrace.

Was she dreaming? She had to be dreaming!

Feeling Maksim's strong arms around her, his lips taking his pleasure and demanding she take her own, was like nothing she'd ever felt before. Nothing like Alan's sloppy, drunken kiss six weeks earlier.

Alan!

She was kissing Alan's enemy in his own house!

"Stop," she whimpered against his lips, shuddering as she pulled away. "Please stop."

He pushed blond tendrils from her face. "Because you're in love with Barrington?"

"No…yes." She shook her head with a tearful laugh. "You just have to go!"

"You just have to come with me."

He wanted her to go out with him? "I don't need your pity—"

"Pity?" His eyes darkened until they were almost black in the snowy, cloud-ribboned moonlit night. "I have been accused of having no heart. I am telling you the truth, Grace. Take this as a warning."

And he kissed her again.

This time he was not gentle. It was a hard plundering of her mouth that bruised her lips and left her dizzy, aching with pleasure.

"Come out with me tonight," he whispered against her cheek. "You cannot refuse me."

Though she'd been standing for five minutes in the below-street-level entrance of her basement flat, she was barely aware of the cold.

But how could she be tempted? She loved Alan!

Didn't she?

"I won't turn on him," she gasped, still trembling with the shock of desire. "Not for any price. You won't kiss a betrayal out of me."

"You think that's the only reason I would kiss you?" The rich moonlight moved against scattered dark clouds above them, wistful and haunted, tracing his razor-sharp cheekbones and chiseled jaw. "You are a desirable woman, *solnishka mayo*."

"*Solnishka mayo?*" she repeated.

"Sunlight," he whispered.

She choked out a laugh, glancing down at her flannel pajama pants, her ratty sweatshirt. She pulled her mother's quilt a little tighter over her shoulders. "You're blind."

"You don't know your own beauty." He stroked her shoulder, running his hand down the quilt as he looked down into her eyes, towering over her. "Let me show you the truth."

"But I can't trust you," she whispered. Prince Maksim was dangerous and ruthless. Though knowing he was forbidden to her just made her want him more....

He leaned down to kiss one cheek softly, then the other, as he spoke against her skin. "I'm not leaving without you."

The touch of his lips against her cheek sent aching tension to her breasts and down deep in her belly. She longed for him to kiss her again. In his arms she couldn't think, she couldn't do anything but feel. She closed her eyes as she felt his hot breath against the tender flesh of her ear. "I...I can't."

"You can and you will," he said. "Let me show you how pleasurable life can be."

With those words he pulled away from her. She nearly protested aloud and her eyelids reluctantly fluttered open. He was at least six inches taller than her, making her feel delicate. "No."

"Stubborn and foolish," he repeated softly, rubbing his thumb lightly against her swollen lower lip. "Why do you resist me?"

"Because...because..." She couldn't think straight with him stroking her lip like that. Grace's whole body ached. "I...don't have anything to wear."

With a sudden grin, he snapped his fingers. A bodyguard—a dark, hulking man who had to weigh three hundred pounds—ambled down the steps to her basement door with two primrose boxes in his arms. He set them near the doorway, then disappeared back up to the street.

An exclamation of shock escaped Grace as she stared at the two recognizably colored boxes embossed with the Leighton coat of arms.

"What have you done?"

"The coat," he said. "The dress."

She licked her lips. "Not the ones from Leighton."

"I knew you wanted them, though you denied it."

Remembering how she'd yearned for the black coat and the teal silk cocktail gown, a shiver swept through her body. She'd been afraid to even touch them in the store. At the thought of wearing them against her skin, her heart pounded.

He's luring me, she warned herself desperately. *Luring me to my own destruction!*

"I guessed your size, but have others in the car if necessary." His eyes met hers. "Women's clothes have always been a mystery to me. I've always been more interested in taking them off."

She gave an involuntary shiver. Then she looked down at the boxes, licking her lips, torn with longing.

He grabbed her wrist.

"Fair warning, Grace," he said quietly. "I will seduce you tonight."

Caught in his gaze, she couldn't breathe. Her heart almost felt about ready to explode from her chest.

"You're welcome to try," she managed over the rapid pounding of her heart. "I will resist you."

He gave her a slow, seductive smile. "I would expect nothing less."

She looked at the Leighton boxes. "And I can't… won't…accept expensive gifts."

"They weren't expensive."

"I saw one of the price tags in the boutique. The coat alone cost ten thousand pounds."

"You are worth far more than that." He stroked her

cheek. "I would pay any price to give you pleasure. Any price to please you."

The reminder of his wealth and power made her tremble. The money that felt like nothing to him was a fortune to her. More than enough to save her family. She closed her eyes. No. She wouldn't think about it. Asking Alan's enemy for help would blacken her soul beyond recognition. She might be weak, but she wasn't a traitor.

"If Alan found out I went out with you, he'd fire me."

"In which case you could come work for me," he said.

"But—"

"Either wear these clothes or go naked." He gave her a slow-rising smile. "Decide. Or I will."

Without asking permission, he pushed past her into her flat, carrying the boxes and pulling Grace behind him. He closed the door. They were alone.

The air seemed to leave the small apartment.

Prince Maksim Rostov—in her flat? She saw him look around at her sagging, plaid, threadbare couch. The day-old Thai takeout in the cardboard container. The blaring television with faded stars sparkling in sequins dancing to ballroom music. The laptop computer set up by her couch. Her cheeks burned.

He turned to her with a sensual smile. "Or we could just stay in."

Stay here—with him?

Ohmygodohmygod. *No.*

"The dress and coat would have to be a loan," she heard herself whisper. "I would give them back to you at the end of the night."

He smiled down at her.

"I'll look forward to it."

A dark force in his eyes pulled her with all the force of gravity. He looked at her as if he'd already undressed her and tossed her naked into his bed.

Bed? Who was thinking about bed?

Going out with him tonight, she was risking everything for a dangerous feeling she couldn't control. But she suddenly hungered to feel something that wasn't grief, loneliness or fear. She wanted to forget. She wanted to disappear into another world.

Her knees shook as she gathered up the boxes. "I'll be right back."

"I'll be waiting."

She hurried to her tiny bedroom, feeling strangely lighthearted. She brushed out her blond hair for two minutes with a hair dryer, then dabbed on some lipstick. She had no bra that would work with the cocktail dress, so she left her breasts bare beneath the dress. As she pulled the aquamarine gown over her hips, the softness of the luxurious silk slid like the whisper of a caress.

She knew she shouldn't do this.

Just one night, she told herself. *One night to forget my problems. I won't let him seduce me.*

She glanced at herself in the mirror and nearly gasped. She looked nothing like the downtrodden, damp, dowdy secretary she'd been just a few moments before. Aside from her old shoes, the scuffed silver pumps which were her only option, she almost didn't recognize herself. Who was the blond, bright-eyed young woman in the mirror?

The teal silk exactly matched the shade of her eyes.

The rose-pink lipstick made her pale skin look creamy. The cut of the gown made her full breasts look exactly right with her small waist, giving her the hourglass shape of a 1950s pinup girl.

Could clothes and makeup really do so much?

It wasn't just the clothes, she realized. It was *him*. His attention was making her blossom like a flower.

One night, she repeated to herself, and her teeth chattered. Just a few hours to feel pretty. She wouldn't let him seduce her. She couldn't. She was in love with someone else, which meant she was perfectly safe. Right?

Coming out of the bedroom, she stopped abruptly when she saw him leaning against the wall of the hallway. Maksim was so dark and handsome and terrifying. His gaze held her own, electrifying her.

"Sorry to make you wait," she said.

He came forward, stalking her like a jungle cat. He looked slowly over her body, from the blue-green silk skimming her curves to the silver drops dangling from her ears, from her long, thick blond hair to her full pink lips. He gave a long, slow whistle.

"You, *solnishka mayo,*" he said in a low voice, "were utterly worth waiting for."

CHAPTER FIVE

As the chauffeur drove through the London streets, Grace watched feather-edged moonlight from the window move over Maksim's sharp cheekbones, his angular jawline. He was the most beautiful man she'd ever seen.

Beautiful. A strange word to describe such a powerful, dangerous man. But he *was* beautiful—hauntingly so. The moonlight caressed his straight nose, the cleft of his hard jaw, the hinted strength and latent brutality of the muscular body beneath the tuxedo and black coat.

He turned to meet her eyes, and his gaze scorched her, his gray eyes like smoke twisting from a deep hidden fire.

Grace suddenly realized…he hadn't lied. *He did want her.*

Innocent as she was, she could feel it.

He wasn't showing pity—or even kindness.

He wanted her.

The Leighton clothes had somehow transformed her into a beautiful, desirable woman. She'd felt downtrodden and invisible—now she felt like a goddess. Or possibly a sex kitten. An answering fire burned inside her with his every touch, every hot glance.

It wouldn't last. Like Cinderella's, her dress would disappear at the end of the night. She couldn't keep these things. She wouldn't let him buy her. She wouldn't let him seduce her.

But…for this one night, she could be the woman these clothes had created. She would have one night of magic. One night to be *seen*.

She would be the princess in the fairy tale.

The limo pulled smoothly to a stop at the curb. Maksim got out of the car and opened her door himself. Holding her arm in his own, steadying her on the icy sidewalk beneath the softly falling snow, he led her down a popular Covent Garden street filled with pubs and restaurants. Her black shearling coat swished against her ankles as she walked. Between the coat and Maksim's hand on hers, she felt warm in the frozen winter air.

"This way." He led her into a stately Victorian building, through a hidden door beside a chic tavern. She saw an elegant foyer, complete with a crystal chandelier, a front desk concierge and a security guard.

"Where are we going?"

"The top two floors of this building were converted into a penthouse." He gave her a brief smile. "A loft."

She stopped dead on the marble floor. "I'm not going to spend the evening alone with you at your house!"

"I don't live here. My sister does." He gave a careless shrug as he led her into a gilded elevator. "It's a bit colorful for my taste."

"So why did you buy it?"

Pressing on the elevator button, he looked down at her. "The Sheikh of Ramdah thought he could steal a pipeline deal from me. Instead I took his company and his favorite home in the bargain. To teach him a lesson."

The coldness in his voice made her shiver even more. "That's a bit ruthless, isn't it?" she ventured.

He gave a grim smile. "I protect what is mine."

When they arrived at the top floor, he knocked on the door. A ponderous, stiffly formal butler opened it to welcome them. His eyes widened. "Your Highness!"

"Oh!" A beautiful black-haired girl suddenly pushed past the butler to fling herself into Maksim's arms. "You're here! I can't believe you're here!"

He hugged her awkwardly, then drew back. "I wouldn't miss my own sister's birthday party."

"Liar," the girl said with a laugh. "You've missed the last two! And don't think expensive gifts make up for your absence. I don't need another Aston-Martin convertible, I need a brother—" She saw Grace and drew back in surprise. "But who's this?"

"A friend," he said.

"Funny, you've never bothered bringing 'friends' around before." She looked at Grace inquisitively, then pulled them both inside. "But I'm being rude. Come in! Come in!"

As the butler took their coats, the girl turned her piercing gray eyes, so much like her brother's, on Grace. "I'm Dariya Rostova."

Of course Grace knew the famous Princess Dariya, the fun-loving party girl who was constantly in the papers with her gorgeous friends. Pale and model slender in her silver sequin minidress, she wore a diamond tiara in her straight black hair.

Beneath her examination, Grace felt shy and out of place. "I'm sorry, I didn't know we were going to a birthday party," she stammered. "I'm afraid I don't have a gift."

Dariya suddenly smiled, and her lovely face lit up with warmth. "It wouldn't have even occurred to Francesca to bring a gift, so I already like you loads better. If you ask me, that woman was a snooty dry stick draped in furs."

"Dariya," her brother warned.

"What's your name?" his sister said, ignoring him.

She cleared her throat. "Grace."

"Well, Grace, you've actually brought the best present of the night." She beamed up at her brother fondly. "Come say hello to everyone!"

Dariya led them into the enormous loft, with soaringly high ceilings and big windows overlooking St. Martin's Lane. In the center of the room, a sharp, metallic chandelier held multicolored orbs for lights. Amid the vast space of the open-walled apartment, the furniture was a cross between 1960s retro and cartoonish avant-garde. Grace looked with dismay at backless chairs that were shaped like ripe strawberries.

"Look everyone," Dariya announced happily. "Look who came! And he even brought a friend. Everyone, say hello to Grace!"

As a cheer of welcome went around the room, Grace felt happy in a way she hadn't felt for months. She suddenly realized how much she'd missed having friends. She hadn't kept up with her old friends since she'd started working for Alan, much less tried to make new ones. She'd given up the idea of friends or hobbies or anything but being Alan's perfect on-call secretary.

But now…

The laughing, friendly group around her reminded Grace of bonfires on the beach when she'd been in school, before her father had died. Before she'd started working for Alan. Back when her life had been simple and easy. She ached remembering the fun she'd had, getting together with friends to eat, drink, talk and laugh.

The only difference being that these people were all impossibly rich and good-looking. And that the party was in an artistic, soaring two-floor loft that had once been the treasured possession of the Sheikh of Ramdah.

"I told you Maksim would come!" Dariya said triumphantly to a young man hovering nearby. "You owe me ten pounds!"

"Best bet I've ever lost. Hello, Maksim. Lovely to meet you, Grace," he said with a grin. "Thanks for putting a smile on my girl's face."

"*Your* girl?" Dariya tossed her dark hair. "In your dreams, Simon!"

Maksim growled something incomprehensible to the aristocratic young man. He was obviously being protective, but it still seemed rude. Grace cleared her throat and turned to Dariya. "So it's your twenty-fifth birthday?"

"Don't remind me," she groaned. She suddenly looked alarmed, putting her hands on her perfect face. "Do I look it?"

Grace laughed, then pointed at the hand-painted banner slung from the high, frescoed ceiling that read, *Happy Twenty-fifth Birthday, Dariya!* It was a charming homemade touch amid all the exorbitantly expensive, bright, sharp modernity.

"Oh. Right." The girl followed her glance with a sigh. "A quarter of a century, and what have I done with my life?"

"I just turned twenty-five on Sunday," Grace said sympathetically, "and I spent the day huddled in my flat in total denial."

"No, really!" Dariya exclaimed. "Not even a party?"

"My boss gave me a gift card for a week's worth of lunches at my favorite Japanese restaurant."

"You had no party," the girl repeated, shaking her head in horror. "You simply can't turn twenty-five without a party! Maksim," she turned to her brother, "tell her it's ridiculous!"

"Ridiculous," he agreed laconically.

"Lulu," Dariya called over her shoulder, "get a party hat, will you? Right. So this party will be for both of us." When Lulu brought the colorfully decorated hat, Dariya took the tiara off her head and stuck the hat in its place. "This will be for me." She placed the diamond tiara on Grace's blond head. "And that will be for you."

"Oh no," Grace gasped, feeling the weight of the diamonds on her head. She'd come without a gift, and now she was going to upstage Maksim's sister, the famous socialite Princess Dariya, during her own birthday party? "That's so generous of you, really, but I couldn't—"

"To be honest, it suits you better." She leaned forward and whispered mischievously in Grace's ear, "It was a gift from my brother, anyway, and not at all my style!"

"Dariya, you promised to dance!" Simon called from the other side of the loft, where a four-person jazz band had started to play.

"In a mo!" She gave Grace one last hug. "Must go dance, I'm afraid. Otherwise he'll pout, but I'm so glad you're here. My brother looks happy. Make yourself at home!"

After she left, Grace touched the top of her head. Was it possible that they were actually real diamonds? The thought shocked her…frightened her. The wealth around her was already far beyond anything she'd ever seen, even working as Alan's secretary. She felt like Alice who'd just stepped through the looking glass to a world where money really did grow on trees. And the tree branches were made of gold. And the berries were all diamonds, rubies and emeralds.

She felt Maksim come up behind her. Wrapping his arms around her, he kissed the crook of her neck. Her nipples instantly went hard, her breath shallow, her mind went dizzy. Then he whirled her around, handing her one of the crystal flutes from his other hand.

She took it with an awkward attempt at a smile. "My first champagne."

"Cristal is not a poor way to start."

She took a sip. The bubbles floated inside her, all soft and lovely and warm going down.

Maksim tilted her head upward with his hand, looking down at her from his towering height. His gaze was dark and intense. She suddenly knew he meant to kiss her again and she couldn't think. Couldn't even breathe.

Everything about him tempted her. Transfixed her. Made her long to really and truly be the woman who could mesmerize him in equal measure.

When would he kiss her?

Kiss her? What was she thinking? Clearly the tiara had constricted the blood flow to her brain!

Nervously she pulled away. She gulped down the rest of the expensive champagne as if chugging a can of soda, then pushed the tiara back crookedly on her head. "This thing isn't real, is it? The tiara's not real diamonds?"

He took a drink of champagne, his dark eyes resting on hers. "Set in platinum."

She swallowed, thinking that she likely could pay off her mother's whole mortgage with the sparkling tiara on her head. And maybe their neighbor's house in the bargain!

"What if I break it?" She gave a weak laugh. "Do you have insurance?"

"Diamonds don't break." Finishing his champagne, he took both flutes and set them on the tray of a passing waiter. He took her in his arms. "The tiara suits you. You should keep it." He slowly lowered his mouth toward hers. "You were born to wear jewels, Grace," he whispered. "Born to be adored and pampered in a life of luxury."

Someone turned out the side lights, leaving the loft lit only by the multicolored globes of the steel chandelier high above. Wide spotlights of red, green and blue shimmered in the semidarkness. In the wide space, she was aware of other people dancing, laughing, swaying to the music. She was in some strange fantastic world of stylish art, youth and limitless wealth.

But it wasn't the luxury that lured her most.

It was Maksim.

"I won't let you seduce me," she whispered, trying to reassure herself. "I won't."

Every inch of her body, down to blood and bone, ached for him to kiss her. Her body arched toward his, taut with longing as her teal silk dress slid like a whisper against his tuxedo.

Pulling her against his hard body, too arrogant to care who might be watching, he lowered his mouth to hers.

He kissed her so deeply that their tongues intertwined, kissed her so hard that with one embrace he bruised and branded her forever as his own.

No! She sagged against his chest, her heart pounding wildly when he released her from the kiss. She couldn't belong to Maksim. She couldn't!

He straightened the diamond tiara, stroking the long hair that brushed her bare shoulders, making her shiver. He took two more flutes of champagne from a passing tray. Then, taking her hand, he led her to the dance floor.

For the next few hours they drank champagne and danced together, their bodies swaying to the music. Time moved strangely, sliding sideways so hours felt like minutes, and minutes felt like eternity. They danced to the soulful jazz music, to the poignant cry of the saxophone, until finally he pulled her gently to the furthest side of the loft.

There, alone in the shadows and away from the others, he pushed her against the wall. He gently bit at her neck, sucking on her ear. She gasped, breathless and desperate for more.

He finally kissed her mouth, his tongue stroking hers deeply, luring her. And suddenly she could barely remember Alan's name, let alone why she should be loyal to him.

"Grace," Maksim murmured between kisses. "It's time to go."

"Go? Already?" she faltered.

"It's past midnight."

"Oh." And like Cinderella, that meant her time was up. The dream was over. She swallowed. "All right. I have a lot of work to do tomorrow, anyway."

"Then you'll be tired." He held her close, so close she could hear the beat of his heart. "I'm taking you to my hotel."

Hotel? A hard shiver racked her body.

"Come with me now," he whispered. "I can wait no longer. I want you in my bed."

She sucked in her breath, staring up into his eyes, caught by his dark, commanding gaze. She'd somehow wandered into a fairy-tale world, a place beyond her comprehension. She'd been drawn from the real world to become a princess in diamonds and teal silk, enslaved by a fantasy prince who compelled her to follow her deepest desires.

He was so handsome, she thought in a daze. Brutally masculine, like a sixteenth-century barbarian warlord. A dark czar from a mist-shrouded medieval age.

"Can you walk," he asked in a low voice, "or should I carry you?"

Walk? Her knees felt weak, whether from champagne or desire she wasn't sure. She glanced down at feet, at the cheaply made silver pumps, scuffed up at the toes, that she'd bought for fifteen dollars at a discount warehouse in Los Angeles. The shoes threatened to break the spell.

He led her from the dance floor. As he said their farewells to Dariya and her friends, Grace could barely speak as she looked up at Maksim.

He intended to take her to his hotel.

Could she resist?

Did she still even want to?

Maksim put her coat over her shoulders, pulling her close to button it up. She felt every brush of his fingertips like an earthquake through her body. He led her back to the elevator. Suddenly they were alone, and she trembled.

"Do you swear," she whispered, "seducing me isn't some backhanded way to hurt Alan?"

He put his hands on her shoulders and looked down at her.

"I swear it to you."

"On your honor?"

He looked away and his jaw clenched. Then he turned to face her.

"Yes," he said tersely.

When she remembered to breathe, she nodded, believing him. He was a prince. He wouldn't look her straight in the eye and lie.

"So why me?" she said. "Why be so nice—"

"Call me nice again and you'll regret it." His dark eyes gleamed as he pulled her from the elevator and out onto the street. "I am selfish. I take what I want. Any man would desire you, Grace. In his arms. In his bed. Any man would want you."

"Alan didn't." As soon as the bitter words escaped her, she wished desperately she'd kept them to herself.

"Barrington is a fool." He stopped on the sidewalk. His mouth curved into a sensual smile. "He lost his chance. Now you will be mine. Only mine."

He slowly stroked up the inside of her bare arm beneath her coat, causing her to give an involuntary shudder of longing.

"Grace," he whispered. "Let me show you how truly selfish I can be."

CHAPTER SIX

DECEIT was part of the art of war.

The truth could be a flexible thing in Maksim's opinion. Stretching it correctly was partly how he'd built a vast empire out of nothing. As a teenager, he'd gotten investors by pretending to already have them. He'd deceived competitors, making them believe deals were finished when they weren't. He'd bought commodities cheap and sold them high because he knew information that others didn't. Information he'd ruthlessly kept to himself.

It was not Maksim's responsibility to do the due diligence of others and reveal any truth against his own best interests. He looked out for himself. He assumed others did the same. Only a fool would blindly trust the word of another.

But that was business. Lying in his personal life—that was something new.

And swearing on his honor…

His neck broke out in a sweat to think of it. He'd never looked into a woman's face and lied against his honor. It made him feel…cheap.

I had no choice, he told himself fiercely. *She gave me no choice.* And this wasn't personal. It was business.

Wasn't it?

If he'd told Grace the truth, it would have ended everything. And he was getting so close. He could feel her weakening by the moment.

Seducing her away from Barrington was the best thing that could happen to her, he told himself. The man was obviously using her own feelings against her, working her like a slave without pay.

And it wasn't as if she were an innocent. No, her kisses were too perfect for that. She'd kissed Maksim slowly, sensually, holding herself back with such restraint. As if she'd been born to enflame a man's senses and make him crazed out of his mind with longing until he would do or say anything to possess her.

Even lie against his honor.

He took Grace's hand in his own. "I gave my driver the night off," he said. "I thought we'd walk."

"All right," she whispered, never taking her eyes from him.

Snow whitened the sidewalk, covering patches of slippery ice beneath. He held her arm tightly as they walked past the pubgoers enjoying last call, making sure she didn't slip and wasn't accosted by some drunken lad seeking a beauty for his bed.

Grace was all his.

Maksim could see their breath joined in swirling white puffs of air, illuminated by the moon in the winter night. He looked at her as they walked down the snowy street toward the southern edge of Trafalgar Square.

She looked so beautiful, he thought, lit up like an angel in front of St. Martin-in-the-Fields. Her light blond hair tumbled down her shoulders, looking like spun silver and gold in the frosted moonlight. The diamond tiara sparkled in her hair, making her a spun-sugar princess. No. There was a layer of grief, of steel, beneath the sweetness. She was no helpless pink princess. No. She was a Valkyrie, from a Gothic northern land.

Her shoulders were set squarely, her hands pushed into the pockets of her long black coat that whipped behind her like a regal cape; and yet there was a softer side to her as she leaned up against him, her tender pink lips pressed together, as if she were trying to hold herself back. As if she were trying not to think.

"Thank you for bringing me to your sister's party," she said softly. "I'd forgotten what it was like to be around friends."

He felt another pang of an unpleasant emotion perilously close to guilt. It had been ruthless of him to take her to the party. But he'd wanted to see Dariya on her birthday. And, he admitted quietly to himself, he'd known it would lower Grace's defenses to meet his family. She would think she could trust him. Another lie.

The only thing that wasn't a lie: *he wanted her*.

"Are you, Maksim?"

He focused on her. "Am I what?"

She looked up at him as he led her by Charing Cross station. "Are you my friend?"

He brought her hand to his lips and kissed the back of it. He felt her shiver beneath the brush of his lips against her skin. "No," he said in a low voice. "I'm not your friend, Grace."

They passed down a slender street full of restaurants and pubs, crowds of young people and a few Chelsea football fans in blue-and-white scarves celebrating loudly over a pint. He took her hand and led her down to the embankment by the river. As they walked, they passed a dark garden.

"I don't want your friendship," he said. "I want you in my bed."

The intimacy of his words, as they passed the quiet darkness of the park drenched in crystalline moonlight, was perfect. She looked up at him, her mouth a round *O*. A mouth made for kissing. A mouth he wanted to feel under his.

Right now.

But as he stopped, leaning down to kiss her, she suddenly turned away, her pale cheeks the color of roses in the moonlight.

"Did you learn to flirt like that in Russia?" she whispered. She gave a sharp, awkward laugh and started walking again. "You have some skills."

So his beauty wished to wait? He would be patient. "I grew up here."

Her eyes went wide. "London?"

"And other places." He shrugged. "We moved around. My father couldn't keep a job. We were poor. Then he died."

"I'm sorry," she said quietly. "My father died five years ago, too. Cancer." She swallowed, looked away. "My mother has yet to recover. She almost never leaves the house. That's why…" She looked away.

"Why what?"

She turned back, blinking hard.

"I'm sorry I misjudged you," she said. "Thinking you'd never known what it was like to struggle or suffer just because you're a prince."

"Yes, a prince," he said acidly. "Distantly in line to a throne that, if you haven't noticed, stopped ruling Russia nearly a hundred years ago."

"But still…"

"Prince of nothing and nowhere," he said harshly. "Money is all that matters. Only money."

"Oh, Maksim." Tears filled her eyes as Grace shook her head. "Money isn't the only thing that matters. It's the way you love people. The way you take care of them."

"And you take care of them with money."

"No. Like your sister said, she didn't need more expensive things, she wanted *you*. Your time and—"

"A lovely sentiment," he said sardonically. "But my sister is too young to remember how we nearly starved and froze to death the winter we lived in Philadelphia. After that, I made sure I could support us. I made sure no one and nothing could ever threaten my mother and sister again."

"You protected your family." Her eyes suddenly glittered, and her hands clenched into fists before she stuck them in the pockets of her designer coat. "I should have stayed in California," she said softly. "I never should have left my mother alone."

A hard lump rose in Maksim's throat. "Being with the people you love doesn't always save them. I made my first million when I was twenty, but it couldn't save my mother from dying."

"Oh, no," she said softly. "What happened?"

"Brain aneurysm. She died without warning. I…I couldn't save her."

He stopped, choking on the words. He had never spoken about his mother's death to anyone—not even Dariya, who'd been barely nine when it had happened.

Maksim waited for Grace to expose the weakness in his argument. To point out that, by his own admission, money was indeed not everything in life.

Instead she reached up to stroke his cheek. The first time she'd deliberately touched him.

"It wasn't your fault," she said softly. "You took care of your family. You protected them. You tried to save your mother. You did everything you could."

A tremble went through him, and he involuntarily turned his face into her caress. He closed his eyes briefly, taking a deep breath.

"You're a special woman, Grace Cannon," he said in a low voice. "I've never met your equal."

She gave a short laugh and looked away. The street-lights shone a plaintive blurry light on the dark, swift river beneath the bare trees of the embankment. "I'm not special. I'm completely ordinary."

"You're special."

"It's the clothes."

"It's the woman inside them." He looked down at her. "Grace. You are just like your name. Grace." His eyes narrowed. "And did you say your middle name is Diana?"

"Don't laugh."

"Your mother believed in fairy tales."

"Yes." She shook her head. "But her two favorite princesses didn't live happily ever after, did they?"

"What about you, *solnishka mayo?*" he whispered. His eyes drifted to her lips. "Do you believe in fairy tales?"

She briefly closed her eyes. "I used to believe in them. I used to believe with all my heart."

"And now?"

Their gazes locked, held in the moonlight. Her pupils dilated as she looked down at his lips, then licked her own.

An invitation no man could resist.

Taking her in his arms, he lowered his mouth to hers. Kissing her was heaven. He was intoxicated by the taste of her. The feel of her. His whole body tightened and he drew back to stroke her face, looking down into her eyes. "Tonight," he said hoarsely. "Tonight you must be mine."

He saw her dreamy expression suddenly change to shock. She shook her head hard, as if clearing the cobwebs from her mind.

She hesitated, licking her lips. Then she pulled away from him. "Please. Don't."

He reached for her. "Grace—"

"I can't," she whispered, backing away from his reach. "Please don't."

As she blindly stepped back, he saw her ankle twist, saw one of her shoes slide on the black ice beneath the snow. He heard the snap of one high heel. Saw her stumble back—

He caught her before she could fall. He cradled her against his chest. She looked up at him with an intake of breath. He could feel the rapid beat of her heart. She was so light she seemed to weigh nothing at all. That damned diamond tiara probably weighed more than she did, he thought. And as he looked down into her eyes, he felt dizzy for a reason he couldn't explain. As if he were the one in danger of falling.

A flash of fire burned through him as he felt her tremble in his arms. And he knew that nothing on earth would prevent him from possessing her tonight.

Grace would be his.

Without a word he carried her toward his hotel. As they were about to turn near Savoy Hill, he paused in a nearby alley to lean her against the rough wall and kiss her, hot and demanding. She was all woman, he thought, warm and pliant and willing...but with an elegant hesitation and restraint that heated his blood. He wanted nothing more than to take her against this wall, to fill her up, to slide inside her and thrust deeply until she screamed his name.

"Don't deny me, Grace," he whispered against her skin after he'd kissed her. "Don't deny us what we both want."

The dreamy look had returned to her eyes. "You're right," she said so softly he almost couldn't hear it. "I can't fight you."

She was looking up at him with desire, yes. But also something else. Faith? Trust? Pushing that disquieting thought away, he carried her around the corner toward his hotel. But when he saw the brightly lit porte-cochère of his luxury hotel, he hesitated again in spite of himself.

He wanted her so badly that his whole body hurt from it. But he also had a sour taste in his mouth. Because of guilt? Because he'd lied? He'd lied to get revenge against

Barrington. To win back the merger. To possibly take back Francesca.

But most of all…he'd lied to get Grace in his bed.

She's no innocent virgin, he told himself again. And she wanted him as he wanted her. Maksim had nothing to feel guilty about. Nothing at all.

The doorman saluted respectfully, pretending he didn't see the captive woman in Maksim's arms. "Good evening, Your Highness."

"Good evening," Maksim replied shortly.

He carried Grace straight to the waiting elevator and upstairs to his penthouse. He would make her moan with pleasure, he told himself fiercely. He was so hard with need he couldn't imagine letting her go now.

He couldn't.

Damn it, he wouldn't!

He unlocked his door with one hand then kicked it wide, carrying her over the threshold like a bride. He walked past the stark black-and-white furniture, the black leather sofa, the large flat-screen television above the fireplace.

The curtains had been left open. Below, he could see the dark Thames beneath moving lights of the barges, and steady traffic across the bridges. He saw the gleaming buildings of the city across the river and, to the far left, the brilliantly illuminated dome of St. Paul's.

A fittingly celestial image for the heavenly things Maksim intended to do to Grace. He couldn't even make it to the bedroom before he started kissing her.

In answer, her lips moved against his with gentle hesitation, a light tease that made him plunder her mouth with greater desire. Her kiss was like nothing he'd ever known before. Women had always kissed him so eagerly and desperately, matching his fire or surpassing it. Her unusual restraint fired his blood, increasing his need until he panted from it.

Still kissing her, he set her down on the big white bed. He paused to look down at her. Her blond hair was mussed and tousled. Her eyes were deep pools of blue green, like clear pools of mountain water from newly melted snow.

He trembled as he reached down to touch her, stroking down her neck to the soft silk of her teal dress, down the valley between her breasts to her flat belly. She was so soft and warm. So beautiful from her rose-pink lips to her unpolished nails. He leaned over her, brushing blond tendrils from her face to kiss her cheeks, her neck, her throat. Finally kissing her mouth, he teased her tongue with his as he cupped his hands over her full breasts. Discovering that she wasn't wearing a bra, that those high, firm breasts were unassisted by fabric or padding and were all her, he nearly gasped. He touched her in wonder and felt her nipples pebble and harden beneath his fingers. It was too much for him.

Lowering his head, he suckled her through the silk.

She gave a small hushed cry, arching involuntarily against his mouth. Wanting more, he roughly pulled down the neckline and tasted her flesh. She fell back against the bed with a shudder, exhaling her breath in a little mewling sound that made him harden to painful intensity. Lying on top of her, wrapping his hands possessively around her naked breasts, he suckled her more forcefully, not letting her go even as she twisted beneath him. His body was hard against hers. Feeling her beneath him, he wanted nothing more than to pull up her cocktail dress, unbutton his pants and push all the way inside her with one hard, deep thrust.

The thought made him groan aloud.

He shoved her dress up to her hips, revealing simple white cotton panties. Even that surprised him, compared to the lacy, tarty panties his lovers typically wore to entice him. The simplicity was just like Grace, and revealed the perfection of her curvy hips, her creamy thighs. She didn't need to even try to seduce, to drive any man mad with need...

"Stop," she suddenly whispered. "Please stop."

He realized he'd already pushed up her dress to her waist and had started to unbutton his pants. Damn it to hell, after promising himself he would take his time and make her explode with pleasure, had he really been planning to fill her with one thrust, to roughly and savagely take her body like an animal?

Yes.

What the hell was this sweet insanity? She caused him to lose control. No woman had ever done that before.

"I'm sorry," Maksim said roughly, pulling away. His hands shook with the difficulty of holding himself back. "I didn't mean to go so fast."

"You're not." She licked her swollen, bruised lips. "I'm just...new to this."

He looked at her with a sudden frown. "How new?"

Propping herself up on her elbows, she admitted, "Completely new."

He sucked in his breath.

"Are you trying to tell me you're a *virgin?*"

Her cheeks went red. "Don't say that word!"

"How else would you describe it?"

Tears filled her eyes. "I'd describe it as being helplessly infatuated with a boss who's barely noticed I'm alive, except for one kiss."

"He kissed you?" he demanded. The ferocity of his sudden jealousy surprised Maksim. He'd never felt jealous before, not even when Francesca had delivered her little ultimatum and taken off with another man as promised. But then, Maksim's claim on Francesca had always been territorial. His possession of Grace felt...personal.

Very personal.

She looked at him, surprised. "Why are you so upset?"

Yes, why? "Because...because it's sexual harassment," he stammered furiously. "He's your boss. It's illegal!"

"Sexual harassment?" Grace laughed, then shook her head with a tearful little hiccup. "One drunken kiss before he passed out on the office couch? Then he met Francesca, who I'm sure is perfect at everything. That's why I wanted you to know," she said in a rush. "In case...in case I'm *not* so perfect. I'm sure I'm very clumsy."

Clumsy?

That explained her restraint. Her hesitation. *She was a virgin.* A shudder of hard desire went through him when he thought about how close he'd been to just ripping off her clothes and brutally taking her.

"Maksim, please. The fact that I'm—that word— doesn't mean anything," she pleaded. "It truly doesn't."

Clenching his jaw, he shook his head.

"You're wrong."

She was a virgin. She was doubly innocent.

He couldn't use her in his vicious power play.

He'd been prepared for anything but this. He could fight anything...but this.

Her naive faith had conquered the would-be conqueror.

"Maksim, nothing has changed between us." As she timidly reached for him, he grabbed her wrist.

"No, Grace. No."

He pulled her up from the bed and straightened her clothes. He wrapped her coat around her shoulders. Within two minutes he'd led her down the elevator, through the hotel lobby and out onto the street.

"Where are you taking me?" Grace whispered.

He hailed a passing black cab. When the cab pulled to the curb, he turned to face her.

"You're going home," he said tersely. "Alone."

He pushed her into the cab, then leaned forward to speak to the driver, giving him Grace's address and a very large tip with the fare.

"Wait!" Blinking out of her trance, Grace protested, "No. Maksim, please——"

He slammed the door. "Just go."

"But——"

"Go!" he ordered the cabbie.

The man pressed on the gas. Maksim watched her go. Grace turned around in the back seat to stare at him through the back window. She looked hurt and bewildered.

Then the cab turned a corner, and she was gone.

And for the first time that night, Maksim felt the chill in the air.

Oh my God, he thought suddenly. What had he done? Why had he let her go?

Why had he shown mercy?

He'd always laughed at the word. *Mercy.* Another name for weakness! And he'd let her go. He'd been weak.

He clawed back his hair. He wanted Grace so badly it hurt. Knowing she was an untouched virgin made him ache, wanting her still more. He wanted to take her in his soft, wide bed, to teach her everything he knew, to fill himself inside her again and again and watch her face slowly shine with the joy of discovery. To take her hard. To take her slow. To take her any way he could get her, *and be her first.*

Growling a curse that made the doorman's eyes nearly pop out of his head, Maksim strode into his hotel to his penthouse. He undid his tuxedo tie and tossed it on his desk before he poured himself a short vodka. Every ounce of his body was howling for him to take Grace…take her now…take her hard and deep.

Why had he let her go?

Mercy. Staring down at the swirling clear liquid in his shot glass, Maksim said the word aloud with derision. He gulped the rest of the vodka, but his body still hurt with need for her. He glanced across the room to his vast, empty bed. He could have had her, but he'd let her go.

Tomorrow, he promised himself grimly. Tomorrow he would regain control. He would show no mercy. He would be ruthless.

Virgin or not, Grace would be his.

* * *

The next morning Grace stared forlornly out the small window beside her desk at work.

The snow that had made London so magical had melted, turning to rain. And the rest of last night's magic had melted right along with it.

From their suite of offices on the thirtieth floor, where the Cali-West Energy Corporation had leased space, Grace looked down at the people on the street, far below the other high-rise office buildings of Canary Wharf. The city seemed foggy and sad.

Or maybe that was just her today. Foggy. Sad. With a deep breath, Grace tried to turn her attention back to her computer screen, but her focus on work kept getting interrupted by her painful memories of last night.

She'd sworn she wouldn't surrender to Maksim.

Then she'd not only surrendered, she'd thrown herself at him—and he'd rejected her!

She rubbed her temples, then tried to straighten her wrinkled beige skirt and oversize brown cardigan. She'd planned to iron them this morning but she hadn't had time. She'd tossed and turned all night, then fallen asleep around dawn and had nearly slept through her alarm. Now she felt exhausted. Every time she thought about last night, she writhed inside. Her cheeks burned hot with shame.

She'd tried to resist him.

She'd really thought she could.

But then when he'd shown such unexpected gentleness, allowing himself to be vulnerable in front of her when he spoke of his family, she'd been helpless to fight him.

But she must have overestimated Maksim's desire for

her. Big surprise there. What did she know about men? He'd wanted her—she was still sure about that. Then he'd changed his mind. One moment he'd been kissing her senseless, peeling her clothes off, his hands roaming all over her as he'd pushed her back against his bed.

The next minute he'd been shoving her into a taxi without so much as a good-night.

She swallowed. The reason for the change was obvious. He'd been turned off by her virginity. What man would want to initiate a twenty-five-year-old virgin?

It was all too horrifying.

Sometime before dawn, she'd gotten up from bed and packed up the Leighton dress and coat and the platinum tiara. She would send them to his penthouse tonight and be done.

Even now she could hardly believe that she'd worn them to a society party, where she'd been lavished with kisses by the most devastating man in the city, probably the *world*.

She was lucky he'd rejected her, she told herself. She stared blankly at the screen.

She'd thought she was invulnerable, but she'd utterly lost herself in the winter moonlight. He'd stolen her soul away, evaporating it from her body like mist under his power.

The intoxicating force of his touch had done such strange things to her, made her weak inside, made her melt in his arms. She wondered if she'd ever truly loved Alan at all. Because if she had, how could she have surrendered to Maksim?

As if on cue, she heard Alan's peevish voice. "Where

were you last night? I came back early and you weren't in your apartment."

She looked up to see him standing over her desk. It was almost ten-thirty and he was just now coming into the office. That was typical. What was unusual was that his pale, handsome features looked irritated as he looked down at her.

"I was out," she replied shortly. There was not a single detail about last night that she felt like sharing with Alan.

"Did you finish the wedding plans?"

Anger—usually such a foreign emotion—suddenly burned through her. Did he think she had no life of her own? Did he really think after doing his shopping, she would rush to spend her whole night planning his wedding and honeymoon?

The answer was clear as he waited with his arms folded. *Yes*.

Clenching her hands under her desk, she took a deep breath. It wasn't enough that she came into work before dawn while he never bothered to arrive before ten. It wasn't enough that she'd spent the past three hours frantically writing his speech for a charity event that afternoon, a speech he'd insisted for weeks that he would write himself—until she'd found the task waiting in her inbox that morning.

"Look at these!" The front desk receptionist appeared with an enormous arrangement of exquisite long-stemmed white calla lilies, which she set on Grace's desk. "Aren't they gorgeous?"

"Oh, thank you," Alan said with a smile and a wink,

immediately reaching for the card. "I can't imagine who—"

"Oh no, Mr. Barrington," the receptionist said with a giggle. "They're for Miss Cannon."

"For me?" Grace exclaimed in shock.

"For you?" Alan said with equal shock. "What…who?"

Drawing the card from the envelope, Grace silently read a single line written in a rough, sharp hand.

"Last night you dazzled me like the sun in winter. Waiting outside now for the bright burn of dawn—M."

Happiness soared through Grace.

She hadn't made a fool of herself after all! Maksim hadn't been disgusted with her for being a virgin! He'd just sent her away in the taxi because…

Because he wanted more than just a one-night stand? Because he was trying to protect her and take things slow?

It was the only possible reason.

And he already wanted to see her again! She suddenly felt like tap-dancing beneath her desk.

She closed her eyes and inhaled the heady scent of lilies. Maksim thought she was worth such extravagant beauty.

And for the first time in forever *so did she*.

"Well?" the receptionist asked slyly. "Who's the prince charming, Grace?"

"Yes," Alan demanded. "Who?"

She looked up at her boss and saw him with utterly new eyes. She'd suddenly had enough. Straightening in her chair, she gave a dismissive laugh.

"For heaven's sake, Alan, I'm your secretary, not your wife. Why do you care who sends me flowers?"

"I don't," he stammered, clearly surprised. "I just want to make sure that you devote the proper time and energy to your work."

"You mean the time I've spent buying gifts for your various girlfriends?" she said coolly. "Or do you mean the time I've worked for you around the clock without pay?"

The receptionist gasped a laugh. At Alan's dirty look, she gulped and scurried away.

He looked back at Grace. "Look here, Gracie…"

She leaned her elbows against her desk. "Or maybe you mean the times I've asked you for a pay raise." She thrummed her pen thoughtfully against her cheek. "All the times you put me off and said we'd talk about it later. When I was promoted to your executive assistant. When I moved to London with you."

He swallowed, licking his lips as he attempted a weak smile. "You know how valuable you are to me—how much I need you!"

"I'm afraid that's not good enough."

He leaned over her desk. "Is this because of Francesca? Because you don't need to feel jealous," he whispered urgently. "Our engagement isn't real."

"You bought her lingerie!" she gasped.

He gave a bitter laugh. "I *thought* it was real. She set me straight last night when I suggested an elopement. That's why I asked if you'd started the wedding plans yet—you don't need to bother. She only agreed to a fake engagement to make some other man jealous. She has no interest in marrying me—or sleeping with me either." He clenched his jaw. "But as long as I play along with her, she'll make sure her father doesn't know, and the merger will still go through."

Francesca was trying to make some other man jealous?

Grace suddenly feared she knew who that man might be. And she didn't like it one bit.

"So don't give up on me." Alan gave her his old charming, Hugh Grant smile. "In a few months, it will all be over. Things can go back to how they were. Just be patient. I'm asking you, Grace. Wait for me."

Looking into his smiling eyes, Grace sucked in her breath.

Oh my God.

He'd known.

All this time she'd thought he was clueless about her feelings. But *he'd known about her crush all along.* He'd used her own feelings against her. Used her for free work. Used her for a nice ego boost or a snog when it suited him.

"Well? What do you say?"

"I'm sorry," she said evenly.

And she was. Sorry that she'd given him all her time and energy. Sorry she'd thrown away better opportunities with both hands, while pretending he was the solution to all her problems!

With a sympathetic smile, he leaned against her desk. "Sorry you have to wait?"

"I'm sorry, but things have to change." She slowly rose from her desk. "I'm dating someone else. And if you want me to remain your secretary, it's going to cost you."

He gaped at her. "Where else would you go?"

"I've had another job offer."

"From whom?"

"That's irrelevant," she said. "Since I had to move from Los Angeles, my mother's had trouble paying her mortgage. I need ten thousand dollars to stay working for you. Call it a retroactive raise."

"Ten thousand?" he gasped. "Dollars? Are you joking?"

"And effective immediately," she continued sweetly, "I expect a raise in pay commensurate with the increased cost-of-living expenses in London."

"Grace!"

"So what do you say?" She paused. "Shall I stay and finish writing your speech for the charity event this afternoon? Or shall I clean out my desk?"

He stared at her.

"Stay," he muttered. "Finish the speech. You'll get your raise with your next paycheck."

"And my bonus?"

"Ten thousand dollars? That will take longer."

"You have until Christmas Eve."

He ground his teeth. "Fine. Would you perhaps like to take the rest of the afternoon off, as well?" he suggested acidly.

"Yes, thank you." She smiled at him. "I'll go as soon as I'm done with your lovely speech."

Alan tightened his jaw, then turned away. "Fine."

She almost felt sorry for him as she watched his hunched shoulders as he returned to his office and slammed the door. Almost.

Getting one afternoon off wasn't even close to all the hours she'd worked for free over the past two years, but…Maksim was outside at this very moment, waiting for her. Grace's feet tapped excitedly as she polished the last few paragraphs of the speech, making sure it was perfect before she e-mailed Alan the finished copy. Her spirits were soaring as she put on her old coat and came triumphantly out of the building.

She found Maksim waiting for her at the curb in an ultra-expensive, black Bugatti Veyron.

"Thank God," he said with a dark gleam in his eye as she climbed into the car. "It was agony waiting for you."

"It was twenty minutes."

He put on dark sunglasses. "I'm not a patient man."

She laughed aloud, happier than she'd been for years. "Thanks for the flowers," she said. "They really lifted employee morale. I just got a raise from my boss."

"You lift *my* morale, *solnishka mayo*," he growled. He reached over to change gears, and his hand accidentally brushed her thigh. "Ready to celebrate?"

"Yes," she breathed.

"So am I," he said, looking down at her steadily in a way that made her feel hot all over. Then he gunned the thousand-horsepower motor, and the Bugatti flew like a black raven through the mist and rain.

CHAPTER SEVEN

GRACE took a deep breath as she stood on the terrace of Maksim's Dartmoor estate, staring out at the snow-dusted fields. They'd left the London rain far behind. Here the moors were wide and haunted beneath the last rays of fading red sun. A thick white mist was blowing in from the sea.

Tears fell unheeded down Grace's cold cheeks. The sound of her mother's happy crying still echoed in her ears as she tucked her cell phone back into her bag.

She'd done it. She'd told her mother that she would save the house from foreclosure. Now Grace would make sure her family never worried about money again. She took another deep breath, grateful beyond words that she'd found her strength. That she'd found herself.

Thanks to Maksim.

Maksim, who'd treated Grace like a princess. She'd never have imagined that any man, let alone someone so handsome and powerful and rich beyond belief, would treat her that way.

Now Grace realized she should accept nothing less. She would never settle again.

She wanted the fairy tale.

She turned from the wide terrace overlooking the carefully tended classical garden and returned through the back door of his eighteenth-century country house. Maksim was waiting.

The inside of the house was every bit as Gothic and misty as the moors outside. Perhaps because the fifty rooms had no furniture—just white translucent curtains that seemed to move against the windows even when they were closed, twisting eerily in an invisible draft that no human skin could feel.

She'd called her mother outside on the terrace, where the cell phone reception was better, and where she could have privacy. She didn't want Maksim to know how desperate she'd been for money. She didn't want him to think of her as someone who needed saving.

She'd been proud to save herself.

She wanted Maksim as her equal. As her friend. As her…lover? She could barely move her lips to form the word, but there it was. Her secret.

She wanted him as her lover.

She wanted him for the fire he sparked inside her. For the way he'd somehow made her become the woman she'd always dreamed she could be. For the dreams suddenly coming true around her, like roses blooming full and red amid the breathless hush of winter.

Grace walked back through the empty salon. Painted cherubs looked down at her from the two-hundred-year-old painting soaring high above the enormous chandelier.

This house was beautiful, large…and lonely.

No one lived here, Maksim had told her. He'd bought

it to use as his weekend escape, but he'd been too busy with work to bother visiting. The caretaker and his elderly wife, who resided in a nearby cottage, were the only ones who'd entered the estate for the last several years.

Until now.

The house seemed happy to finally have company, she thought, then nearly laughed at her own ridiculous thought. The *house* was happy?

What was it about houses that made people so batty?

Grace wiped her eyes as she approached the dining room. She felt like an idiot for crying because she was happy, but as foolish as it sounded, she felt as if her family—as long as they had their home—could survive and be strong.

She entered the dining room, then stopped in shock.

The room was dark, lit by the fire in the marble fireplace—and by dozens of white pillar candles of various sizes and shapes on the floor.

Maksim was lighting the last candle as she entered. He was darkly handsome, wearing a black shirt and black pants. He looked up at her, then straightened as the expression on his handsome face changed to concern.

"You were crying," he demanded.

"Houses," she sniffled, looking with wonder at all the candles. "They don't make a family, except they do, don't they?"

He frowned. "You're not making any sense."

Laughing through her tears, she shook her head. "I'm just happy. I needed money for my house. Thanks to the raise, I'll have it."

"Good," he growled. "About time you moved out of Barrington's basement."

He'd misunderstood her, but she didn't correct him. Moving out of Alan's house *was* a good idea, and as soon as her family's home was secure, that was exactly what she intended to do.

Blowing out the match and tossing it aside, he put his arms around her. "Now leave his office and come work for me."

"Mixing business and pleasure would be a bad idea," she whispered.

He stroked her chin. "I'll buy you a house as your bonus. Any house you want."

She looked around the eighteenth-century country mansion mischievously. "Really? *Any* house?"

He laughed, then he kissed her. His lips were warm and passionate. She felt his rough chin against her skin as his tongue stroked hers, luring her, intoxicating her. She pressed her body against his. When he pulled away, a little sigh escaped her.

"Let me take care of you, Grace," he murmured against her skin.

"I don't want you as my boss," she managed to say. "And I don't want your money. I just want you."

His eyes flickered.

"And I take care of what is mine," he growled.

She was his? The idea of his possession was like a warm blanket wrapped around her. He cared about her. Hadn't he proved that last night when he'd let her go? He could have easily made her a one-night stand, but instead he was wooing her. Courting her in this romantic way.

And she was starting to care about him more than she wanted to admit.

He sat down on a thick white blanket on the floor near the fire. He patted a spot next to him. "Sit down," he said, quirking a seductive eyebrow. When she did, he handed her a flute of champagne.

"Sure, you have champagne," she teased. "But what about furniture?"

Reaching into the hamper, he held out a chocolate-covered strawberry. "I don't need a bed for what I intend to do to you."

She opened her mouth obediently, and he fed it to her. Then she took the next strawberry from the basket and returned the favor. As he suckled the rich chocolate from the lush fruit, he never took his gaze from hers.

She shivered. When she finished the flute of champagne, he took it from her without a word. Gently brushing her hair aside, he kissed her neck. She closed her eyes, shuddering with desire as he nibbled his way down her throat.

"You're so beautiful," he murmured.

And for no good reason, she felt like crying.

"Thank you," she said, opening her eyes to look directly into his. "Thank you, Maksim."

His dark eyes looked surprised. "For what?"

She looked past him, to the translucent white curtains and lead-paned windows overlooking the winter twilight. Shaking with the force of her emotion, she looked into his face.

"It has been a hard few years for my family." She took

a deep breath. "I didn't know what to cling to anymore. Didn't know what to believe in."

Maksim looked at her steadily above the shimmering firelight. His eyes were deep smoke, his strong jawline shadowed with bristle. Surrounded by the flickering white candles on the floor around them, he looked like a dark king from a medieval fantasy.

"Now I do," she said softly, then took a deep breath. "I can believe in you."

He blinked. Hard.

Clenching his jaw, he looked away.

"I'm no saint," he said in a low voice. "I told you from the beginning. I'm selfish. Ruthless."

"You're wonderful." Reaching her hand up to his rough chin, she gently turned his cheek until he looked at her. "I've never met a man like you before. You claim to be selfish and even cruel, but you're not. You're a good man, Maksim. You don't want anyone to know it. You think it's weakness," she said softly. "But I know your secret."

She felt him tremble in her arms. He took a haggard breath, briefly closing his eyes before he looked down at her. His dark gaze shot through her soul. "I've never met anyone like you, Grace. So determined to see the best in people even if they don't deserve it."

"Because of you." She licked her lips with sudden nervousness. "For the first time in my life, I feel brave. Brave enough to…"

Her words dwindled off as the expression in his dark gaze changed, became fired with heat. He stroked her cheek, looking down at her. Their bodies were so close. She could feel every inch of hard muscle, all the strength of his power. Their eyes were interlocked, and in that moment she could hardly say where her soul ended and his began.

"Grace…"

Lowering his mouth to hers, he kissed her. It was a kiss of anguish and longing and such tenderness that a little whimper escaped her.

Then a Russian curse exploded from his lips. He suddenly pushed away from her.

Rising to his feet, he paced in front of her, clawing his hands through his dark hair.

"What is it, Maksim?" she whispered, staring up at him from the blanket. It was the second time he'd pushed away from her. Was something wrong with her? Something about the way she kissed that he didn't like?

Insecurity went through her. She thought of what Alan had told her, that Francesca only agreed to a fake engagement to make some other man jealous.

What if Maksim still loved Francesca?

"It's all right," Grace said miserably. "I understand. I'm not the one you want."

When he spoke, his voice was low. Harsh. "You think I don't want you?"

"It's all right, truly." She shook her head, trying to keep the tears from her eyes. "I'm not remotely your type—"

Falling to his knees, he grabbed her upper arms so tightly that they bruised.

"Not want you? God! Not want you?" he exploded. "All I can think about is taking you, Grace. In the bed, against the wall, on the floor! Not want you? I want to spread your thighs beneath me. I want to caress and suckle and taste you until you explode and shake around me. I want you and every second I physically hold myself back from making love to you is killing me!"

His voice echoed against the soaring ceilings of the empty dining room as it slowly sank in. *He wanted her.*

"Then why do you keep pushing me away?"

He cradled her face in his hands. "Because you are the only sunlight I've known for years," he said in a low voice. "I can't extinguish that warmth in you, Grace. I can't let the world go dark and cold without your light."

"You're afraid to hurt me?"

Clenching his jaw, he nodded.

"Don't be." She took a deep breath. "After my bad experience with Alan, I've decided love is totally overrated." She wouldn't be stupid enough to risk her heart again. No matter how Maksim made her feel. She reached out to stroke his rough cheek, tracing her fingertips down his throat. "I promise you can't hurt me...."

He grabbed her wrist. "Don't," he said harshly.

"Please," she whispered. "Just kiss me."

Their eyes locked.

With a groan, he surrendered.

His lips brushed hers, then bruised her. The rush that spread through her body was unimaginable. He yanked off her coat. He pulled off her oversize brown cardigan. His hands moved urgently over her plain white shirt, undoing the buttons rapidly, pulling the last one until it ripped. He dropped the shirt to the floor and looked at her in the firelight.

"I will try to go slow," he whispered, visibly shaking

as he touched her bare skin. "But the way you affect me, Grace…"

He kissed her again, reaching his strong arms around her, and her white cotton bra fell to the floor. Then suddenly his shirt was off, as well, and pants and skirt all disappeared in a frantic tumble.

And suddenly he was standing before her.

She'd never seen a naked man before. She took a deep breath and looked at him in the firelight. Candles were glowing all around them in the darkness of the empty mansion as she gently reached her hand to stroke him.

He shuddered, jumping beneath her touch.

"You're beautiful," she whispered.

He gasped. Gathering her up in his arms, he laid her gently beneath him on the thick blanket in front of the fire.

She felt the hard muscles of his masculine body, so much bigger and stronger than she would ever be, and as he stroked her naked body in front of the fire she arched beneath his hands. He slowly kissed down her neck, between her breasts, down her belly.

Did he mean to…? He couldn't possibly intend to…?

Moonlight traced the translucent, gauzy curtains. A sudden frozen rain rattled the windows as he pushed her thighs apart.

Lowering himself between her legs, he kissed the inside of her thighs, slowly licking higher and higher. Her cheeks burned and she tried to scoot out of his grasp, but he held her.

Spreading her wide, he tasted her.

Her nipples tightened so painfully that she gasped

aloud. A thousand zinging sensations went up and down her body like lightning shooting out of her fingertips, her toes, her hair. Every nerve was on fire, and she twisted beneath him.

His tongue changed width and pressure, lapping her widely then swirling lightly against her aching nub. She felt dizzy. She was breathless as her body tightened in agony, wanting…wanting…

She cried out as the first burst rolled through her like thunder, starting low and deep inside her and sweeping through her body until she screamed. At that moment he moved his body and pushed himself inside her.

For an instant the pain was wrenching, but pleasure immediately rode behind it, making her shudder in rhythmic contractions around him. As he thrust inside her, she heard his low gasp. With agonizing slowness, he pulled back, then thrust again. She whimpered as increasing pleasure built inside her. Then her hips rose to meet his as he rode her.

He filled her completely. Slowly, steadily, deeper and deeper until he seemed to reach her very heart. The intensity was too much, pleasure so great it was almost pain.

She looked up and saw his hard masculine body over hers, his chest laced with dark hair and his muscles glistening with sweat in the firelight as he thrust inside her. His eyes were closed. She saw the agony on his face as he held himself back, forcing himself to move slowly. His handsome face was taut as he gasped with every slow, deep thrust, filling her to the hilt.

Maksim.

Her prince.

Her lover.

Her...love?

As if he'd heard her thought, he opened his eyes. Their gazes locked, their souls linked. And as he pushed inside her one last time, her world shattered into a million pieces. She shuddered and shook with him so deeply inside her, deeper, deeper, until she felt like she was being ripped in two by his brutally hard body. Her body arched with electricity as she exploded and gasped out his name.

CHAPTER EIGHT

MAKSIM'S intention in bringing her here had been to seduce her. He'd intended to coldheartedly win her loyalty to get information he could use against Barrington. But his conscience had interfered again. He'd tried to resist. To let her go. To push her away.

Until she'd taken him in her soft arms and asked him to kiss her.

In that single instant he'd tossed aside his plans to get information from her. He'd given up his revenge on Barrington. He'd even given up the merger for the sake of possessing her.

He'd given it all up so he could possess her without guilt and be even half the man she believed him to be.

It had taken all his self-control to go slowly. He was determined to make it good for her. But when their eyes met as he slid deeply inside her, when he saw her beautiful face as their bodies joined, he could barely hold himself back from exploding.

He felt her arch and heard her gasp his name; and then he utterly lost control.

Thrusting one last time, he spilled into her with a hoarse, harsh cry that blended with hers. He closed his eyes as his body was racked with waves of pleasure almost too intense to bear.

He collapsed against her. He must have blacked out for a millisecond before he realized he was crushing her with his weight. And he never wanted to hurt her, never, this fragile innocent beauty who'd given him her virginity....

He rolled to one side of her, cradling her softly in his arms, kissing her forehead. She took several deep breaths before she opened her eyes and looked at him. But she did not speak. What had happened between them was too deep for words.

Candlelight and firelight flickered on the lush curves of her naked body. Grace was everything he'd imagined. Just what he'd fantasized about. But she had more than just an innocent beauty—she had an innocent soul.

He was her first.

Maksim gloried in the thought. It filled him with pride and wonder. No other man had ever touched her. No other man had ever thrust inside her—

Then he suddenly stopped breathing.

Distracted by the conflict between his conscience and his overwhelming need for her, he'd forgotten to use a condom. The first and only time he'd ever forgotten.

Turning from her on the blanket, he stared blankly at the high ceiling. Barely visible cherubs smiled down at him from the shadowed depths.

What if there were a child?

"Maksim." Grace rolled her naked body over his. He

felt the soft press of her breasts into his chest as she looked down at him with concern. "Did I do something wrong?"

"No." Wrapping his arms around her, he kissed her on the temple. "Don't think that, *solnishka mayo*. Never think that."

She ducked her head, placing her cheek against his heart. "Do you feel like you've betrayed Francesca?"

Francesca? He was trying not to think about her—something astonishingly easy to do, considering she'd been his mistress for a full year. He set his jaw. "Why ask me about her? Do you feel you've betrayed Barrington?"

She shook her head. "I never loved him. That was infatuation, nothing more."

For reasons he couldn't explain, those words seeped into him, relaxing him like a warm embrace. He stroked her naked back lazily, appreciating the curve of her body and sweet, smooth skin. "I'm glad to hear that. So there's nothing to stop you from coming to work for me."

"But I thought you said I shouldn't endure sexual harassment from my boss?" she teased.

"You'll enjoy it from me," he growled.

"A lovely offer." She sighed, then slowly shook her head. "But I can't desert Alan. I feel sorry for him."

"Why? He's gotten the deal—and the bride."

"But he just found out she never intended to actually marry him. They haven't even slept together. She's just trying to make some other man jealous." She took a deep breath, then lifted her eyes to his. "I think it must be you."

His hand stroking her back stilled.

"It's not a real engagement?"

"The merger is real. Her father doesn't know. But the

engagement will end." She licked her lips. "And you can have Francesca back, if you want her."

For a moment Maksim couldn't even breathe.

He couldn't believe it.

What a joke of fate. The moment he'd decided to surrender to his conscience, the moment he'd decided he wouldn't try to force information out of Grace— she'd tossed the key to destroying Alan Barrington right into his lap.

With this one bit of information, he could destroy the merger.

Part of him had suspected this all along. Francesca had been so furious when Maksim hadn't caved to her ultimatum in October. After a tempestuous year together, a year of screaming breakups and passionate makeups, she'd demanded that he marry her. "Or else," she'd threatened ominously, "you'll lose me." But Maksim never responded very well to threats or ultimatums. In reply he'd kissed her until she sagged in his arms, then he'd whispered, "In that case, I must lose you."

Typical of Francesca to orchestrate her battle by going straight to his enemy. Managing to string Barrington along without even giving him her body— Maksim was impressed. But the fact that she'd never intended to actually go through with her threat to marry him revealed her weakness.

All Maksim had to do was tell the Earl of Hainesworth the truth, and the merger would be his. Along with Francesca, if he wanted her....

"Do you love her, Maksim?" he heard Grace whisper. "Do you?"

He abruptly focused on the sweet, beautiful girl in his arms.

Grace was so different from his former mistress in every way. She was curvaceous, with full cheeks the color of roses, skin that glowed with health, and natural blond hair that looked like blended gold and silver in the candlelight.

Francesca was tiny and thin in ultrachic designer clothes, with fiery red hair that came compliments of an expensive salon. Natural? Francesca was the type of woman who wore red lipstick to bed!

Grace was poor, young and sweet, and so kind-hearted that she let others take advantage of her, while Francesca gleefully bossed the servants and rode all over anyone weaker than herself.

Grace was honest to a fault. Even now, Maksim could see the vulnerability in her eyes as she anxiously looked at him. Francesca savored nothing more than a viciously well-placed lie. She planned her love affairs like a chess match, or possibly like a general leading troops into a war she intended to win.

"She's so beautiful," Grace said, biting her lip. "She's the kind of woman any man would want."

It would be easy to hurt Grace, Maksim thought. And he never wanted to do it.

"I'm with you now." He rose from the blanket and swiftly blew out the candles around them before he nestled back against her, pressing his naked body against hers. He cuddled her in his arms, turning them both on their sides toward the fire.

With a little sigh she relaxed in his arms. In no time

at all he felt the even rise and fall of her breath as she slept peacefully against his chest. Trustingly.

Normally after he'd been with a woman, he couldn't leave her fast enough. But with Grace, he felt different. She made him feel strangely at peace.

He stared at the fire, waving and crackling and dying in the marble fireplace.

He could complete the merger. Get his revenge on Barrington. Get everything he'd dreamed of: he could create and control the largest oil and gas company in the world.

Or…he could do the unimaginable.

He could forget he'd ever heard the information. And keep Grace as his mistress.

He'd planned to spend the winter in Moscow after the merger was done. He could bring Grace to live in his new Rublyovka estate. He rather liked the idea of having her cook for him, bustling about, making him laugh, sharing his bed at night. How better to keep himself warm through the long, cruel Russian winter?

He could open her credit accounts at all the luxury shops in one of the most expensive cities in the world. He could hire a tutor to give her Russian lessons.

And Maksim could give her other kinds of lessons as well. Personally. He suspected the recent virgin would be a quick and eager student….

Her only job would be to be his mistress, enjoy his company and spend his money. She would be happy.

Maksim stared at the hypnotic dwindling of the fire. Could he let Barrington win? Could he let the merger go? Could he give up his dream of world domination—

and let Barrington have it, while he slipped into a distant second place, possibly making his own company ripe for an eventual hostile takeover?

Giving up this merger meant potentially losing everything he'd ever fought for. But the choice before him was plain.

Grace or the merger.

He couldn't fool himself into thinking he could have both. If Grace found out he'd betrayed her, using her careless words in bed against her boss, she would never forgive him.

But if he didn't betray her, would he ever be able to forgive himself?

Maksim held her in his arms as the moonlight flooded through the high windows. The dying firelight flickered in the sleek marble fireplace.

He'd never appreciated this house quite so much before. Never appreciated anything quite so sharply as this moment. He knew it would never come again. She sighed in sleep, her breasts swaying beneath his arms. He felt himself stir. This woman moved him like no other.

Her eyelids fluttered. She looked up at him with dream-drenched eyes.

"I think I love you," she whispered.

His body went absolutely hard. So hard it hurt.

She blinked. "Oh my God, did I say that aloud? I thought I was dreaming."

"You said it out loud," he said tersely.

"I just meant—"

"I know what you meant."

He gripped her.

She'd just experienced sex for the first time, he told himself. That was what she meant. She loved him in the way a man loved a well-cut suit or a perfect steak or watching sports on Sunday; or crushing an opponent to win a big business deal. She loved him in the way a person loves a pleasure they never want to end.

He told himself these things, but he knew they were lies.

"Maksim…" She touched his shoulder.

"Go to sleep," he told her harshly.

The fire had turned to ashes before he heard her finally fall back into slumber. But he couldn't sleep. He lay awake all night, watching as the pink dawn rose over the misty-white moor.

He had to make a choice.

The warm light of dawn sifted through the high windows, revealing the dust motes trembling in the air. He woke her with a kiss. On her shoulder. On her temple. All over her naked body.

She turned over with a sigh, blinking and not quite awake, but she held out her arms for him. Instinctively welcoming him into her soft body. Into her soft heart.

But this time, as he tenderly made love to her in the pink fresh light of dawn, he used a condom.

Horrible. Unbearable.

When could she leave?

Grace glanced at the clock on her computer screen and tapped her toes impatiently on the floor. She didn't want to be at work on Christmas Eve!

Apparently, no one else wanted to be here, either, since she was the only one left in the office. She'd come to tie up a few loose ends before her two-week vacation in Los Angeles. She smiled as she thought of home. She just needed to wait long enough to pick up the check for $10,000 that would save her mother's house.

But Alan was, of course, late.

Grace was trying to focus on compiling the necessary data for Cali-West's fourth-quarter sales reports. But her mind kept wandering to her favorite subject.

Maksim.

The past two weeks had been the most wonderful of Grace's life. Maksim had taken her out nearly every day. He'd taken her dancing. Out to dinner. And it was hilarious how he kept trying to buy her things. Like yesterday, when he'd suddenly pulled her into a car dealership in South Kensington and wanted to buy her a gold Maserati convertible.

"To match your hair," he'd said, then smiled. "Think of it as a hair accessory."

When she'd refused, he'd tried to argue with her. "It's a small Christmas present," he'd said. "A trifle. A token. *A stocking stuffer!*"

He'd really made her laugh with that one.

She'd steadfastly refused, of course. But later that night in his penthouse suite, he'd made her an offer she could not refuse—he'd made love to her all night.

That must be why she felt so tired today. So absolutely exhausted, and even a little bit queasy.

Especially when she thought about leaving Maksim for the next two weeks.

She was falling in love with him.

She'd already fallen like a brick!

So much for her defenses. Thank God he wasn't in love with Francesca as she'd briefly feared, because she'd started to fall in love with him from the moment he'd taken her virginity in that empty house on the snow-swept moor. She'd even stupidly blurted it out.

Fortunately, by some miracle, telling him she loved him just days into their relationship hadn't scared him off!

Perhaps he was starting to care for her, as well.

The thought made her heart leap in her chest. She wanted to buy him a Christmas present before she left, but what did you get a man who truly had everything? Her naked body wrapped in a big red bow?

Grace glanced down at her form-fitting gray cardigan, yellow silk blouse, pearls and gray wool slacks. Her clothes weren't quite so glamorous as the Leighton cocktail dress, but they were fresh and pretty and new. She grinned down at her feet. She even had new shoes, lovely pale-pink pumps of such sturdy quality that they would never break. They squeezed her a little in the toe, but who cared about that? They were beautiful. She'd put her first paycheck since her raise to good use.

She wanted to look nice for Maksim.

A stronger wave of queasiness went over her. Grace glanced at her lukewarm coffee cup, feeling ill. Had she drunk too much wine last night at dinner with Maksim? Impossible, she remembered, she'd had just half a glass. It must have been the chicken tikka, then.

Picturing the spicy dish, usually her favorite, she felt so nauseated that she almost retched over her keyboard. Rising to her feet, she stumbled to the ladies' bathroom just in time.

Afterward, as she came out of the bathroom she still felt a bit sick and in a cold sweat. She was just grateful she was alone in the office.

Then she saw she wasn't. Alan stood by her desk.

Oh, thank heaven! He was here with the check, and that meant she could go! Hang the data for the fourth-quarter reports. No one would compile the information until January, so why kill herself over it? She'd collect her bonus, brush her teeth then go to the penthouse to see about convincing Maksim to come home to California with her for Christmas.

If all else failed, she'd convince him via that big red bow. She giggled. Perfect.

But she still felt a bit dizzy as she walked toward her boss. "I'm glad to see you!"

"Are you, Grace?" Leaning against her desk, Alan's pale eyelashes blinked rapidly as he stared down at her. He looked strangely grim.

Something seemed to be bothering him, but Grace still felt queasy and couldn't dredge up enough energy to wonder what it was. "Alan, if you'll just give me my bonus check, I think I'll head out. You don't mind if the sales figures wait? I'm not feeling very well." When he folded his arms and continued to glower at her, she added weakly, "It *is* Christmas Eve…"

"You can take as much time as you want."

"Oh, thank you—"

"Because you're fired."

She stared at him for a long moment. "What?"

"You heard me. You have exactly three minutes to pack up your desk before I have you thrown out."

"Is this a joke?"

"Yes, a joke. The secretary I trusted most just betrayed my secrets and caused me to lose the deal of my life."

"What?" she gasped. "How?" She frantically tried to remember saying anything to anyone. Had she mentioned any details? The numbers, the price? She shook her head. "I never breathed a word to anyone!"

"Lord Hainesworth just pulled his funding and support," he said furiously. "He found out this morning the engagement was fake. I've lost the deal and now I'll likely lose my position as CEO. The board has been after me for the past year. I've lost everything. My only consolation is...*so have you.*"

Oh my God, what had happened?

"It's got to be some ghastly mistake," she said. "I would never betray you. Please, I need that bonus—"

"Bonus?" He barked a laugh. "You're lucky I don't have you thrown in jail for corporate espionage! You'll never get hired again by anyone if I can help it. No job recommendation. No back pay." His lip curled. "Now get the hell out before I call the police."

"But I didn't tell anyone about the fake engagement," she cried. An icy trickle went down her back. "Except..."

"When you blackmailed me into giving you a raise, you didn't mention that you were already working on your back for Maksim Rostov!"

She sucked in her breath.

"It wasn't like that," she gasped. "How did you find out about—"

"Francesca heard it from her friends." Alan shook his head with a derisive snort. "Apparently he's been flashing you all over town, his cheap little mistress. You've always been so desperate for money, Grace. Tell me. What did you enjoy more—selling him my secrets or selling him your body?"

She felt like he'd just slapped her across the face.

"I didn't sell anything," she whispered. "He wouldn't do that to me."

"No? You think Rostov wanted you for your intelligence?" he sneered. "For your beauty?" He looked her up and down. "You might have gotten new clothes, but you're way out of your league. This was always a game between him and Francesca—always. He dumped her. She wanted him back. And now they're together."

"No!"

"If you really believe he would choose you over her, you're even more stupid than I thought." He turned his back on her. "I'm sending the security guard up here in two minutes."

Numbly Grace gathered up a few items from her desk, putting a half-dead plant and two framed pictures of her family into a box. She left the building, then realized she'd forgotten her old coat. The security guard refused to let her back inside. Her only option would be to call Alan and ask him to bring it down to her.

Instead she left without it.

Outside, there was a biting chill in the gray afternoon sky. Clutching the cardboard box to her chest, she shivered in her thin cardigan and silk blouse.

Alan had to be wrong. Maksim wouldn't have betrayed her!

She pictured his darkly handsome face. The way he'd

teasingly fed her chow mein noodles at his penthouse last week. The way he'd tried to trick her into accepting expensive gifts. He'd made love to her. He'd made her laugh. He'd been her first.

He wouldn't use her careless words in bed against her, the words she'd spoken when she'd been feeling insecure and had been seeking reassurance!

But she hadn't told anyone else about the fake engagement. Who else could it be?

The answer was shockingly clear.

He'd intended all along to seduce and betray her.

No. A sob escaped her. She felt dizzy as she walked toward the nearest Tube entrance. Another wave of nausea went over her and her knees shook as she went down the escalator. As she sat on the half-empty train, she felt the curious and pitying stares of other passengers. She knew what they saw—a woman without a coat, red-eyed and holding a box with a plant and picture frames. Easy to follow that story. Sacked on Christmas Eve.

Just sacked—or also betrayed?

She found all her clothes stuffed in two suitcases sitting outside her basement flat in Knightsbridge. The locks had been changed. Alan had tossed her out.

Pulling her cell phone from her handbag, she dialed Maksim's number.

No answer. After three rings, it clicked over to voice mail, to his terse voice saying, "Rostov. Leave a message."

Another wave of dizziness washed over her. She started to leave a message. "Maksim, I've just heard something that can't possibly be…"

Her phone went dead. She stared down at it in shock. It had been her business phone, paid for by her company. Alan must have had it disconnected.

Grace took a deep breath, trying to control the rising panic.

She placed her family photos in the suitcases, wrapped herself in her warmest, thickest, frumpiest sweater and left the box and plant in a nearby rubbish bin. She managed to get back on the Tube, dragging both suitcases behind her.

Could it be true?

She heard the echo of his voice. Husky. Deep. Slightly foreign. *I have been accused of having no heart. I am telling you the truth, Grace. Take this as a warning.*

Struggling with her luggage, she came out of the Tube stop near his hotel. He was likely not there but busy at his office, as he hadn't answered his phone. She would wait for him in the penthouse and…

Then she saw he wasn't busy in the office.

Maksim was walking arm-in-arm with Francesca.

He looked ruthlessly handsome in a gray suit and coat. The redhead at his side wore an ivory coat and six-inch heels. Grace watched in shock as they passed the smiling doorman and went inside his hotel.

She saw the look Francesca gave him over the shoulder. Flirtatious. Cozy. Affectionate.

And Grace felt her knees go weak beneath her.

Trembling, she stumbled out into the road to flag down a cab. She shoved the suitcases inside and collapsed in the back of the black cab. "Heathrow," she gasped to the cabbie.

She could no longer deny the painful truth. She'd loved him, while he…

He'd taken her virginity to win back another woman.

Grace needed to get home. Her mother would take her in her arms and stroke her hair and tell her everything would be all right. Her mother knew about broken hearts.

Grace nearly cried with gratitude when a desk clerk at the airport managed to switch her seat to an earlier flight.

Crossing the Atlantic that endless day, crammed into a middle seat between two large, snoring men who both hogged the armrests and overlapped her space, Grace kept her eyes tightly closed. If she started crying, she was afraid she wouldn't be able to stop.

She had more to worry about than a broken heart.

How would Grace save the house? How would she support her family? Now that her father's life insurance was gone, her family was nearly destitute. And the economy was tough. How would Grace find employment when she'd just been fired for blurting out a billion-dollar secret in bed?

Grace clutched the thin airplane blanket to her chest. Funny to think she'd been so determined to not accept any gifts from Maksim. She'd returned the tiara and Leighton clothes. She'd refused his offer of the Maserati convertible and a new house and his many other suggestions of jewelry and clothes and luxury trips. She'd been so proud to stand on her own two feet. So proud to show Maksim she wanted *him,* not his money.

But money, it seemed, was all Maksim had ever wanted. Money. Revenge. Another billion or so dollars to pile on top of his fortune. She'd given him her virginity and her heart, but he'd only wanted money.

Money…*and Francesca.*

CHAPTER NINE

"SHE'S not here."

Maksim looked up to see Alan Barrington staring down at him from the doorway of his town house. It was dark and gray, past twilight on Christmas Eve.

He'd been knocking on the door of Grace's basement flat for the past five minutes without answer. He hadn't expected to be so late. He'd promised he would take her to the airport for her late-night flight, but secretly he'd planned to talk her out of going home for Christmas. His private jet was waiting at a small nearby airport to whisk them away to the South of France.

But he was fifteen minutes late. Only fifteen minutes—that was something of a miracle, given all the surprises today! The merger was nearly a done deal. Thanks to Francesca, it had fallen into his lap, and he'd have been a fool to refuse. But he'd left the meeting halfway through. His people could mop up the details.

He wanted Grace.

He'd called her as soon as he got out of the meeting but hadn't been able to reach her. "Where is she?"

Barrington glared at him. "Why would I tell you?"

"Her phone was disconnected. Any idea why?"

The man folded his arms. "The phone went with her job, which she lost this afternoon."

"After all her loyalty, you fired her so quickly?"

"Loyalty? Some loyalty. Isn't it enough you already took one woman from me? Now you want the other one?" Barrington turned his lips into a sneer. "I'm not her pimp."

In three leaping steps Maksim had run up the stairs and grabbed him by the throat. "Are you calling Grace a whore?"

"Let me go!" the slender man croaked.

Maksim released him with a growl. "Apologize."

"Oh, so now you're her protector?" The blond man gasped, rubbing his neck. "You did this. You seduced and betrayed her. Not me."

"I never betrayed her," Maksim said, even as that strange, unpleasant prickle snaked down his spine. Guilt?

"Why bother denying it now?" Barrington snarled. "You've won. You've taken the merger. You've taken Francesca. You've gotten your payback—you've gotten rid of me for good. My shareholders have already issued a statement asking for my resignation."

"Good." But at this moment, Maksim's revenge didn't feel very satisfying.

"What do you care about some secretary?" Barrington looked at him with shrewd, beady eyes. "You have Francesca."

Right. Francesca.

Maksim's capricious ex-lover had shown up at his penthouse that morning, offering him Barrington's head on a silver platter. "I've just told my father the truth," she'd said, weeping artful tears from her lovely green eyes. "I never wanted Alan. It was you, Maksim, always you!"

Maksim's furious retort had been interrupted by the ringing of his cell phone. Francesca's father had moved swiftly. He'd always preferred that his company accept the offer from Rostov Oil; only his daughter's fake engagement had made him consider Cali-West. Within half a day the merger proceedings had been well started, although it would take another several weeks before they would be fully signed, sealed and delivered.

Maksim had accepted the deal. But he'd chosen Grace. He'd never used the information she'd shared. He'd never betrayed her.

But he realized now it'd worked out exactly the same as if he had.

He clenched his fists. "Just tell me where she is."

"Flying to Los Angeles, I expect, with the plane ticket I bought her. I hope it crashes." Barrington slammed the door.

Coming down the steps from the Knightsbridge town house, Maksim dialed his private investigator to get her address. But that wasn't all he discovered about her family's situation.

An hour later he was on his private jet en route to California.

The little yellow cottage gleamed in the predawn darkness, a shining beacon on the cliff above the soft roar of the Pacific Ocean.

Breathing heavily after her uphill walk, Grace crept back into her house, tiptoeing as she walked past the artificial Christmas tree decorated with ornaments from her childhood, gleaming with colored lights.

"Gracie?" Her mother suddenly peeked around the kitchen door. "You're awake early. I expected you to sleep in this morning."

Grace hid the small purchase she'd bought at the twenty-four-hour drugstore half a mile away. "Um. Jet lag. I couldn't sleep, so I went on a walk."

"Oh, poor dear," her mother said sympathetically, then brightened. "I'll make you some coffee. Come chat while I baste the ham."

"I'll be right there, Mom." Grace tried to calm her rapidly beating heart as she went to her childhood bedroom. She changed out of her jeans and back into her soft, comforting flannel pajamas and red chenille robe.

She set the bag down on her nightstand.

Her mother had been so happy to pick her up at L.A. airport last night, so joyful that she'd come home even earlier than expected. The boys had jumped up and down as they got her luggage from the carousel, and even seventeen-year-old Josh had hugged her, saying in a low voice, "I'm so glad you're home."

Her mother had driven them in the minivan back home to the northern beach town of Oxnard, an hour away, then made them all hot chocolate at midnight with marshmallows. Everyone finally went to bed to dream happy Christmas dreams.

Except Grace.

She hadn't been able to tell them that they were about

to lose the house they were sleeping in. She'd lied. No, not lied, she told herself angrily. Lying was for selfish bastards like Maksim. All she had done was put off the truth that would break their hearts. But she'd barely been able to stomach the hot chocolate, which was usually her favorite. A low-grade nausea had been with her for two days. As she went to bed late that night in her old bedroom still decorated with posters of rock bands and old teddy bears, even her breasts hurt.

That's when the dreadful thought first occurred to her.

Nausea…dizziness…exhaustion. Painful breasts.

And so she'd sneaked off before dawn to buy a pregnancy test.

It's a waste of money, she told herself firmly. She and Maksim had only had sex a few times—all right, *many* times—but only just that once without protection. Fate wouldn't be so cruel, would it?

She'd been too carried away, too overwhelmed by sensation to even think of using protection that first time. If she'd thought about it, she would have assumed that a playboy like Maksim would naturally make sure he didn't get his many lovers pregnant. Especially lovers he intended to betray.

Her heart still hurt to think about it.

But the pregnancy test would have to wait. She couldn't take it now, knowing her mother was awake and waiting for her.

Grace went slowly into the kitchen. Sitting at the dining table, she could barely tolerate the smell of the creamy, sweet coffee her mother happily served her. But that was nothing compared to being forced to listen to her mother's delighted praise as she tearfully thanked Grace for saving their family.

"I was silly to live in denial and hide from our problems. You've inspired me with your career, Gracie. I've run this home for twenty years," Carol Cannon said as she put homemade biscuits in the oven. "After raising you four children, I can do anything!" She paused thoughtfully. "I might go back to school to become a tax accountant. I was always good at math."

Grace gulped down a single sip of hot coffee, scalding her tongue. The coffee made her feel nauseous, so she put it down immediately. "I know you can do anything you want, Mom."

Her mother's eyes glistened at her. She leaned forward to kiss the top of Grace's head. "I'm so proud of you, Gracie. I want to come with you tomorrow when you take the check to the bank. I'm so grateful to have such a strong daughter to lean on."

Grace rubbed her temples, feeling like a fraud.

They had no savings. No income now that she'd lost her job. In just one week, they would have to leave their beloved seaside cottage and beg their friends and family for a place to stay. And as there were five of them, including three boisterous teenage boys, they would soon wear out their welcome with even their most devoted friends.

I'll tell Mom tomorrow, Grace promised herself over the lump in her throat. *I just want her to enjoy Christmas.*

The rest of the morning was agony for Grace, as she watched her younger brothers open their presents and saw their joy and the grateful hugs they gave their mother. The gifts would all have to be returned to the store tomorrow. They would need every penny to survive. Seventeen-year-old Josh would have to say farewell to his long-desired iPod. Fourteen-year-old Ethan would be forced to give back his new guitar. And twelve-year-old Connor would tearfully have to return his new drums. Even their mother would return the expensive cashmere sweater the boys had bought for her with their own money earned mowing the lawns of neighbors throughout the fall. When Grace opened her own present from her family, she found a large hardcover picture book about the Trans-Siberian Railroad. Looking up at their beaming faces, she felt like crying.

"Thank you," she said over the lump in her throat. "I love you so much."

"It's 'cause you're such a world traveler," her youngest brother said happily. "I helped pick it out."

At brunch Grace watched her mother serve the platter of ham and scalloped potatoes. The boys cheered the food, but all she could think was that the ham alone was worth two weeks of cheap dinners like ramen noodles and frozen bean burritos.

Tomorrow, she repeated to herself, pasting a frozen smile on her face. *I'll tell them tomorrow.*

But after brunch, when her mother and brothers got ready to attend a Christmas-morning service of songs and carols, Grace pleaded jet lag and stayed home.

Now, finally alone, she stared at the pregnancy test, waiting for the results.

Be negative, she willed with every creative visualization technique she'd ever heard about on morning talk shows. *Be negative.*

Her hands shook as she waited for the results. She squinted in the dark bathroom. Would there be one line? Or two? She thought she saw the lines start to form. She couldn't see.

She ran out into the front room with the sunny windows overlooking the sea. The prewar cottage was small and bright and cozy, with old striped couches and cushions they'd had since Grace's childhood.

She looked down at the test. Negative. It would be negative….

Two lines. Oh my God. Two lines. Positive.

She was pregnant!

She heard a sound and turned to look.

Maksim stood in the open doorway. Brilliant sunlight cast him in silhouette, leaving his features dark. His wide, powerful frame filled the door, instantly filling their cliffside cottage with the force of his presence.

For a moment she thought her knees were going to buckle beneath her. In spite of everything, her heart soared to see him. She longed for him to take her in his arms and tell her everything Alan had said was a lie. To tell her he'd never seduced her to get information about the merger and win back a woman a thousand times more desirable than Grace could ever be.

Thrusting the pregnancy test in her robe pocket, she took a deep breath.

"What are you doing here?"

He stepped over the threshold, his eyes focused only on her. "I came for you."

A shiver spread through her body. She could barely

breathe as she faced him. She gripped her old chenille robe more tightly around her body. "You shouldn't have come."

He strode forward, his face tense. "You shouldn't have left London."

She lifted her chin.

"Why?" she said coldly. "Are there other secrets I might have forgotten to blurt out to you in bed?"

His handsome face closed down, looked grim. "I never betrayed you."

"You didn't take the deal with Exemplary Oil?"

He clenched his jaw. "I took it yesterday."

She briefly closed her eyes. So Alan hadn't lied. Everything he'd said was true.

"You must love her very much," Grace said, her voice barely a whisper.

He shook his head. "Grace, listen to me…."

She sucked in her breath, hating him more than she'd ever hated anyone in her whole life. "What are you even doing here? Shouldn't you be celebrating with Francesca?"

"No, damn you!" His steel-gray eyes blazed as he grabbed her by the shoulders. "I don't want her. I want you!"

"On the side?" She gave a harsh, ugly laugh. "You really think you can have anything you want, don't you? You always intended to seduce me for information, from the moment your car splashed me in the street!"

The rage in his eyes faded. His grip on her shoulders loosened.

"You're right," he said in a low voice. "You were nothing more to me then but Barrington's secretary, and

I thought you were his mistress. I intended to use you to take back what was rightfully mine."

"You took my virginity for that." She fought the angry tears rising to her eyes. She would die before she'd let him see her cry! "What is wrong with you? Don't you have a soul?"

His jaw clenched. "When I made love to you, I gave up my plan," he said, looking down at her. "I couldn't use the information you'd told me in bed. I knew I would lose you. So I kept silent. Francesca was the one who told her father. It would have been foolish and useless for me to refuse the deal she brought to me yesterday." He lifted her chin, holding her in his arms. "But I swear to you. On my honor. I never betrayed you."

She wanted to believe him.

Wanted it so badly it hurt.

But she couldn't.

"You mean the same word of honor," she said evenly, "with which you swore you weren't trying to use me against Alan?"

"My only lie," he ground out. He looked at her, and his eyes glittered. "I hated lying to you. But I made the choice, Grace. I chose you."

He stroked her cheek, looking down at her with emotion. She closed her eyes, her heart pounding at his touch.

"Come with me to Moscow," he whispered. "I want you with me. As my secretary, as my mistress, whatever you—"

Her eyes flew open. "Your…secretary?"

She ripped away from him. After everything they'd

been through together—the romance that had consumed her so utterly that she'd fallen in love with him and was about to have his child—that was still how he saw her. As a secretary?

And now that he'd won the merger with Exemplary Oil, he wasn't even trying to hide it. He was no longer even vaguely trying to pretend that he cared for her.

"You mean because I've helped you steal a billion-dollar deal from my last boss," she said scornfully, "you'll kindly allow me to type your letters and make your coffee in Moscow? Except you'll want different fringe benefits than Alan, I suppose. I assume I'm to spend my evenings and weekends earning my wages on my back?"

His dark brows lowered furiously as he grabbed her shoulders. "You know that's not how it is—"

"You want to hide me away in Moscow, so you can enjoy Francesca in London!" The images she'd seen of Francesca with him outside the hotel went through her. "Marrying her is part of your deal, right?"

"Damn you!" he shouted. "I don't want her! I want—"

"I saw you with her yesterday!" she shouted back.

He dropped his hands from her shoulders. "What?"

Tears filled her eyes. She wiped them fiercely. "After I was fired, I went to your hotel. Stupid me, I actually had faith in all the lies you'd told me."

"They weren't lies, not all of them—"

"Oh, yes, I always get things wrong, don't I?" She could barely speak over the lump in her throat. "Because I'm just a silly little secretary. That's all I've ever been to you."

"You little fool," he ground out. "You know that's not true—"

"Stop trying to have it both ways!" she shouted. "You never cared for me, you just took my virginity, you seduced me, you got me—" *Pregnant with your child,* she almost blurted out, but she stopped herself just in time. Humiliation gnawed at her, causing her cheeks to go hot.

She didn't want to tell him about the baby. Ever.

She just wanted him out of their lives for good.

"I did you a favor to get you away from Barrington," he ground out. "You were letting him walk all over you!"

He'd felt sorry for her?

"Oh, thank you. Thank you so much," she said. Waves of acute misery continued to build inside her, making her feel more ill by the minute. "I wish to God I'd never let you touch me!"

Gut-wrenching nausea waved over her. Covering her mouth, she ran to the bathroom, stumbling on the floor to retch over the toilet just in time.

She heard him come in behind her. His voice was suddenly gentle as he said, "But Grace, you're ill."

"It's nothing—the flu—just go!" She wiped her mouth, looking back at him with eyes of fury. "I hate you!"

"Grace—"

"Just go! You liar, you back-stabbing bastard!" She grabbed a bar of soap and threw it at him. He ducked it easily, enraging her still more.

"I'm not leaving you."

"If I'm sick," she bit out, "it's because looking at your face makes me want to puke! My skin crawls when I think of how I let you touch me." She looked at him with eyes of ice. "You're not a prince—you're not even a *man*."

She'd finally pushed him too far.

He stiffened behind her.

"Fine." His lip curled. "Now that I know your true opinion of me, I won't fight to keep you. I see now there is nothing for me here..."

Turning to go, he stopped.

Bending over the carpet, he picked up something that had fallen to the floor and rolled across the carpet.

The pregnancy test had fallen from the hole in her pocket!

She gasped, rising quickly to her feet. "It's not what you think. It's nothing...an old test...a friend's...left here," she stammered helplessly.

"You're pregnant." He looked at her. "You're pregnant?"

She stared at him. She wanted to deny it, but the lie stuck in her throat.

"Am I the father?"

She gasped at the insult.

"You know you are! Although I wish to God you weren't. I wish any other man on earth was the father but you!"

His eyes focused on her coldly. "And I realize now everything I ever thought about you was wrong. I thought you were special. You're not. You're selfish and deceitful. Jealous and controlling."

She gave a harsh laugh. "More than your precious Francesca?"

"Francesca and I broke up because she tried to push

me into marrying her. You did something far worse. You were going to let me walk right out that door, weren't you? You were going to keep my child a secret. You intended to sacrifice our child's need for a father, and live in poverty without even a home, all for the sake of your own selfish pride!"

He knew the house was in foreclosure? She gasped, feeling as if he'd exposed her vulnerable jugular.

"How did you know?" she whispered.

"I told you. I protect what is mine. That means my child. That means his family." His lip curled. "And whether I wish it or not, that means my child's mother." His eyes were cold as he looked down at her. "You will be my wife."

His...wife?

She sucked in her breath.

His duty bride, the ignored spouse he would leave trapped in a lonely Muscovite palace while he continued to pursue the wickedly lovely Francesca in London?

"No," she whispered desperately. She looked around the sunlit cottage. She desperately wanted her family to keep their home. Then she thought of the tiny life in her womb who needed to be protected. Better to remain in poverty in the warm sunshine of California, near family who loved her, than risk either of them anywhere near Maksim's icy Siberia of a heart!

She shook her head hard. "How many times do I have to say it? I don't want your money!"

"But now you will take it." His voice was low, dangerous. His gray eyes glittered at her as he added maliciously, "As you will take my name. Today."

"No! I won't!"

He grabbed her painfully by the shoulders. "Apparently, I haven't made myself clear. You have no choice."

She was suddenly afraid of him, this dangerous man who seemed to control his anger with such icy reserve.

"Your wife in name only?" she whispered.

He gave a hard laugh. "And now you think to trick your way out of my bed? No. You will be my wife in every way. You will sleep naked in my bed and service me at my will."

It was the final stab to her heart. He'd already made it plain he cared nothing for her. He expected her to surrender her body to his possession, without affection, without love?

"You're worse than Alan," she whispered. "A million times worse. Because, you're not asking me to be your wife. You're trying to make me your household slave, chained to your bed."

He stroked her chin.

"I'm not asking you," he said coolly. "I'm telling you. You are pregnant with my child. You will be my wife. Every jewel and home and luxury you could possibly desire will be yours. You are now mine."

He was offering her money, in exchange for giving her body and soul to a man she hated—a man in love with another woman! "A gilded cage. You're offering me the life of a whore!"

He grabbed her wrist, pulling her hard against his muscular body.

"Have it your way, then. You will be my pretty songbird in a golden cage." He kissed her cruelly, punishing her. As she felt her lips bruise beneath his embrace, a whimper escaped her. He drew away with a hard smile, looking down at her with a gaze like frozen steel. "And, my beautiful one, you will sing only for me."

CHAPTER TEN

MOSCOW, ancient stronghold of czars, was white and frozen in the breathless hush of winter. The sprawling modern city of untold wealth was as brutal as Maksim's will, Grace thought. And in the frosty twilight of New Year's Eve, it was as cold as her husband's icy heart.

Grace stared out the window of her large, elegant, lonely bedroom. After nearly a week in this vast city of old poverty and new wealth, her only outings had been to the doctor and to the exclusive shops of Barvikha Village and Tverskaya Street, driven by bodyguards in a Humvee with darkened windows. She'd shopped beside powerful oligarchs and their pouting trophy girlfriends dripping with furs and diamonds.

She'd seen little of the city. She'd seen traffic, traffic and more traffic on the paved, guarded road to Rublyovka. She'd seen huge billboards on Moscow's ring roads, advertising luxury cars and jewels as they drove past old buildings with aging Communist icons chiseled in stone.

For a woman who'd once hated fancy shops, they were now her only excuse to escape her luxury compound. Surrounded by bodyguards and servants, Grace was never alone.

And yet she was always alone.

She was a captive bride in a guarded palace, and she'd been forced to accept she was completely in Maksim's power. He'd made that clear by coldly marrying her in Las Vegas on Christmas Day.

Once her family came back from their Christmas service, Grace had been forced to tell her mother she was pregnant. Then she lied and said she loved her baby's father. She'd endured her family's delighted surprise and her mother's whispered blessing on their hasty elopement. When she learned they had no ring, Carol had wrenched off the precious ring that hadn't left her finger for twenty-seven years.

"Your father would want you to have this," she'd said to Grace, holding out the simple half-carat diamond ring in rose gold as tears streamed down her face. "He would be so happy for you today. I just wish he could be here now."

Grace had blinked back her own tears two hours later, as she gave her vows to Maksim in the small chapel of the Hermitage Resort, a Russian-style casino owned by his friend, Greek tycoon Nikos Stavrakis. And Grace hadn't been blinking back tears of joy, either. Beneath the candlelight and mournful, painted Russian icons, she'd pledged herself to Maksim for life. Barely looking at her, Maksim had tersely done the same.

After their cold wedding, there had been no sunny honeymoon. Maksim had brought her to Moscow on his private jet and abandoned her in his luxurious palace compound in an exclusive neighborhood outside the city. Grace had no idea where he'd spent his days and nights since they'd arrived. She tried to tell herself she didn't care.

Her only consolation was that her family was safe. They would never lose their home or be worried about money again. Maksim had paid off the entire mortgage and had placed a large sum in a bank account to make sure her family would always be financially secure and her brothers could go to college. They were happy because they believed Grace was, too.

She had been well and truly bought.

I'm sorry I did this to you, baby, she thought, rubbing her flat tummy mournfully. She looked around the large, feminine bedroom with the blue canopy bed and the lady's study beside it. Down the hall, the next room was empty. Maksim had ordered her to create the baby's nursery there, but Grace didn't have the heart. She couldn't accept her new life here. Couldn't accept that this was all the home life her child would have.

As purplish twilight fell softly over the skyline of the distant city, Grace finally saw his armored car pull past their front gate.

Where had he been for the past six days? Where was he sleeping at night? Clenching her hands into fists, she rose from her chair at the window and left her bedroom.

From the high second-story landing overlooking the wide marble floors of the downstairs foyer, she saw Maksim enter the house, followed by assistants and bodyguards. His face was dark and tired. He didn't bother to ask the housekeeper about how his new bride was faring. He didn't bother to even glance upstairs. He simply handed Elena his coat, went into his study and closed the door behind him.

For Grace, it was the final straw.

She ran downstairs. Without knocking, she pushed through his study door.

Sitting at his desk, he looked up at her with infuriating calmness. "Yes?"

She hated his coldness. She envied that he had ice water in his veins instead of blood. She wished she, too, could feel nothing, instead of feeling like her heart was continually breaking anew!

"Where have you been?"

He barely glanced at her as he gathered papers on his desk. "You have missed me, my bride?" he said sardonically.

"I'm your wife. I have a right to know if you've been sleeping with someone else!"

"Of course you do," he said with a cold laugh. "I can tell you I've been working day and night to finish details on the Exemplary merger, sleeping two hours a night on a cot in my office. But of course you will immediately know I have been with another woman. You will immediately suspect I've set up Francesca in a suite at the Ritz-Carlton."

Grace's heart fell to the floor.

"Francesca's in Moscow?" she whispered.

His lips twisted into an ironic smile. "And to think I once believed you had such faith in people."

"You destroyed that!"

"Have no fear, my dear wife," he drawled. "I have no interest in Francesca. How could I, when I have such a warm, loving wife waiting in my bed at home?"

His barb went straight to the heart. She clenched her hands into fists. "Just try getting into bed with me sometime, and you'll see how warm and loving I am!"

Maksim rose wearily from his desk. "Enough." Placing a stack of papers in his briefcase beside his laptop, he started walking toward the study door. "If you have nothing else to discuss, I'll wish you good-night."

She stared at him incredulously. "You're leaving? Just like that?"

He stopped and turned back to her. At the intensity of his expression, she trembled from within.

Then he lowered his head and kissed her softly on the cheek. "*Snovem godem,* Grace," he said softly. "Happy New Year."

She turned her face up toward his, her heart aching with the memory of the man she'd loved in London. She searched his gaze for some remnant of the man she'd laughed with, cared for. *Loved.*

Then he turned from her.

"Don't wait up."

Anguish rose in her heart…then anger. She hated his coldness. How could she have ever thought he was a good man?

"You can't keep me locked up here!"

He glanced back curiously. "Do you not think so?"

"I'm not your slave!"

"No." He gave her a brief, cool smile. "You are my wife. You are carrying my child. You will live in comfort and luxury, with nothing to do but enjoy the pleasure of your own company."

"I'm going insane!"

"How surprising."

She ground her teeth in frustration. "It's New Year's Eve. Elena is going to Red Square…"

Her voice trailed off as she saw him shaking his head.

"There will be half a million people in Red Square. The bodyguards couldn't protect you."

"Protect me? From what?"

He shrugged. "I have enemies. Some hate me for my billions, some hate me for my title. You could be kidnapped for ransom. It's rare but it does sometimes happen. Or perhaps—" he glanced at her keenly "—you'd be tempted to run off in the crowd."

"I won't," she said tearfully. "Please. I just want to live a normal life!"

"Just what every princess wants," he said sardonically. "And cannot have."

He turned away.

"Maksim, please don't leave me here," she whispered. "I can't bear to be left like this."

He paused at the door, not bothering to turn around.

"Have a pleasant evening, my bride."

She stood in shock in his office until she heard the front door slam and the silence as his bodyguards and assistants left with him.

She walked slowly up the wide, sweeping stairs to her lonely bedroom.

He'd left her alone on New Year's Eve.

Was it really possible that Lady Francesca Danvers was in Moscow?

Very possible. The fiery, tempestuous redhead was the woman Maksim had really wanted all along. The woman every man wanted.

She tried to tell herself she didn't care. But still, her heart felt perilously close to despair.

"Can I bring you something to eat, princess?" Elena said softly, and Grace looked up to see the older Russian woman standing in the doorway. She liked the capable housekeeper, who supervised a staff of twenty and spoke fluent English.

But between nausea and fury, food was the last thing on Grace's mind. She shook her head.

"You must eat something, Prince Maksim said, for the baby."

"He's not the boss of me!" Grace shouted, then she felt instantly abashed about her childish behavior when she saw the expression on the housekeeper's face. "I'm sorry, Elena." She paced the luxurious room, then rubbed her forehead. "I'm going out of my mind. I've been trapped in this house for days."

"I'm sorry you're not feeling well, princess. I'm sure His Highness was very regretful to have to leave you alone. He's very busy."

Grace closed her eyes as grief and fury built inside her. Yeah. She could just imagine how he was *busy*.

All week she'd been waiting...for what? For him to

return to the man he'd been in London, the man she'd loved? For him to act like a decent, caring husband?

Well, she wasn't going to wait anymore. She wasn't going to remain jailed here for his convenience!

Grace went to her huge closet and grabbed dark skinny jeans and a snug black cashmere sweater she'd bought at the Leighton boutique on Tverskaya Street. "I'm coming to Red Square with you tonight."

Elena looked alarmed. "Have you asked Vladimir and Igor if it's all right?"

There was no way Grace was going to invite her hulking, overprotective bodyguards to join her tonight! "No. I'll just take the Metro with you."

"It's the train. And, princess, I'd get fired for sure."

"Please, Elena!" She closed her eyes. "I just want a nice, normal life. Just a few hours to breathe fresh air and blend in without big bodyguards hovering over me wherever I go!"

"You don't know this city. You don't speak a word of Russian."

"I do know one word. *Nyet.* And that's my answer to Maksim." She pulled her hair into a ponytail. "*This* princess will have a normal life. I might be his wife, but I won't be his slave!"

Grabbing her warmest coat and hat, she opened the second-story window, peering down at the wide wall. She'd have to climb over on the tree branch and down the other side…

"*Kharasho,*" Elena said, sounding resigned. "You can come with me. Just stay close and don't wander off!"

Grace nearly wept tears of gratitude. "I promise I won't tell Maksim!"

"He will find out," the woman said with a shake of her head, then grumbled, "For a new bride to be home alone on New Year's Eve? Bah!" And she muttered something under her breath in Russian.

Grace tapped her black boots on the floor. Every muscle in her body ached to get out of this luxurious palace. Away from her captivity and loneliness.

Away from the fact that she was with yet another man who was in love with Lady Francesca Danvers instead of her.

Was it Grace's fate to always lose every man she cared about to the same woman?

The painfully ironic thought chased her all the way to Red Square an hour later. They followed the currents and crush of people past the twin towers of the Resurrection Gate, with its mosaic icons of favored saints, into Red Square.

"Stay close," Elena said.

Grace took one look at the colorful onion domes of St. Basil's Cathedral and gasped. Standing still in the packed crowd, she slowly turned around, looked at the Kremlin, Lenin's tomb and the red buildings around the square. She'd dreamed about this ever since the Soviet breakup when she was a girl.

Red Square was lit with a million lights and filled with half a million cheering people. It was more fantastically beautiful than she'd ever dreamed. For one moment it made her forget her pain.

Then she saw a nearby man take his girlfriend in his

arms and kiss her. Watching them kiss and laugh and share an intimate moment just a few feet away suddenly made Grace ache twice as much with loneliness.

She turned back to Elena, but the Russian woman was gone! Somehow they'd been separated.

Struggling not to feel alarmed, clenching her gloved hands into fists and shoving them into her coat, Grace looked around through the white mist of her breath.

She felt so alone, and the night was so cold. Here in the far north of the world, she wondered if winter would ever end.

Suddenly she felt a hand on her shoulder.

She turned and saw Maksim standing beside her!

In spite of everything, her heart leaped to see him, dark as night in his black clothes.

"You little fool," he ground out. "I expressly told you not to come here."

She took a deep breath. "I'm not your prisoner."

He looked down at her grimly. "If you risk my child without bodyguards again, you will be."

The threat made her furious. How dare he insinuate that she'd placed their unborn child at risk, just by living a normal life?

"I'm sick of you trying to control me." Furious, she tossed her head, "And where's Francesca?" she taunted. "Don't tell me you've finished with her already?"

"Damn your jealousy," he growled.

"I'm not jealous," she fired back. "I don't care if you make love to her every night. I don't love you. I don't want you!"

He yanked her into his arms.

"Who's lying now?" he growled.

Her eyes suddenly widened when she saw his intent. "No—"

Lowering his mouth on hers, he kissed her savagely.

Beneath the colorful fireworks in the dark wintry sky, he punished her in his embrace, plundering her lips, mastering her with his strength. She tried to resist, pushing at his chest with her small hands, but in the end her own desire overpowered her in a way brute force could not. Surrendering, she sagged in his arms with a whimper, holding his body against hers as she returned his brutal kiss with equal passion.

Beneath the brilliantly lit onion domes of St. Basil's Cathedral, they kissed in a fiery embrace of hate and longing amid the roar of half a million people celebrating the birth of the new year.

From the day he'd married Grace, Maksim had intended to punish her.

And he'd done it. He'd brought her to Moscow, a place where she knew no one, and he'd deserted her in the same palace he'd once dreamed of bringing her to live as his mistress. Except all the tenderness he'd once had for her was long gone. In its place was cold, hard anger.

He'd rushed to her in California. He'd told her the truth. He'd practically begged her to forgive the single lie he'd told her. A small request considering that he'd been willing to give up what he wanted most for her sake.

He'd treated her with better care than he'd ever treated any woman. *He'd placed her interests above his own.*

And all he'd gotten from her in return were insults—and lies. Then, to top it off, she'd tried to steal his child!

He'd thought Grace was different. That she was special. But he knew the truth now. She might have been a virgin when he first bedded her, but in other ways she might as well be Francesca—selfish, cruel and controlling.

When Elena had told him Grace had accompanied her to Red Square against his orders, he'd been furious. Then he'd been frightened—purely for the baby's sake, he'd told himself.

But when he dismissed Elena and saw Grace looking so forlorn and alone amid the festive crowds of Red Square, anger and desire and fury had finally boiled over him.

And something more. Desire. The desire he'd suppressed for days, trying to finish the hellish, endless details of the merger. The desire he'd tried not to feel, staying away from the bride he despised as a way to keep himself from wanting her.

He hadn't meant to kiss her. He'd sworn to himself when he brought her to Moscow that he wouldn't even touch her.

Then she'd taunted him.

Anger and lust had seized him. And he'd seized her. Now...

His need to punish her blended with his need to possess her. Taking her by the hand, he dragged her from the crowds of Red Square to his waiting car. Closing the privacy screen to block the eyes of his bodyguard and driver, he threw her into the back seat and kissed her hard. Her hat had been long lost. Pulling off her coat and gloves, he pressed her body beneath his, kissing her with angry force. She returned his kiss with matching fervor, biting at his lips until they bled.

"I hate you," she breathed against his skin.

For answer, he ripped her black sweater off her body. Yanking her bra to the floor of the car, he pressed his mouth on her breasts, biting and suckling until the mix of pain and pleasure made her gasp and arch beneath him.

"Hate me if you want. You are mine to do with as I please," he said, licking her nipples. "You will pleasure me."

"I won't…ah," she sucked in her breath as he moved his hand between her legs, over her tight jeans, rubbing her until she gripped his shoulders wordlessly seeking release.

He wanted to rip off her jeans. He wanted to thrust inside her hard and deep, until she begged for mercy.

Until she begged his forgiveness.

By the time they made it home, her lips were bruised with his kisses, her blond hair tousled and tangled, her eyes dazed and bewildered with her unwilling longing. Giving his driver and bodyguard a terse order in Russian, he collected Grace in his arms and carried her roughly into the house.

The palace was quiet. The bodyguards were outside celebrating in the guardhouse by the gate. The rest of the servants had been given the night off.

Maksim intended to carry her to the master bedroom, but halfway up the stairs she reached up to stroke his neck and he could bear it no longer. He placed her down on the curving, sinuous staircase, beside the art deco railing that looked like swirls of melting wax in white limestone. Pulling off her jeans, he undid his fly. He was hard as a rock and aching for her.

He didn't tease her.

He didn't ask permission.

Without warning, without tenderness, he pulled down his pants and thrust himself inside her, all the way to the hilt.

She gasped, then moved beneath him, her full, heavy breasts swaying as she arched her back, pulling him deeper still.

She wanted him as unwillingly as he wanted her. He knew it. But suddenly he wanted far more than just to take his pleasure. He wanted her to take her own. To force her to hold nothing back. To surrender herself completely.

Rolling over, with his own back against the shallow, wide steps, he lifted her on top of him. She gasped as he lowered her over him, impaling her.

"Move," he ordered.

As he commanded, she slowly moved against him, sliding her wet, hot body against his in circles that got progressively tighter and smaller. He felt her muscles clench around him, deep inside her, as she closed her eyes. She stopped, fighting her desperate desire.

He stroked her breasts, then, taking one of her hands in his own, he sucked gently on a fingertip. Her blue eyes met his, innocent, shocked. Her pupils were dilated, her nipples painfully tight, her body so hot and wet around him. And as if she could not resist his will, she started to move again. Her heavy breasts bounced softly as she rode him, pushing her hips harder and faster until he was barely able to hold on to his self-control. He looked up at her beautiful face, at her soft, curvaceous, feminine body that was getting tighter and tighter around him as she started to shudder. And he heard a low scream rising from her throat.

As she moved herself against him, rocking back and forth in rhythm, her core slick and impossibly soft around him, he felt her start to tense and shake, and finally he could take it no longer. With a Russian curse on his lips, he exploded into her with a shout that echoed against the high walls of the foyer, mingling with her own ecstatic cry.

Exhausted, her limp body fell against his own. For a moment he held her, feeling her soft body against his chest, listening to the sound of her breath.

But when his sense returned, he was furious.

At her.

At himself.

He had no self-control whatsoever where Grace was concerned.

He'd sworn to himself that he wouldn't touch her. But this proved his desire was stronger than his pride. Proved she still had control over him.

Proved that no matter what she thought of him, he still cared for her.

Pushing away roughly, he rose to his feet on the stairs, furious at himself. Without saying a word, he rezipped his pants and coldly left her on the stairs.

The palace suddenly felt too confining, and outside

he would be watched by guards. With a deep breath, he climbed two floors to the roof garden. Where he went to find peace. Where he went to be alone.

The rooftop terrace was covered with snow and dead branches of the dormant garden. He took several deep breaths, stretching his arms, trying to clear his head. He stared at his own breath, looking past the treetops and lights of the city toward the distant fireworks in the cold clear night.

He heard her come out though the garden door. He couldn't believe she'd followed him out here. He looked at her with narrowed eyes. She'd put her clothes back on, tying her tattered blouse together as best she could. She hesitated, then finally came up behind him, wrapping her arms around him.

For a moment he was tempted to lean into her arms. His heart hungered for her.

Then she spoke.

"Just tell me the truth, Maksim," she whispered. "Admit that you betrayed me. Admit that you lied and I'll forgive you."

His jaw clenched as he turned to face her. "You'll forgive me," he said tersely.

She swallowed, then lifted her chin. "I will try."

Anger rushed through him, pulling away all his remembered tenderness like an overflowing river ripping sediment from the banks.

"I do not want your forgiveness," he said in a low voice.

"Maksim." Her face was tear stained, her voice a whisper. "Just tell me if you love her. Tell me."

Love her? *Her?* Who?

Then he knew. Of course. She was talking about Francesca. He'd never given Grace any reason to feel jealous, but she continued to grind away at him with her insecurity's endless need for control.

Did he need further proof she thought him a man without honor, a man she couldn't trust?

He'd tried to change her mind in California. He wouldn't try again. He wouldn't allow himself to be vulnerable with her. Never again.

He looked at her coldly. "In two days I will introduce you to all of Moscow as my bride. You must be ready for the ballroom reception. You and the child need rest. Go sleep. In your peaceful, solitary bed."

"Maksim…" she whispered.

For answer, he turned and left her without a backward glance, leaving her shivering and alone on the snowy rooftop garden, in the chill black night beneath icy white stars.

CHAPTER ELEVEN

"LADY Francesca Danvers is here to see you, princess."

Grace whirled around in her chair. "What does she want?"

"Nothing good, I wager," Elena said sourly.

Grace turned back to face herself in the mirror. She hardly recognized herself. Wearing a long, sparkling, champagne-colored gown that caressed her body, with her blond hair piled high on her head, she looked like a princess.

For the past two hours, Elena had been helping her get ready for the ballroom reception that would introduce her to Moscow society. But she wasn't sure she could face the woman her husband still loved. She licked her lips nervously. "Do you know her?"

The Russian housekeeper shrugged as one of the maids brought in a small enamel-and-silver box. "She was here once before, long ago. But old lovers should disappear when a man gets married," she said with a sniff. "Let me send her away. Your reception starts in ten minutes. You don't have time to speak to each and every guest before..."

"She's a guest?" Grace gasped. "Who would have—"

But she cut herself off. She didn't have to ask who would have invited Francesca.

She closed her eyes, willing herself not to cry. It would ruin the carefully applied makeup, and she had to look lovely when she was introduced as Maksim's bride.

He must really hate her, to do this, she thought. How could he stab her in the heart, forcing her to publicly meet his mistress? It hurt so badly she thought her heart might crack in two.

Maksim had made his feelings plain. After they'd made love on New Year's Eve, she'd begged him to justify his actions. She'd been so desperate for a fresh start, she'd offered him almost more than she thought she could bear—her forgiveness. If only he would just admit what he'd done, and promise never to see Francesca again!

But he had refused. And in the two days since, he'd avoided her more than ever.

And yet she still couldn't believe Francesca was in Moscow.

When Maksim had said he'd installed her in some fancy hotel, Grace had assumed he was just trying to hurt her.

But the woman was here. Had he been telling her the truth? Had he been spending all his nights with his mistress?

Why shouldn't he? She thought miserably. He'd only married Grace because she was pregnant. A forced marriage wouldn't necessarily stop him from loving Francesca....

"Ah, you look perfect. You just need one last thing.

His Highness sent this." Elena pulled an antique gold-and-emerald tiara from the enamel box and reverently placed it around Grace's high chignon.

"It's beautiful," Grace said in a low voice.

"It used to belong to the prince's great-aunt, the Grand Duchess Olga." Elena pulled back to see the effect in the mirror then nodded her approval. "Now I'll send that wretched woman away," she added, "and I'll be right back."

"No," Grace blurted out, her mouth suddenly dry. "Send her up."

The Russian woman looked at her dubiously. "Are you sure, princess?"

No. "Yes."

A moment later Lady Francesca was escorted into the drawing room beside Grace's bedroom.

The pale redhead was as beautiful as Grace remembered. Petite and very thin, she wore a pink tweed Chanel skirt suit and white peep-toe shoes with flashy red soles. In her perfectly manicured hands, she carried a white quilted bag with a gold chain handle.

She glanced around the pretty, elegant, feminine room. "I see you've set yourself up nicely," she said with a sniff.

"Please sit down," Grace said nervously, indicating the blue high-backed chair. "May I order some tea?"

"No, thank you." Francesca's cold, kohl-lined green eyes looked right through her scornfully. "This isn't a friendly visit." She set her handbag on the tea table, all business. "I've come to ask you how much money I have to pay you to divorce your husband."

Grace stared at her in shock, speechless.

"Oh, come on," she said impatiently. "You were clever enough to get pregnant. You are hoping to profit from your child. I don't blame you. I'm sure I would do the same if I had no money, skills or beauty. So just tell me how much you expect."

Grace tried to speak, but still couldn't.

Francesca pulled her checkbook and an expensive-looking pen out of her wallet, then looked up at her. "Well?"

"I'm not trying to profit from my child!"

"Because you're a decent mother?" Francesca's red lips twisted. "Can we please skip your fervent protestations? We both know that Maksim should belong to me. Tell me how much it will cost to be rid of you."

Remembering all that she'd suffered because of this woman, Grace clenched her hands into fists.

"I gave up one man to you without a fight," she said in a low voice. "I won't do it again."

"So you did have a desperate little crush on Alan," Francesca drawled, glancing down at her flawless scarlet nails. "I wondered. My dear, don't you realize that a woman like you cannot possibly compete against a woman like me?"

Every word was like a stab to Grace's heart. "I never loved Alan," she said in a trembling voice. "You can have him. But I'll die before I give Maksim up to you!"

"You poor fool. I understand Maksim in a way you never will." Francesca tilted her head. "He doesn't love you. If you were any sort of decent woman, you would let him go. If you won't, you're not a decent woman.

You're a gold digger who deliberately got pregnant to trick Maksim into marriage."

Grace's insides twisted. "I never tried to get pregnant. I never asked him to marry me," she whispered. "He insisted."

Francesca nodded. "So you didn't want to marry him in the first place. Perfect. Then take my check and leave him. Find some other man to marry." She stared at Grace with false sympathy. "Someone more at your level."

"He's my husband and father of my child. Now we're married, I won't give him up." She narrowed her eyes, looking up at the other woman as her shoulders shook with emotion. "Not to you or anyone."

With a sigh, the beautiful redhead closed her checkbook. "Fine. Have it your way." She leaned forward across the tea table. "You're not a bad person. I can see that. So if you love him, let him go."

Grace looked up at her rival. "You love him?"

Francesca's green eyes were clear and direct. "And I can help him. In life. In business. I thought a fake engagement would prod him into setting a date to marry me. But he plays the game even better than I do. He actually married you." She gave a thin red smile. "I told my father about the fake engagement to save Maksim's merger. I can make him the richest man in the world. What can you ever do for him…except be a burden?"

"*Izvenitche, pojhowsta.*" Elena suddenly appeared in the door, scowling. "It's time for the princess to make her entrance at the reception."

Francesca rose gracefully to her feet. She paused at

the door, her eyes narrowed and her red lips pulled back to reveal her sharp white teeth.

"If you love him, Miss Cannon," she said softly, "you'll leave him."

After her parting shot the beautiful redhead swept away, leaving pain and regret racking through Grace in waves.

Maksim had told her the truth. Francesca was the one who'd told her father about the fake engagement. Maksim had tried to tell her he didn't betray her. He'd seduced her, yes, but he hadn't been able to use her words against her. He'd protected her honor at the expense of his own. He'd given up what he wanted most—for her.

But she hadn't believed him.

Instead she'd insulted him. She still winced to remember the horrible words she'd thrown at him when he'd followed her to California.

She'd done everything she could to push him back into Francesca's arms. Could he ever forgive her lack of faith?

He has to, she thought. *Even if I have to beg him for forgiveness.*

But what difference would begging make—if he was in love with another woman? She closed her eyes as a stabbing pain went through her heart. Why would he ever choose her over Francesca, after the way she'd treated him?

"Are you ready, Grace?"

She turned to see Maksim standing in the doorway. She sucked in her breath. He looked devastatingly handsome in his tuxedo, her dark Rostov prince, strong and powerful and very, very dangerous.

"She's ready," Elena said approvingly. She adjusted

the tiara over Grace's high chignon, adding pins to hold it as she said softly, "And the most beautiful princess the house of Rostov has ever seen."

Maksim slowly looked her over and then nodded. "You are beautiful."

Grace's heart fluttered in her chest. "You are, too. So handsome, I mean."

His dark eyes were inscrutable as he held out his arm. "Come."

He led her out of the room to the top of the elaborate limestone staircase where they'd made love with such intensity two days before. At the bottom of the stairs, she heard the noise and voices of their guests, the clinking of crystal. She couldn't face them as Maksim's wife.

Not without knowing their marriage had a chance.

She stopped in her tracks, pulling on his hand with urgency to pull him back into the hallway.

He looked down at her impatiently. "What is it?"

"I should have believed you all along. I'm so sorry, Maksim." Her eyes filled with tears as the words spilled out, rushing over each other. "You never betrayed me. Francesca said she told her father about the engagement. Oh, Maksim. Can you ever forgive me?"

His eyes narrowed. "You have spoken with Francesca?"

"She was here."

His eyebrows rose. "Here? What was she—"

She placed her hand over his. "I don't want to fight," she pleaded. "I want to start fresh. To go back to how we were in London. I believe you now. I'm sorry I didn't have faith—"

"It's easy to believe me now, isn't it?" he interrupted

coldly. "You believe Francesca's words, when you wouldn't believe mine."

This was all going wrong. She'd apologized, begged him to forgive her, pleaded for a fresh start. What else was left? What hadn't she said?

Only one thing, and it terrified her. She couldn't possibly lay her soul bare before him, not when his face was so cold, his body so tense and unyielding.

"Come." He turned away, drawing her once more toward the wide sweeping stairs and the marble-floored foyer where she knew hundreds of society guests were waiting.

She grabbed his tuxedo sleeve, pulling him to her, forcing him to listen.

"Maksim, I…" Her heart pounded in her throat. She licked her lips. "I…I love you."

His steel-gray eyes widened, became deep pools of some emotion she couldn't identify, but it caused yearning and fear to spread through her veins.

"I love you," she repeated, her mouth utterly dry. "And I have to know. Can you ever love me?"

She waited for his answer, and as the seconds ticked by, they seemed to last for eons.

Then his handsome face slowly turned to ice. He shook his head grimly. "It's too late."

"How can it be too late?" she gasped.

"I'll always take care of the child, Grace." He looked away, tightening his shoulders. "But I'll never love you again."

Again?

He'd loved her?

He'd loved her—and she'd thrown his love away!

"No!" she cried. "It can't be too late! I love you. And if you once loved me…"

He gave her a sardonic smile, all emotion gone from his eyes. "And how well you repaid me."

"I made a horrible mistake." She was humiliated by the whimper in her voice, but she couldn't lose him. Not now. Not when she'd finally realized he was truly the man she'd always wanted. "Please, Maksim…"

"Stop begging," he said harshly. "You are a princess. Begging is beneath you."

"I can't lose you." She felt a sharp pain in her heart. "But I already have, haven't I?" she whispered. "You want to be with her."

"Who?"

"Do I have to say her name?"

His jaw clenched as he exhaled with a flare of his nostrils. "I am sick of having to defend my actions where Francesca is concerned. You are my wife. You are pregnant with my child. There will be no other woman in my life. There can't be. How clear do I have to make it?"

"But if there were no baby?" she said, her heart in her throat. "Would you still have married me?"

"That is a pointless question. There is a baby. The decision has been made. Love doesn't matter."

She closed her eyes to block out the pain. "You're wrong," she whispered. "It's all that matters."

Maksim had married Grace out of honor. The honor she'd bitingly, insultingly accused him of never having. And for the sake of honor, he was determined to stand by her side.

But if Grace hadn't been pregnant, he would have gone to Francesca like a shot. His heart was with her. She was beautiful and wealthy and a perfect match for Maksim in every way.

"I will always protect you both," he said in a low voice. "Don't ask for more than I can give."

He would protect her with money and his name. Nothing more.

Grace's own parents had had such a blissful marriage. She thought of how they'd laughed together, teased each other. The way her father had playfully wrapped his arms around her mother's waist while she cooked in the kitchen. Her parents' love had shone through everything, especially their children. Grace and her brothers had shared such a happy childhood beneath the umbrella of their parents' love.

She suddenly realized it had never been their house that had made them a family. The house hadn't made them secure and warm. It had been her parents' love. Their mutual adoration that had endured long after her father had died.

The lump in her throat sharpened.

What kind of home life would Grace's loveless marriage create for their baby?

How would their son or daughter feel, raised by a father who'd been forced to give up his own happiness because of the child's very existence?

Grace suddenly felt like crying.

Maksim held out his arm stiffly. "Come. Our guests are waiting."

Her heart felt shattered in her chest as he escorted her down the limestone Art Deco stairs.

In the wide marble foyer, beneath the soaring crystal chandelier, she saw a swirl of faces. Hundreds of people applauded for her as she was introduced as Her Highness Princess Grace Rostova. Gorgeous women in diamonds and Maksim's billionaire friends cheered in both English and Russian, holding up their champagne flutes in a toast to the new princess.

Grace got a glimpse of herself in the enormous gilded mirror across the foyer. She truly looked like a princess. The tiara sparkled in her hair. The champagne-colored gown moved against her like a whisper. This time, even her shoes were perfect, the twenty-first-century version of glass slippers. Beautiful, rather uncomfortable and very, very expensive.

But she would have done anything to go back in time to when she was just a plain, poor secretary, happy in Maksim's arms and bed. Back to when they'd actually had a chance at happiness.

Back to when he'd loved her. He'd never said the words then, but he'd made her feel them.

Grace saw Maksim's sister waiting for them at the bottom of the stairs. Dariya glowed as she hugged them both. "I'm so glad you're my sister," she whispered to Grace. "Not just my sister...my friend. And you're going to make me an aunt!"

"Thank you." Blinking back tears, Grace did her best to smile. "Your friendship means so much..."

She froze when she saw Lady Francesca Danvers over Dariya's shoulder.

She felt her husband stiffen beside her. She glanced at him. His face had closed down, his mouth a grim line, as he looked straight at Francesca.

"Excuse me," he said shortly.

Grace watched as he crossed through the crowd, grabbed the redhead's wrist and dragged her toward his study. His expression looked furious as he closed the door behind him.

And staring at the closed door, everything suddenly became clear for Grace.

He wasn't having an affair with Francesca. She now knew that to her core. He'd promised fidelity to Grace and he would keep to that vow. He was a man of honor.

He hadn't invited her here. He was determined to remain faithful to the wife he'd never wanted. Family and honor meant everything to Maksim. He would remain faithful to Grace.

But did she want him to?

After so many years of being Alan's doormat, desperate for any sign of tenderness, did she really want to be tied forever to a man who didn't love her?

And worse: did she want to raise their child that way?

Could she raise her baby to be happy in this palace of ice? Could she risk her child's bright, joyful new spirit in this frozen place, knowing he'd always be bewildered by his parents' cold misery and might eventually blame himself?

Grace may have sacrificed herself for her baby's sake, but she couldn't allow the life and warmth to be sapped out of her newborn's soul. She couldn't allow her precious baby to grow up suffocated in an endless winter of unspoken blame.

"What's *she* doing here?" Dariya said sourly. "Can't the woman take a hint?"

"I…I'm not feeling very well," Grace said, rubbing her forehead. "Will you please make my excuses and thank everyone for coming?"

"Of course, absolutely." Dariya peered at her in worry. "You do look pale. I'll go get my brother—"

"No! Don't tell him anything. I want to be alone." She ran upstairs with a hard lump in her throat.

Slamming her bedroom door behind her, she collapsed on her bed.

Love made a family.

She loved their baby. She loved Maksim.

But Maksim loved Francesca.

Grace's eyes fell on her battered old suitcase in the massive walk-in closet. It had taken her to London, back to California, to Moscow. It could take her back home.

"If you love him, let him go," Francesca had said.

Grace loved Maksim. She loved her baby. She loved them both so much and there was only one way to save them. One way to make sure they were both safe and happy. One way to set them both free.

Rising from the bed, she picked up her suitcase.

"How dare you show up here?" Maksim said furiously as he closed the study door behind them. "I expressly told you in London—we're through. We were done two and a half months ago when you gave me your little ultimatum."

Francesca looked up at him with her perfectly lined

green eyes. "But I made up for that, darling, when I got the merger back for you!"

"You only gave back something that should always have been mine."

A tremulous smile traced her red mouth. "I rectified a strategic misfire. You won this round."

He stared at her coldly. He expected at any moment, tears would appear—her carefully manufactured tears that never smudged her eye makeup. She was a master at manipulation.

Unlike Grace. Grace who'd looked so vulnerable just moments before they came down the stairway. She'd truly looked like a princess.

"I love you," she'd said. "Can you ever love me?"

His reply to her had been harsh.

Maksim clenched his hands, remembering the stricken look on her face. Grace had no defenses. It had been coldhearted and cruel of him. But she'd kept pushing him for what he wouldn't, couldn't give her...

"Come back with me to London," Francesca said. "It's time."

"Perhaps you haven't noticed," he replied acidly, "but I have a wife."

Emotion turned her thin face pale beneath the rouge. "I never should have given you an ultimatum. But how long do you intend to punish me for my mistake? Let the gold digger go."

"What did you call her?" he said dangerously.

She threw him a scornful glance. "Oh, please. A secretary? She's obviously a gold digger. I just offered her a blank check to leave you, but she refused. She knows she can cash in for more after the little brat is born!"

He clenched his fists. "You tried to buy her off?"

She sniffed. "I was trying to do you a favor, darling. You can't actually want to be married to her. She's not remotely your type!"

His type?

Pictures of Grace went through his mind. Her openness. Her purity. Her laughter and her tears. The way her thoughts were always revealed on her face. Her care and concern for the people around her. Her soft heart.

Gold digger? She'd made it clear from the beginning that she didn't want Maksim's money. He'd tried to spoil her in London, but she'd made it impossible. Over and over again, she'd refused his offers of gifts for clothes, jewels, cars, houses.

The only time she'd accepted anything was to give her family a place to live, when Maksim had blackmailed her into marriage. A strange feeling almost like shame went through him at the memory.

I had no choice, he told himself. *I had to protect my child. I had to make her marry me.* But the oft-repeated reason rang hollow today.

"I love you," she'd whispered. "Can you ever love me?"

"You're right," he said heavily, clawing his hand through his dark hair. "Grace is not my usual type of woman."

"She's not." Francesca gave him a sly smile. "I am."

She was right. Francesca was exactly his type. A selfish beauty who enjoyed playing games and liked to fight dirty. She liked to insinuate they were special due to aristocratic birth, but there was one thing and one thing only Francesca thought was truly noble: money.

Creeping closer to him, she licked her sultry red lips. "You and I are perfect for each other. Yes, we fought constantly, but only because we pursue our own desires no matter the cost. We're both selfish to the bone. Face it, Maksim, we're exactly alike!"

He stared at her.

"That's not true," he said hoarsely. "I'm nothing like you. Now get out."

"Maksim, don't be a fool. You're throwing away a fortune if you don't marry me!"

"We're done, Francesca. Through." He clenched his fists, staring at her coldly. "If I ever see you again—if you ever upset my wife again—you will regret it." Walking to the door, he flung it open. "Now leave."

"Fine," she ground out, tossing her head and exiting toward the curious party-goers outside. "Enjoy your common little wife. You'll be tired of her before your kid's even born!"

In the echo of her departing steps, Maksim closed the door heavily and sank into a chair at his desk. In his heart of hearts, he knew that he *was* just like Francesca.

Or at least he had been. Until he'd met someone who'd inspired him. Someone who with her sweet kindness and natural beauty had made him believe there was more to life than money.

He heard someone come in, and looked up, ready to snarl.

His sister stood in the doorway, her arms folded.

"About time you sent that woman away," Dariya said.

"And I hope you did it more thoroughly this time. Heaven knows she won't take a hint. Maybe you should toss a Rolex into the Moskva River—she'd be sure to dive through the ice. That would be one way to finally—"

"Where's Grace?" he interrupted.

"She wasn't feeling well, so she's gone upstairs to her room." Her eyes met his. "You have a houseful of guests with no host or hostess at the moment. I thought you'd want to know."

He took a deep breath. "Did Grace see me come in here with Francesca?"

"Yes. Everyone saw it. You might want to come and do some damage control."

Maksim clenched his jaw. "I'll go to her now." His encounter with Francesca had left him feeling strangely dirty. Had he really been like that? *Like her?*

He needed to see Grace. To see her calm face and hear her sweet voice. To have her take him in her soft arms so that he could take a deep, clear breath…

"Let Grace rest, Maksim," Dariya said sharply. "Let her sleep and talk to her in the morning. You need to end the rumors going through Moscow, or your marriage will be over before it's begun."

He clenched his jaw. He didn't blame Grace for fleeing to her bedroom. How could he? He'd left her alone during their wedding reception, abandoning her with hundreds of strangers while he disappeared behind closed doors with his ex-mistress.

No wonder Grace had been so insecure, considering that he hadn't bothered to reassure her. He'd just left her, his lonely, pregnant, deserted wife.

He clenched his hands into fists.

He had to make this right.

He had to see her.

"We're exactly alike," Francesca had said.

But fighting that was the soft echo of Grace's voice from long ago. "You're a good man, Maksim. You think it's weakness...but I know your secret."

Which woman did he want to believe?

Which man did he want to be?

He took a deep breath. "I'll just check on her. I won't wake her if she's sleeping," he promised. "Act as hostess until I'm back, Daritchka, won't you?"

But friends and acquaintances were swarming the foyer. Bewildered at the sudden abrupt disappearance of both bride and groom, they stopped him in his path, asking for reassurance and explanations that Maksim hardly knew how to give. It took him almost twenty minutes to cross the marble floor of the foyer to the limestone stairs.

He went to Grace's bedroom and knocked softly on the door. When he heard no answer, he pushed the door open.

Her room was dark. Only in the faintest trace of moonlight from the window could he see her shape in the Wedgwood-blue canopy bed beneath the covers.

He wanted to wake her but held himself back. Waking her would be selfish when it was only to seek his own comfort.

He was a husband.

He was going to be a father.

Everything had changed for him, but he'd been slow to realize it.

Turning away, ignoring the ache in his throat, he went downstairs and did his duty as host. He spent the rest of the long night entertaining his guests and reassuring them that his new bride had just taken ill due to her delicate condition. But all through the endless hours, he couldn't stop thinking of his pregnant wife sleeping upstairs. Lonely in the bedroom that he'd given her as a way to punish her for calling his offer of marriage "a gilded cage."

At dawn, after he'd finally shoved the last guest firmly out the door, Maksim crept back to her room, praying she would now be awake. If she wasn't awake, he didn't know how much longer he could wait.

He needed to feel comforted by her presence. To tell her he was sorry he'd been so cruel. To tell her…to tell her…

The warm blush of a gray-and-pink dawn filled her bedroom as he pushed open the door. She was still in bed, just as she'd been before.

I won't wake her, he told himself. He would just watch her sleep. Even that would bring him some small peace.

But as he walked forward in the lightening room, something didn't look right. Her body beneath the blanket looked strange. The comforter stretched all the way up to the headboard. He pulled back the blanket and discovered…pillows.

She was gone!

He snatched up the note attached to the pillow. It read:

Maksim,
There is no baby. I faked the pregnancy—don't

ask how—to try and get your money. But I can't
do it. Please divorce me immediately and don't try
to find me. I don't want any alimony. I wish you
every happiness in your life with Francesca. All I
want is for you to be with the woman you love.

    Grace

No baby? She'd faked the pregnancy?

Pain ripped through him, pain so staggering it almost
dropped him to his knees.

He couldn't breathe. The tie on his tuxedo suddenly
seemed to constrict his air, choking him. He ripped it
to the ground in a tear of fabric. He read the note
again. And again.

No baby.

She'd faked the pregnancy.

He crumpled up the note in his fist.

He'd been shocked by her pregnancy, but until this
moment he hadn't realized how much the baby had
come to mean to him. In spare moments between the
bone-crushing work of completing the oil company
merger, he'd daydreamed about their coming baby.
Would he have the Rostov profile? Would he have
Grace's pale-blond hair and blue eyes?

He threw the note across the room. It floated gently
to the floor. Not enough. Grabbing the lamp, he threw
it across the room, smashing it against the wall.

No baby.

She'd lied to him. She'd faked the pregnancy to
marry him for his...

    Money?

His body snapped straight. Grace, after his money?

He recalled all the times he'd tried to help Grace with money. She'd refused. She'd fought everything—jewels, designer clothes, fancy cars, cash, everything. Beyond having food, clothes and a roof over their heads, Grace didn't give a damn about the so-called finer things in life. All the designer clothes and jewels she'd gotten since their marriage were still hanging neatly in her closet. His eyes fell upon the priceless tiara once owned by his great-aunt, the Grand Duchess.

Grace hadn't lied about the baby.

She was lying now.

He looked back at the note.

Please divorce me immediately and don't try to find me. I don't want any alimony. All I want is for you to be with the woman you love.

Francesca must have somehow convinced Grace that Maksim loved her.

And he'd helped her, he acknowledged to himself grimly. He thought of all the times he could have reassured Grace that he wanted both her and the child. The hours he could have spent with Grace, instead of deserting her in his palace. He'd claimed he wanted to protect his unborn son or daughter, and he'd forced Grace to be his wife, but he'd never acted like a decent husband or father.

He'd withheld the security and comfort and affection he could have given his lonely, pregnant wife.

Grace, on the other hand, wanted him to be happy—

even if that meant throwing him into the arms of another woman.

Shame raced through him, and this time he couldn't deny the emotion for what it was.

He didn't deserve Grace's love. He didn't deserve her. But...he *loved* her.

She was like no other woman he'd ever known. Her faith and honesty. Her willingness to sacrifice herself for others. *He loved her.* He loved her and he'd let his anger and hurt pride get in the way of his own happiness...and hers.

How could he have been such a blind, selfish fool?

Maksim had money, power, influence—everything he'd ever wanted when he'd been desperately poor as a child. But all his success had somehow become meaningless without her.

What use was it to be one of the wealthiest men in the world, if he didn't have the woman he loved?

CHAPTER TWELVE

GRACE rubbed the frost off the edges of the train window and looked out at Lake Baikal and the distant mountains. The endless white of the deepest lake in the world was an eerie expanse of snow. Hillocks of razor-sharp ice, ten feet tall, stabbed upward on the edges of the frozen lake.

How many days had she been on the train? Her journey from Moscow blended together in endless dark days and still darker nights. She looked numbly at the tiny village with a few wooden buildings scattered up the hillside. Grace couldn't read the Cyrillic letters on the sign to even know its name.

Siberia.

She'd hoped taking the Trans-Siberian Railway would raise her desolate spirits, as well as make sure that Maksim couldn't find her. He would check at the airport and possibly trains heading west into Europe. He wouldn't look here.

If he bothered to look for her at all.

Her body felt hot in the sweltering train car as she

leaned her forehead against the steamy, half-frosted window. But instead of enjoying her childhood dream, she couldn't stop agonizing about the man she'd left behind.

This train station was just a small platform covered with snow, on which three women wrapped in coats and hats were selling fish, homemade bread and fruit to train passengers. After so many days spent weeping in her packed third-class compartment, hanging out of the window and trying not to smell the stale smoke and sweat, Grace saw oranges and suddenly hungered for the sweet tangy fruit as fiercely and recklessly as Rapunzel's mother had once longed for rampion in the fairy tale.

Putting her thick coat over her old jeans and sweater, she crawled out of her upper berth and got off the train. She traded a few Russian coins to the old woman in furs, then snatched up the fruit. Grace barely managed to peel off half of the rind before she sank her mouth into the juicy fruit. Tears streamed down her face. It was delicious. It was heaven.

But by the next bite, the orange had suddenly lost its flavor. She stared out at the vast white emptiness of the snow-covered lake and craved something far more.

Her husband.

Her heart twisted in her chest every time she thought of how she'd left him. How she'd lied to him!

I was right to lie about the pregnancy, she told herself. *He doesn't really want to be a husband or a father. I can't keep him from the woman he loves. Not when I all I want is his happiness, and our child's...*

But at this moment she wanted Maksim so badly she

could hardly believe she'd had the strength of will to be so unselfish. She yearned for him. For his touch. For his smile. Even for his haughty glare. She would have taken any and all of it.

The night of the reception, she'd snuck out of the house and managed to sell her mother's wedding ring for the equivalent of a hundred dollars in a pawn shop near Yaroslavskiy Station in the center of the city.

Every day of her journey had been full of tears. She couldn't stop thinking about Maksim in love with another woman…thinking of the fact that she'd sold her mother's wedding ring…thinking of her own unborn child who would have no father.

The kindly Russian *provodnika* who was in charge of their train car had grown so concerned she'd started sneaking Grace dried fish and borscht from the first-class dining car. An invisible alliance of women who'd been hurt in love.

Grace wondered suddenly if everyone on earth was secretly hiding a broken heart.

She stared blindly across the white snowy expanse of Lake Baikal. In the distance she saw a black truck driving across the frozen lake toward her. The image blurred as her eyes filled with tears.

She hated what she'd done. How she'd lied to him.

It was the only way to set him free, she tried to tell herself. She wiped her tears with the back of a gloved hand. If Maksim knew their unborn child still lived, flourishing and growing every day inside her, he would have tracked her down to the ends of the earth. And she would not have been able to give him his freedom.

Now her own freedom stretched before her like a death sentence. In a few days, at the end of the tracks, she would reach Vladivostok. From there she'd get cheap passage across the Pacific. She would find some kind of job and raise her child in California's endless sunny days.

And yet the thought of that sunshine was more bleak to her than any rain.

As she took a deep shuddering breath, the black truck whirled to a stop on the other side of the platform in a scatter of snow and ice.

A dark figure come out of it, slamming the door with a hard bang.

He walked toward her, a dark prince coming from the white mist like a Gothic warlord with a long black coat, surrounded by snow and jagged sharp ice like ancient swords left by northern giants.

The orange dropped from her nerveless hands as he reached her.

"Maksim…?" she whispered.

Taking her in his arms, he kissed her fiercely.

"Grace, oh, Grace," he whispered. "Thank God. I was afraid I would never find you."

"But what are you doing here? In Siberia?" Still believing that she was dreaming, she reached up to touch his rough cheek. It was thick with bristle. She'd never seen him so unkempt. "You haven't shaved…"

"This train was my last hope. Oh God. I've barely slept for the last four days. Thank God I've found you." She thought she saw a suspicious glimmer in his eyes as he stroked her cheek. He lifted her chin. "Both of you."

She gasped. He knew she'd been lying!

She tried to open her mouth to lie to his beautiful, powerful face, but she couldn't do it. A sob rose to her lips.

"I'm…sorry," she cried, pressing her face against his chest.

"Sorry?" he said gently, rubbing her back. "Oh, *solnishka mayo*. I am the one who is sorry."

"I tried so hard to let you go," she sobbed. "I wanted you to be happy, and I've failed…."

"Failed?" He laughed softly, shaking his head. "Don't you think I know you by now? You have a heart as big as the world. I knew almost at once that you were trying to sacrifice your own happiness for mine."

"Just as you once sacrificed what you wanted most for my sake." Tears streamed down her face, wet tears that stung as they froze like hoarfrost against her skin. "But, Maksim, I want you to be with the woman you love—"

"I *am* with the woman I love," he said fiercely. He forced her to meet his eyes, and she couldn't look away from the intensity of his gaze, a whirling blend of black and white, of snow and hot steel. "It's you, Grace. Only you. The only woman I have ever loved. The only woman I will ever love."

"Me?" she whispered, hardly daring to believe she'd heard him right.

"My plane is waiting at a private airstrip across the lake." He put his arm over her shoulders. "Let us go home."

"Home." The thought tantalized her. She looked up at him. "Are you sure?"

"I wish to make one thing clear, *solnishka mayo*." Reaching for her hand, he pressed it against his rough cheek. "I didn't marry you just because you were pregnant. Even when I thought I hated you, part of me always knew you were the only one for me. Now I will be yours to the end. You are my princess. My wife." He put his hand on his heart. "I love you with all my heart, and I always will."

And to her incredulous wonder, he kissed her passionately on the train platform on the edge of the misty Siberian forest and endless white lake.

As if from a distance, she heard a burst of applause, then yells in Russian, Chinese and a few other languages she couldn't recognize. Blushing, Grace pulled away from Maksim to see people young and old hanging out of the sliding windows on the train, beaming down at the two lovers, clearly egging them on.

She saw the impish look on Maksim's face as he wrapped them both in his black coat.

"Today is January sixth," he whispered. "Do you know what day that is?"

She licked her lips. "Epiphany?"

"It's also Christmas Eve."

"Christmas Eve was weeks ago!"

"Russians celebrate Christmas on January seventh. One Christmas isn't enough for a winter as long as ours." He glanced back mischievously at the people cheering and hanging out of the train windows. "So let us give our audience one last gift for the season." He stroked her cold cheek, unfreezing her tears with the warmth of his breath. "Let's show them what love really means."

And this time, when he kissed her, it was so long and deep and true that she couldn't hear the applause or the whistle of the train. She couldn't hear anything but the pounding of her own heart roaring in her ears, in perfect rhythm with his.

A year later Grace crept down the holly-decked stairs in their Devonshire house, weighed down with Christmas stockings.

She heard a noise in the room below and froze. She knew her brothers were far too old to believe in Santa, but she had baby Sergey to think about now. Then she giggled at the thought that her four-month-old son might catch her. He was certainly the smartest, cleverest baby on earth, but that was pushing it a little too far, even for a proud mother.

Santa had already brought Grace everything she'd ever wanted.

She only had to look around this house. The country house had seemed so empty and wistful last year when she and Maksim had first conceived Sergey. But not anymore. She'd spent the last few months of her pregnancy consulting designers, buying furniture from all over the world, making it comfortable and bright. She'd done the same for their other homes in Moscow, London, Los Angeles, Cap Ferrat and Antigua, but this house was her favorite.

This house was their home.

She'd gone into labor three weeks early here, while finishing the baby's nursery. Sergey had been born at the hospital in a nearby village at a healthy seven pounds three ounces, and he'd been growing ever since. The baby was happy here and so were his parents. Grace could feel the house glowing with happiness, the wood of the banister warm beneath her touch as she came downstairs to the family room with the old fireplace and their Christmas tree.

She stopped when she saw her husband, still shirtless as he'd slept and wearing only the bright red reindeer flannel pajama pants she'd bought him as a joke, walking their baby son back and forth in front of the shining lights of their twelve-foot Christmas tree.

"He's finally asleep," Maksim whispered, and kissed their baby son tenderly on top of his downy head. "I'll take him up to bed."

She nodded with a lump in her throat. As she watched her husband carry their slumbering baby up the staircase, she wondered what she'd ever done to deserve such happiness. All her dreams had come true.

For her Christmas surprise, Maksim had flown her whole family here from California yesterday to share their baby's first Christmas.

"Oh, my dear," her mother had whispered to her last night, her eyes full of joyful tears as they shared their midnight cocoa, "you're really going to live happily ever after."

Now Grace hung the red stockings—stuffed full of candy, oranges and small gifts—on the marble mantel and stood back to see the effect. She nodded with satisfaction, then placed one last gift in her mother's stocking. Her father's wedding ring. Maksim had tracked it down for her in Moscow two weeks ago. Grace had cried with gratitude, kissing him again and again.

She glanced down at her left hand, which now shone

with a ten-carat diamond surrounded by sapphires, set in gold with a matching wedding band. Maksim had given it to her right after she'd kissed him. "To match your hair and eyes." He'd added with a wicked grin, "I know this time it's a gift you can't refuse."

And she hadn't refused. She couldn't. It fit perfectly with the wedding ring that meant everything to her, the one he'd bought her on Russia's Christmas day last year. She was so happy and proud to be his wife.

And she'd finally found the perfect gift to give him in return. The perfect Christmas present for the man who had everything.

Smiling through the tears, Grace gently placed the small gift in Maksim's stocking. It was a small framed picture of baby Sergey she'd taken last night, while Maksim was in the village doing last-minute Christmas shopping. In the photo, the baby was wearing a T-shirt she'd made herself, with words that read, "I'm going to be a big brother."

Looking at the stocking, picturing Maksim's reaction, she smiled, and tears welled up in her eyes. *Such a ninny I am,* she thought, wiping her eyes and laughing at herself. But was it possible to die of happiness?

Upstairs she could hear her younger brothers waking up. In a moment they would be racing downstairs to open their presents beneath the tree. Her mother would bustle around the enormous, refurbished kitchen, insisting on cooking brunch for them as the staff had the day off. Then she'd sit by the fire, knitting booties for the baby while studying books for next semester's classes.

And Grace could sit on her husband's lap and kiss

him when no one was looking. He would kiss her back, and they would wait with breathless anticipation for their private Christmas celebrations to come during the silent, sacred night.

With a grateful breath, Grace glanced outside through the tall windows at the wide expanse of white fields, the peaceful moment before the world woke. Outside, the first rays of pink dawn were streaking through black trees covered with snow.

It was the winter glow of her heart. Even in the stillness of winter they would forever have the warmth and light of home. And as she heard her husband's step on the stairs coming back to her, she knew the sunshine would always last.

THE CHRISTMAS NIGHT MIRACLE

Carole Mortimer

Carole Mortimer was born in England, the youngest of three children. She began writing in 1978 and has now written over one hundred and eighty books for Mills & Boon. Carole has six sons, Matthew, Joshua, Timothy, Michael, David and Peter. She says, 'I'm happily married to Peter senior; we're best friends as well as lovers, which is probably the best recipe for a successful relationship. We live in a lovely part of England.'

CHAPTER ONE

'IT'S snowing again, Mummy!' Scott cried excitedly from the back of the car.

What an understatement.

It wasn't just snowing, it was blowing and gusting towards blizzard proportions. Which, in fact, the radio station Meg was listening to as she drove along had already warned that it would become some time this evening.

It had just been a flurry of delicate white snowflakes when they had left London three hours ago, pretty in its delicacy, to be admired and enjoyed, but standing no chance of actually settling on the streets of the busy city, even though some of it had clung determinedly to the rooftops.

Unfortunately, the further Meg had driven out of London, the heavier the snow had begun to fall, until it was now a thick layer on the ground, the road in front of her almost indistinguishable from the hedgerow, the snow hitting the windscreen so thickly the wipers were having a problem dealing with it.

As was Meg herself, finding it increasingly difficult to control the car as the wheels slipped and slid on the growing layer of snow, the fall of darkness just over an hour ago making things worse, the headlights just seeming to hit a wall of white rather than light the way.

Scott, at three and a half, and awake after sleeping in the back of the car for the last hour, could only see the potential fun and not the danger of this novelty in his young life.

Something Meg was at great pains to maintain as she glanced at him briefly in the rear-view mirror, her smile warm and loving as she looked at his tousled head of dark hair and still-sleepy features; one of them feeling worried and panicked was quite enough.

'Isn't it lovely?' she agreed as she hastily returned her attention to the road, the car having slewed slightly sideways in that moment of distraction.

She shouldn't have come by car. The train would have been so much easier. And at least if there had been a problem with snow on the rails she would have had adult company in her misery.

Because she hadn't seen another car, or even a truck, in the last half an hour.

Of course, that could have something to do with the warning being given out on the radio station for the last hour by the police for people 'not to travel unless absolutely necessary'. A warning that had come far too late for Meg, already more than two thirds of the way towards her destination.

'Can I build a snowman when we get to Granma and Grandad's?' Scott prompted hopefully, thankfully still totally unaware of their precarious situation.

'Of course, darling,' she agreed distractedly.

The relevant word in Scott's statement was 'when'—
because Meg was very much afraid they weren't going
to make it to her parents' house this evening, as planned.

She could barely see where she was going now, the
headlights of the car only seeming to make the snow
whiter and brighter, and blinding. If she could just see a
house, or even a public house, anything that showed signs
of habitation, then she could stop and ask them for help.

'I need the toilet, Mummy.'

Her hands tightened instinctively on the steering
wheel; this was, Meg had quickly learnt after toilet-
training her young son two years ago, the age-old cry
guaranteed to put any mother into a panic. Because it
always came when you were standing in a long queue
at the supermarket, or sitting on a bus, or trying on
shoes—or in the middle of a blinding snowstorm.

And something else she had also learnt very quickly:
it was no good telling a small child that they would
have to wait a few minutes while you finished what you
were doing—when children said they needed the toilet,
then they needed it now.

Nevertheless, like many other mothers before her,
Meg tried. 'Can you hang on a few minutes, Scott? We
aren't too far from Granma and Grandad's now,' she
added with more hope than actual knowledge; she had
absolutely no idea where they were, as she hadn't been
able to see a signpost for miles.

'I need the toilet now, Mummy,' Scott came back
predictably.

She was already so tense from concentrating on her
driving that her shoulders and arms ached, this added

pressure only making the tension worse. Not that it was Scott's fault. He had been asleep for over an hour; of course he needed the toilet.

But she could hardly pull over to the side of the road, even if she could find it, take Scott outside and just let him go to the loo there. This wasn't the middle of summer, it was the evening before Christmas Eve, with a temperature below zero. She could hardly expect him to expose himself to the elements.

If only she could find somewhere, a building of some kind, a barn, even, so very appropriate for this time of year, somewhere they could go and sit this thing out.

Even as the thought played across her frantic mind she felt the steering go from her completely, the car moving sideways as it slid across the snow.

'Hang on, Scott,' Meg had time to warn before she saw a dark shape looming towards her in the darkness, the car coming to a shuddering halt as it hit an immovable object, the noise of the impact almost deafening in the otherwise eerie silence created by the blanket of snow.

'Mummy? Mummy!' Scott's voice rose hysterically at her lack of response.

'It's all right, Scott,' she soothed reassuringly even as she put up a hand to where seconds ago her head had made painful contact with the window beside her.

Amazingly, although the engine had stalled on impact, the headlights were still on, and when Meg turned she could see Scott strapped into his seat in the back of the car, tears streaming down his cheeks as he tried to reach forward and touch her.

'It's all right, baby.' She choked back her own tears

as she saw and felt his fear, fumbling with the clasp of her seat belt, desperate to get out of the car and go to him, to hold him, to reassure him they were both okay.

But before she could do any of that the door beside her was wrenched open, letting in a blast of icy-cold air, Meg's face white with shock as she let out a scream at the apparition she saw looming there.

'Mummy, it's a bear!' Scott cried from the back of the car.

A big hairy grizzly bear.

A blue-eyed grizzly bear, Meg realized as the man pushed back the hood of the heavy coat he was wearing, snow instantly falling on the dark thickness of his hair.

'Are you okay?' he barked concernedly, the narrowed blue gaze turning to Scott as he began to cry in the back of the car.

'I have to go to him!' Meg muttered anxiously as she scrambled out of the car, the man stepping back as she pushed past him to wrench open the back door and almost fling herself inside. 'It's okay, Scott. We're okay.' She held him close to her, feeling his shuddering tears. 'This nice man has only come to help us.' She hoped.

It would be just her luck to have crashed into the side of the house—yes, she could see it now, the lights burning warmly inside, she had actually hit the side of a house!—of an eccentric recluse who didn't like women and children, and had no intention of helping them, either.

Although at this particular moment she didn't really care who or what the man was; she was too weary, too upset, to do more than look up at him with huge shadowed green eyes and say, 'Is there any room at the inn?'

Which was a totally ridiculous thing for her to have said, she realized, still cringing inwardly a few minutes later when she and Scott, after a quick visit to the loo for her small son, sat together in front of a warm, crackling log fire drinking hot chocolate.

Although their rescuer had simply looked at her with mocking blue eyes and replied, 'Sorry to break with tradition, but, yes, there's room at the inn,' before all but picking her and Scott up in his arms—no little weight, she was sure—and carrying them inside the house.

Well, it wasn't exactly a house, Meg noted as she took a look around her, more of a cottage with its low beamed ceilings and small rooms. Not that it mattered what it was; it was warm, and dry, and out of the snowstorm still raging outside.

A storm their unexpected host had gone back out into after making them the hot chocolate.

Scott, safely ensconced on her denim-clad knees, peered shyly around her shoulder towards the door. 'Where did the man go, Mummy?'

Good question. But apart from 'outside', she had no idea.

'The name's Jed,' the man drawled as he stepped back into the small sitting-room, looking more like a bear than ever, the heavy coat and hood liberally covered in the same snow that dripped off in lumps from the huge boots he wore. 'Yours.' He handed Meg the handbag that she had left on the passenger seat of the car. 'And yours,' he added more gently as he gave Scott a small knapsack that contained the toys he had brought along to play with on the journey. 'Your car keys.' He dropped them into Meg's waiting palm. 'Not that I think anyone is going to steal your car any time soon,' he added dryly as he shrugged out of the heavy coat. 'You dinged the front pretty bad.'

Two things had become obvious during that conversation, or should that be monologue? Because Meg's teeth were still chattering too badly for her to be able to answer him. One, that the man's accent was American, two, that he didn't look much less formidable without the bulky coat.

At well over six feet in height, with shaggy dark hair; his shoulders were wide beneath the black sweater, faded denims fitting snugly on narrow hips and powerful thighs, those deep blue eyes set in a face of teaked mahogany, the squareness of his jaw giving him an air of complete self-assurance.

Meg's arms tightened instinctively about Scott as that vivid blue gaze moved over the two of them with the same deliberation, knowing what he would see: a woman of five feet two inches tall, with a mane of straight dark hair that reached almost to her waist, a small, heart-shaped face, green eyes, with a sprinkling of freckles across her nose, the little boy on her knee with the same colouring and freckles.

And the silence in the room, apart from the crackling of the logs on the fire, was starting to become oppressive.

Meg stirred herself. 'I'm really sorry to have disturbed you and your family in this way, Mr—er, Jed,' she amended awkwardly.

'No family, just me,' he dismissed easily, moving into a crouched position to place another log on the fire.

'Hey,' he murmured steadyingly as Meg and Scott moved further to the back of the chair. 'I realize I haven't been near a barber for a couple of months, but I don't really look like a bear, do I?' He gave what Meg was sure was meant to be a reassuring smile, but only succeeded in making him look more wolfish rather than harmless.

Meg moistened dry lips. The storm and crash must have made her oversensitive; this man was their rescuer, not their attacker. 'I really can't thank you enough for helping us like this, Mr—Jed,' she said again ruefully, placing Scott back on the chair as she stood up. 'Without your help Scott and I may just have…well, I can't thank you enough.' She decided not to go into the details of what could have befallen Scott and herself out there alone in the storm. Scott was probably going to have nightmares about this as it was, without making things worse.

'You're welcome,' he drawled dryly as he stood up to tower over her once again.

Meg blinked up at him. He really was extremely large for this tiny room. 'If you could provide me with the telephone number of a local garage, I'll give them a call and see if they can perhaps tow my car away before taking us to the nearest… No?' she said uncertainly as the man gave a derisive shake of his head.

'No,' he confirmed. 'It's after five-thirty, so the workshop at the garage in town will be closed. And even if it wasn't I doubt very much they would come out in this weather. Don't you?' He glanced pointedly out of the cottage window where the snow was still falling heavily.

She glanced at Scott who, having lost interest in this

adult conversation, was now taking toys out of his bag to play with. Which was probably just as well—there was absolutely no need for him to see his mother's worry.

What was she going to do? The car, from what this man said, was undriveable. The snow was still falling, and even the few minutes she had spent outside between the car and cottage were enough to tell her she couldn't expect Scott to walk anywhere in that.

Besides which, she had absolutely no idea where she was.

Jed watched as the emotions flickered across the woman's face, although 'woman' was perhaps stretching things a bit. Despite the small boy who called her 'Mummy', she didn't look much more than a child herself, barely five feet tall, her face appearing bare of make-up, her only colour the freckles across her nose and the emerald-green eyes surrounded by the longest black lashes he had ever seen, her long, glowing black hair unstyled except for a few wisps on her forehead.

And she appeared to be quietly panicking from her pained expression and continuing pallor.

Not that he was all that happy with this turn of events himself. He hadn't deliberately placed himself out of circulation here in the middle of nowhere to have his peace and solitude shattered by a green-eyed imp and her kid.

But whatever panic she was still feeling over her predicament was placed firmly under control as she introduced herself. 'I'm Meg Hamilton—' she even managed a slight curve of those full lips as she held out a slender hand '—and this is my son, Scott,' she added with a certain amount of pride as she gazed down at the little kid now busily playing with a tractor and some farm animals.

Trust the English, Jed mused ruefully. Even in the middle of a blizzard, good manners couldn't be ignored.

'Jed Cole,' he returned abruptly, searching her face for any sign of recognition of his name as he shook her hand.

'Mr Cole.' But she only seemed relieved to have the formalities covered, as though these minor pleasantries reassured her, at the same time releasing her hand from his.

She didn't recognize either his name or him, then. That, or else she was a very good actress, followed the cynical thought.

Over the last nine months, since his life had suddenly become public property, women had tried all sorts of tricks to meet him, one of them even sneaking into the sports club he belonged to and accosting him in the shower. Apparently all the other men present in the changing-room had been too dazed by the woman being there at all to ask her what she thought she was doing.

Although perhaps dragging a kid along, in the middle of a snowstorm, was going a little far, even for the most ardent fan. And from the totally unknowing look on Meg Hamilton's face, she wasn't one of those.

'Is there perhaps a hotel nearby?' Meg queried with what he thought was more hope than expectation.

'I hate to disappoint you, Mrs Hamilton.' And he really did, already resenting this intrusion into his privacy.

Not that he would have just left her and the kid outside to freeze—he just wished she had chosen someone else's cottage to drive in to.

But having been secluded here for two months

now—not very productive months, he had to admit—
he had got out of the habit of polite conversation. If he
had ever had it. Which he probably hadn't, he acknowledged ruefully. He didn't suffer fools gladly at the best
of times, and driving in this weather, with a little kid in
tow, had to be the height of foolishness.

'No hotel,' he rasped. 'In fact, apart from this cottage,
no anything,' he bit out harshly.

A frown marred that creamy brow now. 'But we can't
be too far from Winston. Can we…?' she added uncertainly, those small, slender hands betraying her nervousness as she ran them against denim-clad thighs.

She should be nervous, risking her own life and that
of the kid's, to drive in weather like this, and for what?
He had no idea, but it wasn't worth it, whatever the reason.

His impatient anger was audible in his tone. 'About
ten miles or so, though it might as well be a hundred,'
he added harshly as her expression brightened. 'You
must have taken a wrong turning half a mile or so away,
because this is a private road that leads to this cottage
only. And even if they get the snowploughs out tomorrow
the road to the cottage will remain snowbound.'

Tell it like it is, why don't you, Cole? he berated
himself disgustedly as tears swam now in those deep
green eyes.

But if she hadn't deliberately come here to meet
him—and he was inclined to believe that she hadn't, her
distress was too genuine—then what was this wom-
an/child doing out here in the middle of nowhere two
days before Christmas?

He scowled heavily. 'Where have you driven from?'

'London,' she said flatly. 'It wasn't snowing when we set out—well, not much, anyway,' she amended with a grimace as her son would have spoken.

Out of the mouths of babes. But Jed accepted that it probably hadn't been snowing anything like this in the capital; he had never known snow to settle for long during his own frequent trips to that busy metropolis. But London was over a hundred and twenty miles away from here, at least.

'Didn't you have the good sense to pull over and stop somewhere when you could see the weather was worsening?' he snapped his impatience with the situation, what was he supposed to do with this unlikely pair of visitors?

'Obviously not!' A flush brightened her cheeks. 'I realize now that I should have done,' she continued awkwardly, those green eyes glittering with anger now rather than tears. 'But I didn't.' She angled her pointed chin challengingly, as if daring him to criticize her again.

It was a challenge Jed had no problem accepting. 'Instead of which, you and the kid there are now my guests!' Unwelcome guests, he could have added, but knew that his tone of voice said it all.

Her mouth set stubbornly. 'The kid's name is Scott,' she corrected tersely, obviously smarting from his comments. 'And I'm sure there must be some way the two of us can get out of here and leave you to your privacy.' The last word came out scornfully.

That privacy wasn't something to be scorned as far as he was concerned; it had been hard won.

But it was hard not to admire this petite woman. Not

only had she kept her head through blizzard conditions—simply pulling over to the side of the road and sitting out the storm could have resulted in her and her son freezing to death—and maintained that calm after the crash, but she still had enough courage left to stand up to her reluctant rescuer.

And he was reluctant, had no idea what he was going to do with the pair of them for what he knew, even if Meg Hamilton hadn't realized it yet, was going to be an overnight stay, at least.

Jed Cole to the rescue. It wasn't a role he, or indeed many of his friends, would ever have imagined him in. Humanity, he had decided this last year—even ebony-haired green-eyed waifs—left a lot to be desired, and should be avoided, if possible.

Something, in this particular situation, he simply couldn't do. Which only increased his bad temper.

'Really?' He dropped down into the unoccupied armchair, draping a leg over the arm as he looked up at her enquiringly. 'I would be very interested to hear it?' He quirked dark brows.

'Maybe we could walk to—'

'There's a blizzard raging outside,' Jed cut in impatiently. 'Some of the drifts are already four feet high; if the kid—Scott,' he amended dryly as she glared at him. 'If he fell into one of those drifts you'd never find him.'

Once again he watched as the emotions raging inside her showed on her face; good manners versus impatient anger this time, rather than her earlier panic at her predicament.

Anger won out as she glared at him. 'I would find him,' she assured him grimly.

He would just bet that she would too, reminding him at that moment of a lioness protecting her cub.

He shrugged. 'You got lost driving a car; what chance do you think you stand on foot?'

That glare turned to a frown as she moved to stand protectively in front of her son before answering him softly. 'Are you deliberately trying to frighten me?'

Jed eyed her speculatively. 'Am I succeeding?' he prompted dryly.

'You're being unnecessarily cruel, if that's what you mean,' she came back tartly.

Giving a good impression of one of the bantam hens back home on his parents' farm as she defended her ground against one of the larger species of live-stock. A defence that was usually successful, he recalled wryly.

'Look, I realize we've inconvenienced you, turning up like this…'

'You drove into the side of the damned cottage,' he reminded with some of the incredulity he had felt at the time. Relaxing beside the log fire, staring broodingly into the flickering flames as he sipped a glass of whisky, he had heard an almighty bang as the whole cottage had seemed to shudder. He had thought the side of the cottage was going to fall in on him.

'Well. Yes… I know, but—' she gave a pained grimace '—I didn't mean to,' she added ruefully. 'And could you please not swear in front of Scott?' she said softly. 'They aren't words I want added to his vocabulary.'

Not only had he been severely 'inconvenienced', he was now being told what he could or couldn't say.

He scowled darkly. 'Is there a Mr Hamilton somewhere anxiously awaiting your arrival?' If there was, he would quite happily pass on the responsibility of rescuing his wife and son to the other man.

She looked stunned for a moment, as if reminded of something she had forgotten as the angry flush faded from her cheeks, making her look all eyes again. Defenceless eyes, Jed recognized uncomfortably.

She chewed on her bottom lip before answering him. 'Yes, there's a Mr Hamilton.'

'Nearby, I hope?' Jed prompted harshly, not happy with the protective emotion this woman was starting to engender in him. If he could just get her back to her life he could return to his.

'And a Mrs Hamilton,' she continued distractedly. 'My parents,' she supplied at his quizzical frown.

Her parents, Mr and Mrs Hamilton. Which meant there wouldn't be a husband rushing to the rescue, because there wasn't a husband.

'I was on my way to see them for Christmas when I—' her bottom lip trembled slightly before she drew in a deeply controlling breath and continued '—before I got lost. Do you think I might use your telephone to call them?' That pointed chin was once again raised challengingly. 'My father hasn't been well, and they would have expected us to have arrived by now.'

Jed frowned. Not 'they will be worried about me and their grandson', just they would have 'expected us to have arrived by now'.

He shook the observation off impatiently; he was probably just reading too much into it. What the hell business of his was it, anyway?

'Sure.' He made a sweeping gesture to where the telephone sat on the table by the door.

The old-fashioned kind of telephone before push buttons. But, then, everything about this cottage was a bit dated, he had discovered when he'd arrived here nine weeks ago. From the sheets and blankets on the beds rather than duvets, to the fire. And he had lost count of the amount of times he had cracked his head on one low-beamed ceiling or another during the first couple of weeks here, before he'd learnt to duck automatically as he stood up.

Not that Meg Hamilton had that problem, he noted a little sourly as she moved to pick up the receiver, her ebony head at least a foot lower than those innocuous-looking, but actually lethal, beams.

No, her nervousness seemed to be for another reason entirely.

He stood up. 'Would you like me to take Scott into the kitchen and give you some privacy for your call?' He had no idea what made him make the offer, only that he sensed her reluctance to make the call.

She gave him a startled look before glancing past him to where her son was still playing with his tractor. 'No, I... That's okay. Thank you.' She gave a brief smile. 'I only need to let them know I won't be arriving in time for dinner, after all.' She picked up the receiver and dialled.

Jed made no answer as he lowered his considerable height back into the armchair. But he thought about what that told him. For instance, if his mother had been expecting him to arrive in the middle of a snowstorm, and he hadn't done so, she would have called out the local police, probably the FBI, plus sent his father and two brothers out to search for him. A bit over the top, maybe, but in those circumstances dinner would be the last thing on his mother's mind.

'Mother?' Meg Hamilton queried tautly as her call was answered. 'Yes, I'm sorry. It will probably be some time tomorrow now. Yes, I realize that. Of course I'll let you know if we intend arriving in time for lunch.' There was a slight pause as she listened to a lengthy reply. 'Did she?' Meg's voice had become somewhat brittle now. 'Yes, I probably should have come by train, too, but I had Scott's things to bring too, and... Yes, I'll definitely call you tomorrow to confirm our arrival.' Her hand, Jed noticed frowningly, was shaking slightly as she replaced the receiver.

It sounded as if his instincts had been correct. Mrs Hamilton, at least, was more concerned with her dining arrangements than she was with the welfare of her daughter and grandson.

He glanced at Scott as he sat in front of the fire arranging his farm animals on the rug. As far as Jed was aware his grandmother hadn't said one word about him.

Jed straightened in the chair as he recognized what he was doing. He would not get involved. This girl and her son would be on their way as soon as he could get them there, and that would be the end of them as far as he was concerned.

He would not get involved.

CHAPTER TWO

MEG deliberately kept her back to the room for several seconds after the call had ended, taking the time to try and compose herself.

Her palms were damp and yet she felt an icy shiver down her spine—not an unusual reaction after talking to her mother.

She had no idea how her mother did it; perhaps the tone of voice her mother used rather than the actual words spoken, she thought. All Meg knew was that after a five-minute conversation with her mother she felt five years old again, rather than a grown woman with a young son of her own.

But that wasn't all of it, of course. Her sister Sonia would be there for Christmas, indeed, as her mother had just told her, was already there, having sensibly taken the train, her skiing trip cancelled because her husband had sprained his ankle on the golf course and so couldn't ski.

Sonia, of the designer clothes, the successful career, and the eminently suitable marriage.

Everything, as their mother was so fond of reminding, that Meg wasn't, and didn't have.

She bought her clothes from a chain store, and her career as an interior designer kept the landlord from the door and the bills paid, with very little left over for anything else. As for marriage, she had Scott instead of the suitable husband her mother would have preferred.

And he was better than any husband she might have had, worth all the heartache of the last three and a half years, she reflected with the same fierce protectiveness she had known from the first moment he had been placed in her arms.

Sonia could keep her wealthy lifestyle, and her suitable marriage; Meg would much rather have Scott.

'I was just about to fix supper when you arrived.' Jed Cole spoke huskily behind her.

Meg drew herself up, turning to face him, putting all thoughts of Sonia and her parents to the back of her mind. There would be plenty of time for her to think of them tomorrow. Or even the day after that, she acknowledged ruefully after a glance outside at the still heavily falling snow.

Right now she had the more immediate problem of being a guest in Jed Cole's cottage—an unwelcome guest, if her guess was correct.

And who could blame him for feeling that way? She hadn't exactly arrived under auspicious circumstances. Crashing into the side of the cottage like that. The poor man must have wondered what on earth was going on.

Where the splutter of laughter came from she wasn't exactly sure, only that it was there, and there wasn't a thing she could do about it. In fact, the more she tried to control it, the worse it became.

'I'm sorry.' She shook her head helplessly. 'I just—I can't believe I actually drove into the side of your cottage.' She was laughing so hard now there were tears on her cheeks.

'Why's Mummy crying?' Scott looked across at her concernedly.

'I have no idea,' Jed Cole answered him grimly even as he took a determined step towards her. 'Will you calm it down?' he snapped. 'You're scaring the kid.'

As Scott didn't look scared, only puzzled by her behaviour, it was more likely she was scaring 'the man' rather than 'the kid', Jed Cole staring down at her uncertainly now, as if he weren't sure whether to shake her or slap her.

Neither of which particularly appealed to her, although she had a feeling he might enjoy it.

'I really am sorry.' She did her best to stop laughing, wiping the tears from her cheeks as she met his gaze. 'You were about to make supper, you said?' The hysteria hadn't completely gone, was still lurking on the edges, but for the moment she seemed to have it under control.

Jed Cole still eyed her warily, those hard hewn features appearing more arrogant than ever, his jaw clenched disapprovingly. 'Steak and fries,' he answered her abruptly. 'There's enough for two if you're interested,' he added tersely. 'Although quite what you're going to feed the kid—'

'His name is Scott,' she repeated firmly. 'And Scott eats what I eat.'

The man grimaced. 'Then I guess there's enough steak and fries for three.' He turned on his heel and left the room abruptly, the sound of another door opening and then closing seconds later.

Meg gave Scott a quick glance. He seemed satisfied that his mother was okay after all and had resumed playing with his toys. 'Scott, I'm going to help Mr Cole prepare dinner. Do you want to come or stay here and play?' There was a guard in front of the fire, and he was playing far enough away not to come to any harm.

'I stay here,' he decided predictably. 'There's no tree, Mummy,' he added with a frown.

No tree. No decorations. No cards. In fact, nothing to indicate it was Christmas Eve tomorrow.

'Not everyone celebrates Christmas in the way we do, Scott,' she explained smilingly. 'And I'm sure Granma and Grandad will have a big tree for you to look at tomorrow.'

The tree would be in the hallway as always, with the decorations all just so, and white lights only because her mother abhorred the coloured ones, with neatly rib-boned and bowed gifts nestled beneath it.

A sharp contrast to the fern they had left behind in their flat, Meg thought wistfully, with its home-made decorations and paper chains, and enough tinsel and multicoloured lights draped around it to illuminate a tree four times its size.

'I'm just in the kitchen helping Mr Cole, darling.' She bent to kiss her son lightly on top of his ebony head. 'Just call if you need me.'

It wasn't too difficult to locate the kitchen in this three-up three-down cottage. The door to the room opposite the sitting-room was open, revealing a small

formal dining-room, meaning the closed door at the end
of the hallway had to be the kitchen.

But even without that process of elimination, the sound
of pots banging and the smell of food cooking would have
told her exactly where she could find Jed Cole.

Jed Cole.

He really was something of an enigma. Even without
that American accent he so obviously didn't belong here.
He was too big, or else the cottage was too small for him.
Besides, the décor and furniture in the cottage were both
well-worn and faded, and even if she didn't buy expensive clothing herself Meg knew a cashmere sweater when
she saw one, and the faded denims had an expensive label
on the back pocket, the shoes he had put on after taking
off the heavy boots made from soft black leather.

'So tell me,' she said brightly as she entered the kitchen
to find him putting steaks, two of them, under the grill.
'Which do you think you would have opted for if I hadn't
stopped laughing when I did—the shaking or the slap?'

Jed eyed her mockingly from beneath heavy dark
brows as he leant back against one of the kitchen units,
arms folded across the width of his chest as he looked
down at her. 'Actually, I'd got around to thinking that
kissing you might do the trick,' he drawled ruefully.

Embarrassed colour instantly stained her cheeks. So
much for her attempt at humour.

'But on second thoughts,' he added hardly, 'I decided
that I'm not into kissing teenage mothers, no matter
what the provocation!'

Meg's eyes widened at this description of her. 'Just
how old do you think I am?'

He gave her a considering look. 'Obviously old enough to legally be the mother of the—Scott,' he amended harshly. 'Just, probably.'

She put her hands on her hips as she eyed him incredulously. 'For your information, Mr Cole, I'm twenty-seven years old,' she snapped. 'And I most certainly did not offer you any provocation.' The wings of colour in her cheeks seemed to burn now.

His eyes narrowed at the slight emphasis she put on the 'you', that steely blue gaze easily holding hers for several long seconds, until finally he gave a shrug and moved away. 'Make the salad, why don't you?' he instructed tersely before checking the steaks under the grill. 'Nothing ever looks as bad with a hot meal inside you.'

'Does that apply to you or to me?' Meg returned ruefully as she moved to take the makings of a salad out of the cooler box in the fridge.

'Both of us!' he came back tersely before turning away to look at the fries.

Meg continued to look at him for several seconds. This really wasn't an ideal situation, for any of them. Jed Cole had just been sitting here in the cottage minding his own business, looking forward to his steak dinner no doubt, and now he had a woman and her young son to feed too.

She moved to look out of the kitchen window, the light reflected outside showing her that the gusting wind was blowing the snow into deep drifts.

'Is there really no way we can get away from here tonight?'

She only realized she had spoken the words out loud

when Jed Cole slammed a knife down on the worktop. 'No way and no how,' he rasped with controlled violence. 'Now if you want to eat tonight, I suggest you make the damn salad.'

Meg had turned as he'd slammed down the utensil, eyeing him warily now as she started to prepare the salad.

'And stop looking at me like that,' he added impatiently.

She straightened. 'Like what?'

'Like a mouse expecting to be mauled by that bear Scott originally thought that I was!' He sighed his exasperation. 'Compared to my usual demeanour I'm behaving like a goddamned pussycat, okay?'

Meg bit on her top lip as it twitched with laughter. At the moment he looked as Scott used to when he'd gone through 'the terrible twos', totally disgruntled at not being able to get his own way.

'Okay,' she agreed mildly. 'Do you want dressing on this salad?'

'Do I want…' He closed his eyes, drawing in a controlling breath before opening them again to glare at her. 'Who the hell are you, Meg Hamilton? And what warped quirk of fate,' he rasped before she could reply, 'landed you on my doorstep?'

'Actually it was the side of the cottage,' she corrected softly as she mixed a mustard dressing together. 'But we won't argue the details just now,' she dismissed brightly.

'We'll save that until later, huh?' he muttered, a grudging respect now in those deep blue eyes as he looked at her consideringly. 'What was with your mother earlier? She seemed more concerned with her eating arrangements than whether or not you and Scott were okay.'

The kitchen, small at best, with barely enough room for the two of them to move around it, suddenly didn't even seem big enough for that, with no room for her to hide, to avoid the piercing intrusion of Jed Cole's gaze.

Because he was right. Not once during that brief conversation had her mother bothered to ask why Meg and Scott had been delayed, merely commenting that her sister had managed to get there, also from London, because she had sensibly come by train.

It simply hadn't been worth the effort of explaining that, unlike Sonia, who had probably got all her Christmas presents for the family in one elegant designer-label bag after being gift-wrapped by the store they were bought from, Meg had all Scott's Father Christmas presents to bring too. Gifts lovingly bought and wrapped by Meg herself, this being the first Christmas that Scott, aged three and a half, had really appreciated and looked forward to. She had even gone to the expense of hiring a car so that she could transport the things here.

The car that was now crumpled into the side of the cottage.

She would have to call the hire company in the morning and explain what had happened, sincerely hoping that the insurance would cover the costs of the damage.

She managed to give Jed Cole a casual shrug as he stood waiting for an answer to his questions. 'Mothers are like that,' she evaded. 'Feeding their family is of high priority.'

Which might have been true of her mother if she did the cooking herself, but ever since Meg had been born, probably before that too, Mrs Sykes—Bessie—had presided over the Hamilton kitchen. But as Jed Cole would never meet her mother, let alone eat a meal in the Hamilton household, he didn't need to know that.

'I'm sure your mother is the same,' she dismissed.

There was a slight softening of his expression. 'For as long as I can remember my mother has always had enough extra food in the house to feed a family of ten, and often has, and if she hadn't she'd send my dad out to kill a cow.'

'She sounds nice,' Meg murmured wistfully, almost able to imagine the warm kitchen and the motherly figure there caring for her family.

'She is.' Jed nodded. 'So's my dad. And my two younger brothers. And their wives, and the numerous offspring they've produced.'

Meg gave him a considering look. 'So why aren't you there for Christmas, instead of—well, here, alone?'

His mouth twisted. 'Maybe because I prefer "alone" to my Mum and Dad, two younger brothers, their wives, and numerous offspring.'

Maybe.

And then again, maybe not.

She certainly hadn't imagined that softening when he'd spoken of his family, or the slightly wistful tone in his voice.

But she didn't have time to probe any further before he snapped, 'Will you stop asking so many questions, woman, and dish the food up?'

In other words, end of discussion about his family.

But that didn't stop Meg's curiosity about them, about

whether or not Mum, Dad, two brothers, their wives and their numerous offspring were sad because one of their number was missing from their Christmas this year.

Somehow, and she didn't know why she felt that way, she had a feeling that they were.

Mistake, Cole, Jed remonstrated with himself even while he inwardly acknowledged that the dressing on the salad was just as he liked it. But he should never have mentioned the idea of kissing Meg. Because now he couldn't take his eyes off her mouth. It was a rather nice mouth, too, the lips full, with a permanent tilt at their corners, as if this woman liked to smile a lot.

As she was smiling now at her small son as they all sat at the dining table and Scott manfully tried to tackle his own small piece of steak, fries and salad.

And she most definitely was a woman, and not a girl, he accepted self-derisively, her smart comeback before dinner that of an adult. And the soft swell beneath the dark green sweater she wore over faded denims was adult too, as was the curve of her hips. And as for those full, inviting lips.

Damn it, he should never have mentioned kissing her, because now he couldn't think of anything else!

Two months he had been holed up here, that was all, and now he was looking at Meg Hamilton as if she were a bottle of water in the desert. A carton of ice cream in a heatwave.

'Is the food not to your liking?'

Jed focused on her scowlingly. 'What?'

She gave him a quizzical smile. 'You were glaring at

your steak as if it had done something to offend you,' she teased.

Oh, very funny. Ha, bloody ha.

It was okay for her to laugh, she wasn't the one sitting here having carnal thoughts about a woman who had arrived on his doorstep in distress, her young fatherless son in tow.

'The food's fine,' he rasped curtly. 'It's all fine.' As if to prove his point he stabbed a piece of steak on his fork and shoved it into his mouth and began chewing.

And chewing.

Maybe cutting the steak down a little in size might have been a good idea, Jed, he berated himself, aware that both Meg and her son were now looking at him, Meg surreptitiously Scott with the frank intensity of a child.

'It's rude to stare, Scott,' his mother remonstrated as she noticed his intensity of concentration.

The little boy turned away obediently. Only to turn back again seconds later when his mother wasn't looking, those green eyes studied on Jed's face.

Obviously he had never seen a man try to eat half a cow in one mouthful before.

'Mr Cole, why don't you have a tree?' Scott finally asked, a frown marring his creamy brow.

Ah, it wasn't the steak that was bothering him at all.

'Or decorations?' The little boy looked disapproving now. 'We like decorations, don't we, Mummy? An' there's no cards, either,' Scott continued before his mother could answer him. 'With robins on. We like robins, don't we, Mummy?' He gave his mother a beatific smile.

As little kids went, this one was a cute little devil, Jed

allowed as he finally managed to swallow the steak. In fact, with his dark hair, green eyes, the freckles on his little nose, he was a tiny version of his mother.

Not again.

Meg Hamilton, even without the extra baggage, was most definitely not his type.

At thirty-eight, he liked his women to be tall and sophisticated, older women, who were only interested in the brief relationship he was willing to give. Meg had the look of a woman who had already taken enough blows to her girlhood dreams, without another selfish bastard coming along to shatter them some more.

'I did explain, Scott—' Meg spoke quietly to her son now '—that not everyone celebrates Christmas.'

'Do you celebrate Christmas, Mr Cole?' Scott questioned guilelessly.

'Well… Yes. Usually.' Talk about putting him on the spot. 'But, you see, I don't actually live here, Scott. I live in a place called New York.' He predicted what the next question would be and answered it. 'Very far away from here, in a place called America.' Where, no doubt, dozens of cards and gifts would be waiting for him to deal with when he returned.

But even in New York he wouldn't have put up a tree and decorations, had never seen the need for them when there was only him living there, the modern chrome and leather of his apartment not lending themselves to such frivolity.

Scott's eyes were wide now, surrounded by the same incredibly long lashes as those of his mother. 'Then why are you here and not there?'

Exactly like his mother, Jed identified impatiently, who had asked him a similar question before dinner.

But the difference here was that with cute little kids like Scott you didn't feel comfortable either fobbing them off or lying to them.

However, at this point in time, Jed really didn't feel like telling the little boy the truth, either. Especially as there hadn't been so much as a flicker of recognition in Meg's face when he'd introduced himself earlier.

He wasn't quite sure where Meg had been for the last nine months while the invasion of his privacy had become a thing of nightmares, so that he had come to England and hidden away in this cottage in order to find the peace and quiet he needed to work. Not that he had worked. Well... not much, anyway. But this escape from instant recognition was better than nothing.

'I think we've bothered Mr Cole enough for one evening, Scott.' Meg came smoothly to his rescue at his continued silence. 'It's almost time for your bath and then bed.'

'Oh, but, Mummy, Father Christmas comes tomorrow night,' the little boy protested.

She smiled. 'All the more reason for you to get lots of sleep tonight. Let's help Mr Cole clear away, and then I'll run your bath—' She broke off, giving Jed a wry look. 'I take there is hot water for a bath?'

He nodded. 'And a shower, of sorts.' He stood up. 'You'll need your bags from the car?' He didn't particularly relish the idea of going back out into the cold and wet, but neither did he think it a good idea for Meg to be wandering about naked upstairs later. It might be fun, but after the thoughts he had been having about the curviness of her hips, and the soft warmth of her body, it probably wasn't the best idea.

In fact, having this unlikely pair here at all wasn't a particularly good idea, but as none of them had any choice in the matter he would have to make the best of it. And that included providing Meg with nightclothes.

'Please.' She nodded. 'Just the one bag in the boot of the car.'

'Travelling light?' He raised dark brows, remembering all the clutter his sisters-in-law always seemed to carry around for their kids.

'We're only staying at my parents' until Boxing Day,' Meg answered him as she collected the plates together, at the same time, it seemed, carefully avoiding his gaze.

They didn't have Boxing Day in the States, made do with Christmas Eve and Christmas Day for the holidays over there, but it seemed to him that Meg had travelled a long way for a three-day, now two-day, visit. Why?

'We're going to see my granma and grandad,' Scot told him brightly.

'So I understand.' Jed nodded, finding himself smiling at the little boy in spite of himself.

Children, especially little ones like this, were not part of his everyday life. Although, despite what he might have said earlier, he was fond enough of his nieces and nephews.

'Do you know my granma and grandad?' Scot looked up at him expectantly.

He gave a shake of his head. 'I can't say that I've ever met them, no.'

'Scott, it really is time for your—'

'Neither have I.' Scott spoke at the same time as his mother, his expression wistful now.

Curiouser and curiouser, Jed mulled frowningly. Scott had to be at least three, perhaps a little older, and yet he claimed never to have met his own grandparents. Jed could understand the lapse where the boy's father's parents were concerned, but not with his maternal grandparents.

What sort of people were the Hamiltons never to have even met their own grandson?

CHAPTER THREE

'Is IT all right if I come in?' Meg hesitated in the doorway to the sitting room.

She had just put Scott up to bed in the guest bedroom—a guest bedroom with a double bed that she and Scott could share, thank goodness. Scott was a restless sleeper, and she hadn't relished being kicked all night in the confines of a single bed with him. Although perhaps she should think herself lucky she was sleeping in a bed at all tonight; she and Scott could so easily have ended up huddled together in the car somewhere.

She shrugged. 'If you're busy I can always...'

'Always what?' Jed Cole came back derisively, lounging in one of the armchairs but putting down the book he had been glancing through. 'Your choices are pretty limited in this cottage.'

A flush heightened her cheeks. She felt strangely uncomfortable now that she was alone with this darkly enigmatic man. Although he was only three, Scott's presence had acted as a buffer between the two adults, making personal conversation almost impossible. Something that was no longer true.

Especially after Scott's statement earlier concerning his grandparents.

And her parents, her whole family, in fact, were something she would rather not discuss.

She grimaced. 'Well, I could always go and tidy the kitchen.'

'All done,' Jed Cole dismissed dryly, almost as if he had guessed what she would do and had nullified it. 'For the main part the cottage is pretty basic, but it does have a dishwasher and washing machine, and, wonder of wonders, central heating.'

Meg had already noted that the entire cottage was warm, that the log fire burning in this room was only for effect and not to provide actual heat. 'Were they here when you bought the cottage or did you have them installed afterwards?' She moved further into the room, feeling slightly shy with this man, as shown by the inanity of her conversation.

Not surprising really. Jed Cole was the sort of darkly handsome man who would wreak havoc with any woman's pulse-rate at the best of times. Here, alone in a cottage with him, the snow on the ground outside creating an eerie silence, she found him nerve-janglingly attractive, his dark good looks, the intensity of his deep blue eyes, combined with the lean strength of his body, making Meg completely aware of him.

Which was quite an admission coming from a woman who hadn't so much as accepted a date in over three years.

Jed Cole shook his head now. 'I don't own the cottage, Meg, it belongs to...a friend of mine,' he dismissed abruptly. 'I've just been staying here for a while.'

Not exactly helpful. And she hadn't missed that slight pause when he'd told her whom the cottage belonged to. 'Do you work in the area?'

He settled back in the armchair, blue gaze hooded now. 'No.'

She gave him a quick glance, not sure whether or not to sit down herself; if they were going to continue this horribly stilted conversation, probably not. 'Perhaps you have friends in the area?'

He grimaced. 'Don't know a soul.'

Hmm, talkative man, wasn't he? Perhaps it would better if she just made her excuses and went back upstairs.

'My turn now,' Jed drawled hardly. 'Why has Scott never met your parents?'

She had known by the narrow-eyed way he'd looked at her at the time that he wasn't going to let that statement pass, but the directness of his question now threw her into some confusion. Most people, most polite people, wouldn't have pursued the subject, but Jed Cole had made no effort to be polite, so why should he start now?

'I was about to have a glass of red wine,' he continued lightly. 'Would you care to join me?'

Why not? She'd had a long and stressful day, and she somehow didn't think it was going to get too much better if Jed Cole was going to start asking her questions like the one he just had.

He stood up now, careful to avoid the dark wooden beams on the ceiling as he did so.

She should have known that he didn't own this cottage. It was like trying to fit a round peg into a square hole; he simply didn't fit.

'Perhaps you'll be able to think of an answer to my question while I go and get the wine,' he told her mockingly as they stood together in the doorway for several seconds.

Several seconds too long for Meg's comfort, her awareness of this man becoming more acute with every minute that passed. Which would never do. Despite what this man might think to the contrary, because she had Scott, she did not get involved in brief, meaningless affairs. Even with attractive men she met in snowstorms.

Neither did she have an acceptable answer to his question, she admitted with dismay. And his slightly mocking smile before he disappeared down the hallway to the kitchen seemed to say that he already knew she didn't.

Well, she did have an answer, but it wasn't one she could give without being unkind to her parents, and she didn't think they deserved that. It wouldn't have been easy for them to accept their daughter turning up on their doorstep with their illegitimate grandchild. Not that she ever had.

'Here we are.' Jed came back with two glasses and an opened bottle of red wine. 'Thought of an answer yet?' he taunted as he poured the wine into the two glasses before handing one to Meg. 'Why don't we sit down, hmm?'

If he was trying to put her at her ease, then he wasn't succeeding.

Although after one glance at his face, at those mockingly raised brows, she realized that perhaps he wasn't trying to do any such thing, that he was a man who rarely, if ever, tried to make things easy for other people. In fact, as Meg was quickly learning, he wasn't a man it was easy to relax around at all. And it didn't help that he was so sure of himself, that he wore his obviously expensive clothing with a complete disregard for their worth—or that he was so rakishly attractive.

Admit it, Meg, she mocked herself, it was the latter about him that bothered her the most. She was alone here, with only the sleeping Scott for chaperon, with a man it was impossible not to be completely physically aware of.

'Still trying to think of an answer?'

And who also happened to be purposefully blunt to the point of rudeness.

'We aren't usually this—inquisitive, into other people's personal lives, in this country.' She eyed him sternly, a look usually guaranteed to subdue Scott, but which only succeeded in making this somewhat older man smile.

He shrugged those broad shoulders unapologetically. 'These aren't usual circumstances.'

No, they weren't, were they? Because in the normal course of things single mothers like Meg wouldn't even be noticed by a man who was probably more at home with highly sophisticated New York types.

Which posed the question Scott had asked him earlier—why was he here and not in New York?

'In that case…' she paused to take a sip of her wine '…perhaps you wouldn't mind explaining to me—'

'Oh, no, little Meg,' he cut in tauntingly, totally relaxed as he watched her from beneath hooded lids. 'You've already asked enough questions for one evening. Or do you want me to repeat the question?'

'That won't be necessary,' she snapped tautly.

'I'm still waiting, Meg,' he prompted softly seconds later at her tight-lipped silence.

She was as disturbed by his use of her first name as she was by his persistence. Although it would be slightly ridiculous, given the circumstances, for them to continue to stand on formality.

This time her sip of wine was more from necessity than for effect. 'You would have to know my parents to understand.'

'Oh, I can believe that,' he drawled scathingly.

'My father has been ill.'

'How old is Scott?' he prompted hardly.

'Three and a half. But—'

'Your father has been ill for three and a half years?' he said disbelievingly.

'Of course not,' she snapped agitatedly. 'I was just… Our parents are in their sixties.'

'Our?' Jed picked up frowningly. 'You have siblings too?'

'One. A sister,' she supplied reluctantly, knowing that the sophisticated Sonia wouldn't have found herself blushing and stumbling in conversation with this wildly attractive man, that her sister would have known exactly what to do and say.

'Older or younger?' he prompted softly.

'Older. Just,' she added with a sigh, knowing she had succeeded in disconcerting him by the way his eyes widened.

'You have a twin sister?'

'No need to sound so surprised.' It was her turn to

mock him now. 'They say everyone has a lookalike some-where in the world, my sister just happens to be mine.'

He frowned. 'You're identical?'

'Yes,' she confirmed brightly. 'Or, at least, we were,' she added slowly.

'Either you are or you aren't,' Jed derided, obviously not one to be disconcerted for long.

'We are,' Meg confirmed abruptly. No need to mention that Sonia had had her teeth whitened and capped, the freckles on her nose minimized, and wore an all-year-round tan. 'But Sonia wears her hair short, and is—well, she's a lawyer. I'm the arty one.' She sighed. 'I'm an interior designer,' she explained as he seemed to be looking at her hands for signs of paint.

'Wow.' He gave a derisive smile as he looked around the room. 'You must be itching to change things in here.'

She wasn't sure she would know where to start.

Well, no, that wasn't strictly true, although the décor in here did run to worn and comfortable rather than elegant or eye-catching. She would take out all the heavy furniture for a start, replace it with—

'Just joking, Meg,' he drawled. 'As I told you, I don't own the place. As long as it has a chair for me to sit on and a bed for me to sleep in, I'm really not too inter-ested.' He sat forward in his armchair, cradling his glass of wine between long, sensitive hands. 'I am beginning to see a pattern emerging, though,' he told her softly.

Meg gave him a startled look. 'You are?'

'I am.' He gave a mocking inclination of his head. 'Twin girls, born to older parents, one twin practical and ambitious, the other more sensitive and artistic. The older twin goes on to make a successful career for herself as a lawyer, an advantageous marriage—she is married? I thought she might be,' he drawled at Meg's nod of confirmation. 'No kids, either, I suspect; plenty of time for that later, if at all. The younger twin, on the other hand, turned out to have an artistic flare, opted for art college in London rather than university before finally getting spat out into the real world, only to end up getting pregnant—'

'I think you have said quite enough, Mr Cole,' Meg cut in abruptly, turning away slightly so that he wouldn't see the sheen of tears in her eyes. 'It isn't polite to discuss people's personal lives in this way.'

'British reserve, you mean?' he derided. 'Yeah, I've heard of that. We have something like it in the States too. It's called respecting other peoples' privacy. But I seem to remember someone asking questions about my family before dinner.'

'It's hardly the same.' She turned sharply to snap at him, having brought those tears firmly under control. She had cried enough tears over the years over her family, without breaking down in front of this man.

Jed Cole looked up at her consideringly. 'Got a little too close to home, did I?'

Far too close. Although he hadn't been right about everything. No, not everything.

'Hey, don't beat yourself up about it,' Jed chided derisively. 'I'm the duckling in my nest of swans too: Granddad was a farmer, Dad's a farmer, my two brothers are farmers.'

'And you, Mr Cole, what exactly are you?' she challenged, still stung by their earlier conversation.

'Well, I sure as hell ain't a farmer,' he assured mockingly.

She already knew that, those strong, slender hands didn't grow crops or tend animals. In his youth maybe, but certainly not for the last twenty years or so.

He gave a confidently dismissive smile. 'We weren't discussing me.'

'We aren't discussing me, either.' Meg drank down some more of her wine before placing the almost empty glass down on the table. 'Offering Scott and I shelter for the night does not entitle you to comment on either myself or my family.'

'No?' he taunted huskily, putting his own glass down on the carpeted floor before getting slowly to his feet. 'Then what does it entitle me to?' he challenged, that vivid blue gaze moving over her slowly, from the tips of her toes to the top of her ebony head, before moving down slightly to rest speculatively on the fullness of her lips.

For some reason he was deliberately trying to unnerve her. And he was succeeding. The atmosphere between them was now charged with expectation, the intensity of his gaze almost tangible against her lips.

He was playing with her, Meg recognized frowningly. It was there in the mocking twist to his mouth, the hard gleam of laughter in his eyes.

She drew in an angry breath. 'It entitles you to my heartfelt thanks,' she bit out tautly.

He gave a brief inclination of his head. 'Which you've already made. Several times,' he drawled.

Her eyes sparkled with her anger. 'Which I've already made several times,' she agreed tightly. 'Now if you will excuse me.' She bent to pick her handbag up from the floor. 'It's been a long day, and I'm very tired.'

'Oh, I'll excuse you, Meg,' he told her mockingly. 'I'm sure that most men would excuse you anything.'

Her mouth tightened. 'Goodnight, Mr Cole,' she told him firmly before turning on her heel to leave.

''Night, Meg,' he called after her tauntingly.

Her shoulders stiffened slightly but she didn't halt her departure, only starting to breathe again once she was out in the hallway with the door firmly closed behind her.

Jed Cole was rude. He was hostile. He was mocking. He was, in a word, infuriating.

He was also one of the most handsome men she had ever seen. And far too sexy for his own good.

'Just exactly what do you think you're doing?'

Jed looked up to watch as a very irate Meg stomped across the snow towards them, her eyes sparkling deeply green, twin wings of angry colour in her cheeks.

Something had put a burr under her saddle, that was for sure, and it appeared to be him. Although he couldn't for the life of him think what he had done; this was the first time this morning that he had set eyes on her.

As to what he and Scott were doing, surely the two huge balls of snow, one placed on top of the other, the bottom one larger than the top, spoke for themselves.

But he was willing to humour her for the moment. 'We're building a snowman.'

'I can see that,' Meg snapped irritably. 'But don't you

think it would have been better to have woken me first and told me what you were doing?'

'Why?' Jed eyed her derisively. 'Did you want to build a snowman, too?' He folded his arms across his chest as he looked down at her.

'No, of course I—' she broke off her angry reply to glare at him frustratedly. 'You—'

'You really should have put a hat and coat on before coming out here,' Jed told her frowningly. She was already starting to shiver as the cold penetrated the red jumper and denims she wore. 'Especially as I made sure Scott was dressed appropriately before I would let him come outside.'

'Isn't our snowman great, Mummy?' The animated little boy was covered in enough snow to be a snowman himself, having insisted on rolling the huge balls of snow until they had become too heavy for him to move and Jed had had to take over. 'Jed says he has an old hat and scarf we can put on him.'

'Mr Cole, darling,' Meg corrected slightly distractedly as she brushed some of the snow from his clothes.

Scott grimaced with what little of his face could be seen beneath the woollen hat and scarf he wore. 'But he said I could call him Jed, Mummy,' he dismissed with the simplicity of a child. 'Jed says we need a carrot and some coal, too, for his face.'

Jed watched the way Meg's mouth tightened slightly at this second 'Jed says' in as many minutes, sensing there was an explosion about to happen if he didn't intervene. 'How about Mummy and I go back into the cottage and get them right now?' he suggested lightly.

'You can look in the wood pile over there for some small branches that might do for arms, if you like,' he added as the little boy looked disappointed not to be included in the task.

'Cool!' Scott grinned before scampering off to the wood pile, totally impervious to the icy cold air that was now making his mother's teeth chatter.

Jed raised dark brows at a still frowning Meg. 'Shall we?' He indicated the cottage.

Her mouth firmed. 'I think we had better,' she muttered disgruntledly before turning and stomping back inside.

Jed followed at a more leisurely pace, sure that she wouldn't approve of the way he was watching her hips and backside move in the tight denims.

Yep, there was no doubt about it, Meg Hamilton was a fine-looking woman, under any circumstances. And Scott was a great little kid.

But they were also a complication he didn't need in his life, now or at any other time, so he had better stop thinking this way. Absolutely no involvement, he reminded himself sternly.

They got as far as the kitchen before she turned on him. 'I don't allow Scott to be overfamiliar with adults,' she told him stiffly.

'That's good.' He nodded tersely. 'I don't believe in being overfamiliar with adults, either.' Although he couldn't guarantee that was going to last too much longer where Meg was concerned. It was a cliché, he knew, but she really was beautiful when she was angry. Her eyes sparkled like emeralds, her cheeks were flushed, even her lips appeared redder. And more kissable.

'You know exactly what I mean,' she told him frustratedly. 'And what do you mean by just disappearing outside with him in that way?' She stood hands on hips now as she challenged him.

'I don't see what your problem is.'

'My problem is that I woke up to find Scott gone, and neither of you to be found in the cottage.' She was tense with fury now. 'If I hadn't heard Scott laughing, and looked out of the window and seen you both I would have thought—'

'What?' he cut in icily. 'What would you have thought, Meg? That I had run off with him? Because if that thought even entered your mind I—'

'It didn't!' Her shocked expression said that it really hadn't. 'It was only that I woke up to find the bed beside me empty.'

'Always a disappointment,' he drawled, starting to relax again.

Meg shot him a reproving glare. 'Speaking for yourself, of course.'

'Oh, of course,' he murmured dryly.

'Humph.' She gave him a narrow-eyed look before continuing, 'Anyway, I woke up and Scott wasn't there. Neither were his clothes. A quick search of the cottage showed me that you weren't here, either. I thought—well, what I thought was that Scott must have woken up, been confused about where he was, and just—just wandered off somewhere. I thought you had gone after him. And that perhaps you had both got lost in the snow. And then I heard Scott laughing.' She choked back the tears. 'And when I looked out the window and saw the two of you happily building what I could clearly see was a snowman, well, that's when I got angry instead of scared.'

'And came straight out of the cottage ready to tear me limb from limb!' he drawled. 'You aren't becoming hysterical again, are you?' He eyed her warily; she was certainly babbling enough to be, had said more in the last five minutes than in the whole of their previous acquaintance. 'Because you know what I threatened to do the last time you became hysterical.' He could see by the sudden colour that flooded her cheeks that she did remember. Clearly.

'Of course I'm not becoming hysterical,' she defended strongly.

'No?' Well, there was no need for her to sound quite that certain. He wasn't sure it was good for his ego. His ego, be damned; women didn't usually make it so obvious they desperately wanted to avoid having him kiss them.

Now who was being irrational? Don't get involved, he had told himself. Firmly. Decisively. Now he felt annoyed that the woman he needed to keep his distance from also wanted to keep him at a distance.

'No,' she acknowledged agitatedly. 'I passed hysterical some time ago.'

'You did?' he grated speculatively.

'I did.' She nodded. 'And then I— What are you doing?' She gasped as he took hold of the tops of her arms. 'You don't need to shake me.' She looked up at him with guileless eyes. 'I told you, I was—' whatever she was or wasn't was cut off as Jed lowered his head and kissed her, something he had been wanting to do since last night.

Her lips felt soft and cool beneath his, but that

coolness was only from the cold outside, he quickly learnt as her mouth became warm and inviting.

It was all the encouragement he needed, his arms moving about the slenderness of her waist as he moulded her curves into his, her tiny hands coming to rest on his shoulders as she clung to him.

'Mummy, did you find the carrot and the—oh…'

Meg came to her senses a lot quicker than Jed did, obviously attuned to her son's voice, pulling sharply away to release herself and turn to where Scott stood in the doorway in open-mouthed fascination, his eyes huge green pools of curiosity.

'No, we haven't found them yet, Scott,' Meg's voice quivered slightly. 'We—I had something in my eye and Mr Cole, Jed, was getting it out for me,' she invented with a smoothness that had Jed staring at her too.

'Something in her eye' my eye, he glowered darkly. Although perhaps her version was better than telling Scott that Jed had been devouring his mother's mouth with a need that had quickly spiraled out of control.

So much for not getting involved.

What the hell had he been thinking?

He hadn't been thinking at all, that was the problem, only feeling. And Meg had felt very good indeed.

'The carrot's in the cool box in the fridge, and the coal is in the bucket in the sitting-room,' he rasped as Meg bent down so that her son could inspect that the imaginary something had definitely gone from her eye.

The face Meg turned towards him was white with strain. 'Where are you going?' she prompted huskily as Jed moved to the door.

'Out,' he barked harshly.

She blinked. 'Out where?'

'Just out!' he bit out tersely, making good his escape, having no real idea where he was going, only that he had to get away from Meg for a while.

And try to get the taste and feel of her out of his head.

CHAPTER FOUR

'THE main roads are clear if you would like to get your things together.'

Meg gave Jed a startled look as she sat at the table playing a game of cards with Scott, not having heard him come into the cottage.

Jed had been gone for over an hour, time enough for her to have helped Scott finish off the snowman, make him some breakfast and a cup of coffee for herself, before sitting down to play a game of Pairs with him.

But during all that time she had been half listening for the sound of Jed Cole's return, not quite knowing what to say to him after what had happened between them, the memory of that kiss still firmly in her mind, only knowing that she felt less alone when he was around.

Well, she was less alone when he was around, obviously. But it was more than that: there was an arrogant confidence about Jed, an assurance, that made her feel nothing could go too wrong while he was there.

Except that he might kiss her again, of course.

She had been too stunned earlier to do anything more

than respond when he'd started kissing her, and by the time she'd stopped feeling stunned she had found she was enjoying it too much to want it to stop.

Quite what to make of that, when she had only known the man for less than twenty-four hours, she wasn't quite sure. But it certainly made her feel shy about facing him again.

Except that now he was back he was telling her it was time for her and Scott to leave.

'You carry on playing, Scott,' she told her son softly. 'I just want to have a word with Mr—Jed,' she quickly amended as he scowled across the room at her.

She followed him out into the hallway as he stepped out of the room, firmly telling herself to forget what had happened between the two of them earlier, that it would be better for everyone if she did.

Except that she couldn't quite keep her gaze from the sensuous curve of his lips, or stop herself from remembering how they had felt against hers, or the slight abrasiveness of his chin, where he was in need of a shave, against the softness of hers.

'What word did you have in mind?' he drawled sarcastically. 'Opportunist? Lecher? Or maybe something worse?' He grimaced self-disgustedly.

'No, of course not,' she snapped impatiently. 'What happened earlier was the result of overheated emotions,' she dismissed with what she hoped was conviction, because she wasn't sure what it was the result of, only that she would never be able to forget it. 'You said we could leave? Does that mean I'll be able to phone the local garage, after all?'

'It means I've just walked down to the main road and back.'

'You have?' she gasped.

'I have,' he drawled. 'And pretty damn slippery it is, too. But I think I may be able to drive my Range Rover down the half a mile or so of this lane, and then the main road has been cleared, so I should be able to drive the two of you the rest of the way to your parents' house.'

Meg's eyes widened at this suggestion. 'I don't think that's a good idea at all,' she protested without thinking, a blush colouring her cheeks as his brows rose speculatively. 'I mean, I really can't put you to all that trouble.'

'And the alternative of having you and Scott remain here isn't putting me to any trouble?' he scorned.

Well, when he put it like that…!

'I wasn't meaning for us to remain here,' she came back sharply, accepting that she and Scott had probably been a nuisance to him since they arrived.

Although he had seemed to be getting on with Scott well enough earlier. That was before he had kissed her, Meg reminded herself, something he obviously deeply regretted if he was willing to attempt driving in the dangerous conditions to get rid of her.

She frowned. 'But if the main road is cleared now, perhaps I can order a taxi.'

'Will you get real, Meg?' Jed rasped his impatience. 'The half a mile down to the main road is almost suicidal, and even though the main road is cleared now, there is more snow forecast for later on today.'

'There is?' She groaned her dismay.

'There is,' he confirmed hardly. 'Now the way I look

at it is we have a small gap in the bad weather during which I can attempt to get you and Scott to your family in time for Christmas. Take it or leave it.'

She had to take it. Of course she did. Except that she was no longer in any hurry to get to her parents' house, not now that she knew that Sonia and Jeremy were going to be there too.

She swallowed hard. 'I don't want to put any of us in danger just for the sake of waiting a while.'

'Believe me, Meg, you're in more danger staying on here than we are attempting that ten-mile drive,' he rasped self-derisively.

What did he…? Surely he didn't mean…? He did, one look at those penetrating blue eyes told her.

'If you could transfer Scott's presents from my car to your Range Rover without Scott seeing you, I'll go and pack our things,' she told him evenly.

'I had a feeling you might,' Jed drawled, his throaty laugh following her up the stairs.

Well, she hadn't exactly handled that well, had she? Not that she had ever made a pretence of appearing cool and sophisticated; it simply wasn't her.

The fact that she had Scott, that all of her time the last three and a half years, when she hadn't been working, had been spent taking care of him, meant that she hadn't had much chance for a social life of her own, except the occasional cup of coffee with another young mother. Oh, she had dated before Scott was born, but she couldn't say any of those men had remotely prepared her for a man like Jed Cole.

If anyone could be prepared for a man like him.

He was older, more assured, probably a lot more experienced too, than any of the young men she had previously dated.

Not that she was dating Jed Cole, she mocked herself derisively. But she was attracted to him, had responded to his kiss, had felt a surge of pleasure at his touch, had no idea where that desire might have taken them if Scott hadn't interrupted them when he did.

But it was just as well that he had interrupted them now that Jed had offered to actually drive them to her parents' house.

Not an ideal arrangement, in itself. After the things she had already told him about her family, her mother's lack of interest, the fact that neither of her parents had ever met Scott, her twin sister Sonia, Meg didn't particularly want to introduce Jed to any of them. Something she would have no choice about once he had driven them to her parents' home. She could hardly expect him to just turn around and drive back to the cottage without so much as offering him a hot drink.

Oh, well, seeing as she had no choice in the matter anyway, perhaps it was a small price to pay for finally reaching her destination.

Although she wasn't quite so sure about that half an hour later as Jed struggled to keep the vehicle from sliding off the lane and into the hedgerow at its side, his face grim with concentration, Meg tense beside him as she sat in teeth-clenched silence, Scott the only one unconcerned by the danger—he had fallen asleep several minutes ago, obviously tired from his earlier exertions building the snowman.

But Meg understood now why Jed had been gone so long on his walk this morning, with drifts five feet high or so on some sides of the lane, only Jed's skilled driving keeping them from disaster.

In fact, she discovered shortly when Jed had turned the Range Rover onto the main road, she had kept her hands so tightly clenched during that hair-raising journey that she had imprints of her nails in the palms of her hands.

'Phew,' she breathed her relief, glad she didn't have to do that again.

Although the same couldn't be said for the man at her side, she knew, when he returned in a couple of hours or so.

'This is better, isn't it?' She relaxed slightly in the leather seat, actually able to see the road ahead now, huge piles of snow cleared to bank its edges.

No wonder she had got so lost the evening before.

'Slightly,' Jed muttered, his face pale from the strain of battling with the slippery lane.

Meg took the silence that followed as an indication that he didn't want to talk any more but concentrate on his driving.

She had no argument with that, couldn't think of anything to say, anyway, that wouldn't sound trite. Besides which, the nearer they got to the village of Winston, the more she could feel her own tension rising.

The truth was, she would have been so much happier remaining in London for Christmas, just Scott and herself, as it usually was. Added to which, she was sure her mother wouldn't have issued the invitation at all—

she hadn't any other year—if Meg's father hadn't recently been ill.

A heart attack.

Her father had suffered a heart attack two weeks ago, only a mild one according to her mother, but even so she hadn't let Meg know at the time, only telephoning her on Sunday with that news and the invitation.

She didn't understand her mother. Never had. Had always found her emotionally distant, her father by far the easiest of her two parents to relate to as she'd been growing up, although his job as a civil servant working in London had meant she'd really only seen him at the weekend, and once she and Sonia had gone to boarding-school at thirteen she hadn't even seen him then.

But if Sonia had been her mother's daughter, then Meg had definitely been her father's, and she had been deeply hurt that her mother hadn't bothered to let her know of his illness sooner. To which her mother had replied, 'There was nothing you could do, so there was no point in bothering you.'

She really was that duckling amongst swans that Jed had mentioned last night, had to admit that as a child she had sometimes wondered if they could possibly be her real family at all; if not for her twin she would se-riously have doubted it.

'We're entering Winston now,' Jed told her grimly some time later. 'You'll have to give me directions from here.'

Meg felt her nervous tension return as she told him to turn right out of the town, a fluttering sensation in her stomach at what lay ahead.

For Scott's sake this visit had to go well, and she was

more than willing to play her part, if only she could be sure the rest of the family would do the same. Because if they didn't, this could be a very short visit indeed.

'Here?' Jed rasped incredulously as she told him to turn into the driveway to the left.

'Yes,' she confirmed woodenly, deliberately not looking at him, knowing he couldn't help but notice the grandeur of the imposing house and grounds they were now approaching down a driveway that had been totally cleared of snow.

But even though she wasn't looking at him she could feel Jed's narrowed gaze on her for several long seconds, probably wondering how this single mother, with a hire car for transport—a damaged hire car that the company had agreed to have towed away as soon as the weather cleared, and only a holdall with her own and Scott's clothes in for their short stay, could possibly come from a family of such obvious wealth.

She might even have found his incredulity funny if she didn't feel quite so nervous about facing them all again.

Oh, she heard from Sonia from time to time, as both of them lived in London, awkward conversations where they said nothing of any importance. She had even met her sister for coffee once or twice while Scott had been at playschool—all right, once!—but she couldn't claim that either of them had enjoyed the experience, too much between them left unsaid.

And their lifestyles were so totally different, Sonia with her socialite friends and showcase house, and Meg with her other young-mother friends and often untidy apartment, so they weren't likely to meet socially either.

She could feel Jed's gaze on her again, so intense now it was impossible to withstand.

'What?' she prompted irritably.

'This is where you were brought up?' he rasped disbelievingly.

Meg looked out the window as the house loomed closer, a huge four-storey mansion in mellow stone that was bigger than the whole building she lived in, and that housed eight flats.

'Yes,' she confirmed heavily. 'Look,' she continued irritably as his silence seemed brooding, 'my mother was a Winston before she married my father. The Winstons had the manor here for generations, the village is named for them, then they built this house a couple of hundred years ago.' She was babbling again, she knew she was, but Jed's silence made her feel uncomfortable. 'My mother was an only child, and so when her parents died she inherited.'

'Was it lonely living out here so far away from the rest of the village?' Jed frowned as he looked round at the bleak, unpopulated landscape.

'Yes,' she confirmed huskily, 'apart from Sonia, it was very lonely.' Once again this man had surprised her with his perception.

Because he had guessed perfectly last night when he'd talked of the older and younger twin, and now, instead of envying her this obviously privileged background, he was commenting on how lonely it must have been.

She blinked back the sudden tears caused by his understanding of the situation. 'Wasn't it lonely on your parents' farm?'

'With two younger brothers and too many cousins to count?' He snorted dismissively.

It sounded wonderful to Meg, the sort of childhood she would have wished for Scott but knew he would never have.

Jed was still scowling as he brought the Range Rover to a halt in front of the house. 'No wonder you decided not to come back here to bring Scott up.'

Meg gave a brief, humourless laugh. 'Believe me, it was never an option.' Her mother barely managed to remember Scott's birthday, and when she did the gift was usually a cheque pushed inside his card, very useful to a child of three.

Jed's mouth tightened. 'I don't think I'm going to like your mother very much.'

She wasn't sure her mother was going to like him, either. There was only room for one bluntly autocratic person in the Hamilton household, and her mother was definitely it.

She gave a rueful smile. 'You don't have to stay too long,' she assured sympathetically. 'In fact, if you would rather not go in at all I shall perfectly understand.' Although strangely, after previously wishing Jed didn't have to meet any of her family, now that they were here she was reluctant to see him go. His bluntness was preferable by far to the cold lack of welcome she knew she would find within.

'Are you kidding?' he came back scathingly as he switched off the ignition. 'I wouldn't miss this for anything.'

Meg wasn't quite sure she trusted that glint of challenge she could detect in those deep blue eyes, but, to be honest, she was too grateful not to be entering the lion's den on her own after all to question his motives.

'Is this Granma and Grandad's house, Mummy?' Scott had predictably woken up at the soothing throb of the engine being switched off.

She turned to give him a reassuring smile. 'It certainly is, darling.'

His eyes were wide as he looked up at the imposing house. 'It's big, Mummy,' he said uncertainly.

'It won't look half as big once you're inside,' she said with more hope than conviction.

Perhaps she should have tried to prepare Scott more for this meeting with her family, but how did you even start to explain to a three-year-old that his grandmother could be a cold autocrat, that his grandfather was too mild to stop her, and that his aunt Sonia—Meg didn't even know how to begin to tell him about his aunt Sonia.

She would just have to hope that the subtle nuances of any adult conversation would go way over his innocent head.

As it was she approached the wide oak front door with all the enthusiasm of the condemned man approaching the block.

'Cheer up, Meg,' Jed encouraged teasingly, obviously feeling no such trepidation as he moved lightly up the steps beside her. 'It may never happen.'

He had no idea.

'You ring the doorbell of your own parents' home?' he questioned incredulously as she did exactly that.

'Well…yes.' She grimaced, sure things were much more relaxed on his parents' farm.

He really didn't have any idea.

She could hear the click of heels on the hall tiles now, her hand tightening involuntarily about Scott's as she prepared herself to face her mother.

'Sonia, I didn't expect you back just yet—' Her mother's voice dried to a halt as, having opened the door fully, she realized her mistake. 'Margaret.' She frowned at Meg. 'I thought you were going to ring me and let me know when you were arriving?' She looked down her patrician nose.

'I was. I should have.' But she had totally forgotten that promised telephone call in the rush of leaving the cottage.

Not that her mother had needed the warning to correct any defects in her appearance. As usual her mother looked perfect, her dark hair styled, her make-up and lipstick applied, the cream cashmere sweater she wore with a black skirt perfectly tailored to her slim figure.

Meg glanced awkwardly at Jed, shaking her head slightly as he mouthed 'Margaret?' at her, a name she had detested since childhood, deciding at eight, after reading *Little Women*, that she wanted to be called Meg instead; only her mother refused to use it.

'There wasn't time,' she apologized awkwardly as she turned back to her mother. 'I didn't think—'

'The oversight was my fault, I'm afraid, Mrs Hamilton,' Jed cut in smoothly as he moved forward slightly to make his presence known.

If he was expecting that to change her mother's

demeanour he was in for a disappointment, Meg
thought with a wince as her mother's gaze moved
past her to Jed Cole, those eyes only becoming more
coldly blue, her expression more frosty, if that were
possible.

God, this was awful. Worse than she could possibly
have imagined. She should never have come. Wished the
ground would open up and swallow her.

Instead, as if programmed, she made the introductions. 'Jed, this is my mother, Lydia Hamilton.
Mother, this is—'

'Jerrod, Jerrod Cole,' he cut in harshly as he took
the limpness of her mother's hand in his much larger
one. 'It's a pleasure to meet you, Lydia,' he added derisively.

And no wonder, Meg frowned, a transformation
having come over her mother's face, the coldness fading
from her eyes to be replaced with incredulity, a slight
paleness to her perfectly defined cheekbones.

'I...' her mother swallowed, looking at Jed uncertainly now, as if she weren't quite sure of herself. 'Do
you mean the Jerrod Cole who wrote *The Puzzle*?'

'Of course no—'

'I'm flattered that you've heard of me, Lydia,' Jed cut
smoothly across Meg's denial.

Meg stared at him disbelievingly.

Jerrod Cole.

Jed was Jerrod Cole?

Well, of course her mother had heard of Jerrod Cole;
probably the whole of the western world had heard of
him. His book, *The Puzzle*, had been at the top of the

best-seller lists for the last nine months, a film of the book was already in production.

But Jed couldn't be that Jerrod Cole.

Could he?

He really hadn't meant to just dump the truth on Meg like that. Margaret? She didn't look anything like a Margaret. He hadn't intended telling her he was Jerrod Cole at all. But Lydia Hamilton's attitude towards her youngest daughter had infuriated him so much he had just wanted to wipe that self-satisfied coldness from her unwelcoming face. And telling her exactly who he was had seemed the best way to do that.

He had never actually disliked anyone on sight before; usually it took him at least ten minutes or so. But Lydia Hamilton's behaviour towards Meg, the way she hadn't even looked at Scott, her own grandson, just made him want to shake the woman. And telling her his identity had certainly done that.

Although a quick glance at Meg showed him that she was as stunned by who he was as her mother, also that she wasn't at all happy with this development, staring at him now as if she had never seen him before.

Which, in fact, she hadn't. Not as Jerrod Cole, anyway.

But, damn it, Meg hadn't recognized him when she'd come to the cottage, and, considering anonymity was the reason he was staying at the cottage in the first place, he wasn't going to go around advertising the fact he was the author Jerrod Cole, now was he?

Although somehow, as a glitter of anger started to

show in Meg's eyes, he didn't think she was going to be too impressed with that explanation.

He abruptly released Lydia Hamilton's hand. 'Although I would really rather you just thought of me as a friend of Meg's,' he added smoothly.

'A friend of…yes, of course,' Lydia looked completely flustered at this stage.

'Perhaps you would like to invite us inside, Lydia?' He spoke hardly now. 'It's getting a little wet out here.' He looked pointedly at the snow that had just started to fall again, landing on their bare heads before melting.

'Of course.' She stepped back so that they could enter.

Which, after another frowning glance in his direction, Meg did, Scott's hand still tightly clenched in hers.

Jed's anger towards Lydia Hamilton turned to cold fury as he looked at the slightly bewildered little boy.

How could she remain so indifferent to such a cute kid? He knew he hadn't been able to earlier this morning when Scott had begged to go outside and make a snowman. Scott looked so exactly like his mother, and surely, somewhere behind that cold mask, Lydia Hamilton loved her youngest daughter.

Maybe not, he decided after another hard glance at the older woman.

Aged in her early sixties, Lydia Hamilton was one of those women who looked as perfect first thing in the morning as she did last thing at night, never a hair out of place, her make-up applied expertly so as to smooth out any lines, the skirt and sweater she wore ultra-smart. Jed somehow couldn't imagine this woman ever getting down on the floor to play with her children the way that Meg did with Scott.

Although she was fast recovering from her surprise, her smile once again cool. 'Please come through to the sitting-room, Mr Cole, and meet my husband, David.'

'Hey, look, Scott, a Christmas tree.' Jed, having detected a slight trembling to the little boy's bottom lip, moved quickly forward to pick him up in his arms and carry him across the cavernous hallway to look at the decorated tree, the urge inside him to actually strangle Lydia for her insensitivity to her grandson firmly held in check. He didn't think Meg would appreciate it if he were to murder her mother in front of her eyes.

Scott cheered up at the sight of the nine-feet-high decorated tree, his eyes soon shining bright with wonder as he gazed at all the meticulously applied decorations and lights.

Relieved that his distraction had worked, Jed was nevertheless aware of the conversation taking place across the hallway between the two women.

'I think you might have told me, Margaret,' Lydia Hamilton snapped softly. 'I felt ridiculous not knowing who the man was.'

Jed would take a bet on Meg feeling something a little stronger than ridicule.

But he didn't regret what he had done for a moment. It had been worth it just to see the cold arrogance wiped off Lydia Hamilton's face.

Meg took her time answering her mother, seeming to choose her words carefully when she did speak, 'Jed likes to keep his anonymity for the main part,' she finally responded huskily.

'Well, yes, I can understand that, but—what are we going to do with him?' Lydia Hamilton sounded flustered again—not a frequent occurrence, Jed would hazard a guess.

'Why, nothing.' Meg sounded startled by the question. 'Jed isn't going to—'

'Lydia, who was that at the door? Meg!'

Jed had put Scott down to turn at the first sound of that masculine voice, just in time to see the pleasure that lit the paleness of Meg's face before she launched herself at the man who had to be her father, a tall, thin man with eyes as green as his daughter's.

'Daddy.' Meg choked emotionally as she hugged her father tightly.

'Daddy', not the formal 'Mother' with which she spoke to Lydia Hamilton, Jed noted with satisfaction, glad there was one person in this household, at least, who was pleased to see Meg. Although that relief was short-lived as he remembered that this man was just as guilty of neglecting his daughter and grandson the last three and a half years as his wife was.

He looked critically at the older man. David Hamilton was still a handsome man, his hair white, with a definite look of Meg about him in the eyes and face, although that face showed the pale unhealthiness of a recent illness, his sweater and trousers seeming slightly too big for his frame too, as if he had recently lost weight.

The illness had been a recent thing, then, Jed decided.

Perhaps the reason Lydia seemed to have relented where her youngest daughter was concerned? It would be too much to hope that it had been for Meg and Scott's sakes.

Jed glanced down as Scott tugged at his trouser leg, going down on his haunches as he saw the little boy was looking shyly at the man his mother was hugging.

'Is that man my grandad, Jed?' he prompted in what he no doubt thought was a hushed voice, but nonetheless which carried in the cavernous hallway.

David Hamilton stiffened slightly before putting Meg slowly away from him and turning to look at the source of that voice.

Jed's move was purely instinctive as he placed a protective hand on Scott's shoulder. Lydia Hamilton's complete indifference to her grandson had been hard enough to witness; Jed felt as if he might actually do someone physical harm—even a recently ill man—if David Hamilton were to hurt the boy too.

'Yes, Scott, I'm your granddad.' David Hamilton spoke gently, his gaze riveted on Scott's small features as he slowly walked over to where they stood. 'Goodness, you look just like your mummy did at your age,' he breathed emotionally, a glitter of tears in those faded green eyes as he bent down to the little boy's level.

'Do I?' Scott breathed excitedly. 'Do I really?'

'You certainly do,' his grandfather assured him huskily. 'Why don't you come with me and I'll show you some photographs of her that I keep in my study?' He held out his arms, earning Jed's approval as he let the little boy come to him rather than forcing the issue.

'David, I don't think you should be exerting—'

'I'm perfectly fine, Lydia,' David cut in harshly on his wife's protest, his gaze still on his grandson. 'Scott?' His voice gentled again as he encouraged the little boy to come to him.

Jed glanced across at the two women who stood together watching this scene, Meg with tears of happiness shining brightly in her eyes, Lydia's expression much harder to read, although Jed thought he recognized concern there. For her husband, he guessed, so perhaps the woman did have some redeeming qualities, after all. Somewhere behind that coldness.

Scott, he was pleased to see, had responded to his grandfather's gentleness, and was now securely held in the man's arms as David straightened and looked at Jed for the first time, as if just noticing him. Which, considering the emotional reconciliation the man had just had with his daughter, his first ever meeting with his grandson, he probably hadn't, Jed acknowledged ruefully.

The older man gave him a quizzical look. 'Jerrod Cole, isn't it?' He held out his free hand in welcome.

'It is.' Jed shook that hand, finding the grip firm. 'But I would prefer it if you called me Jed,' he added lightly.

'And I'm David.' The older man smiled. 'I enjoyed your book very much. Can't wait for the next one to come out.'

That had the effect of wiping the smile off Jed's face. 'I'm working on it, thank you, sir.'

'David, please,' the older man insisted. 'I've had a lot of time for reading recently,' he added ruefully.

'David, how on earth did you know that Margaret's friend is Jerrod Cole?' Lydia prompted with hard suspicion.

Her husband gave her a level glance. 'I recognize him from the photograph on the back of his book, of course,' he dismissed mildly before turning back to Jed. 'I take it you can actually pilot the plane you're standing next to?' he teased.

Jed easily returned that smile. 'I can.'

'Good.' The older man nodded. 'I'll take this young man and show him those photographs now.' He bestowed a warm smile on the patiently waiting Scott.

'I'll come with you,' his wife put in quickly.

'That really isn't necessary, Lydia,' David assured her lightly, but the slight edge in his tone brooked no argument. 'Why don't you take Meg and Jed through to the sitting-room and offer them a drink?' he softly, but again firmly, reminded his wife of her manners.

It was easy to see by the bright wave of colour in Lydia's cheeks as her husband departed with Scott that she wasn't at all happy with this arrangement, but at the same time recognized that she had no choice but to comply.

'Margaret, why don't you take Mr—Jed, through to the sitting-room and I'll go and organize some refreshments before lunch?' She didn't wait for an answer but moved off stiffly down the hallway.

Jed had been studiously avoiding looking at Meg for the last few minutes, first because he had felt like something of an intruder to that emotional reunion with her father, and after that because he had been able to feel the accusation in her gaze as she'd looked at him, obviously none of what had happened in the last few minutes detracting from her earlier anger at his duplicity. Something he knew he was likely to hear about now that they were alone.

Yep, the sparkle in her eyes, the firmness of her mouth, told him he was definitely going to hear about it.

He sighed. 'Meg, why don't you hear me out before you say what you're obviously bursting to say?'

'You're Jerrod Cole,' she accused impatiently, as if that nullified anything else he might have to say in his defence.

'Well, yes, I am aware of that.' He grimaced. 'But I'm also Jed Cole. And it was Jed Cole that you met yesterday—'

'They're one and the same person,' she interrupted irritably.

'No, not really.' He sighed. 'I—' He broke off as the front door suddenly swung open behind them, a gust of cold air and snow preceding the two people who entered.

A tiny woman wearing a long white luxurious coat and matching hat, her face flushed from the cold as she laughed huskily at something her companion was saying.

The man was tall and grey-haired, his handsome face lined beside nose and mouth, teeth very white against his tan as he grinned down at the woman, limping very slightly as he moved to close the door.

Obviously Meg's brother-in-law, Jeremy.

Which meant the woman had to be her sister, Sonia.

The woman had removed her hat now, moving slender, perfectly manicured fingers through the short dark tresses, green eyes narrowing, her smile slowly fading, as she turned and saw that they weren't alone.

There were no impish freckles on her nose, and she didn't have that slightly overlapping tooth to the left of her front teeth, either, but even so Jed recognized her as Meg's twin, Sonia.

Identical, and yet strangely not so, just as Meg had tried to tell him.

And that tall, distinguished man at her side, a man surely old enough to be her father, was her husband, Jeremy.

Jed's gaze shifted to Meg, and he took an instinctive step closer to her as he saw how pale she had become. He wasn't exactly sure why—this was her twin sister, after all—but offering her his support, anyway.

So much for not getting involved—he was involved up to his thirty-eight-year-old neck.

CHAPTER FIVE

MEG felt as if she were somehow frozen in time, as if everything were happening in slow motion.

First that frosty meeting with her mother, then that startling revelation about Jed—a revelation, no matter what he might wish to the contrary, that she hadn't finished talking to him about.

He was Jerrod Cole, for goodness' sake.

She still couldn't quite believe it.

The man had become a publishing phenomenon this last year, the sale of his book *The Puzzle*—what an apt title for such an enigmatic man—outselling anything that had come before it, on both sides of the Atlantic. The film rights had been sold for a record amount of money too.

Meg read the newspapers, but she hadn't yet found the time to buy and read the book everyone was talking about.

Something she should maybe rectify now that she had actually met the author.

Then had come that emotional reunion with her father. An older, thinner, strangely different father.

She couldn't quite say in what way he was different,

only that he was. Maybe because of his heart attack, or maybe for some other reason she wasn't aware of.

Not that he had been any different with her, just his usual loving self. And she couldn't have asked for a better response from him towards Scott.

There was just something not quite right, an unspoken strain between him and her mother, perhaps? Meg had certainly never heard him speak to her mother in quite that firm tone before.

But this unexpected—until last night when she'd spoken to her mother on the telephone—meeting with her sister was certainly an added strain Meg could well have done without.

They had been close once, very close, but time, and circumstances, had ensured that was no longer the case.

Sonia looked no more pleased about the two of them being here together as their gazes met in silent battle. An antagonism in Sonia's face that she quickly masked as she realized they weren't alone, her gaze shifting slightly sideways to where Jed stood at Meg's side, those green eyes widening slightly, not in recognition, Meg didn't think, but rather a female response to an attractive man.

Meg couldn't even bring herself to glance in Jed's direction to see what his reaction was to this sleeker, more sophisticated version of herself.

'Meg, darling.' Sonia finally spoke with bright brittleness. 'How lovely to see you here.' She crossed the room to give Meg a brief hug, touching cheeks, her kiss floating away in the air. 'And this is…?' She gave Jed a look of frankly female appreciation.

Meg fought down the instinct to gnash her teeth together as she easily interpreted that speculative glance for what it was, instead making the introductions as briefly as possible, including Jeremy as he strolled over to join them, favouring his left leg slightly as he did so.

Sonia, unlike their mother a short time ago, received Jed's identity with a few complimentary comments about his book and a narrow-eyed glance in Meg's direction.

No doubt her sister was wondering how Meg, of all people, had managed to meet such a famous and fascinating man.

'And where is little—Scott, I believe you called him?' Sonia prompted with a noticeable coolness in her voice.

Meg drew in a sharp breath, the abrupt reply she was about to make forestalled by her mother's return.

'I'm so glad you managed to get back before the storm started again,' she said evenly as she saw that her eldest daughter and son-in-law had now joined them.

'Only just,' Sonia drawled ruefully. 'If you'll all excuse us while we go upstairs and freshen up before lunch?' she added to no one in particular, taking hold of her husband's arm as the two of them went up the stairs together.

'It's snowing heavily again?' Meg prompted with dismay. How on earth was Jed going to get back to the cottage if that were the case.

'Worse than yesterday,' her father answered as he returned with Scott still in his arms, her son, Meg was pleased to see, more than happy with the arrangement. 'I should go and get your luggage from the car now, Jed, while you still have your outdoor clothes on, before it gets any worse.'

'Oh, but—'

'Good idea, David.' Jed spoke firmly. 'Coming with me, Meg?' he added purposefully.

She looked up at him frowningly. First he announced he was a friend of hers, and now he was proposing they get their luggage from the Range Rover. But he didn't have any luggage. Did he?

She gave a puzzled shake of her head. 'But wouldn't you be better—?'

'I can't carry it all on my own,' he told her teasingly. 'I think she packed enough things to stay for a month,' he confided in her father.

Meg's frown only deepened at this comment. Because Jed knew how untrue that was, had already commented himself on the small amount of luggage she had brought with her. Although there were all of Scott's Christmas presents, of course.

However, there were still a few things she would like to say to Jed—Jerrod Cole—in private.

But apparently there were a few things he had to say to her too. 'Phew,' he breathed in relief once they were safely outside with the front door firmly closed behind them. 'No wonder you were in no rush to get here.' He grimaced. 'Your dad seems okay, but as for the rest of them.' He shook his head. 'Your mother is like a reversed iceberg—the ice is ninety per cent above the surface rather than the other way around,' he explained ruefully at Meg's questioning look. 'Your sister I haven't worked out yet, except that she seems to be married to a man twice her age. Although he seems okay too, so maybe it's only the female members of the family who are a bit odd.'

Meg had stared at him incredulously through this monologue about her family, totally immune to the fresh snow buffeting and gusting about them. 'Do I take it that I'm included in that last sweeping statement?'

Jed grinned unabashedly. 'Oh, no, in comparison, you're quite normal.'

'You're so kind.' Sarcasm dripped off her voice.

His grin widened. 'Come on.' He grabbed her arm. 'Let's go and sit in the Range Rover out of the snow, I'm sure there are a few things you would still like to say to me.' He gave her a mocking glance.

'Oh, just a few,' she agreed as the two of them ran down the front steps to get in the Range Rover, at once feeling warmer as the wind continued to howl outside. 'Jerrod Cole?' she prompted again pointedly.

'Yeah.' He grimaced. 'I usually like to keep quiet about that.'

'Well, in my case, you succeeded,' she assured him disgustedly, still feeling rather foolish for not having recognized him.

Although, in all honesty, not many of the reports of the success of *The Puzzle* had actually included a photograph of the author, and those that had been included were black and white and quite grainy to look at, and Jed's hair had been much shorter, too.

Besides, in her defence, a tiny cottage in the middle of the English countryside was the very last place she would have expected to meet the amazingly successful American author, Jerrod Cole.

'You might have told me,' she said exasperatedly. 'I felt, feel, like such a fool for not recognizing who you were.' The man was a writing phenomenon and he had been out in the snow this morning with her son building a snowman.

God, that seemed like such a long time ago. In fact, part of her, a large part of her, wished she were still back there.

'Then don't,' Jed grated. 'The truth is I wasn't going to tell you at all, was going to deliver you and Scott here, make polite conversation for a short time, and then leave. That is, until I met your mother.' His voice hardened over the latter.

'My mother?' Meg frowned her puzzlement with this statement.

He nodded. 'I didn't like the way she spoke to you.'

'I'm used to it.' Meg shrugged.

'And ignored Scott.' His voice was icy now. 'Even if she disapproves of the fact that you have him, although in this day and age even that's ridiculous, she had absolutely no right to just ignore him like that.' His expression was grim. 'It may not be very commendable, but I wanted, if only briefly, to wipe that haughty look off her face.'

Oh, he had succeeded in doing that all right. He had succeeded in stunning Meg too.

'And what's with the "Margaret" thing?' he continued scathingly. 'You obviously prefer to be called Meg, the rest of the family call you Meg, so why not your own mother?'

'I don't know,' Meg admitted dully. 'Maybe…' She broke off, staring down at her ringless hands.

'What?' Jed prompted shrewdly.

She shrugged. 'Maybe it's too familiar. I don't know.'

She had never known, had never been able to understand why, as a child, she had received hugs and kisses from her father, but not from her mother. Not that Sonia had fared any better in that direction, but it had never seemed to bother her sister as much as it did her; Sonia and their mother were very alike in that respect, emotionally self-contained.

As a child Meg had wished she could be more like them, but as an adult she was very glad that she wasn't.

She wouldn't have been able to be the warm and loving mother to Scott that she was if that were the case.

She wouldn't have enjoyed Jed kissing her as much this morning, if she were, wouldn't, even now, be wondering what it would be like to kiss him again.

Despite what she now knew about his identity, Jed was still the only breath of security in a very unusual situation.

'Familiar sounds fine to me,' he said huskily.

Meg gave him a startled look, her pulse starting to beat more rapidly as she noticed how close he was in the confines of the Range Rover, her gaze easily caught and held by the intense blue of his.

'Admit it, Meg,' Jed murmured softly. 'You were secretly relieved at the way I diverted your mother's attention from you onto me,' he explained as she gave him a guarded look.

Oh, that. For a moment there she had thought he knew, had guessed, she was too attracted to him for her own good, which would be just too embarrassing in the circumstances.

But he was perfectly correct about her relief earlier; her mother really was hard work.

'I'm not so sure about the "just think of me as a friend of Meg's" remark.' She gave him a reproving look, hoping that nothing she was saying or doing was betraying how totally aware she was of him.

He grinned unabashedly. 'Would you rather I had told your mother I'm just the man you picked up in a snowstorm?'

Meg drew in a sharp breath, even while inwardly she admitted, within very wide guidelines, that he spoke the truth.

She glared at him. 'I'll be more than happy to put you down again!'

'In this weather?' He glanced out at the heavily falling snow. 'There's gratitude for you.' Even as he shook his head reprovingly his eyes were laughing at her.

One thing was becoming more and more apparent to her by the second: the snow falling steadily outside was such that Jed was never going to make it back to the cottage today.

'Do you really have some luggage with you?' She frowned. 'Or did you just make that up?'

He grimaced. 'I have an overnight bag with me. I never thought I was going to get back to the cottage today, Meg,' he added as her eyes widened at the admission. 'There's a hotel in Winston; I was going to try and book in there for the night.'

There was no way she could allow him to do that after all that he had done for her and Scott. And if he wasn't to stay in a hotel tonight, then he would have to stay here.

He was so close to her now, the weather cocooning them in a world of silence, that at that moment nothing else seemed to exist but the two of them, the very air between them seeming electrified with expectation.

As if becoming aware of that himself, Jed's eyes darkened, his narrowed gaze moving down to the parted softness of her lips.

Meg instinctively moistened those lips with the tip of her tongue.

'I really can't let you do that.' She didn't get any further, staring up at Jed in fascination as he looked down at her only briefly before lowering his head, his mouth easily capturing hers.

It was as if the time since earlier this morning had never been, her lips parting beneath his as he deepened the kiss, pulling her into his arms, although the stowing box between them stopped them getting as close as Meg would have liked. Wanted. Desired.

His hair felt so thick and silky against her fingers, heat building inside her as she met the fiery passion of his kiss.

A blast of cold air gusted inside the Range Rover as the door beside Meg was wrenched open, Meg pulling away self-consciously from Jed to turn and look at her brother-in-law, Jeremy's teasing expression telling her he knew exactly what he had just interrupted.

'The two of you have been gone so long Lydia sent me out to make sure you hadn't somehow got lost in the snow,' Jeremy drawled, smiling, seemingly impervious to the falling snow.

She had only met Jeremy twice, once when he'd come to the flat one evening to pick her sister up for a date, and the second time when the two of them had told her they were engaged to be married, but on both occasions she had rather liked him.

Although she wasn't too sure she liked the fact that

he had caught her and Jed—well, in an embarrassing situation if not a compromising one.

'Lydia did? Or was it David?' Jed was the one to respond to the other man sceptically.

Jeremy gave him a rueful smile. 'Oh, it was definitely Lydia—her tea is getting cold, I'm afraid.'

Meg watched as the two men shared what could only be classed a male understanding look.

How did Jed do that? Meg wondered with some bewilderment. He had quite effortlessly silenced her mother earlier, immediately charmed her father, remained totally immune to Sonia's sensual charm, and now he and Jeremy were exchanging looks like conspirators in a war.

Jed's mouth twisted ruefully. 'Please tell Lydia we'll be right in,' he drawled dryly.

Jeremy turned to give Meg a friendly smile. 'You're looking really well, Meg,' he told her warmly before closing the door to return to the house.

The implication being that the way she looked had something to do with having Jed Cole in her life.

She shot him a glance. 'We really will have to stop doing that.'

'Will we?' he mused softly. 'Why?'

'Because…well…' she frowned as she pushed back the heavy curtain of her hair '…two strangers caught in a snowstorm together and all that.'

'We're hardly alone, Meg,' he mocked pointedly. 'And I don't think we can be called strangers any more, either,' he added teasingly.

No, they weren't, were they? she accepted a little

dazedly as they got out of the Range Rover to collect the luggage from the back. But she would be a fool to read more into a couple of kisses than there really was. Because as soon as the snow cleared Jed would be on his way. Back to New York, probably. And she would never see him again.

Don't, for goodness' sake, get involved, Meg, she told herself firmly as she helped carry the luggage inside.

At the same time having the feeling her warning might have come too late.

Jed knocked on the door to Meg's room, waiting for her to answer, and when she didn't he opened the door and went inside anyway, sure that she was in there.

She was, lying on one of the single beds, an arm up and draped over her eyes, Scott already fast asleep in the other bed, angelically beautiful, a large red sack draped over the bottom of the bed.

Jed padded softly across the room on bare feet, intending—well, he didn't know what he intended doing, only that he was drawn to these two like a magnet. He wasn't sure what that meant, either.

'It's far too early for Father Christmas,' Meg murmured without moving the arm from over her eyes.

'Damn it, woman, you startled me. I thought you must have fallen asleep,' he said irritably as she shifted her arm slightly to look at him.

'No,' she assured him flatly. 'I'm certainly not asleep.'

Jed stood next to the bed looking down at her. 'Then what are you doing?'

She sighed, her arm falling back to her side, her eyes

closed now. 'I'm lying here trying not to scream. What are you doing?' she demanded with some alarm as he moved to stretch out on the bed beside her.

He lay back with his eyes closed. 'The same as you— trying not to scream. That has got to be the weirdest afternoon I've ever spent. Are you usually that polite to each other?' His own family was noisy and boisterous, a row usually breaking out between a couple of them within minutes of their meeting up again.

'Usually, yes.' Meg frowned.

He gave a disgusted shake of his head. 'And who changes for dinner when it's just family?' he continued disbelievingly, having known himself dismissed a short time ago when the whole family had risen to go upstairs to their respective bedrooms to change for dinner.

Except Meg, of course. She had escaped over an hour ago after giving Scott his tea in the kitchen, coming back to announce, much to Scott's disappointment, that it was now time for his bath before going to bed.

When Meg hadn't returned after an hour Jed had been sure that she must have fallen asleep too, this the first opportunity he'd had to check up on her.

He opened one eye at Meg's continued silence after his last statement, only to find she had propped herself up on one elbow and was now looking at him. 'What?' he asked tersely.

She shook her head, turning away slightly. 'You shouldn't be in here,' she told him quietly.

'Why shouldn't I? We're more than adequately chaperoned.' He gave a pointed look at the sleeping Scott. 'Although I didn't get the impression earlier that would be such a problem, anyway,' he drawled as he turned back to look at Meg. A blushing Meg. 'You should have seen your face earlier when your mother asked if we would be sharing a room.' He had found it difficult at the time to contain his humour at the look of shock on Meg's face; now he gave a teasing grin at the memory.

Although he had to admire the dignity with which Meg had informed her mother that she and Scott would be sharing a bedroom, not Meg and Jed.

But Lydia had still allocated them adjoining rooms, with a communicating door between, the doorway he had just come through.

Meg shook her head impatiently, her face pale. 'I can't imagine what my mother was thinking of!'

Jed raised dark brows. 'Possibly treating you like the adult you obviously are?' he suggested, having found Lydia subdued most of the afternoon, seeming to watch them all rather than taking an active part in the conversation, such as it was.

Although Scott's obvious excitement at the approach of bedtime had more than made up for any awkwardness there might have been between the adults—and there had been plenty of that, the undercurrents in this family so deep Jed hadn't had time to try and work them out yet. It appeared the little boy and his grandfather had become firm friends, which wasn't surprising; David was as warm as his youngest daughter.

'I somehow doubt that.' Meg's mouth twisted sceptically at his suggestion about her mother's motives. 'It's more likely that she meant to be insulting.'

'Hey, I take exception to that,' he chided, enjoying

teasing her. 'I'm not usually considered unacceptable to a woman's parents.' Not that he had ever met any before; his relationships didn't usually run along that line.

'Not to you, to me.' Meg sighed, laying her head back down on the pillow beside his. 'Because of Scott.'

'That's rubbish,' Jed dismissed irritably. 'He's such a cute kid, no one could feel that way about him. He and your father have definitely bonded.' David Hamilton's pleasure in his grandson was undeniable, the two having spent most of the afternoon on the floor playing with Scott's toys.

'Yes.' A smile played over Meg's lips.

Jed turned to give her a considering look. 'Do you ever see his father?'

She frowned. 'Whose father?'

'Scott's, of course,' he came back impatiently, lowering his voice as the little boy moved in his sleep. 'Do you and Scott ever see his father?'

'Certainly not.' Meg sounded shocked at the idea, forcefully so.

Jed held up a defensive hand. 'Just asking, Meg. It wouldn't be so unusual.'

'In this case it would,' she assured him determinedly, moving back to look at him. 'Why do I have the feeling that this is all research to you, and we may all appear in your next book?'

He winced, brought back to earth with a resounding bump. 'I wish,' he muttered harshly.

'What does that mean?' She looked confused.

'It means I'm not even sure there's going to be a next book.' Jed got up restlessly from the bed. 'What do you think I'm doing at the cottage in the first place?' He scowled, hands thrust into his jeans pockets. 'The public, my publishers, both here and in the States, are all clamouring for the next Jerrod Cole book. A book I haven't even written yet, and don't know if I ever will,' he admitted bleakly, putting into words for the first time the doubts he had been experiencing this last year that he could write another book—and fear that he couldn't.

The Puzzle hadn't been his first book, but his seventh, the six previous books also best-sellers, but with none of the same worldwide success or the resulting pressure to produce another runaway hit as *The Puzzle* had been.

Obviously he couldn't write another book like *The Puzzle*, had to write something completely different, but at the same time it had to be something that wouldn't disappoint all those people anxiously awaiting the next Jerrod Cole novel.

Easier said than done. In his case, writer's block had become a total shutdown. So much so that he had left New York to come to England, hoping the change would ease the pressure, accepting his editor's offer of the use of his holiday cottage in middle England, and shutting himself away there for the last two months.

It hadn't helped.

Nothing helped, his growing frustration with the situation only making things worse.

But he had, he suddenly realized, forgotten that frustration for a brief time today as he'd concentrated on Meg and her family.

Meg sat up to look at him concernedly. 'But can't

you—?' She broke off, frowning, as a knock sounded on her bedroom door followed by that door opening.

'Oh!' A slightly disconcerted Sonia stood in the doorway as they both turned to look at her. 'Sorry.' She grimaced, green gaze speculative as it moved from the standing Jed to where Meg still sat on the side of the bed. 'I just wanted to have a quick word with Meg before dinner,' she drawled, recovering quickly. 'But I can come back later.' She smiled knowingly.

So similar to look at and yet so very different.

Meg possessed none of her twin's artifice or sophistication, none of that hard gloss, either, that perfection that should have made Sonia the more beautiful of the two, and yet somehow didn't. Not to Jed, anyway.

He saw the sudden awareness of that in Sonia's eyes as they narrowed speculatively on her sister, telling Jed that this preference of her younger, less confident twin had never happened to Sonia before. That slight, angry flush to Sonia's cheeks, in Jed's opinion, boded ill for Meg.

He moved to where Meg now stood, his gaze challenging Sonia's as his arm dropped lightly about Meg's slender shoulders. 'I think that would be a good idea.' He nodded. 'After all, we wouldn't want to disturb Scott, now, would we?' he added with soft determination.

Sonia's expression became blank as it shifted to the sleeping child. 'No,' she agreed evenly. 'We certainly wouldn't want to disturb Scott.'

Jed could feel Meg's tension beneath his arm, at the same time knowing that the politeness with which the two women had been treating each other all afternoon had been nothing but another façade.

What was it with the women in this family? Having had only brothers as siblings, he wasn't as familiar with this female tension as he could have been, but he had been close to his mother all his life, all her sons were, and the strain in this family was completely unknown territory to him.

Except he knew this wasn't normal, the undercurrents between the three Hamilton women such, he felt, that if any one of them ever came out and told the other two the truth the whole structure would collapse like a house of cards.

The fact that the two sisters were still staring at each other, neither one willing to back down from whatever silent challenge was being waged, only confirmed this belief.

'We'll see you later, then, Sonia.' Jed spoke lightly but firmly, determined to break this impasse.

She flicked him an unguarded angry glance, before drawing in a deep breath and forcing the tension from her shoulders, her smile coolly confident again. 'Later,' Sonia echoed coldly before turning and leaving.

Jed's arm dropped back to his side as Meg moved away from him to stand in front of the window, although he was pretty sure she saw none of the Christmas-card whiteness of the scene outside, several more inches of snow having fallen during the afternoon.

She looked so tiny standing there, that ebony dark hair falling straight and shiny almost to her waist, very slender in the red sweater and black denims. She didn't look old enough to be Scott's mother, let alone to have all the responsibility that went along with that role.

'What the hell was all that about?' His voice sounded harsh in the silence. More so than he had intended, certainly, but it seemed the more he tried to understand this family, the less he actually knew.

Meg didn't answer for several seconds, and then she drew in a deep breath, straightening her shoulders before turning to face him, the smile she attempted reaching no further than the curve of her lips. 'It isn't important,' she dismissed.

Jed felt his frustration with the situation building inside him, his hands clenching at his sides.

It was so unimportant there were tears glistening in Meg's eyes, those eyes huge green pools of emotion in the otherwise pale stillness of her face.

'Why the hell did you put yourself through this?' he rasped impatiently. 'Put Scott through it?'

It was a low blow to bring the child she so obviously adored into the conversation, and Jed couldn't really say that Scott had suffered any harm this afternoon from his grandmother and aunt's complete indifference to his presence, his grandfather attentive enough for all of them. But that wasn't the point, was it? It wasn't going to help anyone, least of all Scott, if his mother made herself ill trying to cope with what Jed viewed as an impossible situation.

And he probably wasn't helping the situation by drawing attention to what might, for all he knew, seem perfectly normal to Meg.

'Oh, to hell with this.' He threw up his hands in disgust. 'It's your dysfunctional family. I'm sure you know how to cope with them.' He turned on his heel and walked back through the connecting doorway, closing it firmly behind him.

He didn't want any of this, didn't need it, had enough problems of his own to cope with.

Meg Hamilton would just have to deal with this herself.

The sooner the weather cleared, and he could leave, the better he would like it.

CHAPTER SIX

JED was wrong.

So very wrong.

Because Meg had absolutely no idea how to cope with all the unspoken strain in her family.

Her mother and father, she had realized as the afternoon had progressed, barely spoke to each other.

They had never been a demonstrative couple, and her mother had always been the parent whose word was obeyed, but there was a distance between her parents now that Meg didn't understand, and her father no longer mildly tolerated her mother's dictates. For instance, several times during the afternoon her mother had suggested that perhaps her father should go upstairs and rest for a while, suggestions he had completely ignored, choosing instead to play with Scott and his toys.

The strain between herself and Sonia was harder to define. Although Jed seemed to have had no difficulty picking up on it.

If not that he was part of the reason for it.

Because that was what was bothering Sonia, she was sure. Meg hadn't been home or involved with anyone since Scott was born, and now, not only had she come home for Christmas, but had apparently brought Jerrod Cole with her. The fact that she wasn't and never would be involved with Jed was something, after he had announced to her family that he was a friend of hers, none of them were likely to believe. And Sonia, being Sonia, was probably wondering just how involved with him Meg was, what confidences she might have shared with him.

As if. Sonia didn't know her at all if she thought she would ever put in jeopardy all that she had striven to achieve.

She looked up sharply as another knock sounded on her bedroom door, tensing instinctively; from not feeling wanted by her family, she had suddenly become very popular. Although another frosty encounter with her mother wasn't something she particularly relished.

She smiled her relief as she opened the door and found her father standing in the hallway, a smile on his face, and a shirt and tie draped over one arm. For Jed, she guessed. Because although he might have packed an overnight bag, she very much doubted he had packed something he could change into for dinner.

'Jed's in the room next door, Daddy,' she told him after a brief glance to make sure Scott was still asleep.

A miracle considering his excitement about the arrival of Father Christmas and the amount of visitors to their bedroom in the last few minutes.

She slipped out into the hallway to join her father. 'Are you really well again, Daddy?' She looked up at him anxiously, her hand resting lightly on his arm.

'I really am,' he returned reassuringly. 'The doctors

say it was only a mild attack. A warning, if you like, to change my lifestyle to something less stressful.'

Her father was eight years older than her mother, had retired some months ago; Meg wasn't sure how much more he could change it.

'Not in that way, pumpkin,' he said gently. 'There are certain things, about this family, that I'm not happy with. Those are the things that need changing,' he added determinedly.

She hadn't been wrong about those changes she had noticed in him, then. She knew he was physically much frailer than she remembered, but emotionally he seemed much stronger, less inclined to acquiesce to her mother for the sake of a quiet life. Could she possibly be another of those things about this family that he wanted to change?

'Yes, Meg,' he gently confirmed her thoughts. 'You're my daughter. And Scott is my grandson. I intend to see a lot more of both of you in future.'

Meg would like nothing better if it meant she only had to see her father; her mother was something else entirely.

Her father squeezed her hand sympathetically. 'It will all work out, Meg. I love your mother very much, but I love my daughters too, and now our grandson, and Lydia will have to come to terms with that.'

She didn't understand what he meant, had never understood her mother's aloofness to her family, even less so now that she was a mother herself.

Her father reached up to gently touch her cheek. 'Things aren't always what they seem, little Meg. Your mother loves you very much, and Sonia, and with time, after getting to know him, she will learn to love Scott too. It's totally impossible not to,' he added fondly.

Meg thought her father was expecting rather a lot. She had felt no softening from her mother towards Scott this afternoon, although at least she seemed to have adopted the attitude 'if you can't say anything nice then don't say anything at all'!

'And now I had better deliver these.' Her father held up the shirt and tie. 'I like him, by the way,' he added teasingly.

'Jed?' She gave him a startled look, uncomfortable with her father not knowing the truth. 'Look, Daddy, this is another case of things not being what they seem. You see,' She broke off frowningly as the bedroom door opened behind her, turning to find Jed standing there. In her bedroom.

'Sorry.' He grimaced as he saw the two of them standing in the hallway together. 'It was getting late, and I was just coming to look for you, David. For those,' he added ruefully as her father held up the shirt and tie. 'Thanks.' He took them before turning to go back the way he had come.

Probably not the best time to try and convince her father that she wasn't involved with Jed at all, that they had only met by accident, literally, the evening before.

Although quite what Jed was doing coming out of her bedroom she had no idea.

'You were saying?' her father prompted.

Meg grimaced. 'Nothing of importance.' Or, in fact, believable, in the circumstances.

Her father nodded. 'I'll just go and change for dinner

myself, then. And don't worry, Meg, everything is going to work out just fine.'

She stood and watched as he strode off down the hallway, admiring his optimism, but very much afraid he was going to be proved wrong.

But once her father had disappeared she wasted no time going through her own bedroom, but went straight to the adjacent door and into the room that connected with hers.

Only to come to an abrupt halt once she was inside, the angry words dying on her lips at the sight of Jed standing beside the bed wearing nothing but a pair of faded denims. In fact, she was having trouble breathing, let alone speaking.

Jed's chest and arms were as tanned as his face, his shoulders wide and muscled, a dark dusting of hair on his chest that went down in a vee to his stomach, not an ounce of superfluous flesh on his body.

Meg couldn't speak, couldn't move as she acknowledged she should have knocked first, that of course Jed would be changing into the clothes her father had brought him.

Jed raised one dark brow at her continued silence. 'I'm pretty sure I'm not the first half-naked man you've ever seen,' he drawled mockingly.

No, of course he wasn't. It was just that his nakedness was so unexpected, so immediate. Added to which, he was gorgeous.

His dark good looks were disturbing enough when he was fully dressed, but like this...

'I'm sorry I interrupted you and your father just now.' He grimaced. 'I thought you were in your room, and then when I heard voices in the hallway...' He broke off as she only continued to stare at him, putting the shirt down on the bed to walk slowly towards her, coming to a halt standing only inches away from her. 'You're very quiet, Meg. Don't you have anything to say now that you're here?' he queried huskily.

Something like kiss me? Take me to bed. Make love to me!

Because at that moment they were the only things she could think to say, when she could have reached out and touched the hardness of his flesh.

But she wasn't going to say any of them.

Instead she shifted her gaze away from him. Probably not a good idea either, as her gaze became riveted on the bed. A double one. Easily big enough for both of them.

'Meg?'

She swallowed hard, drawing in a deep breath as she lifted her gaze to meet his, on the assumption that looking into his eyes was better than looking at the rest of him.

But she was wrong.

Jed's eyes had darkened almost to navy as he looked down at her, that gaze shifting now to the fullness of her lips.

Meg groaned low in her throat as she felt the caress of that gaze, something melting deep inside her even as she raised her face to meet the assent of Jed's mouth on hers, moving into his arms as he pulled her against his naked warmth.

They kissed passionately, ravenously, devouring, tasting, sipping as hunger took control once again.

Jed's skin felt firm and smooth to the touch, so hot,

burning, a fire matched by one deep inside Meg, her whole body seeming to have turned to liquid flames as she clung to him, his lips moving down the sensitive column of her throat now.

'How the hell—' Jed raised his head to look at her, his hands cradling each side of her face as he gazed down at her hungrily, his fingers tangled in the dark thickness of her hair '—am I supposed to go downstairs and eat dinner with your family when it's you I want to eat?' he groaned. 'Every—' he kissed her lips '—delectable—' he kissed her again '—inch—' and again '—of you.' This time he kissed her and didn't stop.

She wanted this. As much as she might try to fight it, she wanted this, wanted Jed.

The throb of his body told her he wanted her too. Now. Urgently.

He finally dragged his mouth away from hers, breathing raggedly, his cheeks slightly flushed. 'What am I going to do with you, Meg Hamilton?' he rasped harshly.

She couldn't move, enjoying the hard curves of his body against hers, the clean male smell of him, the warmth of his skin beneath her touch. 'Do with me?' she repeated dreamily.

Jed reached up to grasp her arms and put her slightly away from him. 'I'm not sure whether you've noticed or not, but I can't keep my hands off you.' He groaned self-disgustedly.

She frowned at his tone. 'I didn't ask you to.'

'No, but—' he gave an impatient shake of his head, his hands tightening on her arms '—I'm something of a nomad, Meg. Never quite know where I'm going to be from one week to the next; have homes in New York, Vancouver and Paris. Your life is fixed here, in England, with Scott and your work. Haven't you already been hurt enough, Meg?' he added gratingly.

By Scott's father, he meant. At the same time warning her that he was no more interested in permanence than Scott's father had been. His warning would be laughable, if it didn't hurt so much.

What did Jed think she was? A single mother possibly looking for a husband for herself and a father for Scott? His talk of his nomadic lifestyle certainly seemed to indicate as much.

As quickly as her desire for this man had raged it turned to anger of equal intensity. 'Really, Jed,' she scorned as she shook off his grasp on her arm, moving away from him, eyes glittering with the force of her anger. 'You flatter yourself if you think that this—' she made a flippant gesture that encompassed everything that had happened between them in the last few minutes '—meant any more to me than it did to you.' She gave a hard laugh. 'I happen to like my life exactly as it is too, have no intention of becoming involved in a permanent relationship. Ever!' she added vehemently.

'Meg—'

'But that doesn't mean,' she continued forcefully, 'that at twenty-seven I expect to remain celibate, either. What, Jed?' she derided hardly as his expression became grim. 'Don't you like having the roles reversed on you? Too bad,' she scorned. 'Because that's the way it is. The way it will always be as far as I'm concerned.' She reached the communicating door in long strides. 'Take it or leave it.' She turned back to echo the words he had used to her this morning at the cottage.

This morning at the cottage. Uncomplicated. Simple. It seemed a lifetime away.

Jed looked at her with narrowed eyes, his mouth a thin line. 'I don't believe you, Meg,' he finally said slowly.

She gave an uninterested shrug. 'Please yourself,' she mocked. 'I usually do.'

He shook his head. 'I don't believe that, either,' he bit out. 'You wouldn't be here at all if that were really the case.'

True. Very true. She had come here for her father's sake. Because he had been ill. Because she'd been sure he'd wanted to meet Scott.

But if she had known, if she had even guessed, that she would meet Jed Cole along the way, then she wouldn't have come. Not even for her father.

Because Jed had guessed right about her. She didn't get involved in casual affairs. Never had. Never would.

So what, exactly, was she doing in Jed Cole's bedroom?

Getting out of it as fast as possible. Away from him. Away from the desire that never seemed far from the surface when she was near him.

'You must believe what you please, Jed,' she told him with dismissive scorn. 'But, in future, don't just walk into my bedroom uninvited.'

'And if I'm invited?' His jaw was squared, cheek-bones hard beneath his skin, blue eyes glacial.

Meg gave a humourless smile. 'Hopefully you will be able to leave some time tomorrow. I believe I can resist temptation until then.' She went back into her bedroom, closing the door firmly, but necessarily quietly, behind her.

The tears of humiliation almost blinded her as she stumbled across the room to sit on the side of her bed, burying her face in her hands as she let those tears silently fall.

For over three years now she had kept herself deliberately aloof from any man that had shown an interest in her, not because she didn't want to love and be loved, but because she had Scott, and any man who chose to come into her life would have to be prepared to take him on too, and not just as an adjunct to her, but for himself. She had seen and heard of too many incidents where this wasn't the case, a child from a previous relationship hurt or rejected in any new relationship. She wouldn't accept that for Scott.

But she had allowed Jed Cole to get under her guard these last two days, only to have him tell her that he didn't want to get involved with her, let alone Scott, on a permanent basis. Honest, perhaps, but no less hurtful for that honesty, leaving her no choice but to defend herself.

She raised her head to look at her sleeping son, once again knowing that overwhelming rush of love for him. He was an innocent, a baby, worth all the pain of rejection she had known this last three and a half years, from her family, from so-called friends, from men like Jed Cole too, who wanted no complications in their life.

Well, you handled that really well, Jed, he told himself disgustedly as he looked at the door Meg had just closed in his face. Very suave.

Very sophisticated.

He didn't think.

But it was true that he couldn't seem to keep his hands off Meg, took every opportunity to kiss her, to hold her, whenever the two of them were alone.

And it scared the hell out of him. She scared the hell out of him.

There was no doubt in his mind that he wanted her, that the feel of her lips and body drove him wild, but he also wanted to protect her, keep her safe from harm. Even from himself, it seemed.

God, he hoped she was right about him being able to leave tomorrow—he needed to get away from Meg before she drove him insane.

But keeping his distance from Meg wasn't easy to do when he was actually staying in her parents' home, something brought starkly home to him when he found himself seated next to her at dinner.

He should have expected it, of course. There were only the six of them seated at the round table, Meg's father seated on her other side, by David's design, Jed felt sure, like two sentinels on guard.

Not that Meg looked as if she needed their protection this evening.

So far in their short acquaintance Jed had only ever seen Meg in thick sweaters and fitted denims, but somewhere in that small holdall that had comprised her own and Scott's luggage she had managed to pack the ubiquitous little black dress. A little black dress that looked sensational on Meg.

Or was it that Meg made the dress look sensational?

Whatever, he had been rendered speechless when she'd strolled into the sitting-room a short time ago to join them all for a pre-dinner drink, eyes darkly lashed, a red lip-gloss making her lips look more inviting than ever.

As if Jed needed any more invitation than just looking at her.

But Meg in that dress was something else. It had a scooped neckline, revealing the swell of her creamy breasts, with short sleeves, stopping abruptly just above her knees to reveal shapely legs and slender ankles above high-heeled black shoes. The dress was made of some sort of stretchy material that emphasized high breasts, slim waist, and curvaceous thighs, her hair free and silky down her spine.

He might have come here completely unprepared for the dressing for dinner code, but Meg certainly hadn't.

He had barely been able to take his eyes off her as she'd chatted to her father and Jeremy in the sitting-room, and now he found himself sitting next to her at the dining table, the dress having ridden up her silky thighs when she sat down, a waft of some elusive perfume stirring his senses every time she moved.

He wanted to rip the dress off her and kiss every naked, perfumed inch of her.

Sad, Cole. Very sad. Like a callow youth with a crush on a teacher. Except he wanted to teach her everything he knew.

'Salt, Jed?' David Hamilton's amused voice interrupted his obsessive thoughts.

Almost as if the other man knew what preoccupied his mind. Maybe he did, Jed accepted ruefully as he took the salt to add to his soup; there was a definite glint of laughter in those green eyes so like those of his bewitching daughter.

But this dinner was all so stilted. Jed frowned as he looked around. The conversation was polite, the table set formally with crystal glasses and silver flatware, the only concession to Christmas in this room the arrangement of poinsettias in the centre of the table, although the other females at the table looked as elegant as Meg, Lydia also in black, Sonia in emerald green, David and Jeremy also in formal shirt and tie.

It was a stark contrast to what would be happening at home on the farm in Montana this evening, everyone crowded into the kitchen, talking and laughing, kids yelling as his mother presided over cooking the turkey with all the trimmings. His brothers and his father would have changed into clean denims and maybe a plaid shirt, the females of the family probably having done the same.

He missed them, Jed realized heavily, missed the shouting, the laughter, the teasing, even the occasional arguments.

'Is the venison not to your liking, Jed?'

He focused on Sonia with effort as she sat on his right, her glittering green dress a perfect match for her eyes, eyes that were openly flirting with him, he recognized.

Venison? He looked down at the plate that had been placed in front of him. When had that arrived? Had he eaten his soup? He certainly didn't remember doing so.

You're losing it, Cole, he berated himself impatiently. Totally losing it.

But venison, for goodness' sake. Who the hell had

venison for dinner on Christmas Eve? The Hamiltons, obviously.

He couldn't help wondering what would be served for lunch tomorrow—peacock, maybe. Possibly not.

'The venison is fine, thanks, Sonia,' he replied as he realized she was still waiting for an answer.

Maybe he would go home for New Year. He had come to England to get away from the calls on his time in New York, and now, ironically, he needed to get away from England, too. Fast. If his rapidly escalating response to Meg was anything to go by.

'Are you in England for long, Jed?' Jeremy was the one to engage him in conversation now.

Almost as if some of his thoughts had shown on his face. 'I'm not sure,' he heard himself reply, and then wondered why he had been so ambiguous. The best thing for him to do was to leave England and go home, back to his roots, well away from the temptation of Meg.

'How did you and Meg meet?' Sonia took up the conversation, speculation in those green eyes now. 'I thought all of Meg's time was spent either working or looking after Scott,' she added with a sideways glance at her sister.

A glance that grated on Jed. 'Not all of it, obviously,' he drawled, easily meeting Sonia's cool gaze.

Her mouth tightened. 'Obviously not. So how did you two meet?' she persisted.

Jed easily sensed Meg's tension on his other side, one of her hands clenched on the table beside her plate. He reached out and placed his own hand over that tell-tale tension. 'Mutual friends,' he answered Sonia dismissively.

'Really?' Sonia looked surprised.

'Yes, really,' he echoed hardly. 'Meg called at my friends' cottage when I happened to be visiting. We've been inseparable ever since.' It was stretching the truth a little, although the last part was definitely true; he and Meg had rarely been apart since they'd met yesterday.

'How romantic,' Sonia drawled.

'Very.' Jed deliberately raised Meg's hand to skim his lips across the knuckles, his fingers tightening about hers as she would have instinctively pulled away from the intimacy. 'Scott's a cute kid, too.'

That hardness disappeared from Sonia's gaze to be replaced by cool blankness. 'As children go, I suppose he is.'

Jed maintained his grip on Meg's fingers, liking the feel of that tiny hand in his much larger one. 'You don't like kids?'

'I don't dislike them.' Sonia shrugged bare creamy shoulders before turning to bestow a smile on her husband. 'Although I have to admit I'm rather pleased Jeremy has children from his previous marriage and so isn't interested in having any more.'

'David, would you care to pour some more wine?' Lydia Hamilton cut firmly across what she obviously considered inappropriate dinner conversation.

And maybe it was, Jed accepted frowningly as a still silent Meg finally managed to free her hand, a hand that had trembled slightly, from his. Inappropriate, but interesting.

One twin was secure in a successful career and wealthy marriage, and obviously didn't want children to interfere with that lifestyle, whereas the other twin was unmarried and obviously not wealthy at all, and could so easily have given up the baby she would have to bring up alone, but instead was prepared to make any personal sacrifice to keep him.

He knew which twin he admired more.

Damn it.

'More wine, Jed?' David prompted lightly, bottle poised over Jed's almost empty glass.

'Why not?' Jed accepted.

Although he didn't think there was enough wine in the whole house to help him fall asleep when he went to bed later tonight.

But at least he wouldn't be alone in that wakefulness; children all over the world would be sleepless tonight as they anticipated the arrival of Santa Claus.

The difference was, his sleeplessness would have nothing to do with a jolly man in a red suit, and every-thing to do with a green-eyed witch called Meg Hamilton.

He could spend the time praying for an overnight thaw.

CHAPTER SEVEN

MEG had never been so pleased to see the end of an evening as she was this one.

The whole thing had been awful, from the embarrassing scene in Jed's bedroom, through that awkward dinner, to the equally awkward conversation when they had moved back into the sitting-room, Meg studiously avoiding so much as looking at Jed after the way he had kissed her hand in front of her whole family.

And goodness knew what he had made of the evening.

Perhaps in future he would know better than to avoid his own noisy family, if he had any sense. Tonight had been awful enough to send him running back into their midst.

Had her family always been like this? She didn't think so. It was the undercurrents of the things not being said creating the tension.

But if she was lucky she would only have to spend one more day here and then she and Scott could leave. Never to return, if she had her way. There must be a way she could arrange further meetings between Scott and her father without putting them through this again. She would find a way.

Although for the moment she had another role to play—Father Christmas to her sleeping son. Which was proving a little more difficult to do than she had anticipated. Because they had decided when they'd brought everything in earlier to hide the presents in Jed's bedroom until later tonight.

They were still there.

She had left him downstairs in conversation with her father, so perhaps if she were to just sneak in and get them… It might be a little embarrassing if he returned while she was doing the sneaking, but if she was quick…

This was ridiculous.

She was a twenty-seven-year-old woman, with a responsible job and a young son; she wasn't going to sneak anywhere in her own family home.

Not after the humiliation she had suffered earlier when Jed had warned her quite bluntly not to expect love and for ever from him. Especially not because of that. She would go where she pleased, when she pleased, and if Jed didn't like it, then tough.

But before she could make a move towards the communicating door her bedroom door opened abruptly, Sonia stepping into the room and shutting the door quietly shut behind her, her face pale as she looked across the room at Meg.

'What have you told Jed?' her sister demanded without preamble. 'Oh, don't worry,' she said impatiently as Meg glanced towards the communicating door. 'I left Jed and Daddy downstairs enjoying a brandy together.'

Sonia was so stunningly beautiful, even her present paleness giving her a look of fragile loveliness.

A look Meg knew was completely deceptive, because Sonia was hard and unyielding, caring for no one else's comfort but her own.

Meg stood up, viewing her sister dispassionately. 'I haven't told Jed anything,' she assured her with quiet dignity. 'And I never will. Not to him or anyone else. That was the idea, wasn't it?' she added contemptuously.

If anything her sister paled even more. 'You think I don't care, don't you?'

'I know you don't care,' Meg cut in purposefully. 'Who better?'

Sonia shook her head, her movements restless as she began to pace the room. 'Can I help it if I'm not like you, Meg?' she finally groaned emotionally. 'Why did you never understand?'

'But I do understand, Sonia,' she said coldly, none of her inner turmoil showing on her face. She and Sonia just didn't have conversations like this, not any more. 'You have what you wanted: your successful career and marriage.' She sighed. 'Admittedly, it's unfortunate that we've all met up in this way, but I can assure you that once we all leave here I don't care if I never see you again.' In fact, she would prefer it.

Sonia stopped her pacing, her face full of unreadable emotion, tears in her eyes. 'I miss you, Meg,' she choked.

Meg drew in a sharp, painful breath at this unexpected admission. Because the truth was, she missed her twin too. Yes, they were different, they always had been, Sonia the adventurous one, Meg usually trailing along behind in whatever mischief Sonia had dreamed up for them to do next. Yes, they were different, but as children, even initially as adults, they had shared a bond.

But it was that bond that now kept them apart.

Meg shrugged. 'You made your choices, Sonia.'

'I made a choice,' her sister corrected. 'And I still don't regret making it,' she assured softly. 'Do you?' she challenged huskily.

'Never,' Meg replied unhesitantly.

'Then why—?' Sonia groaned. 'Can't we be friends again, Meg? Daddy's illness was a shock, it made me realize life is too short, Meg.' Her twin looked at her imploringly.

This wasn't at all what she had expected from the conversation Sonia had said she wanted to have with her.

'I know what I did was wrong.' Sonia sighed emotionally. 'I know I hurt people. I hurt you. But I never meant to, Meg, it just, it just happened, and, it's Christmas, Meg, surely a time for forgiveness if ever there is one?' she encouraged softly.

This was so not what she had expected. And she didn't know what to say, what to do.

She drew in a ragged breath as Sonia continued to look at her beseechingly. 'I forgave you long ago, Sonia,' she admitted quietly. 'I think it's you, and not me, who needs to forgive yourself.'

'I've tried.' Sonia closed her eyes, a single tear escaping down the paleness of her cheek. 'Sometimes I can go for days and not—and not remember what I did.' She looked at Meg. 'But I know, all the time I know, that, given those same choices, I would do exactly the same all over again.'

Meg swallowed hard. 'Maybe acceptance is a form of forgiveness.'

'I want to be your sister again, Meg. And I want, more than anything—' her gaze was unwavering '—to be Scott's aunt.'

She frowned warily. 'You've never stopped being my sister, Sonia.' She spoke huskily. 'As for Scott—you are his aunt.'

Her sister gave a shaky smile. 'So will you try, Meg?' she asked softly. 'Will you try? For my sake if not for yours.'

Meg felt confused and uncertain. There had been antagonism between her twin and herself for so long now that she wasn't sure, in the life she had made for Scott and herself, that there was room for any other relationship with Sonia than the one they already had.

'Are you happy, Sonia?' She looked closely at her sister. 'Are you happy with Jeremy?'

'Oh, yes,' Sonia replied without hesitation. 'Oh, I know that people look at us and see summer and autumn.' Her mouth twisted ruefully. 'That people think I must have married him for his money and social standing, that he married me to have a young and beautiful trophy on his arm, but they're all wrong, Meg.' She smiled. 'I love Jeremy very much. And he loves me. We have a good life together.'

Meg nodded. 'Then that's really all that matters, isn't—?' She broke off, her eyes wide with incredulity as Jed strolled in from the adjoining room, hadn't she told him to knock the next time he came in here?

He raised dark brows as he looked at the two women,

a rueful twist to his mouth. 'Ho, ho, ho.' He looked at the bag of presents he had over one shoulder.

Meg and Sonia continued to look at him for several seconds, and then at each other, and then they both began to laugh.

'Well, I guess I know what you're getting in your stocking this year, Meg,' Sonia finally sobered enough to tease.

It was an intriguing thought, but, no, somehow Meg didn't think so.

Sonia moved gracefully, a glittering green butterfly. 'Happy Christmas, Jed.' She reached up to kiss him on the cheek.

For longer than Meg thought necessary. Oh, she knew Sonia loved to flirt, that it came as easily to her as breathing, but nevertheless Meg couldn't help the shaft of jealousy that ripped through her at this platonic kiss.

'Happy Christmas, Meg.' Sonia moved to hug and kiss her now. 'I'm really happy for you, Meg,' she murmured so that only Meg could hear her. 'I'll see you both in the morning.' And with one last tantalizing waft of her perfume she left Meg and Jed alone in the bedroom.

Not a happy occurrence for Meg after the conversation they'd had before dinner. She watched him warily as he slowly swung the sack of presents down onto the carpeted floor.

'I heard voices in here,' he explained with a grimace. 'And from your reaction earlier to Sonia's suggestion that she would come back later, I thought you might need rescuing.'

Jed Cole to the rescue.

Once again. Except this time she didn't think she had needed rescuing.

She still felt emotional from that conversation with Sonia. It had been the last thing she had expected. Although their shared laughter at Jed's attempt at being Father Christmas was more like the two of them used to be together, so maybe, just maybe, they could start to heal this breach, after all.

'Obviously I guessed wrong—' Jed took her silence for rebuke '—but you needed these presents, anyway, right?'

Yes, she needed them, no longer had to sneak into his bedroom to get them.

'Will you for goodness' sake say something, woman?' Jed burst out impatiently.

She returned his gaze steadily. 'Thank you. I can manage from here.'

'That's it?' he rasped, thrusting his hands into his jeans pockets.

'You've barely spoken a word to me all evening and now you're dismissing me like the hired help.'

She gave him a perplexed frown. 'The only hired help I ever have dealings with is Mrs Sykes, the cook here, and as Scott and I spent a very enjoyable hour down in the kitchen with her earlier, I don't accept your accusation. She's more like one of the family.'

'Which I, obviously, am not,' he snapped.

Meg gave an irritated shake of her head. 'I thought this distance between us was what you wanted?'

He scowled darker than ever. 'You're doing this on purpose, aren't you?' he accused tersely. 'To pay me back for being so bluntly honest with you earlier.'

Her cheeks flamed with colour at this reminder of earlier. 'I think you've had too much wine and brandy.'

'Well, of course I have,' he rejoined irritably. 'What else was I supposed to do when you barely acknowledged I was sitting next to you at dinner?'

'I'm not aware that I did anything.'

'You're driving me insane, is what you're doing.' He reached out to grasp her arms, shaking her slightly. 'You look wonderful in this dress.' His gaze moved over her as impatiently as he sounded. 'I don't know how I managed to keep my hands off you during dinner. I wanted to just clear the table and make love to you there.'

She gave a mischievous smile. 'I'm sure my family would have enjoyed the spectacle.'

Jed gave a self-mocking smile. 'I'm not sure I would have cared at the time.'

She didn't understand this man. One minute he was pushing her away with talk of his nomadic lifestyle, and the next he was telling her how much he wanted to make love to her. But maybe he didn't understand himself, either.

'It's late, Jed.' She gave a shake of her head. 'I'm sure that everything will look different in the morning.' Once he had sobered up a little.

His hands dropped away from her arms. 'If the snow thaws then I'm out of here tomorrow,' he told her flatly. 'How are you going to explain that to your family?'

Why was it her responsibility? He was the one who had given her family the impression they were a couple, not her.

Her mouth firmed. 'I'm sure you'll think of something to tell them by tomorrow. Now would you please go?' she urged, lowering her voice as Scott moved restlessly in his bed, not surprising after the amount of conversations he had been a sleeping witness to this evening.

Scott was a heavy sleeper, and not much disturbed him once he was asleep, but her visitors had been excessive this evening.

Besides, she needed some time to herself to be able to think. Oh, not about Jed—all the thinking in the world wouldn't give her the answers she wanted, or change the fact that he couldn't wait to get away from here.

But she needed to digest and mull over that conversation with Sonia, to decide what to do about it, if anything. Her instinct was to do nothing, knowing that allowing herself to be close to Sonia again would change everything. She had to decide whether she wanted that change before she made any decision. And she needed time and space away from people to make it.

'Yeah, I'll go,' Jed agreed heavily once Scott had settled down again. 'But you are driving me nuts, Meg,' he paused in the doorway to murmur.

'I'm sorry,' she sighed.

He nodded abruptly, Meg only starting to breathe again once he had returned to the adjoining room and closed the door behind him.

Really, her bedroom was starting to take on the appearance of a railway station with all these comings and goings.

Although, of course, this wasn't her bedroom, only one of a number of guest rooms. Because that was what she was now: a guest.

Her own childhood bedroom, the room that had remained hers until she'd gone to live in London, was on the other side of the house. It had remained the same since she was in her teens, her cups and rosettes won at gymkhanas along one wall, some of her own drawings on another, the large bookcase full of books she had read as a child and refused to part with.

No doubt they were gone now, along with everything else in that room that had proclaimed it her room.

She blinked back the sudden tears, a part of her longing for the simplicity of those carefree days, when the biggest decision she had had to make had been the colour of her riding jacket for the day.

Jed was right: the sooner the snow thawed, and she could leave, the better she would start to feel.

Jed had no idea what the time was, or indeed where he was, totally engrossed in what he was writing.

He didn't know how or why it had happened, but at one o'clock in the morning, in the midst of a family with so many emotional problems they were too complicated for him to fathom, the storyline for a book had suddenly hit him as he'd moved restlessly about his bedroom unable to sleep. Not the storyline he had been working on so half-heartedly the last six months, either, but a totally new one, complete, entire, and urgently needing to be written down.

It hadn't taken too much effort to find David Hamilton's library, sitting down at the desk there to begin writing page after page, his own inner excitement telling him that this book was going to be as good, if not better, than *The Puzzle*.

Maybe physical frustration was exactly what he had needed to make his mind fertile again.

Because he was frustrated. Wanted Meg. Wanted her more than he had ever wanted a woman in his life before.

But he wasn't going to get her, knew that as surely as there was no thaw predicted for tomorrow.

Think positive, he told himself firmly. At least he was writing again.

He looked up as the library light was suddenly switched off, throwing him into instant darkness. 'What?' The light came on again as abruptly as it had been switched off.

David's smile was apologetic as he entered the room. 'I'm terribly sorry, Jed. I didn't know there was anyone in here. I thought someone must have forgotten to switch the light off earlier.' He stood beside the desk now, wearing a Paisley dressing gown over wine-coloured pyjamas. 'I'm sorry, have I interrupted you?' He looked down interestedly at the pile of papers covered in Jed's scrawled handwriting.

Jed sat back to flex his tired shoulder muscles. 'I could probably do with a break, anyway.' He grimaced as the hall clock struck three o'clock; he had been working for two hours without stopping—amazing after months of getting nowhere.

'Brandy?' David held up the decanter before pouring a measure into two glasses. 'I'm not really supposed to drink alcohol,' he remarked somewhat shamefacedly as the two men made themselves comfortable in the fireside armchairs. 'But if I stopped doing everything the doctors told me to life would be pretty miserable.

'Unfortunately, the insomnia seems to be something I can do little about. Although this sometimes helps.' He sipped the brandy. 'Is Meg asleep?' he asked mildly.

Jed frowned as he looked down at the rich brown liquid in the glass he cradled in both hands. 'Things aren't—they aren't always what they seem, sir,' he said slowly, his gaze direct as he looked at the older man.

David gave a smile. 'I believe I had a conversation along similar lines with Meg this evening.'

He raised dark brows. 'On the same subject?' he prompted guardedly. 'Or something else?'

The older man's smile widened. 'I don't question my girls about their private lives, Jed.'

Jed gave David a rueful glance. 'Does the same apply to the men in your girls' lives?'

'Ah, well, that's different,' the older man came back dryly, and then chuckled at Jed's uncomfortable grimace. 'I'm not about to ask you your intentions towards Meg, if that's what's bothering you,' he assured lightly. 'I'm sure Meg is mature enough to know what she's doing.'

He wished he did.

Part of him wanted to run as fast and as far away from Meg as he could, and another part of him wanted to barricade himself in a bedroom with her for a week, so they could feast off nothing but each other.

Although he didn't think he had better share that thought with her father.

'And now I think it's time I was getting back to bed.' David drank the last of his brandy before standing up. 'If my memory serves me correctly, young children are apt to wake up very early on Christmas morning.'

Something Jed was made all too aware of only a few hours later as the age-old cry of, 'Mummy, Mummy, he's been! Father Christmas has been!' resounded in the adjoining bedroom, making Jed smile as he imagined Jed's excitement at the sackful of presents.

Although he frowned a little when he saw it was only six-thirty in the morning; he had only been asleep for three hours.

It was his own fault, of course, although he couldn't feel bad about it because he had actually written the first chapter in his new book, had the outline for the rest of it too, only needed the time now to sit down and write it. Only. This last two months in England he had had nothing but time and hadn't produced a thing worth reading.

'Ooh, Mummy, look what Father Christmas has brought me.' Scott sounded awed now. 'It's just like the one I saw in the shop and put on my list to Father Christmas.'

It was no good, Jed decided, he couldn't lie here any longer and listen to Scott's excitement through the walls. He had to be a part of what was going on in the next room.

The bright red sack that had been empty on the foot of Scott's bed the night before was now on the floor beside the bed, Scott delving excitedly into the bulging contents.

Meg looked up to give Jed a welcoming smile. 'Father Christmas has been.' She smiled, looking affectionately at her ecstatic son.

'See, Jed.' Scott lifted up the one present he had already opened, obviously the cause of his earlier excitement—a bright red tractor with a trailer on the back containing several strange looking plastic pigs.

'Hey, that's great, buddy.' He grinned as he sat down on the floor to ruffle the little boy's dark curls.

He had quickly pulled on a pair of jeans and a tee shirt before coming through from his bedroom, but Meg, so recently awakened, was still wearing her night attire: a pair of shapeless cotton pyjamas that should have looked totally unfeminine and yet on Meg didn't, only succeeding in making Jed want to take her in his arms and caress every soft curve he knew was beneath.

Very appropriate for six-thirty on Christmas morning.

'Would you like me to go and get you a cup of coffee?' he offered softly as Scott started to rip into the paper on a second present.

Meg looked surprised at the offer, making Jed realize that, living on her own with Scott, this probably didn't happen too often. If at all. Because he still didn't believe her claim about having relationships without permanence—Meg Hamilton had 'commitment or nothing' stamped all over her. It was the reason she scared the hell out of him.

She shook her head now. 'Stay and enjoy this,' she invited huskily. 'There's nothing as joyful as watching a child on Christmas morning.'

She was right: there wasn't. Jed and Meg were surrounded by presents and wrapping paper as Scott, after half an hour, found and opened the main present, right at the bottom of the huge sack, rendering the little boy speechless for several seconds.

'It's a farm, Mummy,' he finally breathed disbelievingly. 'A real farm.' His little fingers, his knuckles not yet defined, touched the farm buildings, barn, fences and assorted animals, with complete awe.

Meg, Jed saw, was blinking back the tears as she looked at the wonder on her son's face, and Jed felt a certain emotional thickness in his own throat, at the same time knowing a feeling of gratitude to Meg for letting him share this with her.

Oh, he had spent lots of Christmases on the farm with his family, his brothers' children ranging in ages from five to eleven, but the fact was they were his brothers' children, and as such Gary and Ray were the ones who got to share this magic moment with their children. Jed was just a bystander, a favourite uncle who would eventually be asked to install all the batteries in the electronic toys they had received.

This was different. Meg had made it different by inviting him to share it with her.

He stood up abruptly as he realized what was happening to him. He couldn't be— Damn it, he had barely known the woman thirty-six hours.

But as he looked down at Meg's ebony head, the long hair cascading over her shoulders, her face completely bare of make-up, her body shapeless in those unbecoming pyjamas, he knew that his worst fears had been realized.

He was falling in love with Meg Hamilton.

CHAPTER EIGHT

MEG looked up at Jed as he stood beside her, frowning at the suddenly closed expression on his face. 'What's wrong?'

'I'll go and get that coffee now,' he bit out harshly, moving abruptly away and over to the door.

Meg stared after him as he left, wondering what could possibly have happened to cause his hasty departure. Perhaps it had been the talk of Scott's farm, making him feel homesick for his own family. Or, more likely, he'd had enough of domesticity for one morning. Or perhaps he really did just need his first shot of coffee for the day.

Whatever his reasons, she very much doubted Jed was going to confide them to her.

Neither was he going to be able to leave today, she discovered as she left Scott arranging his farm to wander over to the window. The deep snow covered the ground for as far as the eye could see, like a huge white blanket, beautiful in its whiteness, but totally unsuitable for travelling.

Whether Jed liked it or not, he was stuck with them all for another day.

And he obviously didn't like it. He was totally uncommunicative when Meg and Scott made their way downstairs. Just as quiet at breakfast when they all helped themselves to food from the selection of trays set out in the dining-room.

Meg didn't feel too talkative herself when Sonia came and sat down next to her.

She still wasn't sure what to do about that conversation with her sister. Oh, she didn't want the strain between them to continue, had also missed the closeness they had once had. But she knew it was a closeness they would never be able to recapture, that too much stood between them for them to do that.

'Why don't we all go for a walk after breakfast?' Sonia suggested lightly to everyone. 'It will give Scott chance to try out his sledge,' she added encouragingly as no one responded to the suggestion.

Meg had to admit she had been stunned when she and Scott had arrived downstairs and Uncle Jeremy and Aunt Sonia had asked if they could give him his gift now.

Normally the presents under the tree, their gifts to each other rather than from Father Christmas, were opened in the early evening of Christmas Day, before they had a cold buffet dinner.

But Jeremy had explained that their gift to Scott would be of more use to him now rather than later this evening.

Meg had had to agree when Scott had ripped off the paper to reveal the wooden sledge with its gleaming runners, sure Scott was going to burst with happiness as he'd looked at it.

Scott's reaction had been obvious, but she hadn't been sure how she felt about this expensive gift to her son.

An hour later she still didn't know.

'What a good idea,' their father enthused. 'You would like that, wouldn't you, Scott? There's a little hill at the back of the house that's just perfect for sledging.'

'David, I really don't think it's a good idea for you to be—'

'Lydia, I have no intention of pulling the sledge myself,' Meg's father cut lightly across her mother's protest. 'Jeremy obviously can't do it either, with his sprained ankle, but I'm sure Jed will oblige.' He gave Jed a smile.

'Sounds good to me.' Jed nodded in agreement. 'Meg?' His gaze was unreadable as he looked across the table at her.

What a position to be in. She couldn't possibly say no, and so ruin Scott's fun, even though a part of her dearly wanted to.

For three and a half years this family had all but ignored Scott's existence, and now they were all fussing over him as if he were a treasured part of that family— it took a lot of getting used to.

She had no idea what she had expected to happen during this three-day visit, but it certainly hadn't been this.

'Yes, of course we can go sledging,' she confirmed quickly as she realized Jed was still waiting for an answer, receiving a whoop of joy and a hug from her son before he hastily began to eat his breakfast, anxious to get outside and begin.

'Are you really okay with this?' Jed caught up with her as she went upstairs to get her own and Scott's outdoor clothing.

She looked at him sharply as he fell into step beside her, obviously going upstairs for his own coat. 'Yes, of course I am. Why shouldn't I be?'

'I have absolutely no idea.' He sighed. 'I just thought I noticed a slight reluctance on your part earlier. But as far as I'm concerned this is the first normal thing this family has done since we arrived here.'

And he didn't even want to be here, she reminded herself, was only here at all because he had tried to help her and Scott.

'What would your own family be doing now?' she questioned huskily.

He shrugged. 'Sleeping, I guess. There's several hours time difference, Meg,' he added teasingly.

'I totally forgot that.' She gave a slight smile. 'Maybe you would like to call them all later? To wish them all a Happy Christmas? I'm sure my parents would be only too happy for you to use the telephone here.'

'Thanks.' He nodded. 'I'll think about it.'

She had no idea why there was this awkwardness between them now, their conversation so stilted; they had seemed perfectly okay together earlier when they had watched Scott open his presents. Before Jed had left so abruptly on the pretext of getting her coffee.

Because he never had come back with the coffee, her father bringing her a cup half an hour later when he'd come to see how Scott was doing with his presents, lingering to play with his grandson while Meg took a shower.

Not that Meg ever intended mentioning that forgotten cup of coffee; this Jed was nowhere near as approachable as the previous one.

How odd that the relationship with her family, certainly her father and Sonia, had become less strained, and now she and Jed had a distance between them that seemed insurmountable.

She grimaced. 'I'm afraid I don't have a gift to give you later today.'

'That's okay. I don't have one for you, either,' Jed responded lightly as they walked down the hallway to their bedrooms. 'How could we have?' he added harshly. 'We didn't even know each other until two days ago.'

Meg stopped, her hand on her bedroom door, looking up at him uncertainly. 'Jed, if I've done something to offend you today—'

'Why should today be any different?' he cut in dryly. 'We've been offending each other, one way or another, since the moment we met.'

She gave a pained frown. That wasn't quite true. Was it?

Admittedly, they snapped and snarled at each other occasionally, but in between that snapping and snarling they usually ended up in each other's arms.

'Don't look so worried about it, Meg,' Jed advised with a rueful smile. 'It's Christmas Day, after all.'

Yes, and, Jed apart, it was a much better Christmas Day than she had envisaged when she'd left London two days ago.

Jed apart.

Three days. That was all she had known this man. And yet already she knew he would leave a huge gap in her life when he left.

She felt herself pale, her eyes widen, as a startling truth suddenly hit her.

She was falling in love with Jed Cole.

She blinked up at him dazedly, not sure how, or even why, only knowing without a doubt as she looked into the rugged handsomeness of his face that she was falling in love with him. If she wasn't already in love with him.

And that, without a doubt, had to be the most reckless thing she had ever done in her life.

She had gone to art college at great opposition from her mother, had kept Scott to even greater opposition, and now she had managed to fall in love with a man who was totally out of her reach. Totally out of any woman's permanent reach if the things he had said to her yesterday, and his bachelorhood at the age of thirty-eight, were anything to go by.

'Are you okay?' Jed frowned down concernedly, blue gaze searching the paleness of her face.

No, she certainly wasn't okay, might never be okay again, had been stupid enough to fall in love with this man.

But it was her stupidity, and she intended keeping it to herself. There would be plenty of time to feel sorry for herself once Jed had gone.

'Just too early a start to my day, I think,' she dismissed with a shake of her head. 'Sonia's right, a walk in the fresh air is exactly what we all need.'

Jed gave her a puzzled look. 'Are the two of you okay now? I noticed the two of you seemed a little friendlier towards each other at breakfast.'

She wished she could talk to someone, to him, about the reason for the estrangement between herself and

Sonia, to ask his advice about what she should do. But she had made a promise long ago, as Sonia had made one to her, and she couldn't, wouldn't, ever break that promise. Too many people could be hurt if she did.

'Things are—better,' she answered cautiously. 'Thank you for asking.'

'That's good,' he nodded approvingly.

But he made no effort to go into his own bedroom, his gaze guarded as he continued to look down at her.

'They'll be waiting for us downstairs,' Meg mentioned huskily.

'Yes.' Still he made no move to leave.

'You have a sledge to pull up a hill,' she reminded teasingly.

His mouth curved into a smile. 'Did you see the look on Scott's face when he opened his gift and saw the sledge?'

Yes, she had seen it. And worried over it. If Sonia's idea of being Scott's aunt was just to shower him with expensive presents, then this was never going to work.

'It's what it's all about, isn't it,' Jed added softly at her silence. 'Kids at Christmas.'

Yes, it was, and perhaps she was being unfair to her sister.

'Sonia wants to start being Scott's aunt.' She only realized she had spoken her thoughts out loud as she heard herself speak, biting her bottom lip as she realized what she had done.

Jed looked at her searchingly. 'Is that going to be a problem for you?'

She drew in a sharp breath, straightening her shoulders before answering him. 'No, of course not,' she said brightly, finally turning the handle on her bedroom door and opening it. 'One big happy family at last.' That didn't come out right, she realized with a wince.

Knowing Jed had picked up on it too as his frown deepened. 'Meg, what—'

'We really do need to get back downstairs, Jed.' She gave him a bright, meaningless smile before going into her bedroom and closing the door firmly behind her.

None of this had turned out as she had expected.

None of it.

There was that difference in her father, his quiet determination to do exactly as he wished. Her sister's efforts to be friendly. And nowhere, absolutely nowhere in her imaginings had she taken into account meeting Jed Cole.

And falling in love with him.

'Need any help, Lydia?' Jed offered as she trailed behind as they walked up the hill, the other three almost at the top, Meg and Scott having insisted on pulling the sledge, Sonia pushing from behind, Scott chattering excitedly. David and Jeremy had stayed at the bottom of the hill to catch the sledge when it came down.

Jed had to admit he had been surprised when he'd returned downstairs to find Lydia Hamilton had opted to join in the sledge expedition. She seemed more the type to stay in the house where it was warm and watch from a window, if at all.

'Thank you, Jed.' She took his arm gratefully, her fashionable boots not made to climb hills slippery with snow. 'David used to do this with the girls when they were small.' She made stilted conversation.

'Did he?' Not David and I, just David, Jed noted.

Lydia gave him a quick glance, as if sensing his unspoken question, cosily warm in a long coat and hat. 'I usually stayed indoors and waited to dry them out and supply them with warm drinks when they came back in.'

Her tone was almost wistful, Jed noted, as if she longed for the days when her daughters had been small and life had been less complicated.

'Still, you've made the effort today,' he encouraged lightly, wondering if perhaps he hadn't misjudged Lydia Hamilton. When that haughty mask slipped he caught glimpses of a very lonely woman who had always stood outside her family looking in, almost as if she were afraid of the emotion held within.

Or maybe he was just imagining it, he decided ruefully as they reached the top of the hill and Lydia Hamilton slipped easily back behind that mask as she engaged her eldest daughter in conversation about mutual friends of theirs in London, taking little or no notice of her grandson as he prepared for his first sledge ride.

'Ready?' Meg prompted him, Scott already seated on the sledge, Jed having elected to go down on the first run with him.

She looked wonderful.

Wearing ankle boots and jeans, a short thick jacket over her green jumper, a red woollen hat pulled low over her ears, her hair cascading free, her cheeks flushed from her exertions up the hill, green eyes sparkling with fun.

Jed was aware of an actual physical pain as he looked

at her and then at Scott, the little boy similarly attired, his eyes excited as he waited for the off.

Anyone looking at the three of them might be forgiven for mistaking them for a real family, this woman his own, the little boy too.

He, Jed Cole, who had never considered permanence with any of the women he had been involved with over the years, let alone contemplated having children of his own, assuring his mother, whenever she teased him about his single state—which was every time he went home!—that she had enough grandchildren already without his adding to their number.

He had no doubts that his mother would like Meg. Scott too. That she would just gather the two of them in and—

Get a grip, Cole, he instantly admonished himself. Meg wasn't his. Neither was Scott. And they never would be.

He might not have believed Meg when she'd claimed that any relationships she had would be transient ones, but there had been no doubting her sincerity when she'd claimed she didn't intend getting involved in a permanent relationship. Ever!

Now wouldn't that be ironic, if, after years of avoiding the marital trap, he should happen to fall in love with a woman who had no interest in marrying him?

'Jed?' Meg's voice sounded puzzled this time as she still received no response from him.

Well…no, it wouldn't be in the least funny. Falling in love wasn't something to laugh about at all.

He really would have to get a grip, take the draft of the first chapter of his book and skedaddle out of here as fast as his long legs would carry him.

But for the moment he swung those long legs over the sledge, either side of the waiting Scott. 'All set, kiddo?' He waited only long enough for the little boy's excited nod before pushing off with his feet, his arm tight about Scott's waist as they began to slide downwards.

The cold wind rushed by his ears, Scott's scream of joy echoing in his ears, the grin on his own face irrepressible, the two of them smiling like idiots when David and Jeremy brought them to a stop at the bottom of the hill.

He was enjoying himself, Jed realized an hour later. Totally enjoying himself, none of the tensions out here that he experienced inside the house, even Sonia taking a turn on the sledge, although no amount of persuasion would induce Lydia to try it.

'That was such fun.' Sonia laughed lightly as she fell into step beside him as they all trudged back to the house a couple of hours later, not quite so perfectly turned out any more, her hair flattened by her hat, her lips bare of gloss, and looking much better for it, in Jed's opinion. More like Meg.

'It was a great present,' he answered smoothly. Meg claimed that things were better between her twin and herself, but Jed still sensed a certain restraint between them.

'Totally impractical for London, of course.' Sonia ran a hand through her flattened hair. 'But I'm sure Mother and Daddy will be quite happy for Scott to leave it here and use it when he comes to visit.'

He raised dark brows. 'Then you think there will be future visits?'

Sonia's smile faded slightly. 'I hope so.' She gave

him a considering look. 'You don't like me very much, do you?' It was a statement rather than a question.

He shrugged. 'I don't know you.' Although he had a feeling there really wasn't that much to know, no depth of character as Meg had.

'No, of course you don't.' She gave a husky laugh. 'Meg is by far the nicest of the two of us,' she added ruefully. 'Special is probably the word. Yes, Meg is very special.' She frowned slightly. 'She deserves to be happy.'

Jed raised both brows now. 'Are you warning me not to hurt your sister?'

Sonia returned his gaze unblinkingly. 'Do I need to?'

'Did you ever consider that maybe she'll be the one to hurt me?' He avoided answering the directness of her question.

Sonia gave a dismissive snort at his suggestion. 'Meg has never hurt anyone in her life.' She put a hand on his arm. 'And I think, Jed Cole, that you're a man who can be trusted with my sister's heart.'

He should be so lucky.

'Am I?' Once again he was noncommittal.

But before Sonia could answer him a snowball whizzed past the two of them to make contact, several feet away, with Jeremy's broad back.

'Who did that?' he demanded as he whirled round, eyes full of laughter as he bent to scoop up some snow, ready to retaliate.

'I cannot tell a lie.' Meg laughed as she and Scott pulled the sledge. 'It was Jed.'

Jed turned. 'Why, you little—' He didn't get time to finish as a snowball landed on the back of his head.

What followed was a complete free-for-all, snow-balls flying through the air at random, even Lydia joining in this time as one miscalculated snowball from Scott caught her squarely in the chest. There was no sub-stance to her return as it fell far short of its mark, but at least she tried.

'Hot chocolate all round, I think,' she announced once they were back at the house, tired and wet, but glowing.

'Sorry about that.' Meg walked over to join Jed as he stood in front of the window in the sitting-room looking out at the bleak, but beautiful, landscape. 'It was a game Sonia and I used to play when we were children: if we preceded a statement with "I cannot tell a lie", then we knew it was one,' she explained before taking a sip of her hot chocolate. 'What were the two of you talking about?' she questioned softly.

Lightly. Cautiously. As if his reply were important. And yet he couldn't for the life of him imagine why.

'This and that,' he answered noncommittally, contin-uing to stare out of the window.

He sensed Meg giving him a quick, searching glance. 'I wouldn't have thought the two of you had too much in common,' she finally remarked with the same light-ness as before.

And once again Jed sensed the tension behind the words. 'Not a lot, no,' he acknowledged dryly as he looked at her.

Meg gave him a reassuring smile. 'So what did you find to talk about?'

Yes, his instinct was definitely correct: Meg was worried about the conversation he'd had with Sonia.

But why? What on earth could she think her twin might have said to him that caused this concern?

He turned fully to face her, needing to see her face in order to gauge her response. 'You, mostly,' he murmured softly, and was rewarded by a brief flicker of alarm in her eyes before it was quickly masked by a return of that quizzical smile.

'Me?' She sounded surprised. 'What could Sonia possibly have to say to you about me?'

He wasn't enjoying this, Jed decided. He felt uncomfortable at Meg's forced lightness, an emotion totally belied by the way her hands were so tightly gripped about the mug of hot chocolate that her knuckles were showing white.

What he said next was purely instinctive, and completely unpremeditated. 'Meg, what's the secret that you and Sonia have between you that is so big, that it actually drives the two of you apart?'

He knew he had scored a direct hit in the question by the way Meg's face suddenly drained of all colour, the expression in her eyes no longer alarm but actual fear.

Fear.

But of what, damn it?

Because Jed had a feeling that if the secret were ever to be revealed it could be the key to all this family's seething undercurrents.

But he had absolutely no idea what it could be.

What could possibly be so important, of such magnitude, that it had kept Meg from her family since Scott had been born? Sister against sister for the same amount of time. What could have happened…

Jed turned to look across the room to where the little boy sat on the carpeted floor playing with his farm, his grandfather at his side, the two of them animated as they arranged all the animals in the appropriate pens and fields.

How could that innocent little boy, so small and carefree, possibly be the answer?

CHAPTER NINE

MEG saw the look Jed gave in Scott's direction, the speculation on his face as he continued to stare at her young son.

A speculation she had to divert away from Scott and back onto her. 'I think someone's been putting whisky in your hot chocolate, Jed,' she taunted. 'Or else your writer's block has finally broken and your imagination is running wild.' Oh, that had got his attention, that frown focused on her again now.

Which was exactly what she had wanted.

He gave her a considering look. 'As a matter of fact I was up half the night writing,' he admitted slowly.

'There you are, then.' She smiled teasingly. 'An overactive imagination and lack of sleep. You're probably hungry too after all that sledging this morning.' Too much, Meg, she realized with an inward wince as that look of speculation returned to Jed's shrewd gaze.

She literally held her breath as she waited for his reply, not wanting to have this conversation. Not now. Not here. Not ever, if she could possibly avoid it.

And it seemed, as Jed's features finally relaxed into a smile, that this time she was going to escape unscathed.

'I've been wondering about that,' he drawled. 'After the venison for dinner last night, what are we actually having for Christmas lunch?'

Meg laughed at his expression, the tension slowly starting to ease out of her at this change of subject. 'Turkey, of course,' she reassured teasingly. 'It's traditional, after all.'

'Oh, of course, and this family is big on tradition,' he said dryly.

'Some of the time we are.' She nodded.

'And does everyone fall asleep this afternoon, full of Christmas cheer?'

'We're usually full of white wine, actually,' she drawled. 'But yes, it's tra—'

'Traditional,' Jed finished lightly, his own features relaxing into a smile as Jeremy limped over to join them.

Much to Meg's relief, the conversation focused less on her as Jeremy began talking to Jed about some of the business trips he had made to America over the years, his property developing business taking him all over the world.

Nevertheless, Meg was still rather relieved when lunch was announced, sitting between Scott and her father this time, with Jed on Scott's other side, giving him no opportunity to engage her in personal conversation again.

But two hours later, all of them stuffed with turkey and Christmas pudding as well as white wine, as everyone else began to doze in armchairs, even Scott fast asleep on his grandfather's knee, Jed having disappeared upstairs as soon as the meal was finished. Meg took the opportunity to leave them all for a while. Too restless to sleep, she went down to the kitchen instead to share a cup of coffee with Bessie Sykes, the familiar warmth of the kitchen reminding her of the times she used to do this as a child.

Maybe because of that, it seemed perfectly natural, once she left the kitchen some time later, for her to go up to what had been her old bedroom, curious as to what her mother had done with it. She wanted to see whether it had been turned into yet another guest room, or maybe just a junk-room to store unused pieces of furniture until they were needed again.

She was wrong, it was neither of those things.

It was exactly the same as she had left it the last time she had stayed here over three years ago.

Nothing had been moved, nothing had been changed, the rosettes still pinned to the wall, her drawings on another, her books still on the shelves along one wall, her canopied bed, with its antique lace drapes and cover, was made up too, as if she might sleep in it that very night.

Meg was white with shock as she stepped dazedly into the room, her hand trembling slightly as she touched the music box on her lace-covered dressing-table, lifting the lid to watch the golden unicorn as it circled in time to the music.

There was no dust in here, no spider's webs, no air of neglect, the room seeming somehow to have been waiting for her return.

She closed the lid on the music box absently, moving

to the side of the bed, the pot-pourri on the bedside table smelling of fresh roses when she touched them.

Her knees felt weak as she sat down abruptly on the side of the bed to look around her.

She didn't understand.

What did all this mean? Who kept her room like this? Not Bessie, surely; she had enough to do in the rest of the house without cleaning a room that wasn't used any more. Besides, the cook/housekeeper would never have done all this without being instructed to do so. And that instruction, surely, had to have come from Lydia.

Meg really didn't understand.

Why would her mother, so cold and remote, although not quite so much today, have bothered not only to leave Meg's room as it had always been, but to keep it so…

'Is this your bedroom?'

Meg was too bemused by her discovery to do more than turn her head slowly in Jed's direction, feeling slightly numbed even as she nodded.

He strolled into the room, much as she had a few minutes ago, pausing when he reached the display of cups and rosettes she had won so many years ago.

He turned to look at her, his expression unreadable. 'Do you still ride?'

She shook her head. 'Not for the last few years; there isn't much opportunity in London.'

He shrugged. 'Maybe you should take it up again; you were obviously good. I'm sure Scott would enjoy learning to ride.'

'Maybe,' she agreed distractedly, some of the shock starting to wear off now.

What was Jed doing up here? This bedroom was on the other side of the house from the adjoining bedrooms they had been allocated yesterday, so what was he doing here.

He turned fully, leaning back against the bookcase. 'I was just going downstairs to see if I could get a cup of coffee from Mrs Sykes,' he explained as if reading her thoughts, 'when I saw you crossing the upper gallery.'

Meg frowned. 'You followed me.'

'I followed you.' He nodded, his tone gentle. 'I thought you could maybe use some company—was I wrong?' he asked huskily.

She swallowed hard, one of her hands tightly clenched in the lace cover on her bed. 'No, you weren't wrong. I thought—I thought all this—' she looked around at the beautiful feminine room '—I thought it would all be gone.' She blinked back sudden tears. 'And instead, instead I found...' She broke off, her emotions too fragile for her to continue.

'Instead you found that it's been kept exactly as you left it, yes?'

Jed moved to sit on the side of the bed beside her.

'What does it mean, Jed?' she choked, fighting to hold back the tears, knowing she hadn't succeeded as they fell hotly down her cheeks.

He reached up to gently smooth the tears from her cheeks. 'I think what it means,' he said huskily, 'is that your mother is a very complex and emotional woman that only your father truly understands.'

Her father... That conversation she had had with him last night, when he had told her that her mother loved her. This bedroom, the way it had been kept exactly as it was, surely had to mean that was true. But then why didn't her mother show that love. Why did she hold herself so aloof.

'Your mother isn't like you, Meg,' Jed soothed at her silence. 'Her emotions, whatever they might be, are kept firmly under control.'

Sonia claimed she wasn't like her, either. And yet this last couple of days Meg had discovered an emotion in both of them that she hadn't thought either was capable of. That emotion was love. Maybe they didn't in the open, giving way that Meg did, but they did love.

As she loved Jed, she suddenly saw with startling clarity. Not could. Not would. But did.

She loved the way he looked, his sense of humour, the fun he had with Scott but at the same time gentle with him, the understanding he showed her parents, the warm way he talked of his own family. But most of all, she loved him, his forcefulness when necessary, the way he had of making problems seem trivial by making her laugh at them, his intelligence.

The way he kissed her. She groaned low in her throat as he began to do exactly that.

He felt so good, tasted so good, that at that moment nothing else seemed to matter but him.

They were hungry for each other, lips and hands seeking, receiving a response that neither of them tried to deny, Meg's body turning to liquid fire as Jed touched her, and she knew he felt the same as she caressed the hardness of his back.

'You're so beautiful, Meg,' Jed rasped as he pushed her jumper aside. 'So small, perfect, and beautiful.' He groaned before lowering his head to capture one roused nipple between his lips, his hands caressing her waist and thighs.

She was on fire, needing him, all of him, wanting him so much.

A need he felt too if the heat of his body was anything to go by, his body hard with wanting her, that hardness demanding against her as he moved to lie above her.

She could feel his desire, felt her own response, her fingers feverishly entangled in the darkness of his hair as her neck arched in pleasure at the feel of his lips and tongue against her sensitized flesh, a pleasure that was building inside her, crying out for release.

A release she knew impossible as she opened her eyes to look up and see the lace canopy of her bed.

Not here, this couldn't happen here, amongst the memories of her childhood. She couldn't.

'Not here, Meg,' Jed raggedly echoed her thoughts as he began to kiss her lightly, soothingly, her neck, her cheek, her eyes, her nose, and finally her lips, his hands cupping each side of her face as he looked down at her. 'It isn't that I don't want you—I can hardly claim that at this moment, can I?' he added self-derisively, his body hard with need of her. 'I do want you, Meg, more than I would have believed possible.' He gave a pained frown. 'But this—this room…' He looked around at the trophies of her childhood.

'I feel the same way, Jed.' She reached up to touch the heat of his cheek, her smile rueful. 'It isn't right for me either. Perhaps—perhaps we should just go back downstairs and forget this ever happened?'

Forget?

He very much doubted he would ever forget the feel and taste of this woman.

But he didn't want to just make love to her for a short time, wanted days, nights, weeks with which to know her, to learn every pleasure they could give each other.

He fell back on the bed beside her, looking up at the lace canopy overhead, not knowing what to do about this woman, not knowing what to do with Meg Hamilton.

That he wanted her was in no doubt.

That she wanted him too was undeniable.

But what else did they both want? Everything? Or nothing? He couldn't go any further with this relationship until he knew the answer to that.

And he didn't think she could, either.

'We'll go downstairs.' He nodded, turning to look at her. 'But we won't forget it, Meg.' He touched one of her flushed cheeks, her eyes still dark with arousal. 'We'll talk later, hmm, when everyone else has gone to bed?'

She avoided meeting his gaze now. 'If that's what you want,' she replied noncommittally.

Jed put a hand beneath her chin to raise her face to his. 'We will talk, Meg,' he told her firmly. 'Really talk.'

He could see the slight panic in her expression he had seen earlier when she'd questioned him about his conversation with Sonia, frowning as he again wondered at the reason for it. Scott. Scott was the answer, he felt sure, but he had no idea in what way.

Or whether Meg would trust him enough, cared for him enough, to tell him.

Although none of that concern showed as they joined in the giving of presents from beneath the tree, Scott obviously enjoying his role as Father Christmas as his grandfather gave him each gift to bring in to the receiver.

This wasn't something they did in Jed's family, usually giving all the presents on Christmas morning. But this giving of the tree presents in the evening certainly carried on the anticipation of the day.

But if Meg had moved to sit as far away from Jed as possible, avoiding meeting his gaze too whenever he chanced to look her way, which was often, then Scott was certainly enjoying himself, receiving by far the most presents, several more from his mother, a ride-on tractor and trailer from his grandparents. David's doing, Jed felt sure as he watched the little boy's excitement; Lydia probably didn't have any idea of the hopes and dreams of a three-year-old boy.

Jed had even received a couple of gifts himself, a very good bottle of red wine from Sonia and Jeremy, and a first edition from David and Lydia. Again David, Jed felt sure as he warmly thanked them both.

Meg's gifts from her family, considering the rather frosty welcome she had received yesterday, were also surprising. She received a set of expensive oils from Sonia and Jeremy, and a beautiful cashmere sweater the same colour as her eyes from her parents.

'I took your father along to the shop for colour reference,' her mother explained distantly as Meg thanked them.

But there was one more small gift to be delivered, Scott's smile shy as he moved purposefully towards his grandmother.

Jed felt his own stomach muscles clench as he saw the suddenly strained look on Meg's face, the slight movement she made with her hand, as if she would like to stop Scott, that hand dropping back to her side as she decided against it.

Jed turned quickly back to look at Lydia, willing her, whatever the gift was Scott carried, not to hurt the little boy who was her grandson.

Lydia looked confused as Scott stood in front of her holding out the gaudily covered present, obviously clumsily wrapped by his own little hands. 'For me?' she said huskily, obviously completely unprepared for this. 'But I thought you and Mummy had given me a bottle of my favourite perfume?'

It was the most Lydia had spoken at one time to Scott since his arrival, and Jed could see that Meg was blinking back the tears, but the slight movement she again made to go to her son's side, in an effort of protection, Jed felt sure, was checked by her father's hand placed on her arm this time, David giving a slight shake of his head as Meg look up at him, his gaze firmly fixed on his wife.

Jed felt his own tension deepen, moving to stand at Meg's other side, knowing what she was feeling, dreading; if Lydia said or did anything to hurt Scott...

He would strangle the woman himself if she did, Jed decided fiercely.

'We did, Granma.' Scott nodded, his smile still shy.

'But we went to the shop and bought it; I made this for you myself.' He still held out the gift.

Lydia swallowed hard as she reached out to accept the gift, her face very pale beneath her make-up.

And the breath of every other person in the room was cautiously held, Jed realized as he looked at them in turn, Sonia's scarlet-tipped nails digging into Jeremy's sweater-covered arm as she clung to him, David's arm about Meg's waist now as she leant weakly against him.

Jed turned sharply back to look at Lydia, ready to leap forward and scoop Scott up in his arms if this all went terribly wrong.

'Mummy said she thought you already had one,' Scott began to chatter as his grandmother started to upwrap the present with shaking hands. 'But I made this at kindergarten for you. Do you like it?' he prompted with the innocent excitement of the very young as the unwrapped paper revealed a star painted in gold.

A slightly misshapen star, obviously made with very small, inexperienced fingers. But to Jed's eyes it was all the more beautiful for being that.

But would Lydia, a woman who never looked less than perfect herself, from her styled hair to her elegant shoes, be able to see that?

Jed felt Meg's hand slip into his, his fingers tightening reassuringly about hers as his gaze remained on Lydia.

No one moved, no one spoke as Lydia stared down at this personal gift from her grandson, the tension slowly building in that silence.

'It's for the tree.' Scott's voice began to wobble in a little uncertainty as he received no response to his gift.

Jed looked across the top of Meg's head at David, the other man deathly pale as he continued to look at his wife, but still he remained unmoving.

Couldn't he see—why didn't David do something? Anything to stop what was about to happen.

And then Lydia looked up, her face ravished with an emotion Jed had never seen there before, her eyes brimming with unshed tears.

'It's beautiful, Scott,' she gasped brokenly. 'So, so very beautiful.' The tears were falling heavily as she slid off her chair onto the carpeted floor, taking Scott in her arms to hug him as if she would never let him go. She looked up finally, attempting to smile reassuringly at her grandson. 'Let's you and I go and put it on the tree right now,' she encouraged as she stood up, the star in one hand as she reached out the other for Scott's.

'Can we?' The excitement was back in Scott's voice as he took his grandmother's hand. 'Can we really?'

'Of course we can.' His grandmother had eyes only for him as the two of them left the sitting-room together.

Jed looked quickly at Meg. There were tears on her cheeks too as she slipped beneath her father's arm, releasing Jed's hand to hurry after the unlikely pair.

Jed crossed the room in long strides, not sure what was going to happen next, only that it was going to be something momentous. And that he had to be there, for Meg, and for Scott, when it did.

CHAPTER TEN

MEG came to an abrupt halt in the cavernous hallway to stand back as her mother and Scott approached the tree together.

Her mother's tears just now had disturbed her a little. Never, in all her twenty-seven years, had she seen her mother cry, and she wasn't sure what they meant now either, only that her mother had voluntarily touched and spoken to Scott for the first time—more than touched him; she had hugged him as if he were the most precious thing in the world!

Of course, Meg already knew that he was, she just didn't know what to make of her mother thinking so too.

She turned slightly as she felt Jed's presence beside her, his narrowed gaze intent on her mother and Scott as they attempted to put the star as high up the tree as Scott held in Lydia's arms could reach.

'Do you think I should go and—?'

'No,' Jed breathed softly, turning briefly to give her a reassuring smile. 'The two of them seem to be doing just fine on their own.'

They were, yes, her mother, with Scott still in her

arms, standing back now to enjoy their handiwork, both their faces raised in wonder.

The star was no less misshapen than it had been when Scott had brought it home and insisted on wrapping it several days ago, and the glitter was no more evenly spread on its tips, and yet at that moment it was the most beautiful decoration on the tree.

'It's beautiful, Scott,' his grandmother told him chokingly. 'Absolutely perfect. Thank you so much.'

Meg felt her heart squeeze tight with emotion as Scott smiled shyly at his grandmother.

This had to be all right. It just had to be.

'What do you think, Meg? Jed?' her mother asked without turning to look at them. 'Doesn't Scott's star look absolutely wonderful on the tree?'

'Wonderful.' It was left to Jed to answer as the two of them strolled over to join them, Meg too stunned at her mother calling her Meg for the first time to be able to speak at all.

Even more so as her mother reached out and tightly clasped her hand. 'What a truly lovely son you have, Meg,' she said emotionally. 'You must be very proud of him.'

'We're all proud of him,' Meg's father echoed smilingly as he, Sonia and Jeremy came out to join them in the hallway.

'Oh, David,' her mother choked tearfully.

'My name is David too,' Scott told them excitedly as he was gathered up into his grandfather's arms. 'Sometimes, if Mummy gets cross with me, she says, "Scott David Hamilton, that was naughty!"'

The adults' laughter at this broke the tension, much

to Scott's confusion, and Meg's embarrassment. He hadn't realized he had said anything funny.

'I know, Daddy,' Sonia said laughingly. 'Let's all go and sing Christmas songs off-key around the piano, like we used to.'

Meg gave her twin a surprised look; Sonia had always hated those family singsongs at Christmas. Or, at least, she had always said that she did.

'What a wonderful idea,' their mother, another one who had always claimed she found the singing of Christmas carols tedious, agreed warmly. 'We'll start with "Jingle Bells",' she added firmly. 'I'm sure you know "Jingle Bells", don't you, Scott?' she queried as she led the way into the music room, Meg's father, Sonia and Jeremy following behind.

'What is going on?' Meg asked Jed, slightly bemused by this turn of events. And initiated by Scott giving his grandmother a gift Meg had tried to discourage him from bringing here, sure that her mother would be horrified by the imperfection that had made it all the more precious to Meg herself.

The fact that her mother seemed to feel the same way about it still stunned her.

'I have no idea,' Jed drawled, his hand light on her elbow as he turned her in the direction of the music room. 'But I should just enjoy it, if I were you.'

She did, the seven of them singing Christmas songs and carols for over an hour, her father playing the piano, the rest of them standing around it as they sang. To Meg's surprise, Jed had a rich baritone, which he put to good use.

But the embarrassment she felt every time she

looked at him was still acute; they had almost made love earlier this afternoon, and it was something she just couldn't forget.

Although Jed claimed he didn't want her to, that the two of them would talk later. Quite what that talk was going to entail—apart from the fact that any relationship between the two of them was going to be impractical and necessarily short-lived. As Jed had already pointed out, he lived wherever the fancy took him, and she was firmly rooted in London, by her work, and Scott. No, there could be no relationship between the two of them once they left here, and, as they both already knew, there could be no relationship between them here. Impasse.

But for the moment she had more surprises where her mother was concerned, Lydia insisting on coming down to the kitchen with them when it came time for Scott's tea. Much to Bessie Sykes surprise, Meg felt sure; the only time Lydia usually entered the kitchen was to discuss menus with her. Now she sat at the scarred and much-used wooden table encouraging Scott to eat his boiled egg and soldiers.

When her mother also came up to watch Scott enjoy his bath Meg felt she could contain her curiosity no longer. 'Mother, what—?'

'Not now, Meg darling,' her mother cut in softly. 'We'll get Scott to bed first, hmm, and then I think I would like to talk to all of you before dinner.'

That sounded rather ominous, but in the circumstances Meg had no choice but to acquiesce. Sitting on the side of her bed long after her mother had departed and Scott had fallen asleep, she wondered what her mother could possibly want to talk to all of them about.

But it was Christmas, after all, and perhaps a time for miracles.

'Everyone else is waiting downstairs.'

Once again Jed had come through the communicating doorway to her bedroom uninvited, but after this afternoon it would be churlish to deny him entry.

'What do you think is going on, Jed?' She gave a pained frown.

He shrugged. 'I think the thaw has probably set in in more ways than one.'

Her eyes widened before she got up and moved to the window. Jed was right—the snow was starting to melt as the temperature rose, green grass showing where the snow had already melted in patches.

Which meant Jed would be leaving soon.

But it was what she wanted, wasn't it? Jed gone, a return to her flat in London, so that she could get on with her life as she had before?

No, of course it wasn't what she wanted.

But what she wanted she knew she couldn't have, and if she had nothing else she would keep her pride.

She forced herself to smile as she turned to look at him. 'That's good news, isn't it?' she said brightly. 'You'll be able to leave in the morning now.'

'So will you,' he rasped, his eyes dark and unfathomable, his expression unreadable too.

'I'm not sure.' She shrugged. 'I may stay on another couple of days or so.' She hadn't really thought about what she was going to do after today, only intent on establishing that, just because Jed was leaving, it didn't mean she had to do so too.

Although staying on wasn't such a bad idea. Scott would love it, and her mother seemed different, since Scott had presented her with his handmade star, so perhaps she would give staying on some more thought.

It was going to be so awful when Jed got in the Range Rover and drove away.

So awful that for a moment Meg felt as if her knees were going to buckle beneath her.

He would return to the cottage, possibly even New York, and she would never see him again.

Her chest ached at the thought, her throat felt constricted, those tears that had seemed so close to the surface the last few days now blurring her vision.

'It's going to be okay, Meg,' Jed assured confidently, obviously misunderstanding the reason for those tears. 'I'm sure this talk with your mother is going to change everything.'

Perhaps that part of her life was finally going to make sense—she certainly hoped so. And until two days ago she would have been content—more than content—with that. But knowing Jed had changed all that. Now it felt, with his imminent departure, as if the bottom had dropped out of her world.

Well, it wouldn't be the first time.

And she had survived before; she would survive again.

She straightened determinedly. 'Yes, of course it is.' She nodded briskly, stepping away as Jed seemed far too close for comfort. For her control. If Jed should so much as touch her she might just break completely. And she was determined not to do that. 'If you would like to go downstairs, I'll join you all in a few minutes.'

He raised dark brows. 'You aren't going to change into that black dress again, are you?' he asked.

Her eyes widened. 'Why?' She hadn't intended to, had packed a red dress to wear this evening.

Jed shrugged. 'You look edible in that dress.' He grimaced wryly.

Meg felt her cheeks warm at the admission. 'No,' she assured him. 'I'm not wearing the black dress this evening.' The red dress, if anything, was even more figure-hugging than the black one.

'That's something, I suppose,' he drawled. 'Although I was wondering, as I'm not family—in fact, as we both know only too well, I'm actually a complete stranger—if it might not be better if I didn't join you all until later?'

His reluctance made sense, of course it did. Her family might not be aware of it, but he was really nothing but an innocent bystander—a reluctant one at that—dragged into their midst out of the snow.

But she would miss him there at her side, knew she had come to rely on his silent support over the last few days. Not a good idea, when usually she could rely on no one but herself.

Although she had a feeling, if she wanted, that might be about to change.

And she couldn't deny it would be wonderful to have the love of her family again.

Except that Jed was the man she loved.

She forced herself to give him a reassuring smile. 'Of course.' She nodded. 'I'll just explain to everyone that you're working; they're sure to understand.' It might also have the benefit of being true; she was sure Jed had been working on his book again this afternoon. 'Or perhaps you would like to go into the library and call your family?' She remembered her suggestion of earlier. 'I'm sure they would love to hear from you,' she encouraged at his continued silence.

She had been talking because of that silence, didn't understand why he had suddenly gone quiet; so far in their acquaintance she had never known Jed at a loss for words.

Perhaps it was that he would really rather leave now. The thaw was such that the main roads were sure to be clear enough to drive, and it was only ten miles or so to the cottage. Yes, maybe that was it. Jed just didn't know, with everything else that was happening, how to tell her he was leaving.

'You know, if you would like to go now, I'm sure that no one will mind,' she told him brightly, her heart squeezing painfully inside her chest just at the thought of it.

'Thanks, Meg,' he rasped harshly. 'That really makes me feel wanted.'

Wanted. She wanted him so badly she could barely breathe.

Although it seemed her remark had angered Jed. But then, nothing she seemed to say right now sounded in the least right to her, either.

'Oh, come on, Jed,' she attempted to tease. 'Admit it, you'll be glad to see the back of the Hamilton family.'

There was no answering smile on his face. 'It's certainly been different,' he allowed dryly.

'I'll bet it has.' This time her humour was genuine,

trying hard to imagine how she would have felt in his place, sitting quietly in the cottage minding his own business when someone drove into the side of that cottage, that someone turning out to be a single mother and her young son, offering, in desperation to regain that privacy, to drive them to the family home, only to become embroiled in the seething emotions of that family.

No wonder he wanted to leave.

'Time I got changed, I think,' she added firmly in an effort to hold back ready tears. 'Otherwise the family is likely to send out a search party. Too late!' She grimaced as a knock sounded softly on her bedroom door, her father entering after pausing briefly.

'We're all having champagne downstairs, if you would like to come down and join us?' he invited lightly, although the shrewd narrowing of his gaze told Meg he had picked up on the tension between Jed and herself.

'I haven't had time to change yet.'

'Oh, I shouldn't worry about that, Meg,' her father dismissed. 'It's only cold buffet for dinner, and I think we've all decided to stay exactly as we are.'

Her eyes widened at yet another change; this family always dressed for dinner.

'I believe Jed would like to stay up here and carry on with his writing.'

'Oh, no, that won't do.' Her father frowned. 'That won't do at all.' He looked steadily at the younger man.

Meg had no idea what silent words passed between the two men, only knowing that they did, Jed shrugging before announcing that he had changed his mind, that the champagne sounded inviting.

'But—'

'Leave the man alone, Meg; everyone is entitled to change their mind when there's champagne being served,' her father teased.

Except they all knew that wasn't the reason Jed had changed his mind.

And that it would only cause more embarrassment if Meg were to persist in the subject.

She gave Jed an apologetic look as they all went downstairs, receiving an encouraging smile in return, that ache in her chest only deepening at his silent support.

She hoped, for Jed's sake, if not her own, that he would be able to leave in the morning.

Jed put a hand lightly under Meg's arm and squeezed slightly as the two of them followed her father into the sitting-room where the rest of the family sat.

Meg had annoyed him earlier when she'd said he could leave now if he wanted to, but he held that annoyance in check, knowing that it wasn't his own emotions that were important just now.

But that didn't mean he wasn't still angry, or that Meg's obvious eagerness for him to leave hadn't hurt.

He followed her across the room as she chose to sit in a chair slightly away from the rest of the family, positioning himself at the side of her chair as David brought them both a glass of champagne.

'Come and sit over here, Meg,' her mother encouraged huskily, patting the space beside her on one of the two sofas in the room, Sonia and Jeremy sitting on the other one.

Jed hoped, as he and Meg moved closer into the family circle, Meg on the sofa, Jed sitting on the carpet beside her, that the fact that Lydia now called her daughter by the name she preferred had to mean something. He hoped, for Meg's and Scott's sakes, that it meant the frost between Lydia and her children was about to melt.

'First of all—' Lydia gave them all a shaky smile '—I would like to drink a toast to my wonderful husband, David, who is so much wiser and braver than me, the person responsible for us all spending this wonderful Christmas together. Thank you, David.' She held up her glass and drank, the rest of the family following her example with murmurs of 'Daddy' or 'David'. 'And to my two beautiful daughters,' Lydia continued emotionally. 'My lovely Sonia, so beautiful and accomplished. And Meg…'

Jed found himself holding his breath as he waited for what she had to say about her youngest daughter. In his eyes Meg was by far the most beautiful of Lydia's twin daughters, her inner beauty making her shine from within. But he still had no idea whether Lydia was able to see that.

'My lovely, lovely Meg.' Lydia turned to her daughter, eyes glowing with emotion. 'I'm so proud of you, Meg,' she continued huskily. 'Beautiful, warm, so filled with love, and such a wonderful mother to Scott, the sort of mother I should have been to my two daughters and was never able to be. To my two wonderful daughters.' She lifted up her glass in toast to them, the men in the room following her example.

Jed felt some of the tension ease from his shoulders, not knowing what was coming next, but more confident that it wasn't going to be anything that would hurt Meg.

Because he didn't want her hurt, happened to echo every sentiment that Lydia had just said about her. She was beautiful and warm, loved all her family in spite of their coldness towards her, and her love for her son was indisputable.

He only wished that she loved him in the same way.

But, despite what had happened between them earlier, her suggestion that he leave tonight instead of in the morning certainly didn't indicate as much.

But if Meg could be reunited with her family he would be happy for her, would have plenty of time to lick his own wounds once he was back at the cottage.

'I have one last toast I would like to make,' Lydia continued shakily, her hand reaching out to tightly grip David's as he stood supportively at her side. 'David and I had a long talk earlier, and decided to tell you all about—'

'It's all right, Lydia, I'll do it,' David said huskily. 'To our dearly loved and remembered son, James David.'

Jed felt Meg's start of surprise, a quick glance at Sonia's pale face telling him that she was as stunned by this announcement as Meg obviously was.

David and Lydia had a son? Had had a son, Jed realized as he saw the naked emotion on Lydia's face.

'James David.' Lydia sipped her champagne, not looking at any of them now but at her hand, tightly clasped within David's.

'Mummy, I don't understand,' Sonia was the one to prompt frowningly.

Lydia looked across at her daughter, her eyes swimming with unshed tears. 'We should have told you and Meg this years ago, your father wanted to, but I—I begged him not to.' She drew in a sharp breath. 'Two years before you and Meg were born your father and I had a son, a beautiful little boy, called James David, but he—he only lived for a week,' she explained emotionally. 'He was born prematurely, and, although the doctors did everything they could, he—he died.'

And that the pain of that loss was still raw within this previously emotionally aloof woman was obvious to Jed.

He couldn't even begin to imagine what it must be like to have, and then lose, a child. It must be awful, totally beyond imagination, totally beyond comprehension.

And he could see by the pain on Meg's face that she more than understood those emotions. Who better, when she had a young son of her own?

Lydia drew in another deep breath, straightening slightly. 'When I found out over a year later that I was pregnant again, with twins this time, I…I didn't think I could cope, couldn't bear it if I had to go through the pain of that loss again. And when our two daughters were born, again prematurely, weighing no more than three pounds each, my emotions simply shut down. Self-preservation, I think,' she added self-derisively.

Jed reached out and tightly clasped Meg's hand in his as he saw how badly she was shaking.

And no wonder. To learn that you had a brother, but he had died at only a week old, must be mind-numbing.

But for Lydia, he now realized, it had been so traumatic that she had been afraid to love her own daughters, too afraid that if she did she might lose them.

'To make matters worse, I was sent home, but because you were so small the two of you were kept in hospital for weeks,' Lydia continued softly. 'It was—I can't even begin to describe my feelings then. Again I came home without a baby in my arms, and although we spent every day at the hospital with you, it wasn't the same.' She shook her head, very pale.

The bonding, so necessary to this already bereft woman, simply hadn't taken place, Jed realized.

'By the time you were allowed home, I was...I wasn't very well, and your father had to do everything for you,' Lydia continued evenly, her thoughts far away now, back in the nightmare her life must have seemed then. 'But, of course, that couldn't continue, he had to return to work, and I—I was simply too ill by that time to care for you. We engaged a nanny, and I—I withdrew from you even more. It wasn't that I didn't love you, never that, I just...'

'Oh, Mummy.' Meg choked, releasing her hand from Jed's to turn to her mother, her arms going around her almost protectively. 'How awful for you. How absolutely awful.'

Sonia crossed the room swiftly, joining in the hug, the men left to look on helplessly, all of them knowing instinctively that this moment was for these three beautiful women only.

'You have to believe that I love you,' Lydia sobbed emotionally. 'That I've always loved you. I've just been too afraid to show it, too cowardly.'

'Never that,' Meg assured her firmly. 'You're the least cowardly woman I know.'

Lydia reached out and gently touched her cheek. 'You were such beautiful babies, such lovely children, but at the back of my mind was always the fear that— It's no excuse.' She shook her head with self-disgust. 'David, my darling David, decided after his heart attack that things had to change, that they would change, but even then I continued to fight him. I've been so wrong,' she choked.

'It's because of the way I've been that we aren't a closer family, that Meg, alone and so afraid when she knew she was expecting Scott, chose to keep his birth a secret for almost six months, and even after that stayed away from us all this time rather than let us help her. For that I will never forgive myself.'

Meg had chosen not to come to her parents when she had had Scott? That wasn't the impression he had got— that Meg had deliberately given him. But why had Meg stayed away. For all that Lydia had been emotionally distant, it seemed that they had offered to help her.

'If your father hadn't insisted on inviting you here for Christmas, then we would probably still be estranged.' Lydia frowned. 'All these years David has stood by and watched, loving me, loving his daughters, but not knowing how to bring us all together. It took nearly losing him a few weeks ago to bring me even partially to my senses, and even then I still held you both at a distance when you got here. But Scott, darling Scott—' her voice quivered with emotion '—although I tried to fight it, to fight loving him, was the one to bring all my barriers crashing down around my ears.' She gave a shaky smile. 'He is so beautiful, so like I imagined James would look at that age.' She broke off, too emotional to go on.

Jed felt an uncomfortable witness to this woman's heartache, and he could see by Jeremy's expression that he felt the same intrusion. This moment belonged to these three women alone.

And David, he acknowledged as Lydia turned to include him in their circle, the four of them now hugging each other so tightly there was no room for anyone or anything else.

'It's going to be so different now. I'm going to be so different. If you will let me...?' Lydia looked at them all uncertainly.

'Well, of course we'll let you,' Meg assured her with a shaky laugh. 'You're our mother, for goodness' sake.'

'Of course you are.' Sonia hugged Lydia before sitting back. 'But as this is a time for sharing secrets—'

'Sonia.' Meg cut her off sharply as she looked across at her sister.

'It's okay, Meg,' Sonia assured huskily. 'I've spoken to Jeremy, and—'

'It is not okay,' Meg rasped angrily as she stood up abruptly, her eyes deeply green in the paleness of her face.

Sonia sighed. 'Meg, I have to.'

'No, you don't.' Meg glared down at her twin, her hands tightly clenched at her sides. 'We made a pact, you and I, a pact I've kept, and I will not let you do this.'

Jed stared at the two women, as Lydia and David were now doing too, wondering what pact they could possibly be talking about. Whatever it was, Meg looked ready to do physical damage to keep it.

Sonia reached out an appealing hand. 'Meg, darling.'

'No.' Meg stepped away from that hand, breathing hard in her agitation. 'If you do this, Sonia, I swear I will never, ever forgive you.'

Sonia was as pale as her twin now, her hand dropping limply back to her side. 'I don't want to hurt you, Meg.'

'Don't you?' Meg scorned. 'Then you have a very strange way of showing it.'

'But it's all right, Meg,' Sonia insisted firmly. 'I've explained to Jeremy, and he understands.'

'I don't care whether he understands or not.' Meg was shaking with angry emotion. 'I don't understand. Do you hear me? I will never forgive you for this. Never.' She turned and almost ran from the room.

Leaving a stunned silence in her wake.

Jed was the first to move, getting abruptly to his feet, his expression grim as he quickly followed Meg from the room, having no idea what was going on, only knowing that Meg was in pain and he needed to go to her.

CHAPTER ELEVEN

MEG was quickly throwing her things into a bag when she sensed Jed had entered the bedroom, not bothering to turn and look at him, only knowing she had to get away from here. Had to call a taxi, wake Scott up, and get as far away from here as she possibly could.

Never to return.

Her hands clenched on the jumper she had been about to throw into her bag, her pain a physical thing.

To have finally made her peace with her mother, to understand her at last, had been something she had thought would never happen.

But what Sonia was about to do made any thought of a family reconciliation impossible.

'Meg, what's going on?' Jed queried softly from behind her.

What was going on? Sonia was about to shatter Meg's life into a thousand pieces, that was what was going on.

'Meg?'

'Will you just leave me alone?' She turned on him fiercely, two bright wings of angry colour in her cheeks.

He frowned darkly. 'I'm trying to understand.'

'Why?' she challenged scathingly. 'You're leaving in the morning, Jed, so why do you need to understand anything about this dysfunctional family?'

He flinched as she threw his own phrase back in his face. 'I asked you this once before: what secret do you and Sonia share that is so big it pushes the two of you apart, and you have chosen to estrange yourself from your own family because of it?'

She glared at him. 'I don't believe that is any of your business.'

'I'm making it my business,' he came back tautly.

'And I'm refusing to answer you.' she came back challengingly.

Jed became suddenly still. 'Why?' he looked at her searchingly.

'It has something to do with Scott, doesn't it?' he added with soft shrewdness.

Meg felt her face go paler even as she refused to drop her gaze from his. She had seen that speculation in his gaze earlier today as he'd looked at Scott, had managed to divert his attention then, and had no intention of satisfying his curiosity now, either.

'Did you and Sonia argue about Scott's father—is that it?' He frowned.

Meg gave him a confused look. 'What?'

Jed frowned. 'Were you involved with him and then found out that Sonia had been involved with him too—?' He broke off as Meg began to laugh. 'I'm trying to make sense of this; what the hell is so funny?' His frown deepened darkly.

Nothing. There was absolutely nothing about this

situation that was in the least funny. But Jed was so far off the mark with his speculation that it seemed funny.

Her laughter was hysteria rather than amusement, tears falling down her cheeks at the same time as she laughed.

'Let's go through to the other bedroom,' Jed muttered as Scott moved restlessly in his sleep, taking hold of Meg's arm before she had time to protest and pulling her into the adjoining bedroom, closing the door softly behind him.

Meg's tears were falling in earnest now, hot, scalding tears that burned her cheeks, her anger turning to despair.

How could Sonia do this to her? How could she just think she could tell Jeremy the truth and everything would be all right?

Because it wouldn't. There was no way Meg would give up without a fight. And it would be a fight that would rip this family apart like never before.

'Tell me, Meg,' Jed urged forcefully as he shook her slightly. 'For God's sake, tell me.'

She shook her head. 'I can't,' she choked. 'I promised that I wouldn't.'

'A promise Sonia is no longer going to keep,' he reminded softly.

Meg looked up at him, pain blinding her. 'How could she do this?' She shook her head dazedly. 'How can she even think about…about…' She sat down heavily on the bed, her face buried in her hands as the sobs racked her body.

'Meg, if you don't tell me what's going on—' Jed sat down beside her, his hands on her shoulders '—if you don't tell me then I swear I will go back downstairs and demand the truth from Sonia.'

She shook her head as she looked up at him, emotional exhaustion etched on her face.

'Meg, please.' Jed's hands fell from her shoulders. 'How can I help you if I don't know what's going on?'

'You can't help me.' She shook her head. 'No one can,' she added dully. 'And why would you even want to?' She gave a humourless smile. 'We mean nothing to you.'

'You mean something to me,' he cut in harshly. 'You and Scott both mean something to me. And if someone is trying to hurt you, then I—'

'You, what?' Meg cut in dismissively. 'You may be the rich and famous Jerrod Cole, but no amount of money can make this right.'

He stood up abruptly, looking down at her with narrowed eyes. 'That's it, I've had it,' he rasped. 'I'm going downstairs to talk to Sonia. I somehow don't think she will be as reluctant as you are to tell me the truth,' he added scathingly.

Meg watched him as he strode angrily to the door, her heart constricting as she realized she didn't want him to go, that she couldn't bear it if he left her now.

'Scott isn't my son,' she burst out emotionally, icily still as Jed slowly turned to face her. 'Scott isn't my son,' she repeated brokenly.

Jed stared across at her, unspeaking, unmoving, his expression unreadable, too.

Giving her no indication as to how he had reacted to her stark announcement.

Meg stood up restlessly, no longer looking at Jed as she began to speak again. 'Sonia had just attained her certificate to practise law, became involved with one of the junior partners in the law firm who had taken her on. A married junior partner, his wife the daughter of the senior partner,' she added dully. 'I'm sure you can guess what happened next.'

'Sonia found out she was pregnant,' Jed rasped.

'Yes,' Meg sighed. 'The two of us were sharing a flat in London at the time, sharing expenses, and when Sonia told me about the baby, that she didn't intend having it, I was horrified.' She swallowed hard. 'I persuaded her to keep the baby, told her that I would help her, that she wouldn't be alone, was convinced that once it was born she would love the baby and want to keep it.'

'But she didn't,' he murmured softly.

Meg turned away, vividly remembering the night at the hospital when Scott had been born, the way her sister had turned away from him, refusing even to hold him, Meg the one to take the newborn baby into her arms, a feeling of absolute love overwhelming her as she'd looked down at him.

But still she had been convinced that Sonia would change her mind, that it had been just a question of getting over the shock of Scott's birth, that in time her sister would grow to love her beautiful son, as Meg already had.

It hadn't happened. Scott had been given in to Meg's care when the two had been discharged from hospital, her sister resuming her job, with another law firm, and her social life, as if Scott hadn't existed. Within six months she had announced that she had met Jeremy and intended marrying him.

Leaving the question of Scott's future in the balance.

Meg hadn't carried Scott inside her, hadn't given

birth to him, but in every other way there was she had been his mother, loved him and cherished him, cared for him, played with him, laughed with him. And there had been a lot of laughter, her love for him absolute.

Sonia's announcement that she intended getting married had thrown Meg into a complete panic at the thought of losing this beautiful child.

But she needn't have worried, because Sonia had assured her she wouldn't be taking Scott with her, that Meg could keep him if she wanted to. But only if she promised never to tell anyone Scott wasn't her own.

And she never had. Had chosen to distance herself from her parents because she didn't want to lie to them, her relationship with Sonia these last three years strained at best, neither of them ever wanting anyone else to know who Scott's mother really was. Sonia because she was afraid she might lose Jeremy if he knew the truth, and Meg because she might lose Scott.

But Meg hadn't cared about any of the sacrifices she had made. Because Scott was her son. In every way that mattered, he was hers.

And she wasn't about to give him up now just because Sonia had had a belated attack of conscience.

'No, she didn't,' Meg confirmed woodenly. 'And she isn't going to take him away from me now.'

Jed's eyes narrowed. 'You think that's what she wants to do?'

Her brows rose. 'Don't you?'

'No, I don't,' he said after a brief moment of thought.

Meg gave a pained frown. 'But you heard her, she's discussed it with Jeremy.'

'She said she had told Jeremy about Scott,' Jed corrected firmly. 'Not that she wanted to take him away from you. Besides, do you really think your parents would just stand idly by while she did that to you and Scott?' he reasoned.

'But...' He was right. Jed was right, Sonia hadn't said anything about wanting Scott, only that she had told Jeremy the truth about him.

As she had just told Jed. Although it was difficult to gauge his reaction.

If he had one. After all, he would be leaving himself soon, much relieved to get away from this complicated family, she suspected.

And who could blame him?

But could he possibly be right about Sonia not wanting to take Scott away from her...?

There was only one way to find out.

Jed watched the emotions flickering across Meg's face before she rose and left the bedroom. Jed remained unmoving for several long seconds, still slightly dazed himself by what she had just told him.

What sort of woman was she, that she could take her sister's unwanted newborn son as her own?

She was the woman he loved, he acknowledged achingly. More than ever, now that he knew what she had done, the sacrifices she had made to keep Scott for her own. And the fact was, he knew that she didn't regret any of it, that if the circumstances were presented to her she would do it all over again.

She was an amazing woman.

Totally unselfish.

Totally adorable.

And he wanted to gather her up in his arms, to love, cherish and protect her, and never let her go, ever again.

Weren't they the words to the marriage ceremony?

Close enough, he realized, slightly stunned. Because that was what he wanted with Meg. Marriage. Nothing less would do.

And now was not the time to tell her that.

In fact, it couldn't have been a worse time, he acknowledged. That was him, Jed Cole, the master of bad timing.

He wanted to go downstairs right now, gather her up in his arms, and make everything right for her. But he stopped himself from doing that, knew that he didn't have the right to do that, that Meg hadn't given him that right.

That maybe she never would.

'Jed?'

He turned to see David Hamilton standing in the bedroom doorway, his handsome face lined with strain. 'Meg?' he questioned gruffly.

David gave a rueful smile. 'Jeremy and I left Meg, Sonia and their mother discussing the plans for Meg to formally adopt Scott.'

Jed raised his eyes briefly heavenwards, breathing a heavy sigh of relief as he turned back to the older man. 'Your youngest daughter is an amazing woman.'

'Isn't she?' David nodded emotionally. 'But in her own way, Sonia is just as amazing,' he said quietly. 'To know, to accept, that you can't be the mother that is needed, necessary, and to give that child up to someone who is, is very brave indeed.'

Was it? Perhaps, Jed allowed. Sonia had been twenty-three when Scott was born, abandoned in her relationship, possibly frightened of what the future might hold for her as a single mother.

Although that didn't change the fact that Meg hadn't hesitated to go through that herself for a child who wasn't actually her own.

'Yes.' David seemed to read some of his thoughts. 'But twins are a strange entity, are joined in a way that other siblings are not,' he continued frowningly. 'In some ways, Scott was always Meg's as much as he was Sonia's. Do you understand what I'm saying or does it all sound like nonsense?' He frowned at Jed.

Yes, he did understand what David was saying, and in some way that might be true. It was a little too deep for Jed to think about right now, Meg his only concern. 'Is she going to be all right, do you think?'

'Oh, yes,' the older man assured him confidently. 'Lydia and I will make sure of that. Scott has become very precious to all of us, and he will remain with his mother.'

Jed didn't doubt that the older man would keep his word, or that Lydia would ensure that he did. She surely knew better than anyone what it was like to lose a child you loved.

But that didn't stop Jed from pacing the bedroom restlessly as he waited for Meg to come back upstairs, needing to talk to her again, if only to hear from her own lips that she was going to be okay.

As it was she was the one to knock on his bedroom door, her expression somewhat shamefaced when he opened the door to her.

She grimaced. 'I believe I owe you an apology for some of the things I said to you earlier.' She sighed. 'They were unnecessary, and my only excuse—'

'Meg, I don't give a damn about any of the things you said to me earlier. And will you stop talking to me like a polite stranger?' he added impatiently, pulling her into his bedroom and firmly closing the door behind her. 'We may once have been strangers, although I don't believe that is any longer true, but we have certainly never been polite to each other,' he added ruefully.

'Oh, now I'm sure that isn't true,' Meg came back. 'We must have been polite to each other when we first met. No, perhaps not,' she added teasingly as she obviously remembered the circumstances of that first meeting.

Jed lightly cupped the sides of her face with his hands, looking down at her intently. 'Your father said… is everything all right now?' he probed huskily.

'Yes.' Her face lit up with joy. 'I'm going to adopt Scott and then he can never be taken away from me.'

Jed shook his head as he looked down at her. 'Do you know—do you have any idea—? My God, Meg.' His arms moved about her as he pulled her tightly against him. 'You are the most amazing woman I have ever met,' he told her forcefully as he buried his face in the perfumed darkness of her hair. 'I can't think of another woman I know who would have done what you did.' He groaned. 'And I want… I want…'

'Yes?' she prompted huskily as he seemed lost for words.

Because he was lost for words, had no idea how to tell this beautiful and wonderful woman, when they had only known each other three days, that he loved her, wanted to marry her, wanted her and Scott with him for all time.

CHAPTER TWELVE

NEVER in their acquaintance had Meg ever known Jed at a loss for words.

As he still seemed lost.

But she was already so happy, felt as if a great weight had been lifted from her shoulders now that the truth about Scott had finally been told and Sonia had agreed to Meg formally adopting him as her own.

It was like a dream come true for her, after years of worrying that Sonia might change her mind at any moment and decide she wanted Scott back after all. Now, that fear taken away, she felt as if she might conquer the world, or, at least, get Jed to talk to her.

'Tell me, what is it you want, Jed?' she questioned confidently.

'You,' he told her purposefully. 'I want you, Meg Hamilton.'

She wanted him too, even more than she had this afternoon, if that were possible, the truth seeming to have liberated her in more ways than one.

Okay, so he was a world-famous author, had homes all over the globe, but that didn't mean they couldn't...

Oh, goodness, he was a world-famous author with homes all over the world.

'I have no idea what you're thinking, Meg—' his arms tightened about her, his expression determined '—but I want you to know my intentions are strictly honourable.'

Strictly honourable. What did that mean?

'As in marriage,' he continued firmly. 'As in allowing me to be Scott's father. As in being my wife for the next thousand years. As in—'

'Jed, what are you talking about?' She gasped, confused, this the last thing she had expected.

'I want to marry you, Meg Hamilton. I love you, I want you, and I need you,' he said huskily. 'I realize you can't feel that way about me yet, but if you give me a chance, I'll do everything in my power to ensure that you do. I love you, Meg, and I'm not leaving here without you.' His expression was grim.

Meg stared at him. Jed loved her.

She hadn't believed that possible, had been so sure he would leave in the morning and she would never see him again. And now, now he was offering her the sun, the moon, and the stars all rolled into one, in his love for her.

Jed gave a shake of his head. 'I told myself from the beginning that I wouldn't get involved. I should have known by the mere fact that I had to tell myself that that it was exactly what I was going to do,' he muttered self-disgustedly. 'I know I was a grouch when we first met, I always am if my writing isn't going well, which it most certainly wasn't, but I'm not usually like that. Well, I am sometimes, but I'll try not to be, I really will.'

'Jed, you were perfectly entitled to feel grouchy

when we first met; I had just driven into your cottage,' Meg cut in, huskily, her happiness such now that she thought she might burst with it. Jed loved her.

'My editor's cottage,' he corrected. 'And I shouldn't have been so bad-tempered; you were a young woman and her son stranded in the snow.' He gave a self-disgusted shake of his head. 'But you frightened the hell out of me—not when you drove into the cottage,' he dismissed impatiently as she winced. 'You, you were what frightened me. I had never before desired a woman while at the same time wanting to protect her, from myself, if necessary.'

This really was all too wonderful to be true.

'And I know you've told me that you don't want a permanent relationship.'

'That was because of Scott. Any man I loved and who loved me would have to be told the truth about Scott,' she explained as he frowned. 'And it must surely be difficult enough taking on another man's child; I can't see any man wanting to take on a child who doesn't even belong to his wife.'

Jed's expression softened. 'You're looking at him. And I wouldn't be taking on Scott, I would be his father, as you are his mother. What can I say, Meg? I love the kid almost as much as I love you.'

She could see that he did, and that he had no doubts about that love.

'Jed—' she reached up to touch the hardness of his cheek '—I don't think of you as a grouch, I think of you as an amazingly kind man who has been there for me every time I needed him these last three days.'

'I don't want your gratitude, damn it.' He broke off,

giving a self-derisive grimace. 'The grouchiness may need a little working on,' he admitted ruefully.

Meg laughed huskily, her gaze steadily meeting his. 'Don't work on it too hard—I may not recognize you if you do. Because the truth is, Jed, I love you. I love you just the way you are.'

He became suddenly still, looking down at her uncertainly. 'This isn't another one of those "I cannot tell a lie" things, is it?'

'No,' she laughed again. 'We haven't known each other very long.'

'Time has nothing to do with it,' he told her firmly. 'I began to fall in love with you the moment I opened that car door in the snowstorm and saw you.'

She had probably done exactly the same thing, despite the fact that Scott had thought Jed was a bear.

Jed shook his head. 'I've been fighting against the emotion ever since, and—Meg, did you just say that you love me?' He looked slightly dazed as that realization hit him.

'I did.' She laughed softly. 'I love you, Jed,' she told him again, enjoying the freedom of being able to say those words. 'I love you, I want you, I need you,' she told him intensely. 'The thought of your leaving in the morning, of never seeing you again, has been making me totally miserable,' she admitted shakily.

'And I was furious because you couldn't seem to get rid of me fast enough.'

She looked up at him, her eyes a clear, unwavering green. 'That was my pride talking. No more misunderstandings, Jed,' she promised him.

His arms tightened around her, holding her close against him. 'Will you marry me, Meg? Will you and Scott marry me?'

'Yes,' she choked emotionally, knowing he offered her earth's version of paradise. 'Oh, yes, Jed.'

'Then I guess we did have a Christmas gift for each other, after all,' he murmured throatily, his lips only centimetres away from her own. 'Each other,' he groaned as his mouth claimed hers.

Meg had no doubts that he was the other half of her, her love, her soul mate, the person she wanted to spend the rest of her life with.

Jed held the telephone receiver to his ear, his other arm firmly around Meg as she lay curled against him in the library chair.

She was so small and beautiful, so warm and loving.

'Hi, Mom?' he prompted as his call was answered, barely able to hear his mother over the talk and laughter he could hear in the background. 'Mom, I just called to wish you all a Happy Christmas, and to tell you that I'm bringing my fiancée to meet you in a couple of days.' He held the receiver away from his ear as his mother screamed excitedly on the other end of the line.

Meg.

His fiancée. Soon to be his wife.

It couldn't happen soon enough as far as he was concerned, wanting Meg and Scott with him for all time, knowing with utter certainty that was what they would have together: for ever.

'I only have one condition to this marriage.' Jed turned to kiss Meg once he had ended the call to his family.

'We've only been engaged for an hour and you're making conditions already?' She looked up at him teasingly, eyes bright with love, her family having warmly accepted their announcement that they were to marry each other, another bottle of champagne opened as they had toasted the happy couple.

He nodded unrepentantly. 'Next Christmas we spend with my family. I don't care if we have to fly all your family over to join us, but next Christmas we spend on the farm.'

'Scott is going to love your parents' farm.' She smiled indulgently.

'So am I.' Jed grinned. 'We don't need to dress for dinner there. In fact, we may not even come down for dinner at all,' he added sensuously.

Meg laughed up at him. 'I don't care where we are, Jed, as long as we're together.'

Together.

After years of enjoying his solitude, of revelling in it, he now wanted to spend every waking hour and night with this woman, to love her, and to be loved.

The best gift of all.

THE ITALIAN BILLIONAIRE'S CHRISTMAS MIRACLE

CATHERINE SPENCER

Some people know practically from birth that they're going to be writers. **Catherine Spencer** wasn't one of them. Her first idea was to be a nun, which was clearly never going to work! A series of other choices followed. She considered becoming a veterinarian (but lacked the emotional stamina to deal with sick and injured animals), a hairdresser (until she overheated a curling iron and singed the hair off the top of her best friend's head, the day before her friend's first date), and a nurse (but that meant emptying bedpans!). As a last resort, she became a high-school English teacher, and loved it.

Eventually, she married, had four children and always, always a dog or two or three. How can a house become a home without a dog? In time, the children grew up and moved out on their own and she returned to teaching. But a middle-aged restlessness overtook her and she looked for a change of career.

What's an English teacher's area of expertise? Well, novels, among other things, and moody, brooding, unforgettable heroes: Heathcliff, Edward Fairfax Rochester, Romeo, Rhett Butler. Then there's that picky business of knowing how to punctuate and spell, and all those rules of grammar. They all pointed her in the same direction: toward breaking the rules every chance she got and creating her own moody, brooding, unforgettable heroes. And that's where she happily resides now—in Mills & Boon® novels, of course.

CHAPTER ONE

DOMENICO didn't usually involve himself with tourists. They were not, as a rule, vitally concerned with the wine industry except as it applied to their drinking habits. That morning, though, he happened to be crossing the yard to his office at the rear of the main building just as the latest batch of visitors filed from the vineyard toward the public section at the front. All but one headed straight for the tasting room. *She* remained outside, earnestly questioning his uncle Bruno who, at almost sixty, had forgotten more about viticulture than Domenico himself ever hoped to learn.

Although professional enough not to dismiss any question, regardless of how trivial it might be, Bruno was not one to suffer fools gladly. That he appeared as engrossed in the conversation as this visitor, was unusual enough for Domenico to stop and observe.

Tall, slender and rather plain, the woman looked to be in her mid-twenties. And, he surmised, noting the slightly pink tint to her fair skin, newly arrived in Sardinia and not yet acclimatized to the sun. Unless she wanted to spend the rest of her holiday in bed with sunstroke, she should be wearing a hat. Tying up her hair in a careless ponytail that left her nape exposed was asking for trouble.

His uncle must have thought so, too, because he guided her to a bench set in the shade of a nearby oleander. More curious by the second, Domenico lingered just within earshot.

Catching sight of him, Bruno waved him over. "This is the man you talk with," he told the woman. "My nephew, first he speaks the good English to make better sense for you. More important, what he does not know about growing grapes and turning them into fine wine, it is not worth knowing."

"And my uncle never exaggerates," Domenico said, smiling at the woman. "Allow me to introduce myself, *signorina*."

She looked up and, for a moment, his usual urbanity deserted him. Suddenly bereft of speech, he found himself staring like a goatherd.

She was not beautiful, no. At least, not in the conventional sense. Her clothes were modest: a denim knee-length skirt, white short-sleeved cotton blouse and flat-heeled sandals. Her hair, though shiny as glass, was a nondescript brown, her hips narrow as a boy's, her breasts small. Nothing like the annoyingly persistent Ortensia Costanza, with her vibrantly dramatic good looks and ripe curves. If Ortensia exemplified blatant female sexuality at its most hungry, this delicate creature fell at the other end of the spectrum and almost shied away from him.

She was, he decided, the kind of woman a man could easily overlook—until he gazed into her large, lovely eyes, and found himself drowning in their luminous gray depths.

Recovering himself, he continued, "I'm Domenico Silvaggio d'Avalos. How may I help you?"

She rose from the bench with lithe grace, and offered her hand. Small and fine-boned, it was almost swallowed up by his. "Arlene Russell," she replied, her voice pleasantly modulated. "And if you can spare me half an hour, I'd love to pick your brain."

"You're interested in the wine industry?"

"More than interested." She allowed herself a quick, almost rueful smile. "I recently came into possession of a vineyard, you see, but it's in rather sad shape, and I need some advice on how to go about restoring it."

Smiling himself, he said, "You surely don't think that is something that can be dealt with in a few words, *signorina*?"

"Not in the least. But I'm committed to doing whatever I have to, to make a success of it, and since I have to start somewhere, what better place than here, where even a novice like me can recognize expertise when she sees it?"

"Spend an hour with the girl," his uncle muttered, reverting to Sardu, the language most often spoken on the island. "She is thirsty as a sponge for information, unlike those others whose only thirst is for the wine tastings they're now enjoying at our expense."

"I can't spare the time."

"Yes, you can spare the time! Invite her to lunch."

Her glance flitted between the two men. Although clearly not understanding their exchange, she correctly identified the irritation Domenico now showed on his face.

Her own mirroring utter disappointment, she murmured, "Please forgive me, Signor Silvaggio d'Avalos. I'm afraid I'm being very thoughtless and asking far too much of you." Then turning to his uncle, she rallied another smile. "Thank you for taking the time to speak with me, *signor*. You've been very kind."

As opposed to me, who's behaving like a world-class boor, Domenico thought, an unwelcome shaft of sympathy at her obvious dejection piercing his annoyance. "As it happens," he heard himself saying before he could change his mind, "I can spare you an hour or so before my afternoon appointments. I won't promise to address all your concerns in that time, but at least I can direct you to someone who will."

She wasn't deceived by his belated gallantry. Picking up the camera and notebook she'd left on the bench, she replied, "That's quite all right, *signor*. You've made it plain you have better things to do."

"I have to eat," he said, sizing up her too-slender length, "and from the looks of it, so do you. I suggest we make the most of the opportunity to kill two birds with one stone."

Although her pride struggled to fling his invitation back in his face, practicality overcame it. "Then I thank you again," she said stiffly. "I'm most grateful."

He took her elbow and turned her toward the Jeep parked next to the winery's huge rear double doors through which, soon, the harvested grapes would be brought for crushing. If she was nervous about hopping into a vehicle with a stranger, she hid it well, asking only, "Where are we going?"

"To my house, which lies a good five kilometers farther along the coast from here."

"Well, now I really feel I'm imposing! I assumed we'd eat in the winery's bistro."

"That is for the tourists."

"Which is what I am."

He put the Jeep in gear and started off along the paved road leading to his estate. "No, *signorina*. Today, you are my guest."

He was a master of understatement, Arlene decided.

She'd learned from the tourist brochures she'd collected that Vigna Silvaggio d'Avalos, a family-owned vineyard and winery going back three generations, was one of the best in Sardinia and that it boasted a prime location on the coast at the northern tip of the island, just west of Santa Teresa Gallura.

The elaborate coat of arms adorning the wrought-iron gates at the estate's entrance hadn't really surprised her. It, as well as the building whose handsome facade housed a state-of-the-art winery, tasting room, shop and garden bistro, were more or less what she expected of an operation touted as producing "internationally acclaimed wines of impeccable quality."

But when he drove through a second set of wrought-iron gates, and followed a long, winding driveway past what appeared to be private residences set in spacious grounds, to a pale stucco building perched above the beach, she was hard-pressed not to behave like the gauche tourist he undoubtedly took her to be, and stare open-mouthed. What he so casually referred to merely as his "house" struck her as being nothing less than palatial.

Screened from the others in the compound by an acre or more of gardens planted with lush, flowering vegetation, it rose from the landscape in a series of elegant angles and curves designed to take full advantage of the view. To the one side lay the breathtaking Smerelda Coast; to the other, acres of vineyards climbed up the hillside.

Escorting her through the main entrance hall to a wide covered veranda below which the sea shone green as the emerald for which it was so aptly named, he indicated a group of wicker armchairs upholstered with deep, comfortable cushions. "Have a seat and excuse me a moment while I take care of lunch."

"Please don't go to a lot of trouble," she protested, well aware that she'd already put him out enough for one day.

He smiled and retrieved a remote phone from its cradle on a side table. "It is no trouble. I'll order something to be brought down from the main house."

Well, of course he will, idiot! she reproached herself, reeling a little from the impact of that smile. Had she really imagined he'd disappear into the kitchen, don an apron and whip up something delectable with his own two hands? And did he have to be so unapologetically gorgeous that she could hardly think straight? Tall and dark, she might have expected and managed to deal with, but his startlingly blue eyes lent added allure to a face already blessed with more masculine beauty than any one man deserved.

After a brief conversation, he replaced the phone and busied himself at a built-in bar. "There, it is done. What would you like to drink?"

"Something long and cool, please," she said, fanning herself against a heat which wasn't altogether the fault of the weather.

He dropped ice into two tall crystal goblets, half-filled them with white wine he took from the bar refrigerator, and topped them off with a squirt of soda. "Vermentino made from our own grapes," he remarked, taking a seat beside her and clinking the rim of his glass gently against hers. "Refreshing and not too potent. So, Signorina Russell, how did you come by this vineyard you speak of?"

"I inherited it."

"When?"

"Just ten days ago."

"And it is here, on the island?"

"No. It's in Canada—I'm Canadian."

"I see."

But he obviously didn't. He quite plainly wondered what she was doing in Sardinia when her interests lay on the other side of the world.

"The thing is," she hastened to explain, before he decided she was just another dilettante not worth his time, "I'd already paid for my holiday here, and because this inheritance landed in my lap so unexpectedly, I thought it best not to rush into anything until I'd talked to a few experts of which, it turns out, there are many here in Sardinia. I've never been the rash, impulsive type, and now didn't seem a good time to start."

"You have no experience at all in viticulture, then?"

"None. I'm a legal secretary and live in Toronto. And to tell the truth, I'm still reeling from the news that I now own a house and several acres of vineyards in British Columbia—that's Canada's most western province, in case you don't know."

"I'm familiar with B.C.," he informed her tersely, as if even an infant still in diapers would have a thorough geographical knowledge of the world's second largest country. "Have you seen this place for yourself, or are you relying on secondhand information about its condition?"

"I spent a couple of days there last week."

"And what else did you learn, as a result?"

"Nothing except that it's very run-down—oh, and that an elderly manager-cum-overseer and two rescued greyhounds are part of my legacy."

He rolled his altogether gorgeous eyes, as if to say, *Why me, oh Lord?* "May I ask what you propose to do about them?"

"Well, I'm not about to abandon them, if that's what you're suggesting."

"I'm suggesting nothing of the sort, Signorina Russell. I'm merely trying to establish the extent of, for want of a better word, your 'undertaking.' For example, exactly how many acres of land do you now own?"

"Seven."

"And the kind of grapes grown there?"

"I don't know." Then, before he could throw up his hands in disgust and tell her to go bother someone else because she'd tried his patience far enough for one day, she added, "Signor

Silvaggio d'Avalos, I realize this might be difficult for you to understand, growing up as you have, so surrounded by the business of cultivating grapes and turning them into wine that you probably started assimilating knowledge from the cradle, but I am a complete novice and although I'm willing to learn, I have to start somewhere, which is why I'm here with you, now."

He listened, his expression impassive. "And you're very sure you have the stamina required to fulfill your ambitions, are you?" he inquired, when at last she stopped to draw breath.

"Very."

He regarded her, his gaze unnervingly intent. "Then if what you have told me is correct, I must warn you that even if you were an expert, you would be undertaking a project of massive proportion whose success is by no means guaranteed. And by your own admission, you are anything but expert."

"Well, I didn't expect it would be easy," she floundered, so mesmerized by his brilliantly blue eyes that it was all she could do to string two words together. "But I meant what I said. Succeeding in this venture is very important to me for all kinds of reasons, not the least of which is that there are others whose welfare depends on it. I am determined to go through with it, regardless of the difficulties it entails."

"Very well." He leaned one elbow on the arm of his chair and cradled his jaw in his hand. "In that case, take out your pen and let's get started on what you need to know at the outset."

In the half hour before their lunch arrived—cold Mediterranean lobster in a creamy wine sauce, avocado and tomato slices, and bread warm from the oven, followed by a fruit and cheese platter—she wrote rapidly, stopping every now and then to ask a question and trying hard to focus on the subject at hand.

Despite her best efforts, though, her mind wandered repeatedly. The questions he fielded from her were not those she most wished to ask. Whether or not she might have to rip out all her old vines and start over from scratch, which varietals she should plant in their place, how much it would cost and how long before she could expect to recoup her losses and make a profit, didn't seem nearly as engrossing as how he'd come by his very remarkable eyes, where he'd learned to speak such excellent English, how old he was, or if there was a special woman in his life.

Although she made copious notes of every critical scrap of information he tossed her way, her rebellious gaze repeatedly returned to his face. To the slight cleft in his chin, and the high slash of his cheekbones which seemed more Spanish than Italian. To the tawny sheen of his skin and his glossy black hair. To the dark sweeping elegance of his brows and the way his long, dense lashes so perfectly framed his vivid blue eyes.

"So, I have not managed to discourage you?" he inquired, as they sat down to the meal.

"You've made me aware of pitfalls I might not otherwise have recognized," she told him, choosing her words carefully, "but no, you have not discouraged me. If anything, I'm more determined than ever to bring my vineyard back to life."

He considered that for a moment, then said, "Tell me more about this great-uncle of yours. Why, for example, did he allow his vines to fail so drastically?"

"I suppose because he was too old to look after them properly. He was eighty-four when he died."

"You *suppose?* Were you not close to him during his lifetime?"

"No. I didn't even know of his existence until his lawyer contacted me regarding his estate."

"He had no other relatives? None better equipped than you to rescue his property from ruination?"

"I don't know."

"Why not?"

She stared at him, frustrated. *I'm supposed to be the one asking the questions, not you!* she felt like telling him. "Because he was from my father's side of the family."

"You did not care for your father and his kin?"

Kin. An old-fashioned word which, coupled with his charming accent, gave one of the few indications that English wasn't his mother tongue. "I barely knew my father," she said, wrenching her mind back to the matter at hand. "He died when I was seven."

He raised a lofty brow. "I remember many relatives and events from when I was that age."

"Probably because, unlike mine, your family stayed together."

"Your parents were divorced?"

"Oh, yes, and the war between them never ended," she said, remembering all too well her mother's vitriolic outpourings to Arlene's hesitant requests to visit her father or speak to him by phone. "I was four at the time, and my mother made sure I lived too far away from my father to see him often."

Domenico Silvaggio d'Avalos shook his head disapprovingly. "I cannot imagine such a thing. When a man and a woman have created a child together, his or her welfare comes before any thought of the parents' personal happiness."

"A fine philosophy in theory, *signor*, but not so easy to live by, I suspect, if the couple in question find themselves irreconcilably opposed to one another's wishes and needs."

"All the more reason to choose wisely in the first place then, wouldn't you say?"

She laughed. "You're obviously not married!"

"No," he said, and turned that unsettling gaze on her again. "Are you?"

"No. But I'm realistic enough to know that if ever I am, a wedding ring provides no guarantee that the marriage will last."

"I do not call that realistic," he said flatly. "I call it defeatist."

"Then that makes you an idealist who's more than a little out of touch with the rest of the world."

"Hardly," he replied. "My parents have been happily married for thirty-nine years, as were my grandparents for almost half a century. And I have four sisters, all blissfully happy in their marriages."

"But you're still single."

"Not because I have anything against marriage. My father's health isn't the best and I took over the running of this company sooner than I might otherwise have done, which has kept me fully occupied and left little time for serious romance. But I'll know the right woman when she comes along and I will commit to her for the rest of my life, regardless of whatever difficulties we might encounter—and they will be few, I assure. I'll make certain of that before putting a ring on her finger."

"You have a list of requirements she must meet, in order to qualify as your wife, do you?"

"Of course," he said, as if it were the most natural thing in the world. "Happiness, like sexual compatibility and physical attraction, will run secondary to suitability."

"You make it sound as if you believe in arranged marriages."

"I don't disbelieve in them."

"Then I pity the woman who becomes your wife."

It was his turn to laugh. "Pity yourself, *signorina*," he declared, tossing down his napkin. "You're the one willing to sell her soul to a lost cause."

"On the contrary, *signor*. I'm doing exactly as you claim you will, when you take a wife. I'm sticking with my decision, regardless of the difficulties I'm facing. The only difference is, I'm taking on a vineyard instead of a husband."

He regarded her for an interminably long, silent minute. Finally he said, "Well then, since you refuse to let me deter you, I suppose I must do all I can to assist you."

"I think you've already done that." She indicated her notebook. "You've given me some very valuable pointers."

"Theory is all very well in its place, *signorina*, but it in no way replaces hands-on experience. That being the case, I have a proposition which you might find interesting. One, I'd go so far as to say, you can't afford to refuse. I'll take you on as a short-term apprentice during your time here—say from eight in the morning until two in the afternoon. It will mean you spend a good portion of the day working instead of enjoying the usual tourist activities, but if you're as determined as you say you are—"

"Oh, I am!" she exclaimed, her attention split evenly between the purely practical benefits of his offer, and the thrilling prospect of spending more time with him.

"Then here is what I suggest we do."

He proceeded to outline a course of instruction geared to get her started. That he was showing extraordinary generosity to a total stranger did not, of course, escape her notice, but Arlene couldn't help noticing not just *what* he said, but how he said it; on his finely carved lips as they shaped his words, and his precise enunciation.

Nor was that her only thought. He spoke with the passion of a true professional about the wine industry. Would he prove an equally passionate lover, she wondered.

"Signora?" His voice, deep and faintly amused, snapped

her attention back to where it properly belonged. "Are we done for now, or is there something else you'd like to know?"

Nothing to do with viticulture, certainly!

"No, thank you." Flustered, she'd stuffed her notebook into her bag and pushed away from the table. A quick glance at her watch showed it was almost four o'clock. The two-hour lunch he'd promised her had lasted well into the afternoon. "My goodness, look at the time! I had no idea it was so late, and I do apologize. I'm afraid I've overstayed my welcome."

"Not at all," he replied smoothly, rising also.

She was tall, but he was taller. Well over six feet. Slim and toughly built, with a midriff as unyielding as a flatiron. A tailor's dream of a body, narrow in all the right places; broad and powerful where it should be.

Escorting her back to the Jeep, he inquired, "You have other plans for the rest of the day, do you?"

"Nothing specific. We arrived only yesterday and are still getting our bearings, but I should head back to the hotel."

"You did not come to Sardinia alone?"

"No."

"Then I am the one who must apologize for monopolizing so much of your time." He slammed her door shut, and climbed into the driver's seat. "Tomorrow the grape harvest begins, which means we'll be out in the fields all day. Wear sturdier shoes than those you presently have on. Also, choose clothing that'll give you some protection from the sun. You have very fair skin."

Fair? Beside him, she felt colorless. Insignificant. But that he'd noticed her at all would have left her glowing had he not concluded with, "In particular, make sure you wear a hat. Neither I nor anyone else working the vines needs the distraction of your fainting from heatstroke."

His obvious and sudden impatience to be rid of her had quashed her romantic fantasies more effectively than a bucket of cold water thrown in her face. "Understood. You won't even know I'm there."

"You may be sure that I will, *signorina*," he replied with unflinching candor. "I shall be keeping a very close eye on you. You will learn as much as I can teach you in the short time at our disposal, but it will not be at the expense of my crop."

CHAPTER TWO

"SO THERE you have it. What do you think?" Eyeing Gail, her best friend and travel companion, whom she'd found stretched out on a chaise by the hotel pool, Arlene tried to gauge her reaction to this abrupt change in plans.

"That he's right." Gail slathered on another layer of sunscreen. "It's a heaven-sent opportunity and you can't afford to turn it down."

"But it does interfere with our holiday."

"Not mine," Gail returned cheerfully. "We came here to unwind and I'm more than happy to spend half the day lazing here or on the beach. In case you haven't noticed, both are littered with gorgeous men, which is probably a lot more than can be said about what's-his-name from the vineyard."

"Domenico Silvaggio d'Avalos." Arlene let each exotic syllable roll off her tongue like cream, and thought that one glance at his aristocratic face and big, toned body would be enough to change Gail's mind about which of them had stumbled across the better deal.

"What a mouthful! How do you wrap your tongue around it? Or are you on a first-name basis already?"

"Not at all. He's very businesslike and quite distant, in fact."

"Well, I don't suppose it really matters. Just as long as you leave here knowing a heck of a lot more about running a vineyard than you did when you arrived, he doesn't have to be witty or charismatic, does he?"

"No."

Arlene did her best to sound emphatic, but something in her tone must have struck a hollow note because Gail removed her sunglasses, the better to skewer her in a mistrustful gaze. "Uh-oh! What aren't you telling me?"

"Nothing," she insisted, not about to confess that, in the space of three hours, she'd almost fooled herself into believing she might have met Mr. Right. Gail would have laughed herself silly at the idea, and rightly so. There was no such thing as love at first sight, and although a teenager might be forgiven for believing otherwise, a woman pushing thirty was certainly old enough to know better. "I find him a little... unsettling, that's all."

"Unsettling how?"

She aimed for a casual shrug. "I don't know. Maybe 'intimidating' is a better word. He's larger than life somehow, and so confidently in charge of himself and everything around him. I don't quite know why he's bothering with an ignoramus like me, and I guess I'm afraid I'll disappoint him."

"So what if you do? Why do you care what he thinks?"

Why? Because never before had she felt as alive as she did during the time she'd spent with him. "His mood changed, there at the end," she said wistfully. "I could hear it in his voice and see it in his expression, as if he suddenly regretted his invitation. He seemed almost angry with me, although I can't imagine why."

Gail popped her sunglasses back in place and turned her face up to the sun. "Arlene, do yourself a favor and stop analyzing the guy. Bad-tempered and moody he might be, but as far as you're concerned, he's the means to an end, and that's all that matters. Once we leave here, you'll never have to see him again."

She was unquestionably right, Arlene decided, and wished she could find some comfort in that thought. Instead it left her feeling oddly depressed.

That night at dinner in the main house, the reaction of his brothers-in-law to what he'd done was pretty much what he expected. Mock disgust and a host of humorous comments along the lines of, "Where do you find these lame ducks, Dom?" and, "Just what we need at the busiest time of the year—the distraction of a useless extra female body cluttering up the landscape!"

His sisters, though, twittered like drunken sparrows, clamoring for more personal information.

"What's her name?"

"Is she pretty?"

"Is she single?"

"How old is she?"

"Don't just sit there looking stony-faced, Domenico! Tell us what makes her so special."

"What makes her special," his uncle Bruno declared, stirring up another flurry of over-the-top excitement, "is that she could be The One. Trust me. I have seen her. She is lovely."

The squeals of delight *that* comment elicited were enough to make him want to head for the hills. His mother and sisters' chief mission in life was to see him married, and the last thing they needed was Bruno or anyone else encouraging them. "Don't be ridiculous, Uncle Bruno," he snapped. "She's just an ordinary woman in the extraordinary position of finding herself with a vineyard she hasn't the first idea how to manage. I'd have made the same offer if she'd been a man."

But she wasn't a man, and no one was more conscious of that fact than Domenico. Throughout their extended lunch, he'd been struck by the sharp intelligence in her lovely gray eyes. But it took more than brains to succeed in viticulture, and given her small, delicate bones, he wondered how she'd begin to survive the tough physical demands of working a vineyard.

Not my concern, he'd told himself, more than once. Yet he admired her determination and he'd enjoyed their spirited debate on marriage, enough that he'd been tempted to ask her out to dinner, just for the pleasure of getting to know her better. Until she let slip that she hadn't come to the island alone, that was—and then he'd felt like a fool for not having figured it out for himself. If she was not a raving beauty, nor was she as plain as he'd first supposed. Rather, she possessed a low-key elegance of form and face that any discerning man would find attractive.

Too bad another had already staked a claim to her, he'd thought at the time, covering his irritation with a brusqueness he now regretted. She'd almost flinched at his tone, as he spelled out what he expected of her when she showed up tomorrow morning. If it weren't that she was in such dire straits, she'd probably have flung his generous offer of help back in his face. He would have, in her place.

Aware that his family continued to stare at him expectantly, he said, "At the risk of ruining your evening and dashing all hope of marrying me off before the last grape is picked, I feel compelled to point out that this woman is already spoken for. Not only that, she's here for only two weeks, after which our relationship, such as it is, will come to an end."

"But a great deal can happen in two weeks," Renata, his youngest sister, pointed out, ogling her husband. "Our honeymoon lasted only that long, but it was all the time we needed for me to become pregnant."

"Lucky you," Domenico replied testily, amid general laughter. "However, my ambitions with this woman run along somewhat different lines, so please don't start knitting little things on my behalf."

That gave rise to such hilarity that, so help him, if he'd known at which hotel Arlene Russell was staying, he'd have phoned and left a message saying something had come up and he'd had to cancel their arrangement.

Domenico Silvaggio d'Avalos was already directing operations when Arlene showed up as planned at the back of the winery, the next morning. Stepping away from a crowd of about thirty men and women being loaded into the back of two trucks, he eyed her critically, then gave a brief nod of approval. "You'll do," he decided.

"What a relief, *signor!*"

Either he didn't pick up on her lightly sugared sarcasm, or he chose to ignore it. "Since we'll be working closely for the next several days," he announced briskly, "we'll dispense with the formality. My name is Domenico."

"In that case, I'm Arlene."

"Yes, I remember," he said, rather cryptically she thought. "And now that we've got that settled, let's get moving. Those people you see in the trucks are extra pickers hired to help bring in the harvest. Stay out of their way. They have a job to do. If you have questions, ask me or my uncle."

She'd have saluted and barked, *Yes, sir!* if he'd given her half a chance. But he herded her into the Jeep and followed the two trucks up the hill to the fields, talking on his cell phone the entire time. When they arrived, his uncle was already assigning the extra laborers to their designated picking areas under the leadership of one of the full-time employees, but he stopped long enough to welcome Arlene with a big smile. "Watch and learn, then you go home the expert," he shouted cheerfully.

Hardly that, she thought. But hopefully not a complete nincompoop, either.

"Although some cultivators bring in machinery to get the job done quickly, we handpick our grapes," Domenico began, wasting no time launching into his first lecture.

"So I see. Why is that?"

"Because mechanical harvesters shake the fruit from the vines, often damaging it. This can result in oxidization and microbial activity which, in turn, causes disease. Not only that, it's virtually impossible to prevent other material also being collected, especially leaves."

Oxidization? Microbial? Whatever happened to plain, uncomplicated English?

Covering her dismay at already finding herself at a loss, she said, "But isn't handpicking labor intensive, and therefore more expensive?"

He cast her a lofty glance. "Vigna Silvaggio d'Avalos prides itself on the superiority of its wines. Cost is not a factor."

"Oh, I see!" she replied weakly, and properly chastised, wondered how she'd ever manage to redeem herself for such an unforgivable oversight.

Unfortunately her woes increased as the morning progressed. Although recognizing that she'd had the extreme good fortune to find herself involved in a world-class operation, what struck her most forcibly as the hours dragged by was that her back ached and the sun was enough to roast a person alive.

Under Domenico's tutelage, she picked clusters of grapes using a pair of shears shaped like pointed scissors. She learned to recognize unripe or diseased fruit, and to reject it. Because bruised grapes spoil easily, she handled the crop carefully, laying the collected clusters in one of many small buckets placed at intervals along each row.

Not that she'd have understood them anyway, but none of the migrant workers had much to say for themselves. They bent to their task with dogged persistence, seldom sparing her so much as a glance. Once assured that she wasn't about to lay devastation to his precious crop, Domenico essentially ignored her, too, and Bruno was too far away to offer her a word of encouragement. Over the course of the morning, however, four women found occasion to stop by separately, each offering a friendly greeting and, at the same time, subjecting her to a thorough and somewhat amused inspection. Even if they hadn't introduced themselves as his sisters, she'd have had to be blind not to see their resemblance to her mentor.

"Don't let my brother wear you out," Lara, the first to pay a visit, counseled, her English almost as flawless as Domenico's. "He's a slave driver, especially at harvest time. Tell him when you've had enough."

Not a chance! Arlene knew from the way Domenico periodically came to check on her that he was just waiting for her to throw in the towel—which she would have done, if her pride had permitted it. But despite a dull, persistent ache above her left eye which grew steadily worse as the morning passed, she refused to give him the satisfaction.

The sun was high when a van rolled to a stop on a dusty patch of rocky ground some distance away from the fields. At once, the sisters converged on it and started unloading its contents onto a long table set up under a canvas awning supported by a steel frame.

As everyone else working the fields downed tools, Domenico

approached Arlene. "Time for a break and something to eat," he declared, in that lordly take-it-or-leave-it manner of his.

By then, the pain in her head was so severe, starbursts of flashing light were exploding before her eyes and she wasn't sure she could crawl to where the women were laying out baskets of bread and platters laden with cheese, thinly sliced smoked meat and olives. But either he was blessed with second sight, or the stabbing agony showed on her face because, just when she feared she'd pass out, he grabbed her hand and hauled her to her feet. "Still want to run a vineyard?" he inquired smoothly.

"You bet," she managed, and disengaging herself from his hold, managed to totter off and collapse in the shade of the awning.

Following, he eyed her critically. "How much water have you drunk since you got here?"

"Not enough, I guess." She squinted against the painfully bright glare of the sun beyond the awning. "I did bring a bottle with me, but I finished it hours ago."

"You didn't notice the coolers at the end of each row of vines? You didn't think to ask what they were for?"

"No." She swallowed, the smell of warm yeasty bread, olives and sharp cheese suddenly causing her stomach to churn unpleasantly.

He let fly with an impatient curse and strode to the table, returning a moment later to thrust at her another bottle of water, this one well chilled. "It didn't occur to me you'd need to be told to keep yourself properly hydrated. I assumed you had enough sense to reach that conclusion unaided."

Another of his sisters, this one well into pregnancy, happened to overhear him. "Domenico, please! Can you not see the poor woman has had enough for one day?" she chided, hurrying forward with a plate of food. "Here, *signorina*. I've brought you something to eat."

Arlene grimaced, by then so sick from the pounding in her head that she was afraid to open her mouth to reply, in case she threw up instead.

With a sympathetic murmur, his sister lowered herself carefully to her knees. "You are in distress, *cara*. What can I do to help you?"

She tried to shrug away the woman's concern but, by then, even so small a movement was beyond her. "I have a bad headache here," she mumbled, pressing her hand to her temple, and hating herself for her weakness almost as much as she hated Domenico for witnessing it.

"More than just a headache, I think," his sister said, glancing up at him. "It is the *emicrania*, Domenico—the migraine. She needs to be looked after."

"I can see that, Renata," he snapped.

"Then drive her down to the house and let Momma take care of her."

"No!" Horrified by the idea, Arlene managed to subdue another wave of nausea long enough to articulate her objection without embarrassing herself.

Renata took ice from a cooler and wrapped it in one of the linen cloths lining the bread baskets. "Do you have a rented car, *cara*?" she asked, placing it gently at the base of Arlene's skull.

"Yes, but not here. My friend dropped me off this morning."

"Just as well, because you're in no shape to drive." Once again, Domenico hoisted her to her feet, this time showing more care than he had before. *"Avanti!* Let's go."

"Go where?"

"I'm taking you back to your hotel before you pass out. I

don't imagine your *friend* will appreciate having you flat on your back—at least, not in your present condition."

If she hadn't felt so lousy, she'd have challenged him on his last remark. Instead she submitted to being bundled into the Jeep, leaned her head against the back of the seat and closed her eyes.

To his credit, he drove carefully down the rutted track from the vineyard so as not to add to her discomfort, but when they reached the paved road, he wasted no time covering the miles into town. Beyond a terse, "Which hotel?" he mercifully made no other attempt at conversation.

Once arrived, he ignored the hotel's No Parking sign, stopped the vehicle right at the front door, and came around to help her alight. "What's your room number?"

By that point almost blind with pain, she sagged against his supporting arm. "Four twenty-two."

"You have a key card?"

"Yes." She fumbled without success in her tote.

He muttered indistinctly under his breath—something unflattering judging by his tone—found the card himself, and hoisting her off her feet, strode past the doorman and across the lobby to the elevator just as its doors swished open and Gail emerged.

Stopping dead in her tracks, she let out a horrified gasp. "Heavens, Arlene, what happened? You look like the wrath of God!"

"Step aside, *per favore*," Domenico ordered, when she continued to block his entrance to the elevator. "I wish to take her to her room."

"Hold on a minute!" Gail replied, clearly not the least bit fazed by his autocratic manner. "You're not taking her anywhere without me."

"Indeed? And who are you?"

"Arlene's roommate."

"*You're* her friend?"

"*You're* her mentor?" she shot back, imitating his incredulous tone. "The one who's supposed to be teaching her everything there is to know about growing grapes?"

"I am."

"Well, congratulations! You're doing a fine job, bringing her home dead drunk in the middle of the day."

"I'm doing nothing of the sort!" he snapped. "What kind of man do you take me for?"

"You don't want to know!"

"Gail," Arlene protested weakly, "it's okay. I have a headache, that's all, and just need to lie down until it passes."

Gail's face swam into her line of vision. "Sweetie, what kind of headache has you practically passing out?"

"A migraine," Domenico interjected on an irate breath. "Perhaps you've heard of it."

"Oh." Her tone suddenly less confrontational, Gail backed into the elevator. "I'm...um...sorry if I came on too strong. I'll help you get her upstairs."

"Close the shutters," Domenico instructed, when they reached the room. "I understand it helps to have the room darkened."

While Gail scurried to obey him, he lowered Arlene to the bed farthest from the window, then sat on the edge of the mattress and stroked a cool hand down her forehead. "Close your eyes, *cara*," he murmured, and even in the depths of her misery, the shift in his attitude was not lost on her. Whatever had given rise to that unspoken edge of hostility between them yesterday and which had continued into this morning, melted in the deep, soothing warmth of his voice.

"I've never seen her like this before," she heard Gail whisper from the other side of the bed. "Shouldn't we call for a doctor?"

"She doesn't usually suffer from migraines?"

"Not that I'm aware of, and if anyone would know, I would. We've been best friends ever since college."

The mattress shifted slightly as he rose to his feet. "Stay with her and keep the ice pack at the back of her neck."

Panic lacing her voice, Gail hissed, "You're just dropping her off, then *leaving*? What if—?"

"I'll be back," he said, as his footsteps receded quietly over the tiled floor.

As soon as she heard the door click shut behind him, Arlene struggled to sit up. "Gail…? I think I'm going to be sick."

"Oh, cripes!" Gail slipped an arm around her shoulders and eased her to her feet. "Okay, sweetie, come on. I'll help you to the bathroom."

They made it with seconds to spare. Wrenching and horrible though it was while it lasted, vomiting seemed to ease the stabbing ferocity of the pain just a little.

After rinsing out her mouth and splashing cold water on her face, Arlene lay down on the bed again and managed a feeble smile. "Don't look so worried. I promise not to pull a repeat performance."

"I'm going to hold you to that," Gail said, crossing to peer through the peephole as a knock came at the door. "You just took ten years off my life. Now lie still and look pale and interesting. Your Sir Galahad's back, and he's not alone."

"How is she?" Domenico inquired, the minute he set foot in the room.

"About the same," Gail told him. "But she threw up while you were gone."

Oh, please! Arlene whimpered silently. *Haven't I suffered enough indignity for one day, without your sharing that with him?*

"Then it's as well I summoned professional help. This is Dr. Zaccardo," he added, as a middle-aged man with prematurely gray hair advanced to her bedside.

"It is as you suspected." After a brief examination and a few pertinent questions, the doctor stepped back from the bed and nodded so energetically at the other two that Arlene shuddered inside. "I will leave this medication with you," he continued, reaching into his medical bag for a small bottle. "See, please, that she takes two tablets immediately and, if necessary, two more at six, this evening. However, treatment now is such that a migraine is usually dispelled in a matter of hours. If she shows no improvement by nightfall, you will contact me, but I do not expect to hear from you. By tomorrow, she will be herself again. *Arrivederci, signor, signorine.*"

With that, he was gone as quickly as he'd arrived, leaving Arlene to deal only with Domenico who didn't seem disposed to leave with equal dispatch. Instead while Gail brought her two pills and a glass of water, he went to the desk and wrote something on the pad of paper supplied by the hotel.

"If you're concerned at all, you can reach me at any of these numbers, and this one is Dr. Zaccardo's," he told Gail. "Regardless, please call me this evening and let me know how she's doing."

"I'm sure she'll be fine."

"I want to hear from you anyway. You'll be staying with her, of course?"

"Of course."

"Until later, then."

* * *

The next time Arlene was aware of her surroundings, the room was completely dark except for the soft glow from a lamp next to the armchair by the window, where Gail sat reading.

Cautiously Arlene blinked. Dared to turn her head on the pillow. And let out a slow breath of relief. No flashing lights before her eyes. No stabbing pain above her left temple. Nothing, in fact, but a cool, delicious lassitude—and a gorgeous bouquet of pink roses on the coffee table, some distance away.

"You're awake!" Gail exclaimed softly, setting down her book and coming to the bed. "How're you feeling, sweetie?"

"Better," she said. "Much better. What time is it?"

"Just after eight. You slept for over six hours. Do you need more medication?"

She sat up carefully. "I don't think so. But I'd love some water."

"Sure." Gail plumped her pillows, then filled a glass from the carafe on the desk.

Arlene sipped it slowly, letting the slivers of ice linger a moment on her tongue, then slide down her throat.

"Well?" Gail watched her anxiously.

"So far, so good." She indicated the roses. "They're lovely, Gail, but you should've saved your money. I'm not going to die, after all."

"Oh, they're not from me! *He* sent them. They arrived a couple of hours ago. Here, see for yourself." She handed over a card, signed simply *Domenico*. "Not long on sentiment, is he?"

"Apparently not." Nevertheless, a sweet, ridiculous pleasure sang through Arlene's blood that he'd cared enough to send her flowers in the first place.

"Pretty good at dishing out orders, though. I suppose I'd better give him a call and let him know you're feeling better."

She retrieved the notepad from the desk, punched in one of

the numbers he'd written down, and almost immediately began, "Hi, it's Gail Weaver.... Yes, I know what time it is.... Well I did, as soon as she woke up... Just now... Well, I will, if you'll stop interrupting and let me finish a sentence...! No, she says she doesn't need them.... Because she's a grown woman, Mr. Silvaggio de Whatever, which means she, and not you, gets to decide what she puts in her mouth.... I don't know. I'll ask her."

She held the phone at arm's length. "Do you feel up to talking to his lordship, Arlene?" she inquired, loud enough for half the people in the hotel to hear.

Arlene nodded, unable to keep a straight face. When was the last time anyone had spoken to him like that, she wondered.

"Hello, Domenico," she said, picking up the handset on the bedside table.

"I hear you're recovered." Seductive baritone verging on bass, his voice stroked sinfully against her ear and vibrated the length of her body. "I'm greatly relieved."

"Thank you, both for your concern and for the flowers. If a woman has to suffer a migraine, waking up to pink roses does make it a little easier to bear."

"I'm glad you're enjoying them."

A pause hummed along the line, which she took to mean the conversation was at an end. "Well, I'll say good night, then—"

He cut her off before she could finish. "Arlene, I blame myself for what happened today. Expecting you to work as long as others who are used to our climate was unforgivable of me, and I apologize."

"There's no need. You heard my friend Gail, a moment ago. I'm a grown woman. I could, and should have spoken sooner. As it was, I put you to a great deal of trouble at a time when you've got your hands full with the harvest. It won't happen again."

"Are you saying you've changed your mind, and won't be returning to the vineyard?"

"Of course not. I'll be there tomorrow morning at eight—at least, I will unless you've changed *your* mind."

"Not at all," he said, his voice dropping almost to a purr. "Until tomorrow morning, then."

CHAPTER THREE

DESPITE her objections, Arlene spent the next four days in Domenico's office. With thick, whitewashed plaster walls, stone floor, recessed windows and heavy beamed ceiling, it served both as a business center and a boardroom. At one end of the vast space stood a large desk, filing cabinets, and high-tech computer station and communications system, but she spent most of her time at the other end, seated beside him in comfortable club chairs at a handsome conference table.

"You're coddling me," she accused him, when he told her she wouldn't be helping with the harvest again. "You think I don't have what it takes to handle the job."

"On the contrary, I'm trying to give you as broad a base of information as possible in the short time at my disposal so that, when you take over your own property, you'll have a better idea of what your priorities should be. I suggest you let me decide the best way to go about doing that."

So it was that, with the door closed on the bustle of activity taking place outside, she studied slide shows illustrating various irrigation methods, ideal sun exposure, elevations, climate and soil conditions for growing grapes. She learned about different varietals and the importance of choosing those best suited to her particular location, as well as determining the trellising system to support them.

Domenico drew up spreadsheets itemizing general expenditures, and a calendar outlining a typical work year in a vineyard. He supplied her with catalogs and names of reputable companies she could call on when it came time to buy seedlings and equipment. Recommended videos she'd find helpful, online courses she could take, and offered advice on the kind of help she should hire.

Just when she thought she'd never begin to assimilate the mountain of facts he threw at her, he'd call a break and they'd help themselves from the thermos of coffee, which always waited on the serving bar separating the two halves of the room. Then it was back to work until around one o'clock, when the same van that delivered lunch to the field workers, stopped by, and the driver brought in a covered tray for the two of them. Unlike the food prepared for the pickers, though, hers and Domenico's was more elaborate and served on colorful porcelain, with linen napkins and crested silverware.

On the fifth day, he took her back to the fields and showed her how to use a refractometer to measure the sugar content of the grapes. "One drop of juice is all you need for an immediate digital read-out," he explained, demonstrating. "Good wine is calibrated at a sugar level of 22BRIX."

"Bricks?"

"B-R-I-X," he amended, spelling it out for her.

She opened her ever-handy notebook. What's that?"

"The scale used by vintners to measure the sugar solution in the fruit."

"And what did you say this thing is called…?"

"A refractometer."

She examined the small, hand-held instrument more

closely. "I think I might have seen one of these among the other equipment, when I went to visit my property, but it looked pretty old and beaten-up compared to this."

"Throw it out and buy another," he advised. "Accuracy is crucial when it comes to determining sugar content. You could lose an entire crop if you harvest too soon or leave the grapes on the vine too long. As the sugar content rises, so does the pH. Harvesting has to be timed to maximize sugar content while minimizing acidity."

To an outsider witnessing these sessions, it would have appeared to be all business between him and her. And indeed, where viticulture was concerned, it absolutely was. But underneath, something less tangible was at work. Without a single overt word or gesture, an invisible tension grew between them that had nothing to do with grapes or wine, and everything to do with the tacit awareness of a man and a woman separated from the rest of the world by a thick wooden door that shut out all sight and sound of other human interaction.

The faint scent of his aftershave, of her shampoo, permeated the air in mingled intimacy. His voice seemed to take on a deeper timbre when he addressed her. He turned her very ordinary name into an exotic three-syllabled caress. Ar-*lay*-na.

Sometimes, she'd glance up from diligently filling yet another page with notes, and catch him studying her so intently that heat raced through her blood as if she had a fever. Other times, he'd touch her, not necessarily on purpose and never intimately. Yet even the most accidental brushing of his hand against hers was enough to send tiny impulses of sensual awareness shooting up her arm.

Simply put, she was enthralled by him. By the authority with which he imparted knowledge, and his patience as he explained the complicated science of viticulture. By his intelligence and integrity.

The respect he generated among his employees impressed her deeply. Nor was it limited to those working close by. She'd soon realized that his holdings extended far beyond Sardinia's shores. He was, as his uncle once mentioned in passing, an international celebrity in his field.

Most of all, though, his evident devotion to his large family touched her where she was most vulnerable. As a lonely, unwanted child herself, she'd ached for the siblings that played so large a role in his life. Yet within that close family circle, he remained his own person. Independent, and confident in his masculinity, he exuded a charismatic charm unlike any other man she'd ever met. That he also happened to be blindingly handsome was merely the icing on a very delectable cake.

But however strong the intuition that told her he was equally attracted to her, once she was away from him, the uncertainty crept in. Possibly her imagination was leading her astray, spurred by the intimacy of just the two of them, alone for hours at a spell. What she took to be glances laden with an erotic subtext might simply be his way of giving her his undivided professional attention. For all she knew, the way he smiled at her, as if they shared something special and personal, could be the way he smiled at all women.

Was she the victim of her own wishful thinking? Or was there something…?

"There's something!" Gail assured her, when she confided her doubts to her friend. "I could've told you that, the night he phoned to see how you were feeling after the migraine. I was listening in to the conversation between the pair of you, remember?"

Laughing, Arlene said, "I recall your panting furiously after he hung up, and gulping down ice water straight from the carafe!"

"What else did you expect? Cripes, Arlene, talk about *steamy!* That man was so hot for you, I thought the phone was about to explode in my ear!"

"That's ridiculous! We'd met for the first time just the day before."

"Which, it would appear, is all the time it took. Admit it, kiddo. Just when you were ready to give up on men, you've finally met one who stirs your little heart to beat a whole lot faster."

"That doesn't mean he feels the same way about me."

"How do you know? Have you asked him?"

The very idea made her break out in a cold sweat. "I wouldn't dare."

"Why not? You know he's not married, so why not just go with the flow and see where it leads? What do you have to lose?"

"His respect, for a start. And for all I know, he could be involved with someone else."

"Or he could be waiting for a sign of encouragement from you."

"What's the point of encouraging him, when we both know I'll be leaving here in another nine days?"

"The point is that you might be shutting the door on a rather glorious thing called love at first sight."

"I don't believe in that," she said stubbornly, all the while knowing she was deluding no one but herself.

Gail sighed, obviously exasperated. "There are hundreds of people in the world who do, and who prove it by living together happily ever after."

But there were couples who mistook sexual attraction and infatuation for the real thing, and lived to regret it, and she ought to know. She'd been the product of such a mistake—the only child of parents who hated each other by the time she was born.

I sacrificed myself and stayed with him because of you, her mother had reminded her often enough. *If I hadn't fallen pregnant, I'd have left him within six months of marrying him and saved myself five years of misery.*

"But if you're convinced it's not possible in your case," Gail continued, "then leave love out of the equation, and just live for the moment. As long as you're careful, holiday romance, with a little lust thrown in for good measure, never hurt anyone."

But Arlene had never been susceptible to lust, mostly because, until Domenico, she hadn't met a man who inspired it. "I don't believe in that, either," she said. "It's too risky."

Gail rolled her eyes. "This, from the woman who threw everything away to take on a broken-down vineyard, a couple of greyhounds and a crabby old man? Give me strength!"

Just as she was ready to leave on the Friday, Domenico asked her what plans she'd made for the weekend. "Because," he said, "if you're interested, I'll take you to visit some of the other vineyards on the island. It never hurts to get someone else's viewpoint. The more you see and the more people you talk to, the better off you'll be when you start working your own fields."

Knowing Gail had hooked up with a local tour guide who'd promised to take her scuba diving, Arlene accepted the invitation, and did her best to subdue the flush of pleasure riding up her neck. "Thank you! I'd like that very much."

"Then I'll pick you up around ten and we'll make a day of it."

Once back at the hotel, she agonized over what to wear. The sensible blouse and baggy pants that had been her standard uniform for most of the past week? The unflattering cotton sun hat that made her look like a wilted weed?

"Definitely not," Gail decided, when asked her opinion. "You're used to the sun now, and you've picked up a nice tan from lazing on the beach every afternoon. Book yourself into the hotel spa this afternoon and splurge—nails, facial, hair, the works. Heaven knows, you've earned it. Go glam, and let him see what he's been missing."

"Glam" had never been Arlene's forte, but the mirror told her Gail had a point. Not only had the sun given her skin a honey glow, it had painted pale blond streaks in her light brown hair.

Four hours later, she emerged from the spa, so buffed and polished her own mother wouldn't have known her.

Such a pity you're so plain, Arlene, she used to say, *but considering what you have to work with, there isn't much you can do about it.*

Until today, she'd have agreed. But not anymore. Nails painted a soft coral, skin shimmering like amber silk and hair expertly trimmed and enhanced by golden highlights, made a world of difference to the girl her mother had once dubbed "painfully drab."

Giddy over her transformation, she stopped by the boutique in the hotel lobby and found the perfect dress to go with her new look. Full skirted, with a fitted bodice held up by spaghetti straps, it was made of soft polished cotton the same deep turquoise as the sea.

"Perfect!" Gail agreed, inspecting the finished results. "You'll knock his socks off."

The thing was, Arlene wondered nervously, would she know what to do about it, if she succeeded?

* * *

He showed up right on time, driving not the Jeep, as she'd expected, but a sleek silver roadster. He wore pale gray trousers, a blue shirt open at the neck and black leather loafers, which even to her inexperienced eye were clearly handmade.

"You look very lovely, Arlene," he said, stepping out of the car to afford himself a head-to-toe inspection, "but your hair…" He fingered a strand and shook his head. "This will not do."

She stared at him, too disappointed to be offended. "You don't like it?"

"It is beautiful, and I won't be responsible for spoiling it."

With that, he disappeared into the hotel. Turning to watch, she saw him enter the boutique, then emerge a couple of minutes later with a long white silk scarf. "For the wind," he explained, draping it over her head, then crossing the ends under her chin and tossing them over her shoulders. "There, now put on your sunglasses, and you'll look exactly the part—an international celebrity, leaving her yacht for the day to travel about the island incognito, with her chauffeur at the wheel of her car."

He was joking, of course. No one in his right mind would ever mistake Domenico Silvaggio d'Avalos for a lowly chauffeur, any more than she'd ever pass for a celebrity. Not even the chinos and boots he wore around the vineyard could disguise his aristocratic bearing, let alone the discreetly expensive clothes he had on now. His watch alone probably cost more than she earned in a month.

He ushered her into the car, and within minutes they'd left the town behind and were headed west along the coast toward Sassari, where they made their first stop. "This vineyard also grows the Vermentino grape as we do," he said, pulling up before a castellated building fronted by an enormous courtyard. "The owner, Santo Perrottas, and I went to school together in Rome, and have been good friends since we were boys."

That much was obvious from the warm welcome they received. Although not in the same class as Domenico, Santo was nonetheless a handsome, charming man. When he learned the reason for their visit, nothing would do but that Arlene sample his wine, not in the tasting room used by the public, but in a private garden screened by espaliered vines already turning color and stripped of their fruit.

"I've heard of British Columbian wines," he commented, as they sipped the straw-colored, aromatic Vermentino. "They have won gold medals in international competition, I understand."

"Not from grapes grown on my land, I'm afraid," she said ruefully. "I inherited a vineyard that's been neglected for some time."

"Then you're in good hands with Domenico. He is a true expert in the art of cultivating healthy vines. And you, my friend," he added, turning to Domenico with a wry grin, "how lucky are you, to have come across such a *bellezza*! Why could she not have turned up on my doorstep, instead of yours?"

"Why do you think? Because she's as smart as she is beautiful. And because you're married."

Arlene felt a blush creeping over her face. She wasn't used to such flattering attention. Not that they meant it, of course. They were just being polite and charming because that was expected of men who moved in the elevated stratum of society they frequented.

From Sassari, Domenico drove south, stopping at three other vineyards on the way, where they were again warmly welcomed and pressed to stay longer—for lunch, for dinner, for the night. But he refused each invitation, and for that,

Arlene was glad. Although she appreciated the hospitality, he was an excellent teacher and much of what she heard and saw, she'd already learned at Vigna Silvaggio d'Avalos. The true pleasure of the day for her was seeing his island through his eyes as he pointed out ancient ruins and breathtaking scenery.

Shortly before one in the afternoon, he drove inland for several kilometers to a village perched on a wooded slope overlooking the Mediterranean. Leaving the car on the outskirts, they walked along winding streets so narrow, the sun barely penetrated between the houses, and it seemed to Arlene that people could reach out of their bedroom windows and shake hands with their neighbors across the way. In a tiny square shaded by palm trees, they ate lunch at an outdoor restaurant, and were on their way again within the hour.

They reached Oristano just after four, and after a quick tour of the town, headed north again, following seventy-five kilometers of magnificent coastline and arriving in Alghero, on the Coral Riviera, just as daylight faded. Even so, the beauty of the city was apparent.

"It is the jewel of northwest Sardinia, if not the entire island," Domenico told her, after they'd parked the car and were strolling through the cobbled streets of the medieval citadel. At that hour, the bars and restaurants were just coming alive after the afternoon lull, with people gathering in social groups at outdoor tables, to sip wine and exchange gossip. "If you had more time here, I would bring you back to enjoy the beach and see more of what the town has to offer. As it is, we'll have dinner here and enjoy together what's left of today."

If you had more time here.... It had become a frequent refrain, during the day. Rose quartz beaches, secluded coves, forested hills, silent olive groves, archaeological ruins and seldom traveled roads leading to the wild interior: they'd have been hers to discover with him, if only she had more time.

Instead she had to make do with this one glorious day of fleeting impressions. Of smiling glances and shared laughter. Of his hand clasping hers to prevent her stumbling over the uneven paving stones. Of the wind whipping the ends of her scarf like the tails of a kite, as the car sped along the dusty roads. Of the sun touching the square line of his jaw and throwing deep bronze shadows under his high cheekbones. Of the scent of myrtle and sea pine capturing her senses.

These were the memories she'd take with her to her new home in British Columbia; these and the knowledge he'd shared with her. Did he know how indelible an impression he'd made, she wondered, angling a covert gaze at him as he led her purposefully past wonderful old palazzos and churches to a restaurant with tables set out under a colonnaded terrace? Or that no matter how many years passed, she'd never forget him?

Street signs, she noticed, were in Italian and what she thought might be Spanish, but which turned out more accurately to be Catalan. "You're on the right track, though," Domenico said, after they were shown a table set with dramatic black linens, white votive candles in crystal holders and wineglasses with stems as slender as flower stalks. "Alghero is more Spanish than any other place in Sardinia. In fact, it's nicknamed 'Barcelonetta,' meaning Little Barcelona. Not so surprising, when you consider it lay under Aragonese rule for the better part of three hundred years, starting in the mid-fourteenth century."

"The first time I saw you, I thought *you* looked Spanish, except for your blue eyes" she admitted.

"Many Spaniards—Italians also, for that matter—have blue eyes, so once again, your instincts were on target. My father's family came from northern Spain in the early 1880s. I'm told I resemble my great-great-grandfather."

"He must have been a very handsome man."

"*Grazie.* And to whom do you owe your looks, my lovely Arlene?"

"Oh, you don't have to say that," she protested, flushing. "I know I'm not very pretty."

He reached across the table and took both her hands in his. "Why do you do that, *cara*?" he asked gently. "Why do you turn away from the truth and try to hide your quiet beauty from the rest of the world? Are you ashamed of it?"

"Nothing like that," she said, her breath catching in her throat at the intensity of his gaze. "I'm not being coy or fishing for compliments. I just know mine's not the kind of face that would launch a thousand ships."

"And who convinced you of that? A man? A rogue who broke your heart and left you with no confidence to believe what is so plain to the rest of the world?"

"It was my mother," she said baldly.

He let out a soft exclamation of distress. "Why would a mother speak so to her child?"

"I think because I take after my father."

"Then trust me when I tell you that your father also must be a most handsome man, as you surely realize."

"Not really. I hardly knew him."

"Ah, yes," he said. "Now I remember. Your parents divorced when you were very young, and he died shortly after. But you have no photographs of him?"

Her laugh emerged shockingly harsh. "My mother would never have permitted one in the house."

He lifted his glass and surveyed her silently a moment. "You might as well have been left an orphan," he finally commented.

In truth, that's how she'd often felt, but he was the first to put it in words. "I hope you know how lucky you are, to be part of such a united family."

He started to reply, then seemed to think better of it and reverted to his role of mentor, instead. "Tell me what you think of this wine?"

"I'm enjoying it."

"No, no, Arlene," he chided. "I expect better of you than that. Tell me what it is that makes it so enjoyable."

She squirmed in her seat. A connoisseur of wines she was not. She knew what she liked, but that's about as far as it went. "It's Vermentino."

"Not good enough! All you had to do to reach that conclusion is read the label."

"It's refreshing."

"And...? What do you notice about the finish?"

"It has nice legs?" she offered haltingly, tilting her glass.

He threw back his head and burst out laughing. "*Dio*, I have failed as a teacher! You'll have to come back for a second course of instruction."

Oh, if only! she thought, her heart seeming to swell in her breast as she feasted on the sight of him. On his flawless teeth, and the lush, downward sweep of his generous lashes. On his eyes, dark as sapphires in the candlelight. How could any woman be expected to keep her head around such a wealth of masculine beauty?

Sobering, he leaned toward her. "Try again, my lovely lady. Inhale the bouquet. Take a slow mouthful and let it acquaint itself with your palate."

Feeling horribly self-conscious, she complied.

"Well? Tell me what you discovered."

"It's light," she ventured. "Fruity—but not overpoweringly so. And…with a hint of almonds?"

"Exactly! The perfect accompaniment to the seafood platter I recommend we order as our main course."

The moon had risen by then, illuminating the ancient domes and towers of the city, and casting deep shadows in the square beyond the restaurant. With the votive candles flickering between them, she and Domenico lingered over a fabulous selection of scampi, crayfish and mussels, served with a salad and a basket of the delicious bread she'd come to expect from the island.

"You left room for dessert?" he inquired, when at last there was nothing left but empty shells and crumbs.

"Heavens, no!" she exclaimed on a sigh. "I'm literally stuffed to the gills!"

"Then we'll finish with something you've yet to experience," he declared, gesturing to their waiter. "So far, you know only the regular Vermentino, a young, slightly bitter wine, served ice cold. Now, you must try its cousin, the *liquorosa*, more aged, sweeter and not so chilled."

"I think I've had enough for one day." Two glasses of wine was pretty much her limit, and they'd already consumed an entire bottle with their meal. If she had anymore, she'd either wind up under the table or throwing herself at him.

"Relax, Arlene," he said gently. "It is not my intention to get you drunk, merely to extend the pleasure of this evening as long as possible."

"I'd have thought you'd had enough of me by now."

"You are mistaken."

Three words, simply spoken, that was all. Yet they intoxicated her beyond anything alcohol could hope to achieve.

The candle flames swirled dizzily before her eyes. The blood surged heatedly through her veins. Clinging to her vanishing sanity, she began, "You know everything about me—"

"Not everything," he murmured. "The best, I suspect, is yet to come."

"The point is," she almost panted, "I know next to nothing about you, so now it's your turn to talk. Tell me about you."

"What would you like to know?"

"Your deepest, darkest secrets," she said, injecting a teasing note into her voice to disguise her inner turmoil.

Tell me you cheat on your income tax, that you're wanted by the police and have a prison record, that you're an inveterate womanizer...anything to bring me to my senses, please!

He looked long into her eyes. Set down his untouched wine. Rose from the table and held out an imperious hand. His own voice suddenly hoarse, he said, "Why bother to tell you, when actions speak so much louder than words?"

CHAPTER FOUR

ON THAT note, he walked her out of the citadel to where he'd left the roadster, drove past a marina in which the masts of million-dollar yachts reached for the stars, and followed a road through a pine forest to an isolated stretch of coast.

"At this very moment," he said, finally breaking his silence and drawing her onto the beach, "what I most want is to hold you in my arms and kiss you, here in this quiet place, with nothing but the sea and sky as witness."

"Why?" she asked him.

"Because, at this moment, I find you more desirable than any other woman I have known."

He ran his hands down her bare arms and, catching her hands, pulled her toward him. The heat of his body reached out to envelop her. The height and breadth of him blotted out the pale moonlight and sheltered her from the cool sea air. The strong, steady thump of his heart reassured her. She was safe with him. He would let nothing hurt her.

He stood close, imprinting her with the evidence of his arousal. His gaze seared her, stripping her to the bone. His breath winnowed over her face, taunting her. Not until he'd reduced her to mindless anticipation did he at last, and with excruciating slowness, lower his mouth to hers.

She didn't have to be an expert to recognize that, when it came to a kiss, he was. The very second his lips found hers, she was lost. Lost in a reality that exceeded all fantasy. Tossed in a storm of emotion that left her shaking. Caught up in a turbulent wanting that screamed for more…for everything he was willing to give her.

…*nothing wrong with a little lust, as long as you're careful,* Gail had said.

But "careful" had no place in Arlene's world just then. The only thing that ruled was hunger, and it raged at her without mercy. Her mouth softened beneath his, eager and willing to accept him into its heated depths. Her tongue engaged with his, instinctively understanding the ritualistic prelude to greater intimacy and signaling her acquiescence. She clung to him, threading her fingers through his hair. Whimpered softly, an inarticulate little sound beseeching him to take all of her.

He did not. Instead he dragged his mouth away and stepped back, leaving the cool sea air to flow over her limbs and infiltrate her heart. "It grows late. I must take you home."

His abrupt mood swing almost flattened her. He didn't mean what he said. He couldn't, not when, just nanoseconds before, his body had broadcast a blatantly different story.

"No," she whispered, clinging to him. "I'm not afraid. I trust you, Domenico. You don't have to stop—"

"Yes, Arlene," he said flatly, his voice rough as the granite decomposition of the soil that produced his grapes. "Oh, yes, I do."

Despair welled up in her throat, colder than ice. She'd disappointed him. Been too clumsy, too eager, too…too *everything!* Humiliated, she spun away so that he wouldn't see the tears glimmering down her face, and started back to the car.

He kept pace with her. Held open her door. Without a word,

he again draped the scarf over her bent head, then climbed into the driver's seat. One quick turn of the ignition key and the car roared to life, its headlights slicing through the dark to play on the densely packed trunks of the pine trees.

The drive from Alghero to the small town where she was staying was both mercifully long, and cruelly, short. The roadster swept in a wide arc to the forecourt of her hotel and stopped, all the while muttering impatiently as if it couldn't wait to be rid of her and on its way again.

She opened her door. Swung her legs to the pavement. "Thank you very much for a lovely day," she said over her shoulder, reciting the words like a child well-coached by her mother. "Thank you, too, for all your kind help. I'm most grateful. Goodbye."

His silence had continued throughout the journey from the beach, but at that, he finally spoke again. "Tomorrow…"

Three syllables only, they were enough to paralyze her in mid-flight. But she didn't turn. Didn't dare look at him. Hardly dared to breathe, let alone hope. "What about tomorrow?"

"Take the day off. Spend it with your friend. You've hardly seen her since you arrived."

Another, more vicious wave of disappointment swept over her. *And you've seen altogether too much of me and don't want to spend another minute in my company! Why don't you just come out and say what you mean, Domenico?*

His voice grazed the back of her neck, stilling her retort before she could air it. Seeped into her pores, electrifying her. "I'll pick you up later…eight o'clock…for dinner…something different from tonight."

Long after the car had growled away, its red taillights swallowed up by the night, she stood immobile and forced herself to breathe. She didn't know what he'd meant by his cryptic remark about "something different," nor, at that moment, did she care. All that mattered was that it wasn't over between them, after all.

Storming into his villa, Domenico poured himself a *grappa* and paced the covered veranda outside his living room, cursing himself for being the king of all fools. The minute his mouth touched hers, he'd known kissing her was a mistake and that the kindest thing he could do was never see her again.

He'd told himself that over and over again, throughout the return trip to her hotel because, as he'd learned when he was still in his teens, smart men avoided involvement with women who didn't understand the rules of the game. And that Arlene hadn't a clue about them became apparent the minute his lips touched hers.

The passion he'd awoken in her with just one kiss had stunned him. He could have taken her, there on a public beach, and she would not have refused him.

I trust you...you don't have to stop, she'd said, her voice thick and urgent with need.

That he *had* stopped was scarcely to his credit. Sexually he desired her in every way a man could desire a woman. Even thinking of how she'd felt in his arms—soft, compliant, sweetly responsive—was enough to stir him to painful arousal. But that word "trust" had awoken in him the voice of conscience and it would not be silenced.

How was it, he'd found himself wondering, that a woman approaching thirty retained such willingness to believe in the goodness of others, when all she'd known as a child was rejection?

And there, in a nutshell, lay the real problem, because he would not, *could not*, be the one to reject her again. However much he might want it, and however mutually pleasurable it might be at the time, they would never make love because her tender heart would end up being badly bruised.

She wasn't the casual type. For her, intimacy would mean love and marriage—and he wasn't in the market for either. Best to avoid further hurt and end things with her now.

He knew exactly the words to say. Rehearsed them all the way back to the hotel until he had them down pat. *It's been a real pleasure, Arlene, but I've taught you as much as I can, so consider yourself free to enjoy the rest of your holiday. Goodbye and good luck!*

Kind, but final, leaving no room for misinterpretation.

She'd beaten him to it. Served up her little farewell speech with perfect composure, and let him off the hook—or so he'd thought until he heard the confusion in her voice and saw how her chin quivered despite her best efforts to control it. Until he saw her walking away from him, her spine so stiff with pain and hard-won dignity that it undid all his good intentions.

Suddenly, without thought for the complications he was bringing down on himself, he'd blurted out an invitation he never saw coming. One that promised nothing but trouble he didn't need.

Dinner alone with her was out of the question. Candlelight and wine made for a dangerous combination. Throw in a little music, a little star-shine, the dark intimacy inside his car, and the end result was a recipe, if not for disaster, then for lasting regrets. Even he wasn't made of stone.

"You're bringing her for dinner?"

"Here?"

"With us?"

The squeals of excitement that greeted his announcement the next day would have put a screech owl to shame.

"Don't make something out of it that isn't there," he warned his mother and sisters grimly. "There's nothing serious going on here. She's just starting out in this business, that's all, and the more she talks to people whose entire lives revolve around a vineyard, the more she'll learn."

"We understand," they crowed, their ill-concealed glee giving the lie to their words. "You're just being a good friend. There's absolutely nothing else going on."

As he drove past the main house on his way to collect her, he saw through the lighted windows the hive of activity taking place inside, and knew he might as well have saved his breath. Nobody had believed a word he said.

Well, it was up to him to prove them all wrong. He'd keep the mood light. Hospitable but impersonal. Pleasant without being overly familiar. In other words, treat her exactly as he'd treat any other colleague.

He arrived a few minutes early and was waiting in the hotel lobby when she came out of the elevator. If, yesterday, she'd been pretty as a picture in her sea-green sundress, tonight she was a study in classic elegance. Instead of leaving her hair to flow loose around her face, she secured it at her nape with a black velvet bow. She wore a straight black ankle-length skirt, open-toed black sandals, a simple, long-sleeved white lace blouse and pearl studs at her ears.

"I forgot to return this to you," she said, handing him the scarf he'd bought for her.

He bent and dusted a kiss on her cheek. A big mistake. The faint trace of her perfume reminded him of the wild violets that grew on the island in spring, but the softness of her skin struck a more intimate note and put a dent in his resolve to keep his distance. "It's yours to keep, Arlene, but you won't need it tonight. I put the top up, on the car."

She trembled slightly under his touch as he guided her outside. "Where are you taking me this time?" she asked, as he drove away from the hotel and turned the car toward the west.

"To dinner with my family."

"Your *family?*" she echoed, clearly shocked.

"That's right. You've already met my uncle and sisters. Tonight, you'll meet the rest." *As in, parents, in-laws, nieces, nephews, dogs, cats and anyone else he could drag into the mix!*

"I see." He felt her thoughtful gray gaze turn on him. "Why?"

He hadn't anticipated that question and had to scramble for an answer that would neither mislead nor offend her. "Because…because being welcomed into someone's home is the best way to really get a feel for a foreign country. Hotels and such are fine in their place, but they don't paint a true picture of the culture."

In the light thrown by a passing street lamp, he saw a frown marred the smooth width of her forehead. "I think what you're really saying is that you feel sorry for me, and I have to tell you, I don't need your pity, Domenico."

Dio! He'd forgotten she was as perceptive as she was lovely. "Of all the feelings you arouse in me, Arlene, be assured that pity is not one of them. If that's the impression I gave you, then I chose my words badly, so let me put it this way: I'd like you to spend an evening with my family because I believe you'll enjoy it, and I know for a fact *they* are eager to meet you."

"Why?"

"Do you realize how often you ask me that?"

"I'm sorry if it annoys you."

"I didn't say it annoys me."

She lifted her shoulder in a delicate shrug. "Then answer the question."

So much for keeping things light and pleasant! Tension, brittle as spun glass, arced between them. "Because I like you," he said, the annoyance she'd accused him of suddenly becoming a fact. He wasn't used to being so easily outmaneuvered. "I like you very much. I admire your intelligence and your determination. To be sure, we haven't known each other more than a few days, but we share common interests and I look upon you as a friend. That's it, pure and simple. I have no ulterior motive. We Sards are hospitable people. We welcome friends into our homes. Is that so very difficult for you to understand?"

"No," she said, in such a small, crushed voice that he swore silently for speaking to her so harshly. "I guess I'm being hypersensitive, and I apologize. I tend to react like this when I'm unsure of myself, and I don't mind admitting I'm finding the prospect of being paraded before your relatives rather daunting."

His anger died as swiftly as it had arisen. "You have nothing to worry about. You'll worm your way into their hearts with no trouble at all."

Just as you'll worm your way into mine, if I let you, he almost added.

A sobering thought. One best kept to himself.

She was a mess; a bundle of nerves. Overnight, she'd had time to consider his last-minute invitation, and it had left her fluctuating between elation and the unwelcome suspicion that he was merely being kind, just as he would be to a stray dog he found on the side of the road.

"Calm down," Gail had told her. "Stop looking for a hidden

agenda that isn't there, and just enjoy the evening for what it is—a date with a sophisticated, handsome man who clearly enjoys your company."

"But what am I supposed to wear? 'Dinner' could mean anything from a hamburger at a beachside fast-food outlet, to a five-course meal at a private club," she fretted.

"Assume it's the private club, but keep it simple, just in case you're wrong."

The trouble was, Arlene thought now, eyeing him furtively as he navigated the curves in the road, nothing to do with Domenico was simple. He was the most complex man she'd ever come across, and she'd known from the start that she was hopelessly out of her depth in trying to deal with him. Discovering she was about to take on the entire Silvaggio d'Avalos family as well was enough to give her the shudders.

"This is the main house where my parents live," he said, turning into a driveway and pulling up under the portico of a villa which, like his, exemplified wealthy good taste. "My sisters also have homes here, and so do I, as you already know, but we're spread out far enough not to get under each other's feet."

She wished they'd stayed spread out tonight. The house alone intimidated her, and never mind the couple who lived there, but when a manservant opened the door and she saw the mob gathered inside like a receiving committee, her heart sank. Her only comfort was that she'd dressed appropriately. The women all wore floor-length skirts or evening slacks and tops in lustrous fabrics, and the men, suits and ties.

The grand entrance hall where they waited comprised a vast space with a high curved ceiling supported by massive beams, very much in the style she'd come to recognize as typical of Sardinia. The floor was slate-gray, the walls white, the refectory table centered beneath a heavy wrought-iron chandelier so severely plain, it could have come from a monastery. Yet what might otherwise have struck her as stark and rather forbidding was softened by a huge colorful flower arrangement in the middle of the table, muted light from alabaster wall sconces, and vivid oil paintings on the walls.

Soon enough, her other worries eased a little, too. From his aristocratic-looking parents to the smallest child, most spoke at least a smattering of English, and even if they hadn't, there was no mistaking the warmth of their smiles and the way they embraced her into their midst.

Immediately Domenico introduced her, Federico Silvaggio d'Avalos, his tall, handsome father, stepped forward and kissed her hand as gallantly as if she were royalty. "We are honored to welcome you into our home, *signorina*."

His mother, Carmela, well into her fifties and still stunningly beautiful, kissed her on both cheeks, exclaimed at how chilled her face was, and promptly ushered her into a large, elegant salon furnished in pale silks and richly inlaid woods. "We're so happy Domenico brought you to meet us, my dear. Come sit by the fire with me, and get to know my large, noisy family."

A flurry of other introductions followed. The pregnant sister who'd been so sympathetic the day Arlene came down with the migraine, joined her on the sofa. "Hello, again, Arlene. I'm Renata, and this is my husband, Vittorio. Not that you're expected to remember everyone's names," she added, with a laugh. "Even we forget who's who, sometimes, there are so many of us."

"That's true." Another sister put in mischievously. "All four of us girls have married and given our parents grandchildren." She paused. "You're not married, though, are you, Arlene?"

"No."

She smiled sunnily. "What a coincidence. Neither is Domenico."

Apart from the black glare he shot her way, and despite all the trappings of wealth and privilege—the women's jewelry, the plush comfort of Persian rugs, damask upholstery as soft as swansdown, and hand-carved wood polished to a satin shine, not to mention the servants hovering unobtrusively in the background—the atmosphere in the room was relaxed and convivial.

Although the older children were more interested in teasing each other than joining in the adult conversation, the younger ones swarmed around Arlene in wide-eyed curiosity. When one of them, a toddler about eighteen months old, stumbled and fell, his grandmother scooped him onto her lap and comforted him, not caring in the least that he drooled down her shot silk blouse.

A grizzled old dog of indeterminate breed dozed by the fire, but no one shooed him away. No irate parent ordered the children to be quiet, or go play in another room. When the noise level grew too loud, the adults simply raised their voices over it.

Long past her initial nervousness, Arlene basked in the scene. She'd crossed the threshold into their home, a stranger, and in no time at all, they'd accepted her unconditionally. They plied her with questions about her life in Canada, and her newly acquired vineyard. Much to his chagrin and to general laughter, they showed her a photograph of Domenico lying naked on a fur rug when he was a baby, and regaled her with amusing accounts of his boyhood exploits.

This, she thought, soaking up every minute, is what a real family is all about.

Dinner lasted a full three hours, a magnificent feast of traditional Sardinian dishes. *Burrida*, a spicy fish soup, followed by delicately poached sea bream, both served with ice-cold Vermentino bearing the Silvaggio d'Avalos label. Next, a full-bodied red Cannonau, also from the family winery, for the main course of spit-roasted lamb, artichokes and *malloreddus*, small gnocchi-like pasta. For dessert, deep fried ricotta cakes drenched in honey, washed down with a sparkling Moscato from the Gallura hills. And finally, rich dark coffee and tiny, exquisite chocolates filled with minted lemon cream.

Arlene never could have consumed so huge a meal had it not been for the leisurely pace. As it was, she was able to relax between courses and enjoy her surroundings without appearing overly curious.

The dining room itself was a feast for the eyes. Large and square, with French doors opening to a terrace, it sported a table that easily could seat thirty. The musical ping of fine crystal, the discreet clink of heavy sterling on monogrammed china all added to a setting which might have been best described as majestic were it not for the infant high chairs interspersed at regular intervals among the formal furnishings.

"You have a lovely home," Arlene confided to Domenico's mother, during a lull in the conversation.

"Thank you, *cara*. It's really much too big for just two people, but my children refuse to let me and their father move to something smaller. They claim this is the only place they can all fit around one table at the same time." She glanced at Renata, and Gemma, Domenico's second youngest sister who was also pregnant. "And since the babies keep coming, I suppose they have a point. Do you have brothers and sisters, Arlene?"

"No. I'm an only child."

Only, and lonely—at least until tonight. But Domenico's family had drawn her so seamlessly into their familial web of affection that, for once, she was not on the outside looking in. For once, she felt as if she belonged, even if it was only for a few hours. Not that they fawned over her or gave the impression that they were putting on a show for her benefit. They simply included her.

So many things touched her as the meal progressed. Insignificant things to most people, probably, but to her they spelled all that had been missing from her own upbringing. Lara's husband Edmondo, for example, who left his own food to grow cold while he patiently coaxed his six-year-old son Sebastiano into trying the slivers of lamb he'd been served.

...I didn't say you had to like it, Arlene. I said you had to eat it, and you'll sit there until you do...

Or Domenico's father reaching across the table to clasp his wife's hand, proof that marriage didn't have to spell the end of love between a man and a woman.

And perhaps most moving of all, Domenico lifting a suddenly fractious niece from her booster seat and cradling her against his shoulder until she fell asleep with her thumb popped firmly in her sweet little rosebud mouth—a sight so unbearably beautiful, so overflowing with affection, that it brought tears to Arlene's eyes.

It was as they all lingered over coffee that the subject arose of a viticulture convention in Paris. "This coming weekend, isn't it?" Renata asked, of no one in particular.

Her uncle Bruno nodded. "That's right. Three days, starting on Friday.

A lively discussion followed, covering speakers, vintners, manufacturers, suppliers and anything else remotely connected to the business of turning grapes into wine.

"You're presenting this year, as usual, Domenico?" his brother-in-law Ignazio inquired.

He nodded, careful not to disturb his sleeping niece. "Once only, on Friday."

Michele, the second eldest sister and the quietest, looked up from wiping honey off her seven-year-old daughter's chin. "You should take Arlene with you. It would be an invaluable experience for her."

"I'm afraid that's out of the question," Arlene said quickly, not about to wait for Domenico to shoot down the idea. If there'd been one flaw in an otherwise perfect evening, it was that he'd remained distinctly aloof from her, as if wanting to make it clear, both to her and his family, that they weren't a couple. Not that he'd totally ignored her. It would have been better if he had. Instead he'd watched her, his blue eyes as sharp and clinical as a surgeon's scalpel. "I'm flying home on Saturday."

"Registration's closed now, anyway," he said.

"Not to you," Lara argued. "Never that. You could show up with twenty extra attendees at the last minute, and they'd be accommodated." She turned to Arlene. "That's the kind of clout our brother wields in vintner circles. They practically kiss his feet when he shows up, he brings such cachet to the occasion."

Fortunately the conversation swung to the pleasures of Paris in October, and soon after, the party came to an end. First the grandchildren were rounded up and bundled into cars by their parents for the short ride home, then it was Arlene's turn to take her leave.

"Come and see us again before you go home," Domenico's mother said kindly, again kissing her on both cheeks.

"Most certainly," his father added. "Don't wait for an invitation. Our door is always open."

"Thank you," she managed, swallowing another sudden clutch of tears, because she knew she wouldn't be coming back. As he had so often throughout the evening, Domenico was again watching her, as if waiting for her to put a foot wrong when she said her goodbyes.

Why? Had she shamed him, in her black skirt and white blouse, with not a single jewel but her pearl earrings to redeem their plainness? Had he decided she wasn't quite good enough to associate with his family? Not sophisticated enough? Or had his aim always been to show her that she didn't fit into his life, and never would?

There was only one way to find out. "Okay, Domenico," she said, the moment they were on the road. "You don't have to pretend any longer. It's nobody but just the two of us now, so 'fess up. What's the real reason you took me to meet your family tonight?"

CHAPTER FIVE

COVERING up his jolt of surprise at the question, Domenico said, "Have you forgotten we already dealt with that subject, Arlene?"

"Remind me again. I'm not sure I remember it accurately."

"I thought it would be an enjoyable experience for everyone involved."

"Including you?"

"Of course including me."

"Then please explain why you spent the entire evening staying as far away from me as possible. Did you have a change of heart once we arrived, and decide you'd made a mistake in inviting me, after all?"

"No."

"I don't believe you. I think you were afraid I'd embarrass you—or worse yet, you hoped I'd embarrass myself."

Inhaling sharply, he slammed on the brakes, brought the car to a skidding stop on the gravel shoulder at the side of the road and turned to face her. Expert though he was at keeping a poker face, even he couldn't hide his shock. "How the devil could you have done that?"

She shifted in her seat, a slight movement only, but enough for the rustle of silky underthings to whisper alluringly over her skin. "Oh, I don't know," she said, giving another of her elegant little shrugs. "Tucked my napkin in the top of my blouse, and not known which fork to use, perhaps. Or knocked back too much wine and slid under the table in a drunken stupor before the main course was served."

Her reply shook him to the core. Never in his life had he lifted his hand to a woman, but assaulted by so many conflicting emotions he couldn't begin to sort, let alone control, he actually grabbed her by the shoulders and shook her. Not hard, to be sure, and in frustration rather than anger. Nevertheless, her lovely gray eyes turned glassy with unshed tears, and her sweet, vulnerable mouth dropped open in shock.

His mind grew dark. Black and empty as a cave buried deep below the earth's surface. Search though he might, he could find no words to justify his behavior, no lodestar to restore him to himself. Never more at a loss than he was at that moment, he gave up trying to excuse the inexcusable, and once again submitted to the instinct which had driven him for days. He hauled her into his arms and crushed her mouth beneath his.

At first, she resisted, holding herself stiff as a board. Desperate to soften the blow he'd dealt her, he cajoled her by cupping the back of her head in one hand and stroking the other up her throat to caress her jaw.

A tear slipped free. Slid pearl-like down the heated curve of her cheek. He trapped it with his tongue and, finally, the right words, the *only* words that mattered, spilled from him. "I could never be ashamed of you," he whispered into her mouth. "You are the finest thing that ever happened to me. If I stayed away from you, it was because I was afraid to stand too close."

"Why?" Once again, her favorite question emerged, this time uttered on a sigh.

He answered by deepening the kiss, with no thought of pulling away, or of letting matters end there. The hunger he'd tried so hard to contain rampaged through his blood, sending coherent thought tumbling into obscurity. At that moment, he was a man driven beyond reason.

She melted in his embrace. Leaned into him and let her head fall back in utter surrender. The scent of her skin filled him. Drove him beyond the bounds of sophisticated seduction that had always been his trademark.

He knew that stretch of the coast like the back of his hand. Knew that, a few meters ahead, a rough track led into the shelter of the pine trees lining the side of the road. With one arm looped around her shoulder, he left-handedly shifted the roadster into gear, steered it under the dark canopy of branches and killed both engine and headlights.

Stripped of moon and stars by the foliage, night closed around the vehicle, veiling it in cool secrecy. Inside, though, a fire raged, fusing desire into a mass of molten passion as primitive and unplanned as it was unstoppable.

He put his hands on her. Shaped her through the fine lace of her blouse. He found the buttons. Undid them. Pushed aside the silky camisole she wore underneath, to discover the silkier perfection of her breasts.

Her flesh surged against his palm and she let out a tiny gasp of pleasure. It drove him to further madness. Lowering his head, he captured her nipple in his mouth and ran his hand the length of her slender body to her ankles.

Her narrow skirt resisted his intrusion but he, consumed by raging desire, would not be stopped. The sound of a seam splitting made little impression compared to the thundering of his heart.

Her legs were bare and smooth as cream. Freed from the

demure confinement imposed by her skirt, they fell slackly apart and turned his invasion into an invitation. The breath seized in his throat at her damp softness; at the warm, sleek privacy to which she gave him access. Already hard, he felt himself pulsing against the fabric of his trousers. Teetering so close to the brink of destruction that he gave no thought to dignity or decency.

An owl swooping suddenly out of the night to brush the tip of one pale wing close to the windshield, saved him from himself. Restored to belated sanity, and appalled at his lack of control, Domenico smoothed her clothing into place and, awash in self-disgust, flung himself away, his chest heaving.

In all the years since he'd lost his virginity at fourteen to a woman twice his age, he'd never once sunk to the level of a backseat Casanova. That in this case there was no backseat and he'd had to make do with two front seats separated by the gearshift console, was a moot point. The fact was, Arlene deserved better than to be subjected to the kind of impatient fumbling that had left her with a torn skirt and a level of sexual frustration that probably matched his own. She deserved a little respect—and a very large apology.

"I am sorry," he said. Then, knowing he owed her more than that, added, "Not for finding you irresistible, but for showing it so clumsily, and for every other mistake I've made where you're concerned."

"What kind of mistakes?" she whispered into the darkness.

"Letting my pride dictate my actions. That first day, when you mentioned having to meet up with a friend, I jumped to the assumption that you were here with a man." He laughed grimly. "I was eaten up with jealousy."

"I'd never have guessed."

"No," he said. "I'm good at hiding my thoughts and feelings. But the truth is, I wanted to punish you, and I did. The next day, I endangered your health by allowing you to work yourself into a state of complete exhaustion. Your migraine attack was my fault."

She found his face in the darkness and touched his cheek tenderly. "Even you can't take credit for that, Domenico. I should have had enough sense to quit before things came to such a pass. I chose not to, and suffered the consequences."

"I knew better, and should have been more vigilant."

"You've been nothing but helpful and kind and wonderful to me."

He caught her fingers and kissed them. "I'm a proud, stubborn man, Arlene. I go after what I want with single-minded determination. Don't fool yourself into believing otherwise."

She let her hand trail lightly down his chest. "Do you want me?"

"Yes, I want you," he said, halfway between a laugh and a groan.

"Then take me."

Sorely tempted, he let a beat of silence pass before answering. "Not here. Not now."

"Then when?"

He paused again, weighing the options. He could take her back to his place. They'd be completely alone. It was an unwritten rule among his family that each respected the other's privacy and never showed up on the doorstep without invitation. But there was always the risk of her being seen in the car, and he wasn't ready for the speculation that would arouse.

He could take her to a hotel. But that smacked too much of a cheap one-night stand, and he'd decided years ago he'd never stoop to such lowlife measures. Which left him with

what was probably the best and wisest course, and that was
to do nothing at all, and so spare them both the pain of having
to sever the strands of involvement when it came time for her
to leave the island.

Do it, his conscience prompted. *Let her down gently, and
walk away before you break her heart.* "You could come with
me to Paris," he heard himself suggest.

"I can't afford it," she said.

"I can."

He felt her withdrawal as acutely as if a cold wind had in-
filtrated the car. "I won't take your money."

"You won't have to. I'll be traveling by private jet. It will
cost me no more to add an extra passenger than it will to include an extra guest in my hotel suite."

"Even so, what about Gail? I can't just abandon her."

He heard the longing in her voice. Seduced by it, he said,
"She'll meet you in Paris on Sunday morning and you'll fly
home together from there."

"Our tickets are for Saturday and don't include a stopover
in Paris. We came here via Rome."

"Tickets can be changed, *cara,*" he said, firing up the car
and backing it onto the road. "In fact, you can achieve just
about anything, if you want it badly enough."

The glow from the illuminated dials on the dash showed
her lips pressed together in a way he'd come to recognize
meant she was giving serious thought to the idea. "I don't
know about that," she finally said. "But I do know I want you."

At the time, Arlene had been very certain that she knew exactly what she wanted, and also what she'd be getting: one
glorious weekend with Domenico Silvaggio d'Avalos, the
most exciting man she'd ever known. Not that he'd said it in

so many words, but even she wasn't naive enough to think he was promising anything beyond that.

But when he learned she'd never been to Paris, he changed their plans and suggested they leave Sardinia on the Wednesday so that he'd have time to show her something of the city before the convention began. The prospect of four whole days and nights with him left her giddy with anticipation, and if the sensible voice of caution warned her she was getting in over her head, she hushed it. She'd broken the cautious, sensible mold, the day she'd decided to accept her inheritance.

She didn't see him again until the morning of their departure. "After Paris, I'm heading to Chile for a couple of weeks, which means I'll be tied up for the next few days, making sure everything's running smoothly on the homefront before I leave," he told her, when he returned her to her hotel on the Saturday night.

"I understand," she said, steadfastly ignoring his not-too-subtle reminder that, after the coming weekend, they'd be going their separate ways. "As it happens, I've got a few things to take care of, myself."

Placing his hand in the small of her back, he walked her through the hotel lobby in such a way as to shield her torn skirt from the night clerk's inquisitive stare. "Then it's arranged. I'll have your friend's new flight information delivered tomorrow, and pick you up here at eight on Wednesday morning. We'll be in Paris in time for lunch."

"Sounds wonderful."

As the elevator door whispered open, he dropped a swift, hard kiss on her mouth. "Until Wednesday, then."

Euphoria carried her through the next three days. By Tuesday, she'd refurbished her wardrobe with clothes more suited to private jets and October in Paris, than the beaches of Sardinia. Returning to the millionaire's playground of Alghero, she and Gail scoured the town and found a couple of consignment boutiques stocked with designer fashions in her size. But that they cost her only a fraction of their true value didn't change the fact that she spent more on clothing in two days than she had in the previous two years.

"Think of it as an investment in your future," Gail counseled, when she fretted about the balance owing on her credit card. "This is, after all, as much a business trip as a naughty weekend. You could make some very valuable contacts at the convention, and it's important you project a suitably professional image."

"To the tune of hundreds of dollars?"

"Well, you know what they say. If you want to make an omelet, you have to break a few eggs."

The trouble was, enough clothes to make a four-day, four-night splash in Paris added up to a lot more than just a few eggs. One smart cranberry-red suit, two silk blouses, a pair of tailored slacks, a cashmere sweater, reversible wool cape and basic black velvet dinner dress, plus the two pairs of shoes and ankle-high black suede boots she toted back to the hotel, called for an entire poultry farm!

And that was before she succumbed to the temptation of a misty-mauve, long silk-knit dress and a sinfully gorgeous evening gown shimmering with celadon beading—"because," as Gail reminded her when she hesitated about buying it, "even run-of-the-mill conventions always wind up with a banquet of some sort on the Saturday night, and there's nothing run-of-the-mill about your man and the company he keeps."

Surveying the contents of her suitcase on the Tuesday evening—the "gently used" designer items, supplemented by Gail's silver pumps, matching clutch bag and fake purple pashmina shawl—the full impact of what Arlene had let herself in for finally hit home. She was risking financial and emotional bankruptcy—and for what? A no-promises tryst with a man who hadn't even bothered to pick up the phone and call her since Saturday. A man so dangerously attractive that she was practically guaranteed a broken heart at the end of it all. What use would her fancy new clothes be to her, then?

"I'm a nobody trying to keep up with a very big somebody," she wailed.

"You're an idiot," Gail said bracingly. "Mr. Wonderful puts his pants on one leg at a time, just like any other guy."

But Domenico wasn't at all like any other guy, and the truth of that was driven home with a vengeance, the second he escorted Arlene on board his sleek Gulfstream jet, early on Wednesday morning. The spacious cabin, with its wide aisle, ample headroom, thick carpet and leather seating arrangement spelled the ultimate in luxury and comfort.

She had been too wound up to eat anything before leaving the hotel, but the scant two hours it took to fly from the airport in Olbia to Le Bourget in Paris allowed enough time for a steward to serve them a light breakfast of chilled champagne and orange juice, warm, delicious rolls, fresh fruit and wonderful rich Italian coffee.

"To Paris!" Domenico said, raising his glass in a toast as the shoreline of Sardinia receded below them.

She nodded, not quite believing she was sitting across from him, a fine, monogrammed serviette on her lap, and a mimosa in a crystal flute clutched nervously between her fingers. Her previous flying experience had been all about paper napkins, packaged snacks and plain orange juice from a disposable plastic glass. But then, she'd never before agreed to what Gail had gleefully described as "a business weekend spiked with sweaty, delicious passion between the sheets, with the sexiest guy to walk the earth since Sean Connery strode around as James Bond."

Sexy, yes, but observant, too, and watching her, Domenico said, "You're very pensive, Arlene. Is something wrong?"

In a word, yes! A sleepless night had merely intensified her doubts. Plain, ordinary Arlene Russell didn't belong in a private jet with a man like him. "I'm rather overwhelmed, I guess. I've never been whisked away to one of the great capitals of Europe by someone I've only just met."

"If you're having second thoughts about coming away with me, rest assured I'll not pressure you into doing anything you're not ready for. You will set the pace of our time together, *cara*, not I."

"That's hardly the agreement we made last Saturday. I'm not about to repay your generosity by..." She stopped, unable to put into words what they both knew she meant.

He suffered no such qualms. "By not sleeping with me? Arlene, please! Just because I find you desirable doesn't mean you owe me sexual favors. Over the next few days, you'll meet some of the foremost viticulturists in the world. I'll consider myself well rewarded if you make the most of that opportunity." He shrugged then, and smiled. "And if we happen also to make love? Well, that will be a bonus."

Avoiding his gaze, she stroked her hand over the butter-soft leather arm of her seat. "I wondered if perhaps you'd changed your mind about that. We haven't spoken since Saturday, and when you picked me up this morning, you were very...businesslike."

"You mean, I didn't kiss you?"

He was altogether too good at divining her thoughts. Flushing, she said, "Not even on the cheek."

"Is that what's left you so much at odds?" He laughed, and leaning across the table, caught her chin and brought his mouth to hers. "You taste delectable," he murmured, when at last he drew away again. "And if you think I've kept my distance because I've had a change of heart, you couldn't be more mistaken."

Her mood lifted at that, and she found it easier to focus on the here and now, and leave the future to take care of itself. If this magical few days was to mark the grand finale of her experience with this incredible man, she wouldn't let her insecurities cloud it. Twenty years from now, she wanted the details etched so clearly in her memory that it seemed they had happened just yesterday.

As the jet began its descent over Paris, Domenico pointed out famous landmarks she'd only ever read about, or seen on television or in the movies. Her face pressed to the window, she caught her first glimpse of the Eiffel Tower, the Arc de Triomphe, the bridges across the Seine, Notre Dame, Sacré-Coeur. The names and images unfolded below, gilded with autumn sunlight and the romantic ambience which had defined the city for centuries.

When they emerged from the airport, a chauffeur-driven Mercedes waited to take them to their hotel. Arlene hoped it would be modest enough that her beleaguered credit card could cover the cost of staying there, because she had no intention of letting Domenico pay. It was enough that he'd taken care of their travel arrangements and used his influence to get her registered at the convention.

She realized how fruitless her hopes were when the car drew to a stop and she found herself standing before the legendary Paris Ritz. Even she knew it was among the most expensive and luxurious hotels in the world. Frozen with dismay, she clutched Domenico's arm and skidded to a stop. "The convention's being held *here?*"

"I never stay in the convention hotel, *cara*," he said, calmly propelling her inside the beautiful eighteenth-century building. "Too crowded, too noisy and not nearly enough privacy."

"But I can't afford this place!"

"I can."

"That's not the point!"

"Then what is?"

"That I have my pride. I've gone along with everything else you've suggested, but I refuse to let you pay for my accommodation."

He glanced meaningfully at the people milling around the ornate lobby. "We will not discuss the matter here, Arlene. It can wait until we are alone."

But that didn't happen until she found herself in a suite of rooms overlooking the Vendôme Gardens, and the sheer magnificence of the setting alone was enough to render her speechless. Elegant antique furniture, priceless *objets d'art*, paintings, Persian rugs, huge floral arrangements—try as she might, taking it all in was impossible. Simply put, she had never in her life *seen* anything so exquisite, let alone found herself immersed in it.

Stunned, she turned to Domenico. "What am I doing in this place?"

"This," he said, and kissed her for the second time that day; a long, achingly beautiful kiss.

She struggled to keep her head, to stand by her principles. But however magnificent the Ritz, it couldn't hold a candle to Domenico Silvaggio d'Avalos when he set out to seduce. She could walk away from the trappings of the rich and famous, and never know a moment's regret. She could not walk away from him.

Not that she didn't try. Tearing her mouth free, she whispered, "I don't belong here, Domenico."

"Then leave," he said, holding her tighter. Trapping her in his magnetic aura.

"You don't understand…!"

"What don't I understand, Arlene?" he murmured, drawing out her name on a long breath, and turning it into an endearment.

"I'm afraid. Out of my element. I don't know where all this is leading."

"Then we'll be afraid together, because I don't know that, either."

She sighed, her gaze locked helplessly with his. "I don't believe you know the meaning of fear. You're invincible."

He shook his head. "I'm just a man, *tesoro*," he said quietly, stroking her face. "Because I happen to have more money than some doesn't make me better or worse than they are. It doesn't define who I am. Leave if you must, but do it because you don't wish to stay with me, not because of my wealth, and not because you're afraid I'm trying to buy you. I have a standing reservation on this particular suite, and as I believe I told you last Saturday, the price remains the same regardless of how many guests occupy it. And if it matters at all, there are two bedrooms. I'll be sleeping in mine until, or unless, you invite me to share yours."

How could she leave, after that? How could she turn away from his candid blue gaze, or doubt his decency, his integrity?

Sensing he'd won her over, he led her by the hand to the tall salon windows overlooking the gardens. "Let's not waste any more time standing here arguing over trivialities, not when the sun's shining, and all Paris waits to meet you." He fingered her light sweater, which had been more than adequate for Sardinia's weather. "Put on something warmer, and I'll introduce you to one of my favorite cities."

They began with a trip on a *bateau-mouche*, one of a fleet of long tour boats that plied the waters of the Seine. As the vessel glided by the Ile de la Cité and the Ile Saint-Louis, she sat beside Domenico on the glass-covered deck and breathed in the history of the dazzling monuments.

The names of the people who'd immortalized the ancient city branded themselves on her brain. Marie Antoinette... Victor Hugo... Charles Dickens... Toulouse-Lautrec... The list was endless, fascinating.

The wind had picked up and turned the morning chilly when at last they disembarked on the Left Bank. Copper leaves from the chestnut trees swirled around her ankles as Domenico hurried her along the street to a tiny riverside bistro, and she was glad she'd changed into the slim-fitting black slacks and scarlet turtleneck sweater. With her cape thrown over her shoulders and her feet snug in their suede boots, she almost felt as if she belonged in chic, elegant Paris.

"So how did you enjoy the *bateau-mouche*?" he wanted to know, after they'd been shown to a table next to a blue and white enameled woodstove, and were enjoying a glass of red wine, which the waiter poured from a carafe on the counter dividing the kitchen from the eating area.

"Amazing! The most breathtaking experience of my life! If I didn't see anything else, I'd go home satisfied with what I saw this morning."

"Oh, that was just the aperitif, Arlene," he promised, the heat in his eyes rivaling that thrown out by the logs in the stove. "The best is yet to come. Now tell me what you'd like for lunch."

"You decide," she said, so exhilarated that she wondered why she'd ever entertained a moment's hesitation about being with him. "I'm happy to leave myself in your hands."

After scrutinizing the chalkboard listing the day's offerings, he chose oyster stew, a rich, steaming dish served in individual casserole dishes, accompanied by a baguette fresh from the *boulangerie* next door, and a dish of unsalted butter.

"What do you think of the wine?" he asked at one point.

"Nice legs!" she replied mischievously, and just like that set a lighthearted tone she'd not often experienced with him before then.

As a result, their simple lunch in that unpretentious little bistro marked a shift in their relationship. They laughed and talked as easily as if they'd known each other for months instead of days.

The sexual tension remained, of course. She knew that, for her, it always would. It was as much a part of her as breathing. But for the first time since they'd met, she relaxed enough to stop worrying about what he might be thinking of her, or how he might be feeling about her, and simply had fun with him.

He sensed the change in her. "Still feeling overwhelmed?" he asked, trapping her hand in his, as they lingered over the last of their wine.

Knowing he was referring to her comments during the flight, she shook her head, her heart so full, so grateful, that for a moment she couldn't speak.

"No more doubts or fears that you've let yourself in for more than you bargained for?"

"None," she managed, over the lump in her throat.

"I'm glad," he said. "I want to see you smile more often, hear you laugh the way you have this last hour, as if there's no place you'd rather be than here, with me."

"There isn't," she admitted. "We haven't known one another very long, but you've become very…important to me."

Important? The inadequacy of the word made her shudder. He'd become crucial to her very existence! He filled all the empty corners of her heart. She was captivated by him. Had been almost from the moment she first set eyes on him.

"How long we've known each other isn't an issue," he murmured, his gaze seeming to devour her. "What counts is not settling for the safe and ordinary, but being brave enough to recognize and hold on to the remarkable whenever it happens to come along, and despite the risks it might entail." He stopped and tilted his head to one side, his brows lifted in inquiry. "You're smiling again. Why?"

"Because you struck a chord with your remark about settling for the safe and ordinary," she said. "Until recently, that's what I feel I've always done."

"How so?"

She hesitated a moment. Sharing her past didn't come easily. But he squeezed her hand and said quietly, "Tell me, Arlene. I'll understand."

"All right." Quickly, before she lost her nerve, she plunged in. "You know about my parents' divorce and how I never really got to spend any time with my father."

"Yes," he said. "You lost him when you were very young, and from what you told me, it doesn't seem your mother was able to fill the hole his death left in your life."

"It wasn't that she couldn't, Domenico, it was that she wouldn't. The only reason she fought my father for custody was that she knew he wanted me. She remarried when I was eleven, and decided that she didn't want to be saddled with a child anymore. I spent the next seven years trying to prove I deserved her love but eventually had to settle for her tolerating me, instead. The day I graduated with honors from high school, she informed me that, at eighteen, I should be living in my own place, and kicked me out of the house. I'd hoped to become a lawyer, but I couldn't support myself and afford law school as well, so I settled for becoming a legal secretary."

She stopped rather abruptly then. Adding the rest—that she'd turn thirty in February, that her biological clock deafened her with its frantic ticking and she longed to have a baby, but that until she met him, she'd resigned herself to remaining single because she hadn't met a man she could love with her whole heart—was best kept to herself. Domenico didn't strike her as a man given to panic, but her baring her soul that far would surely send him running out the door in a cold sweat. It was enough that she'd already confided to him things she'd previously shared only with Gail.

"Such a woman," he stated unequivocally in the pause that followed, "is a poor excuse for a mother."

Arlene shrugged. "I came to terms with who my mother is, years ago. I can't change her. The only thing I have control over is my own destiny."

"That's all any of us can do," he observed.

"Yes, but it took inheriting my great-uncle's vineyard for me to realize that. The challenges in my new life—and yes, the risks, too—have shaken me out of my comfort zone and made me realize I was suffocating on the safe and dull and merely tolerable. I want to *live*, not simply exist. I want to know the thrill of accomplishment, even if it's sometimes flavored with setbacks. I'm not saying I think I should always have the best, or be the best, because that's not how life plays out. But I'll do without before I'll settle for second best again."

"Which is exactly as it should be." He wove her fingers more tightly in his. "Thank you for trusting me enough to share what I know are painful memories. They give me greater understanding into what makes you the woman you are today."

She laughed rather uncertainly. "Oh dear! I thought men preferred women with a little mystery to them."

"A little, perhaps, but you've whet my appetite. I very much want to learn more about you, Arlene."

"Well, not right now, if you don't mind," she said lightly. "Not with Paris waiting to be explored."

Rising, he pulled her to her feet and draped her cape snugly around her shoulders. "Then let's get on with it, *cara mia*. How would you most like to spend the rest of the afternoon?"

"Visiting Notre Dame," she replied, without a moment's hesitation. Ever since she was a girl and had read Victor Hugo's classic novel of the tragic hunchback, Quasimodo, she'd dreamed of climbing the towers, and looking out over the rooftops of Paris.

"Then Notre Dame it will be," he said, and led her to the street again.

The reality of the cathedral, its majesty and atmosphere, so far exceeded her expectations that she couldn't imagine anything else the day had to offer could match it. Until, with dusk fast approaching, she and Domenico returned to the Ritz, and she found herself preparing for the evening ahead—and the night that would follow.

CHAPTER SIX

HE COULD see in her face, and the way she moved—gingerly, as if everything hurt—that the grueling climb up and down the towers, coupled with a very long day, had exhausted her. Not that she'd been willing to admit it.

"Of course it wasn't too much for me," she'd insisted gamely, after it was over and she'd gazed her fill at the Paris skyline, her expression filled with a wonder that was almost childlike in its purity. "I wouldn't have missed it for the world."

She had stamina, he'd grant her that. And it looked as if she was going to need it. From everything she'd told him and what he'd gathered from his contacts in the area, she'd inherited not the bucolic paradise she envisioned, but a disaster that could ruin her. The so-called "help" she thought he'd given amounted to nothing compared to what she'd need when she finally confronted the difficulties facing her.

He couldn't protect her from that, but he could see to it that these few days in Paris were as idyllic as his considerable power and money could make them. She'd need a few perfect memories to sustain her, once she was flung into the arduous and unforgiving business of viticulture. Right at that moment, however, she was fading visibly.

"I couldn't get a dinner reservation before nine," he told her, which was a lie. Regardless of the hour, there was always a table for him at Clarice's, the elegant little restaurant he often patronized, as much for its exceptional cuisine as its convenient location to the hotel. "We've got nearly three hours before we have to leave, and I suggest you use some of that time to relax."

"I think I will." She flexed one knee and winced. "In fact, I think I'll soak in a nice, hot bath."

"Excellent idea," he said, sternly turning his thoughts away from the image of her long, lovely body in all its naked glory.

He waited until she'd shut herself in her room before attending to the calls waiting to be answered, as indicated by the flashing light on the telephone. Ten in all, nine of which he returned, and one he ignored. That Ortensia Costanza was also in Paris for the convention didn't surprise him, but he had no intention of allowing her to interfere with his time there.

Unbuttoning his shirt, he ambled to his own bathroom, shed the rest of his clothes and stepped into the shower. Jets of hot water pummeled his body, sluicing away the dust of the day, and dulling the edge of weariness travel always induced. Drying off, he shaved, combed his hair and helped himself to the bathrobe the hotel supplied.

Left to his own devices, he'd have ordered a meal delivered to the suite and watched something mindless on television, an indulgence he seldom allowed himself in the normal order of things. He suspected that, had he asked, Arlene might have gone along with the idea, but lounging around in a state of semiundress was a temptation he wasn't about to fool himself into believing he could withstand.

On the other hand, he wasn't a complete barbarian, and the bottle of Krug he'd had sent up wouldn't remain at optimum temperature indefinitely. Confident she'd still be relaxing in the bath, he collected the wine and two glasses, and let himself into her bedroom. "Are you decent in there, Arlene?" he said, tapping on her bathroom door.

She let out a muffled yelp of surprise. "Of course I'm not decent! I'm in the tub!"

"Hidden under a blanket of bubbles, I'm sure."

"Well…yes."

"Good enough." Not waiting for permission, he pushed open the door and strolled to where she reclined in the marble tub with only her head visible above a snowy mound of froth. She'd turned off the bank of lights above the vanity and left the room swathed in the flickering shadows of lavender-scented candles.

Sputtering, she regarded him from wide gray eyes. Steam curled around her face and left tendrils of hair clinging damply to her forehead. "What do you think you're doing?"

"It's customary to enjoy a little champagne when bathing at leisure at the Paris Ritz," he said blandly, pouring the wine and offering her a glass.

One slender arm emerged from the bubbles, a modest amount of body, to be sure, but enough for his first inkling that perhaps he'd underestimated his powers of resistance. He cleared his throat and backed to the vanity, a safe distance away. "*Salute*—or, as they say in France, *à la vôtre!*"

"I don't believe this," she muttered, eyeing him mistrustfully.

"Then simply enjoy it, *cara*. And stop looking so fearful. I promise I haven't laced the wine with an aphrodisiac. You're not going to lose your inhibitions and leap all over me."

Her gaze remaining fused with his, she took a tentative sip. "Is this how you treat all the women you entertain here? Catching them at a disadvantage, and plying them with alcohol?"

"The only women I've entertained here are my sisters. Fond of them though I am, serving them champagne in the bathtub doesn't fall under the heading of brotherly obligation. They have husbands to take care of things like that. You, however, have only me."

"Is that how you view me? As an obligation?"

"You know very well that I do not. I've made no secret of how very attractive I find you, and how much I desire you. Not even you, Arlene, can mistake that for obligation."

She swallowed and concentrated very hard on the bubbles rising in her glass. "You must find me laughably unsophisticated that I'd agree to come away with you for the weekend, yet be so self-conscious about your seeing me naked."

"But that's the whole point, Arlene," he said gently. "I see only as much of you as you care to show me, and I can say in all honesty that, at this moment, it amounts to very little."

But enough for his imagination to complete the picture and send the blood surging to his loins. Glad of the dim light, he adjusted the layer of thick terry cloth covering him and willed his nether regions to behave. A pointless exercise, of course. A man's greatest weakness was his inability to control or disguise his arousal.

Fortunately she was too concerned with maintaining her own modesty to worry about his. "This place we're going for dinner," she said, running her finger over the rim of her glass, "is it very dressy?"

"It's not black tie, if that's what you mean, but yes, I'd say it's moderately dressy. Does that present a problem for you?"

Her suds-draped shoulder peeped out of the bubbles in a brief shrug. "Not really. I just don't want to embarrass you."

They'd had this conversation once already, just last Saturday, and he thought he'd made it plain enough then that nothing she said or did could ever embarrass him. Yet looking at her now, he saw an abyss of uncertainty in her eyes, and he knew exactly its cause. "Do yourself a favor, Arlene, and forget everything your mother taught you," he said, a flash of anger at the woman's willful destruction of her only daughter's confidence taking him by surprise.

She stifled a laugh. "That's unusual advice. I'm sure neither you nor your sisters follow it."

"My sisters and I are blessed with a mother who has our best interests at heart. It would appear the same can't be said about yours, and I venture to guess the reason is that she's jealous of you."

"Oh, hardly! My mother is the epitome of chic. I'm a terrible disappointment to her."

"In what way?"

She wrinkled her elegant little nose. "I'm plain."

"That," he said flatly, "is a matter of opinion. Of greater interest, at least to me, is what makes her so unfeeling. Can you imagine telling a child of yours she was plain, even if you believed it to be true?"

"Never!" Her eyes blazed with fierce intensity and she sat up slightly out of the water so that it lapped in soapy little waves against the top of her breasts. "If I had a daughter…*oh, if I had a daughter…!* I would tell her every day how beautiful she was—or him, if I had a son—and it would be true because, in my eyes, they would be beautiful! The most precious, beautiful children in the entire world!"

Realizing too late that he'd struck a nerve, he stared at her, taken aback by her impassioned response. "You crave a child," he said.

She shrank up to her chin under the drift of foaming bubbles, as if trying to hide her most shameful secret. "I'd like to have a baby, yes."

"What's stopping you?"

"A husband, for a start. I'm surprised you'd even ask, given your views on marriage and families."

"Are you saying you've never met a man you'd even consider marrying?"

Her lashes fluttered down, lustrous gold-tipped veils shielding her eyes. "You ask too many questions, Domenico, and this water's growing cold."

And he was treading on dangerous territory. Marriage and children were topics he avoided discussing with women, lest they leap to unwarranted conclusions about his intentions.

Glancing at his watch, he said smoothly, "It's time you finished getting ready, anyway. We've got only about forty-five minutes before we have to leave."

The breath of relief she let out as the door closed behind him sent a drift of foam sailing over the side of the tub to the marble floor. The water might have grown cool, but her blood raced fast and hot through her veins.

She'd almost had a heart attack when he showed up without so much as a by-your-leave. Not because he might have caught her naked as the day she was born, but because he'd surprised her in a fantasy woven around him that had left her nipples hard as pebbles and the secret flesh between her thighs tingling.

She wasn't a virgin. Afraid she might be missing something spectacular, she'd succumbed to the pleadings of a man she'd dated when she was twenty-two. They'd "done it" in his bed, in his apartment. He'd said all the right things, and been very proud of his performance. And left her wishing she'd stayed home with a good book. The best she could say about the experience had been that it was over quickly. She had no idea how it felt to climax.

She'd decided then that sex was vastly overrated and highly

undignified, and no one she'd met since had persuaded her to think differently. Until she met Domenico, and with him….

She pressed her hands to her flaming cheeks, mortified. She'd taken shimmering pleasure in letting him touch her intimately. Had known a coiling tension that left the skin behind her knees dotted with goose bumps. A quiver had spread from the pit of her stomach to her womb, leaving her trembling on the brink of discovery. And all this in the front seat of his car.

So much for dignity! Yet she'd felt not a scrap of shame, and not a moment's regret beyond the fact that it all ended much too soon. *I want you,* she'd whispered.

Well, here he was, hers for the taking, and how did she respond? With a pathetically coy show of reluctance that bordered on outright deception. There were names for women who played that kind of game, and she didn't like to think of them being applied to her.

"So start being honest with yourself and with him," she murmured to her flushed image in the bathroom mirror. "If you really do want him, stop dithering and make the first move before you run out of time."

The truth of that stayed with her, prodding her to action all the time she was smoothing body lotion over her limbs and fashioning her hair into a sleek chignon. It whispered to her as she drew a mascara wand over her lashes and slipped into delicate cream silk underwear—she'd always had a weakness for pretty lingerie, as if being glamorous underneath made up for looking so plain on the surface. It nudged her memory as she sifted through the items in her closet.

The night she'd lost her virginity, she'd worn a sweater whose neck fit so tight that it had become stuck over her ears when Whatever-his-name-was had tried to take it off. One of her earrings had flown across the room and she'd stood there, helpless and humiliated, with half her face squished into a shape nature never intended, while he struggled to free the other half.

She wasn't about to suffer a repeat performance again tonight. Too much was at stake. Domenico might consider her untutored in the art of love, but he didn't have to find her ridiculous, as well. Her choice of what to wear would be dictated by how gracefully she could shed it—or he could remove it. Because, one way or another, she would wake up tomorrow morning his mistress, and if her reign had to be short, she would make sure it was also very, very sweet. For both of them.

In the end, she decided on the misty-mauve silk-knit dress. Long but simply styled, it was dressy without being ostentatious, and clung smoothly in all the right places. Gail's purple pashmina shawl, silver pumps and clutch bag, and a pair of her dangling crystal earrings provided the finishing touches.

That she'd chosen well was immediately apparent when she joined Domenico in the salon. "I'll be the envy of every man who sees me with you tonight," he said hoarsely, holding her at arm's length, the better to examine the gown's classic Empire lines. The evening was off to a good start.

Clarice's lived up to every idealized concept Arlene had ever harbored of what an intimate, elegant Parisian restaurant should be. Framed oil paintings, illuminated by discreet spotlights, glowed against burgundy damask wall panels above rich mahogany wainscoting. Winged armchairs, upholstered in faded tapestry, snugged up to round tables covered by thick white linen cloths whose hems swept the carpeted floor. Candlelight glimmered softly on sterling place settings and sparkled on crystal.

A harpist half-hidden behind a lacquered screen filled the

room with melody. The white-aproned waiters were discreet, melting into the shadows when they weren't needed, and appearing silently the very second they were.

She and Domenico dined at leisure on artichoke soup with wild thyme, and lobster terrine. On boneless breast of duck artfully arranged on Belgian endive sautéed in butter and sprinkled with slivers of toasted almond. On apricots from Turkey and *crème fraîche* drizzled with vanilla sugar. And with every delectable mouthful, every sip of exquisite vintage wine, she was aware of his compelling gaze reminding her of the deadline she'd set herself.

It was close to midnight when they returned to the Ritz. The witching hour, she thought dizzily, unable to suppress a nervous shiver as he closed the door to their suite and slipped the lock in place. During their absence, someone from housekeeping had replenished the flower arrangements and left crystal brandy snifters and a bottle of cognac on a silver tray.

"A nightcap?" Domenico inquired, and she was tempted to say yes, if only to prolong the moment of unvarnished truth when she revealed how deeply she ached for him.

But drinking herself into oblivion was not her style and would solve nothing. "Thank you, but no. I've had enough for tonight."

"You enjoyed the evening?"

There it was: the perfect opening for her to go up to him, take his hand, look him straight in the eye and say something along the lines of, *It was wonderful, Domenico, but it's not over yet.* "Very much," she said, and faked a yawn behind her hand.

The smile he turned on her made a mockery of her attempt at subterfuge. "You're exhausted."

"Yes. It's been a very long day." An endless day, she thought, finding it hard to believe it was only this morning that she'd woken up in Sardinia. She'd lived a hundred thrilling lifetimes since then—and died a thousand tiny deaths inspired by her chronic fear that she wouldn't measure up to expectation.

He poured an inch of cognac into a snifter. "You should go to bed."

"Yes." Still, she hesitated, mustering her courage. Willing herself to say simply, *I'm ready, Domenico. Please make love to me tonight.* Mutely imploring him with her eyes to help her. To make it easy for her to cross the line and take that final step.

Cradling the brandy balloon between his fingers, he came to her and kissed her. On the cheek. "I'll say good night, then. Sleep well."

She swallowed, the sting of tears so close to betraying her that the best she could manage was a choked, "Thank you," before fleeing the scene.

Coward! she upbraided herself, making her way through her bedroom to the bathroom. But its carrara marble floors and fixtures, its gold plated taps and fittings offered no comfort. They were as alien to her world as the notion that she could boldly seduce a man into her bed.

Idiot! she could almost hear Gail saying. *Stop selling yourself short, and seize the moment. It's not too late.*

But she'd smeared her mascara with tears, and the chignon she'd so carefully constructed was coming undone. As a femme fatale, she left a lot to be desired. Better to sleep on it and see what tomorrow brought.

Glad to have reached a decision she could adhere to, she washed her face, brushed her teeth, and put on her pretty pink nightgown before hanging up her dress in the vast wardrobe. Whoever had replaced the bouquets in the salon had also turned down her bed, she noticed, and left a chocolate and a single red rose on her pillow.

Chocolate and red roses; the food and flowers of lovers.

Dark melting sweetness on her tongue, just like his kiss. Petals smooth and cool as velvet flesh brushing against hers…

Suddenly irresolute, she swung her gaze to the door separating her from him. If she were to open it now, and go to him, letting her state of undress speak for itself, would he understand and spare her having to ask? Would he welcome her? Or had she tested his patience too severely?

Only one way to find out! Gail's voice teased across the miles.

Tentatively she turned the knob and eased open the door. Peeped out, and…

And nothing. A small table lamp cast enough light for her to see that the salon was empty and the door to his room closed. The brandy he'd poured remained untouched in its glass.

Relief warred with disappointment. Once again, she'd been spared making a decision. Or so she believed. But he was an invisible magnet, drawing her helplessly closer. Her bare feet sighed over the Persian rug. At her touch, his door swung open.

Outside his open window, the night wind whispering through the branches of the trees in the Vendôme Gardens lured her across the threshold. The moon sailing above the slate rooftops of Paris cast a blue sheen over the big wide bed—and him, half-covered by the top sheet, impervious to her presence.

She approached him stealthily, ready to flee if he stirred.

Except for the steady rise and fall of his chest, he remained immobile. His hair, black as ink, fell across his forehead. His lashes, disgracefully long, sprayed thick and lush above his cheeks. Textured by moonlight, the contoured skin of his shoulders, his arms, revealed underlying muscles honed to sleek perfection.

She touched him. She couldn't help herself. Her hand took on a mind of its own and came to rest lightly against his chest. He was warm, vital.

And awake. *"Ciao,"* he said, his eyes dark gleaming pools in his face.

She let out a gasp. The die was cast. There was no sneaking back to her own room; no pretending she'd wandered into his by accident. "I didn't mean to wake you," she whimpered, and went to snatch back her hand.

His own shot out and captured her wrist, holding her firmly in place "I was not sleeping, Arlene. Far from it," he said, and to prove his point, slid her hand from his chest and over the flat plane of his stomach to the thick, hot ridge of flesh resting against his belly. "I was thinking about you and wondering how long I'd have to wait to possess you."

She almost fainted with fright. In the space of a heartbeat, she'd gone from laying an innocuous hand on his chest, to holding his penis. It throbbed against her palm, silky and determined. Eager and urgent.

What did he want her to do next?

The possible ways she might seduce him had occurred to her. Of course they had. But not once had she envisioned this. Her focus had been on letting him know with a glance, a word, that she was ready to take the next step. With enticing him into her room, then letting him take it from there.

How had she, whose experience in the art of lovemaking was about on a par with a beginner pianist, skipped straight from recognizing the correct sequence of simple notes, to performing a complicated overture she'd never played before?

"Arlene?" His voice swam out of the shadows, as much a caress as a question. *Ar*-lay-*na*...

"I don't know what to do," she said on a tight breath. "I want so badly to please you but I don't know how."

"You please me immeasurably, simply by being here. As for what happens next, why don't we begin with this?"

Releasing her hand, he drew her down next to him on the bed. He touched her lightly, tracing a path from the inside of her arm to her shoulder. He stroked up the side of her neck to her ear and drew circles around its perimeter with his fingertip.

She closed her eyes, caught in a web of sensation so pleasurably hypnotic, every cell in her body relaxed. His lips mapped a leisurely tour of her face, drifting from her eyelids to her nose; from her cheekbones to her jaw. By the time he settled his mouth on hers, she was trembling. When his tongue nudged the seam of her lips, she accepted him with the desperation of a starving woman.

If this was all he gave her, it would be enough, she thought, almost afraid of the strange, delicious sensations gathering force in the distant corners of her body. But he was less easily satisfied. Trailing his tongue to her ear, he probed deeply.

The effect was devastating and instantaneous. Jolted from passive acceptance, she moaned and clawed at him, digging her nails into the solid bulk of his shoulders. Her insides turned a slow somersault. A sharp, electric spasm clutched between her legs.

Blindly she turned her face and nudged his mouth with hers, craving again the dark penetration of his predatory tongue. Begging to taste him, to be possessed by him.

He curved one arm around her waist and pulled her closer. Her body rolled sweetly against his, discovering the smooth texture of his torso, except for a dusting of hair on his chest, and a denser, silkier swatch arrowing from his navel to his groin. His legs meshed with hers, became tangled in the folds of her nightgown.

He plucked at it. "This has to go, *tesoro*."

It did. Abetting him, the silky fabric slithered willingly away from her body and left her naked before him. After, a moment of pure, still silence hung in the air, eventually broken by his indrawn breath. "You are touched with moonlight," he murmured huskily, "and you are beautiful."

The next moment, his mouth was at her breast, hot and damp, and his hand was skimming past her hips. He touched her, sweeping his finger between her thighs to stroke the cloistered folds of her femininity. With tactile finesse, he induced another spasm, this one so exquisitely acute that she arched off the mattress with a muffled cry.

He soothed her, murmuring something in Italian, something unintelligible yet oddly reassuring, and touched her again, repeatedly. A roaring coursed through her body, building in intensity until, suddenly, the motherboard that was her brain short-circuited into a thousand dazzling sparks.

"Domenico!" she sobbed, urging him past caution with hands grown clever in their desperation. Opening her legs wide, she pulled him on top of her with superhuman strength, and guided him to where her flesh throbbed and ached for his complete possession.

For one glorious instant, his penis pulsed against her, steely silk straining against supple, molten satin. Then, cursing, he flung himself away to sheath himself swiftly, expertly, in a condom. Then, "I'm here," he ground out, turning to face her again. And he was. Above her, around her and most of all, deep inside her. Answering her feverish need with his own. Driving into her in a ritual that was at once more primitive and more refined than anything she'd ever thought to know.

Cupping her bottom in his hands, he lifted her hips and buried himself to the hilt. Instinctively she wrapped her legs around his waist, trapping him. Wanting all of him.

The blood thundered in her veins. Her vision blurred, grew red and hazy. She was dimly aware that his breathing had grown ragged, that his chest heaved as if he wrestled with odds far beyond the scope of mortal man to control.

"Stay with me," he muttered hoarsely, his thrusting rhythm growing frenzied. And to make sure she did, he slid his hand between their bodies and touched her again, just once.

It was enough. She peaked a second time, a long, exquisite explosion that destroyed him and her both. He buried his face at her neck. His body tensed, shuddered, and with a mighty groan that echoed to the farthest reaches of her soul, he climaxed.

Many minutes passed before he moved or spoke. She didn't care. She could have remained all night bearing the weight of his body. Its warmth, the beat of his heart against hers, his breath fanning damply against her skin, they were all she needed to be utterly, completely happy.

Not him, though. When at length he stirred and clicked on the bedside lamp, the searching gaze he turned on her had her reaching to cover herself with the sheet. "What?" she said fearfully. "Shall I go back to my own room?"

He stroked her face tenderly. "Why would you do that, *cara mia*, when so much of the night remains and there is room to spare in my bed?"

"I'm afraid I disappointed you."

"Disappointed?" He rolled the word around on his tongue as if it were a new and rather unpleasant taste.

"Well, you probably guessed I'm not very good at this."

"Perhaps you're not," he said, flinging off the sheet and subjecting her to intense scrutiny. "Perhaps you need more practice. Come here, my darling."

Squirming under his gaze, she begged, "Turn off the light!"

"No," he said. "I want to watch you, the next time I make you come."

And he took her again, this time putting his mouth where before he'd touched her only with his finger, and what would have shocked her yesterday took her to new heights of ecstasy now. The tension built in her until she shattered into a million pieces and thought she'd never find herself again.

"Yes," he said, kissing away the tears rolling down her face and stroking the hair from her brow. "Just so, my lovely."

When he entered her, she closed her eyes, but he would have none of it. "Look at me, Arlene," he commanded. "See for yourself how much you please me."

And he thrust into her faster, more urgently. The sweat gleamed on his skin. His eyes turned midnight-blue. He growled low in his throat, a fierce primeval sound. A man engaged in a battle he couldn't win, yet fighting to his last, desperate breath to tame the hunger bent on destroying him.

His orgasm was a terrifying, beautiful thing beyond description. Watching him, she felt herself drowning in passion. He'd done more than captivate her. He'd stolen her heart forever. She'd fallen hopelessly, helplessly in love with him.

The realization struck like an arrow, so terrifying and glorious that she surged up against him, her eyes wide with shock.

CHAPTER SEVEN

MISUNDERSTANDING, Domenico froze. "Did I hurt you, *tesoro*?"

"No," she was quick to reply.

But she knew he would, if she didn't control her runaway imagination. Falling in love with him wasn't an option. For her, it meant commitment, marriage, children. And within hours of meeting her, he'd made it clear enough how he felt about all that.

I'm waiting for the right woman to come along.

You have a list of requirements she must meet, in order to qualify as your wife, do you?

Of course. Happiness, like sexual compatibility and physical attraction, will run secondary to suitability....

And therein lay the problem. Plain, ordinary Arlene Russell no more measured up as suitable wife material for a man like him, than she belonged in a corporate jet or a plush suite at the Paris Ritz. From the very beginning of her association with him, she'd been miles out of her depth, socially and economically. To delude herself into believing otherwise, just because they'd had unbelievably fabulous sex, would invite nothing but a badly broken heart.

On the other hand, what was so marvelous about the emotional limbo she'd occupied for so long? Wasn't she the one who'd declared so positively that life without risk, without adventure, sapped the spirit from a person and left her numb? Why else had she consigned her safe, dull existence in Toronto to hell, and chanced everything on a fresh start in a new place?

To backslide now and let fear negate the splendor of the passion she'd shared with Domenico would be a crime. In one respect, at least, he'd elevated her from the ordinary to the sublime with his persuasive finesse.

"Arlene? What is it? What are you thinking?"

Snapping out of her introspection, she looked up and found him watching her. No trace remained of the tempest that had consumed him. His breathing was normal and his eyes, which minutes before had grown dark with passion, were once again a sharply focused, uncompromising blue.

"That I owe you so much more than I can ever repay," she said. "Until tonight, I had no idea making love could be so incredible."

He lowered his lashes in a long, slow blink. "What are you trying to say, Arlene? That you came to me a virgin?"

"No. But would it have mattered if I did?"

"Only insofar that I'd have tempered my own desire with more consideration for your needs. A woman's first time with a man should be memorable for its tenderness and I..." He shook his head in evident self-disgust. "I was caught up too much in my own pleasure to give proper thought to yours."

She touched a hand to his face. "Don't say that, Domenico. No woman could ask for a better lover—not that I'm exactly experienced in that department, as you probably guessed, but I do know wonderful when I see it."

He turned his head and pressed a kiss to her palm. "I wish I *had* been your first."

"Well, you were, in a way," she confessed, so completely under his spell, she could hold nothing back. "I never reached a climax until tonight, and I'm so glad that it happened with you. You've made me complete as a woman. Given me faith in myself. I'm grateful to you for so many things, not just what you've taught me about the wine industry, or for bringing me here, and taking the time to show me this beautiful city, but for what you've taught me about myself."

Still buried inside her, he turned on his side and cradled her next to his powerful body. "I am the grateful one, my lovely Arlene. I wish there was time for us to learn more about one another. If so, we might discover—"

"Hush." She covered his lips with her fingertips, knowing well that promises made in the warm aftermath of loving tended to fall apart in the colder light of day. "I wish it, too, but things are what they are. I don't want to look ahead to next week, or next month. I want to savor every second of the time we have *now*, so that, when it's over, I remember only how good it was between us."

"I will make it good for you," he declared huskily, sweeping his hand up her back. "I will make it perfect."

She drifted to sleep on that promise, lulled by the comforting warmth of his embrace and the soothing stroke of his big, strong hand. She didn't move again until early light pierced the room and she opened her eyes to find him spread-eagled on his half of the bed, leaving her lonely on hers.

Her mouth felt swollen, she ached in places not mentioned in polite society, and the musky scent of sex clung to her skin. Not that she minded; they were the prized mementos of an unforgettable night.

The morning after, though, could be a treacherous time, and her first instinct was to sneak away to her own bathroom and repair some of the damage before he awoke. But she couldn't resist taking a minute to commit to memory how he looked in sleep, with his lean jaw softened by the dark smudge of new beard growth, and his hair falling in undisciplined strands over his forehead.

Somewhere within the long, elegant lines, broad shoulders and deep chest of the mature man lurked the faint image of the boy he'd once been, before the years had sculpted him to hard masculine perfection. The thought brought a different ache, one that struck at her heart. If things had been different and she'd been the kind who'd measure up as his ideal wife, she might have had his child. A boy who looked like him, with the same black hair and thick eyelashes and olive skin.

Suddenly he opened his eyes and caught her staring. "*Ciao*, again," he said, bathing her in a sleepy smile. "Good morning, *cara mia*."

"Oh, my!" Blushing, she tried to turn away. "I didn't want you to see me looking like this."

"And how is that?"

She hunched her shoulders and tried to poke her mussed-up hair into some sort of order. A useless undertaking. It defied any attempt to lie flat and behave. "Morning-after messy," she muttered.

He slung an arm over her hips and nuzzled her spine, from her nape to the small of her back, then all the way up again. "On you, I like morning-after messy. I like it very much."

And I like you, she thought, her entire body vibrating in sensory delight. *Far more than is good for either of us.*

He nibbled her earlobe. "I have two pieces of very good news for you. First, I'm taking you out for breakfast. Second, we have an hour before we must leave." He pulled her around to face him and kissed her. Very, very thoroughly. "How do you suggest we pass the time?"

It was pretty clear what he had in mind. He was powerfully aroused. So big and hard, she couldn't take her eyes off him.

He cupped her breasts and wove delicious circles around her nipples with his thumbs. "It's quite all right to touch, *cara*," he murmured. "I don't bite."

She'd never been so bold with a man. Never had the opportunity, and wasn't sure exactly how to go about it. But he, sensing her hesitation, took her hand and closed it around him. "It's your fault I'm in this shape," he continued in that same mesmerizing tone. "It's only fair you do something about it, don't you think?"

Instinctively she clasped him tighter. He was smooth as silk, the conformation of him so stunningly beautiful that she forgot to be bashful. To give back a little of the pleasure he so unstintingly brought to her was her only thought—if, indeed, her brain was able to formulate anything as structured as thought, when she was dissolving under his continued ministrations.

Spanning both her breasts with one hand and squeezing gently, he slid the other between her legs and found the liquid core of her. "Yes," he breathed, fixing her in a heavy-lidded gaze as she started to tremble. "Just so, my lovely. Show me how much you like the way we are together."

Oh, "like" didn't begin to cover it! With every word, every glance, every erotic suggestion and touch, he drew her more deeply under his spell. Left her so mindless with desire that she cared about nothing but that moment. The ramifications of investing so much of herself in this man, what it meant— a future too bleak to contemplate without him in it, the heartache of finding love at last, only to have it unrequited—those she pushed aside, to be dealt with another day. For now, all that mattered was living to the fullest every thrilling second of the present, and weaving it into a tapestry of memories so vivid, time could never fade them.

Morning-after love, she discovered, was different from that inspired by moonlight. It came cloaked in leisure, in the easy melding of two bodies already familiar with each other. The tension built slowly, sweetly, a dazzling raindrop of passion sliding smoothly to the edge of reason and clinging precariously until it could hold on no longer and shattered into a million rainbows.

Afterward, he carried her into his shower. They soaped each other, washing away the scent of love, then wrapped themselves in big bath sheets. She sat on the deck surrounding the bathtub and dried her hair, all the time watching in dreamy fascination as he shaved; admiring the easy play of muscles in his back and arms, his gleaming olive skin and dark hair. He stood with his long, strong legs splayed, his hips tilted forward a little as he concentrated on his task, completely at ease in her company.

Sliding once again into the addictive world of make-believe, she thought, This is what marriage to him would be like—the unselfconscious sharing of small intimacies and always, never far from the surface, the knowledge of deeper intimacies to come.

Pointless thinking, certainly, because the plain fact was, Arlene Russell and Domenico Silvaggio d'Avalos came from such vastly different worlds that they might as well live on separate planets. Take away the glamour of the moment, the simmering fire of sexual awareness between them, and they were left with no common meeting place; no happy medium that would allow them to honor their commitments and not sacrifice what they shared together.

He splashed water over his face and mopped it dry. "Time to get a move on, *cara*," he said, putting an end to her dismal conclusions. "Make sure you wear something comfortable. We have a distance to go before breakfast."

Carpe diem, Arlene, she told herself bracingly. Stop wishing for the moon. Just seize the day and relish every moment!

She thought he'd take her to a neighborhood bistro within walking distance of the hotel. In fact, he took her by hot air balloon to a château in the country. His driver dropped them off next to an open field just south of the city, and before she could catch her breath, let alone decide if she was ready for the experience, she found herself bundled into the big wicker basket, and they were lifting off the ground.

"Your first ride?" the pilot, Simon, inquired, laughing at her white knuckled grip on the waist-high rim of the basket as the ground crew released the last line, and he fired the burners into the dome of the nylon envelope to gain more altitude and catch the prevailing wind.

And possibly my last! she thought. How could such a fragile contraption be safe?

But her apprehension faded as they drifted serenely over the sun-dappled landscape. Because they traveled with the wind, she was comfortably warm. Domenico stood beside her, his arm at her waist, and that was all she needed to feel safe.

For an hour, they sailed over sleepy villages, quiet country roads and lazy winding rivers. The autumn foliage glowed bright yellow and burnt orange in the early morning sun. She saw a woman hanging laundry on a line, children on their way to school who stopped to wave, a fox running beside a hedge, rabbits scurrying to hide in a patch of bushes. When they passed over farmland, the pilot used a different technique, somehow reducing the noise made by the burners to avoid frightening the livestock grazing in the fields.

Finally they cleared a wooded area and there below lay the château, its stone facade perfectly reflected in the surface of the lake fronting it. Built along classical lines, with a steep mansard roof, tall chimneys and long, elegant windows, it stood at the end of a long avenue lined with ancient chestnut trees, amid acres of gently rolling land.

Deer leaped for the cover of the trees as the big red and blue striped balloon made a slow descent. "Hold on tight," Domenico warned, bracing her firmly at his side. "Even with a pilot as experienced as ours, landings can sometimes be a little rough."

Simon brought the craft down so skillfully and gradually, however, that the basket bumped gently over the grass until the ground crew with whom he'd been in radio contact was able to bring it to a final stop and hold it steady.

She climbed out and was surprised when one of the crew produced a hamper containing a bottle of champagne and crystal flutes. "It's customary to raise a toast at the end of a flight," Domenico explained, accepting two glasses and passing one to her.

But Arlene hardly needed champagne. She was content to drink in the perfection of the scene before her. Timeless and dignified, the château rose up against a sky tinted the pale, cool blue of approaching winter. The sun glinted on its many windows and cast sharply defined shadows over its lawns. A hush hung over the land, broken only by an occasional burst of birdsong.

Leaving her wine untouched, she wandered away from the men, lost in her own thoughts. The peaceful setting spoke to her in ways Toronto never had, and brought home to her in a flash of insight one of the reasons she'd been so quick to accept her inheritance. She'd lived in the city most of her life, but it had taken a great-uncle she'd never met to teach her she was a country woman at heart.

Domenico came up behind her and wound his arms around her waist. "So what do you think?" he asked, resting his chin on her hair.

"That it's the most beautiful place I've ever seen. It'll inspire me when I tackle restoring my house on the lake, though mine will never be as grand as this." She turned her head and pressed a kiss to his cheek. "Thank you for bringing me here, Domenico, and for all the other wonderful memories you've given me."

Whatever he'd been about to reply, he suddenly changed his mind, and tucking her hand in the crook of his elbow, said instead, "Let's go inside. You must be starving and I know I am."

They walked along a gravel path that wound around to the château's main entrance where a butler of sorts waited to greet them. Tall, slender and silver-haired, he was as elegant as the house itself.

He ushered them inside to a graciously appointed room overlooking the lake. Rich cream silk draperies hung at the windows, the floors gleamed with a patina resulting from centuries of polishing, and the antique furniture might have come from a museum. But more than all that, it was the single table for two, set next to the fire roaring in the huge stone fireplace, which put paid to Arlene's perception that Domenico had brought her to some exclusive hotel catering to the very wealthy.

"What is this place?" she whispered, the minute the butler left them alone.

"A country house," he said.

"Whose?"

"Mine."

Her jaw dropped.

He laughed. "Why the surprise, *cara*?"

"Well, for a start, you live in Sardinia."

"Most of the time, yes. But when I want solitude, I sometimes come here."

"So who looks after the place the rest of the time?"

"Emile, whom you just met, and his wife, Christianne. Also their three sons. They oversee the estate for me, with hired help from the village when it's needed."

"I thought you were devoted to your family."

"I am. But as I already told you, we don't live in each other's back pockets. I have my retreats, and they have theirs."

Retreats, she wondered. *As in more than one?*

"Now you look shocked, *cara*. Does that mean you don't approve?"

Still trying to come to grips with what she'd learned, she said, "It's not a question of approving, so much as being taken aback. I know people who have a place in the country, but that usually means a cabin or a cottage, not something a French king might once have lived in."

"I believe the original château did once belong to royalty," he said offhandedly, as if owning a chunk of history was no more important than buying a new pair of shoes, "but what you see now was built in the mid-nineteenth century."

"How did you come by it?"

"I heard that it was on the market." He shrugged. "It took my fancy, so I bought it."

At that point, the butler, wheeling in their meal on an elaborate serving wagon, put an end to the conversation. When it resumed, over a delectable clafoutis made with tiny black cherries, they talked about other things, specifically what she should expect the next day, when the convention began.

"It will be tiring, and very intense. Unfortunately I can't be with you all the time because of meetings I scheduled several weeks ago, but I'll introduce you to people I know, and we'll meet for meals."

"Don't worry about me," she told him. "I'll be fine on my own and certainly don't expect you to hold my hand all the time."

"Not even if I want to?" he said, dazzling her with his smile.

Please don't be so charming! she wanted to tell him. *Don't make me fall in love with you any more than I already have.*

When they'd finished eating, he showed her other parts of the house: the ballroom with its glittering crystal chandeliers, the spacious, elegant reception rooms; the upstairs suites with their claw-foot bathtubs, four-poster beds and carved armoires; the dining hall with its mirrored walls and long, polished table.

Finally after a visit to the kitchen to thank Emile and Christianne for their hospitality, they took a walk outside, and Arlene could see how it would take three grown men to oversee the grounds and keep them looking so pristine. Nothing marred the surface of the ornamental pond. The cobbled courtyard was swept free of leaves, the rose garden neatly pruned ready for winter.

But it was at their last stop in the greenhouse—the *orangerie*, Domenico called it—that she realized there was a dimension to him that had nothing to do with wealth. A man worked at one end, painstakingly washing the leaves of a lemon tree with a small paintbrush. At their approach, he turned, and she saw at once that he had Down syndrome.

Recognizing Domenico, he broke into a beaming smile

and burst into speech, the words falling over themselves in his delight. Although her French was passably good, she couldn't understand everything he said, but Domenico had no trouble at all. After introducing him as Emile and Christianne's eldest son, Jean, he focused all his attention on what the man was so eager to tell him. Arlene didn't have to understand the words being exchanged to realize that Domenico ranked only slightly lower than God in Jean's estimation, and that keeping the greenhouse in perfect order for his idol was his passion in life.

They spent perhaps half an hour with him, during which time he showed Arlene his prized citrus trees and presented her with a sweet-scented lemon blossom. Although Domenico accompanied them, he left it up to her to make what she could of the conversation. Only when Emile came to announce that their driver was waiting did he step in and, counteracting Jean's disappointment that their visit had been so short, brought it to a close with enviable diplomacy.

"Thank you for being so patient with Jean," he said, taking her hand as the chauffeur drove the car down the long avenue of chestnut trees and took the road back to the city.

She looked at the fragile lemon blossom resting in her lap. "How could I not be, Domenico? He is a sweet and gentle soul."

"Not everyone sees him or his brother that way."

"His brother has Down syndrome, too?"

"Yes. Emile and Christianne desperately wanted children, but couldn't have their own, so they decided to adopt. When they learned how difficult it was for older children, especially those with a handicap, to find placement with parents who would love them despite their difficulties, they decided it was God's will that they give their love to such a child. Jean was seven when they brought him home. Two years later, they adopted Léon."

"And the youngest?"

Domenico smiled. "God changed His mind. Christianne fell pregnant when Léon was five, and gave birth to a healthy baby boy. Hilaire will turn forty in December."

"How did they all end up here, or were they already in residence when you bought the place?"

"No. I heard of them through an associate. There'd been several very unpleasant incidents in their village, which is some distance from here. The details aren't important. It's enough to say the entire family's lives were made miserable because Jean and Léon were different.

"They needed a fresh start, some place where they wouldn't be at the mercy of ignorant louts. I happened to have such a place, and I needed staff to run it."

"That's a beautiful story," she said, her voice cracking with emotion. "And you're a remarkable man."

"There's nothing remarkable about lending a hand when it's needed. What's money for, after all, if it can't be put to good use?"

"Not every man with money has your moral integrity, Domenico."

"Then I'd say he's bankrupt where it matters the most. The wealthy don't own exclusive rights to decency and kindness."

She shouldn't be surprised by his revelations, she thought. He'd done nothing but surprise her, from the moment they'd met.

They reached Paris just after two and spent a couple of hours in the Louvre museum, then toured the picturesque old streets of Montmartre before heading back to the Ritz around six o'clock.

After such a long, wonderful day, they decided against going out for dinner that night. Instead Domenico had a meal brought up to the suite. "Nothing too special, so don't feel you have to dress up," he told her, when she went to change her clothes. "In fact, be comfortable and wear your bathrobe."

"I will, if you will," she said mischievously.

He laughed. "I thought you'd never ask!"

To her, "nothing special" meant a hamburger or pizza. She should have known better than to expect he'd think along such mundane lines. When she returned to the salon after her bath, she found a linen-draped table, with flowers, lighted candles and the hotel's signature sterling and china. On a cloth covered serving table were chafing dishes hidden under silver domes, and wine chilling in a silver ice bucket.

They dined on creamy wild mushroom soup, pheasant with poached pears, and strawberries dipped in chocolate. In Arlene's opinion, the only thing more delicious was Domenico in a bathrobe, with his hair still wet from the shower and his jaw freshly shaved.

"Has it been a good day?" he asked her, after the remains of the meal had been taken away and she sat curled up next to him on the sofa.

"Oh, very! But it's made me realize that although you know a great deal about me, I still know next to nothing about you."

"Not much mystery there, Arlene," he said. "I was born in the house where you had dinner with my family, got into all the trouble boys usually manage to get into, eventually grew up, went to the U.S. to study, earned a master's degree in viticulture and enology at California State University, then came home again and took over the family business because my father developed a heart condition that forced him into early retirement. That about covers it."

"I don't think so," she said, cataloging not just the events of that day, but all the others that made up the time she'd spent with him. "You're a lot more complex than you make yourself out to be. You just don't want to talk about it."

"Well, why would I, when I could be making love to you?" he whispered against her ear.

And just like that, she forgot everything but the sublime pleasure he so easily aroused in her. She didn't need to know anything else.

Or so she believed, at the time.

CHAPTER EIGHT

AT FIRST, it all went well enough. She woke up early on the Friday, eager to begin the day, eager to make him proud. She didn't dwell on the fact that, on Sunday, she'd be saying goodbye to him, because perhaps it wouldn't come to that. Perhaps what they shared was too glorious to be snuffed out, and instead of coming to an end, they'd find they were just beginning.

She dressed carefully, teaming one of her silk blouses in a subtle black and white pinstripe with the cranberry-red suit. She pinned up her hair in a neat coil, inserted her pearl stud earrings and stepped into her new black leather pumps with the smart two-inch heels.

The chauffeur stood waiting, with the engine purring and car door already held open, when she and Domenico came out of the hotel. Seated next to her in the back seat, he looked at once supremely relaxed and ultra-professional in a dark gray suit, white shirt and burgundy tie, with only the soft gleam of his gold cuff links and watch to soften their severity. A leather attaché case rested on the seat beside him.

She sat with her knees pressed together nervously and her handbag and a new notebook clutched to her breast. Now that the moment was almost upon her, she wasn't quite as sure of herself.

The mob scene when they arrived at the convention hall did nothing to boost her morale. Although Domenico had told her English would be the common language for all organized events, the babble of foreign tongues assaulting her was enough to send her running for the hills. She didn't belong in such a well-heeled, cosmopolitan gathering; couldn't even identify half the languages being spoken. Not that it mattered. She didn't know enough about viticulture to hold a conversation with anyone, anyway.

Domenico, of course, suffered no such qualms. Grasping her elbow, he steered her confidently through the crowd, which parted for him as if he were Moses commanding the Red Sea.

"Wait here," he ordered, depositing her next to a table overflowing with brochures. "I'll be right back." And promptly disappeared.

In fact, he was gone nearly fifteen minutes, during which time she pretended an interest in the first pamphlet she could lay hands on—which, she gathered from the address on the back, was written in Hungarian but might as well have been Swahili for all the good it did her.

"Sorry," he muttered, when he finally returned. "The trouble with events like this is that you can't avoid running into people you know."

She could. His was the only familiar face among hundreds.

"Here's your registration package," he went on, handing her an embossed binder beside which her spiral notebook looked pitifully inadequate. Program, pens, felt markers, paper, ministapler, calculator—the binder had it all. "Over breakfast, I'll mark the sessions you'll find most useful. You'll see there's a floor plan showing where each takes place. After we've eaten, we'll attend the keynote address together, then you'll be on your own until lunch. We'll meet back here at noon, but in case you're detained or can't find me, here's my cell phone number." He handed her a business card. "Tuck it some place handy."

And with that, they were off, caught up in the tide of humanity flowing toward the room where a buffet of brioches, croissants, coffee and juice waited. He had warned her it would be hectic. In fact, it was bedlam.

Somehow, though, she survived the morning, managing not only to acquire much useful information, but also finding herself swept up in an enthusiasm generated by the conventioneers themselves. To hear them talk, the wine industry was the most thrilling and satisfying occupation in the world, and by lunchtime, she believed them.

When the sessions ended, she found Domenico already waiting for her at their appointed meeting place. Unfortunately he wasn't alone. The woman with him didn't quite hang around his neck like a second tie, but she made it very clear she'd like to.

"You survived," he said, his face lighting up in a smile when he saw Arlene. "How was it?"

"Incredible. I'm really fired up."

"That's what I want to hear." He took her arm and gave it a discreetly intimate squeeze as he introduced her to his companion. "Arlene, this is Ortensia Costanza, one of my neighbors in Sardinia. She and her family own a winery on the west coast of the island."

"A neighbor, *and* a friend," the woman corrected, her eyes skating over Arlene's cranberry suit as if she recognized it as one she herself had turned in to the consignment boutique in Alghero. Which was impossible, of course. She was at least four inches shorter than Arlene, with breasts twice the size. "A very *dear* friend, in fact. Shall we go into lunch, Domenico? Raffaello is saving us a table."

"By all means."

Deftly, he maneuvered Arlene into the huge dining room, and with a brief word of introduction to the other seven already seated, took his place next to her. The flamboyant Ortensia noticed, and was not pleased. Taking the only remaining vacant chair, she said, "I don't recall seeing you here before, *signorina*."

"No. I'm new to the business."

"Indeed." She allowed herself a small, malicious smile. "And Domenico's taken you under his wing, has he?"

"Yes."

"And exactly what is your area of interest?"

The same as yours, she felt like replying. *The difference is, I'm the one he's making love to every night.* "I don't have one," she said. "I'm quite literally starting from scratch."

Her admission sparked a flurry of interest among the others at the table, but conversation became more general as the meal progressed.

"You're on this afternoon, Domenico?" one woman inquired, and when he nodded, smiled at Arlene and said kindly, "You mustn't miss that, my dear. Domenico alone is worth the price of admission to this event. You'll learn more in two hours with him than a whole day with anyone else."

"Don't listen to Madeline," Domenico said, with a laugh. "I pay her to say things like that. You'll do better to stick to the original plan."

"Certainly," the bosomy Ortensia chipped in. "The more basic, the better for someone like you. Domenico's presentation will be far too advanced."

Quite possibly so, but Arlene had no intention of missing it. Scanning her program, she made a note of when and where he'd take the podium.

The rest of the afternoon passed quickly and by the time

she took her place in the room where he was to speak, she'd accumulated enough information on the pitfalls and rewards of getting a vineyard up and running that she could almost write a book for beginners.

The room was packed to capacity and she, seated well to the rear, felt comfortably inconspicuous. Domenico didn't notice her when he arrived, but she was instantly aware of him. The very second he strode through the door, a buzz of anticipation rippled over the audience. In a hall full of self-assured, successful entrepreneurs, more than half of them probably millionaires several times over, he stood just a little bit taller. Impossible to overlook, impossible to forget.

Ortensia Costanza had been right on one count, though. Most of his dissertation was far above Arlene's head, but she didn't care. It was enough to watch him, to listen to the rich cadence of his voice. To dream about the night ahead, when there'd be only the two of them, and everything he said, everything he did, would resonate within her.

But first, she discovered, there was the evening to get through.

"We're invited to a private dinner party," he told her, loosening his tie and stretching out his long legs in the back of the car, during the ride back to the Ritz. "I know you're exhausted, *cara*, and if you'd rather I go alone—"

"No," she said quickly. "I want to be with you."

He put his arm around her shoulders and pulled her close. "And I, with you—and no one else. But there are obligations in these affairs that can't go ignored."

"I understand, Domenico, really."

"It's not yet six o'clock, and we don't have to leave the suite until eight. You'll have time to unwind and take a nap."

Not likely, she thought. She wasn't about to waste precious time napping. She could catch up on her sleep all next week, if necessary. For now, a hot bath would be enough to revive her.

But her feet were killing her, and once back in her room and she'd shucked off her shoes and stripped naked, she changed her mind. The bed looked awfully inviting, and lying down for half an hour didn't seem like such a bad idea, after all.

Snug though she felt beneath the comforter, she hardly expected to sleep, not with her mind in overdrive after the stimulation of the day. But she must have dropped off because the next thing she knew, Domenico was murmuring soft and low in her ear, "Wake up, my lovely."

Her room was dim, lit only by the lamplight spilling through the open door from the salon. "It's time to get ready?" she mumbled, her voice rusty with sleep.

His hand lay cool against the swell of her breast, but his mouth on hers was hot and demanding. "I didn't say that," he breathed, and slid into her, a lovely, slow, sensuous invasion that ran through her blood like warm honey.

There was nothing quite like love as an aperitif, to neutralize the unpleasant effect of finding Ortensia Costanza was among the guests at the private supper club where the dinner was held. Arriving on Domenico's arm, Arlene positively floated on a cloud of euphoria. Her black velvet dinner dress was exactly right for the occasion, a statement in sophistication that required no adornment beyond Gail's crystal earrings.

Naturally enough, much of the conversation revolved around business. Markets came under scrutiny; international wine awards were discussed, future trends predicted. But they were, for the most part, a cultured, mannerly group of people, and didn't forget the newcomer in their midst.

Encouraged by their interest, she told them how she'd

come by her vineyard. Apart from Ortensia, who affected utter boredom with the subject, they peppered her with questions and advice.

"You've done well by your distant relative," one man, a fiftyish American, observed as the party was breaking up. "That area of British Columbia is garnering huge respect worldwide for the quality of grape it's producing. We in the Napa Valley will have to look to our laurels."

His wife nodded agreement. "Jimmy's right. Everyone who's anyone in this business is buzzing about your neck of the woods. You're a lucky woman."

"Lucky and charming," her husband said. "It's been an honor to meet you, Arlene. Where did you find this young woman, Domenico?"

"I didn't. She found me," he said, bathing her in a smile that made her toes curl inside their borrowed silver evening pumps.

Ortensia, who'd remained silent until that point, suddenly spoke up, her voice as sour as her expression. "You always did have a talent being in exactly the right place at exactly the right time when some poor soul needs you, Domenico."

At that, a brief uncomfortable silence filled the room, before he replied. "And you, my dear Ortensia," he said, his tone of steely disfavor erasing any scrap of affection from the endearment, "never have learned when to keep your unasked-for opinions to yourself."

Then dismissing her, he turned to their hosts with an apologetic smile and a murmured word of thanks for the evening. Taking their cue from him, the others dispelled the lingering tension in a spate of goodbyes, and made their way to the fleet of cars waiting to take them back to their various hotels.

"That was unpleasant, and I apologize," Domenico said, tucking Arlene's cape around her shoulders against the brisk

October night as they walked the few yards to where his driver was parked. "Ortensia is a spoiled, self-indulgent woman who is used to being the center of attention. I'm afraid she didn't take kindly to your upstaging her, but please don't take it personally. She'd have been just as disagreeable had it been any other woman."

He was wrong, Arlene thought. Ortensia was more than spoiled, she was eaten alive with jealousy because she wanted Domenico for herself. And that, in Arlene's opinion, made her attack very personal indeed.

The clock showed it was after three in the morning. Worn out from the hectic day and long evening, Arlene lay fast asleep in his bed, but Domenico paced the salon floor, wide-awake and irritable. Most of the people who'd attended the dinner party were good friends he saw only once a year, and always before, he'd looked forward to a long, stimulating visit with them. Tonight had been different. He'd chafed at its leisurely progress, his thoughts obsessed with the fact that he was running out of time with Arlene and could ill afford to waste four precious hours.

He'd thought he had all the answers where she was concerned, that when their time together came to an end, he could walk away from her and not look back. She was an innocent who'd been thrown by an unknown relative into an unknown situation, and by sheer luck she'd ended up on his doorstep, seeking his help. That didn't make her his responsibility, he told himself for what seemed like the hundredth time. He'd given her the benefit of his advice and experience. The rest was up to her. She'd either make a go of her vineyard, or she wouldn't.

Or was *he* the innocent, to have believed he could play with fire and not get burned? He'd had no thought of a permanent involvement with her when first they met. Had been certain the attraction between them was a passing thing. Pleasurable, of course, just like others before her, but never meant to last.

He'd felt secure in knowing he was expert at ending such affairs gracefully. There'd be no emotional meltdowns when it came time to say goodbye. They'd go their separate ways with good memories and no hard feelings, no lingering regret, no deep abiding sense of loss.

So when had it all begun to change? The first time he kissed her? When he'd almost seduced her in the front seat of his car? When he'd stopped having sex with her, and instead started making love to her? Had it begun the day they met and a worm of jealousy had poisoned him because he thought she'd come to Sardinia with another man? Or had it taken Ortensia Costanza to make him realize that, as far as Arlene was concerned, he was in so far over his head, he hadn't a hope of extricating himself?

He didn't have the answer. The only thing he knew for sure was that he wasn't immune, after all, to the weaknesses he'd witnessed in his friends. The confused mass of emotion she aroused in him left him as susceptible as the next man, and no more able to separate his life into neat compartments, than he could command the sun not to rise every morning.

She preyed on his mind, night and day. He was worried about her, afraid for her. She faced at least four years of back-breaking labor before she could expect to see a return on her vineyard. With her limited knowledge, and probably limited resources, too, the pitfalls of the undertaking were huge and could ruin her both financially and mentally.

From his perspective, she'd been rejected enough by her monster of a mother, and he was filled with a fierce, burning desire to make sure that no one ever hurt her again. He wanted to protect her. Be part of her life, a strong shoulder for her to lean on when she needed it. And in his book, all that added up to only one thing: he'd fallen in love with her. Except "added up" didn't quite fit because, contrary to what he'd always believed, it wasn't a mathematical equation arrived at by logic and conclusion. It was irrational, impractical and bloody inconvenient!

Dio, where was his legendary cool detachment when he needed it most?

"Domenico?" Her voice, soft with sleep, whispered to him across the room, and spinning on his heel, he found her standing in the bedroom doorway. "What's wrong?"

"Nothing. I'm having trouble sleeping, that's all."

She'd put on the shirt he'd worn to dinner. It swamped her slender frame. The sleeves hung inches below her hands, the tail almost to her knees. Her skin was rosy, her hair a silken sun-streaked tangle, and she looked adorable.

"Go back to bed, Arlene," he said brusquely. He had things to work out in his head, and that wouldn't happen with her making further inroads on his emotions.

"Not without you," she said, coming to him and resting her hands between the lapels of his bathrobe, quite literally putting her finger on the heart of the matter. "I miss you."

"Arlene...please!" In an agony of indecision, of a need that floored him, he grasped her wrists and pushed her away. "Just go!"

She shook her head. "Not until you tell me what's really bothering you."

"Ortensia," he said, latching on to the first thought that sprang to mind. "I'm furious with her. She was an embarrassment tonight—a disgrace to Sardinia with her churlish behavior toward you. There's no telling what next might have come out of her mouth, if the party hadn't ended when it did."

It wasn't a complete lie. He'd wanted to throttle the woman for making Arlene the target of her frustrated resentment. He knew she'd set her sights on him, and he'd tried to let her know as diplomatically as possible that she was never going to succeed. His mistake! He should have spoken bluntly, a long time ago. Perhaps then, tonight's unfortunate scene could have been avoided.

"I don't care about Ortensia," Arlene said softly, untying the belt at his waist and pressing a damp kiss to his chest. "I care about you. Come back to bed, Domenico, and let me show you how much."

She mesmerized him with her artless seduction. Against his better judgment, he let her lead him back to the bedroom. She stripped off his bathrobe and as he stood there, naked and painfully aroused, she sank to her knees and took him in her mouth.

He almost came. So nearly lost control that he yanked her to her feet with an abrupt curse.

"Oh!" she breathed, collapsing against him on a forlorn sigh. "I want to please you, but I've never done that before, and—"

If she had, he'd have killed the man! "Stop it!" he said harshly. "For the love of God, Arlene, stop apologizing for not being perfect!"

And driven beyond reason by the desire running rampant through him, he ripped his shirt off her body, pushed her down on the bed and drove into her. Furiously. Once, twice, three times. The fourth time, she peaked, gloving him so tightly and sweetly that he could hold back no longer. Without thought of contraception or the possible consequences of such an oversight, he gave in to the forces tearing him apart, and spilled free inside her in a powerful rush.

He was lost, and he knew it.

* * *

They didn't make it to the Saturday program. Wrapped in each other's arms, they slept late, stirring only when the sun was high. They ordered breakfast in bed, vowing to catch the afternoon sessions, but raspberry-stuffed crepes and mimosas weren't enough to satisfy their appetite, and somehow the morning wasted away in slow explorations more delicious than anything the hotel chef could hope to produce. Still insatiable for each other, they made love again in the deep marble bathtub, their bodies slick and eager, awash in sensation and soap.

Eventually they dressed and made it out to the street for a final tour of Paris. There'd be no time tomorrow; she was meeting Gail early in the morning for their eleven-thirty flight to Toronto. Domenico took her to the top of the Eiffel Tower, and showed her the elegant shops favored by the glitterati along the Rue du Faubourg Saint-Honoré and Avenue Montaigne. Over her objections, he bought her a cashmere shawl and bottle of perfume at Hermès.

Then, as the shadows lengthened, they climbed the hill to Sacré Coeur, and sat on the cathedral steps, eating ham sandwiches he'd picked up at one of the many cafés in the area. The air was brisk, with a hint of frost, but she didn't need her cape, tailored wool slacks and suede boots to be comfortable. Domenico's smile, his touch, his voice warmed her from the inside out.

Strolling back through the Latin Quarter, they browsed the many artworks displayed in the streets of Montmartre. When she stopped to admire an oil painting, a tiny unframed canvas no more than six inches square, showing the city at sunset, again nothing would do but that Domenico negotiate a price with the artist. A short while later, he spotted a handsomely bound book on the history of Paris, filled with photographs of the places they'd visited together, and presented her with that, too.

"You've already done so much for me," she protested. "Please don't feel you have to buy me gifts, as well."

But, "No one should leave Paris without at least a couple of souvenirs," he said.

Because he was to receive an award, they had to attend that night's banquet, to be held at the Hotel George V, and in a way, she was glad they wouldn't be alone. It would be too easy for misery to creep in and spoil their last night together. Better to be among a crowd; to dance with him and weave a few more golden strands into the magic they'd spun together.

She was glad she'd succumbed to the temptation of the beaded celadon evening gown, even if she never had occasion to wear it again. It was worth every euro she'd spent on it, just to see Domenico's face when she joined him in the salon, and hear him exclaim softly, "You are beautiful!"

"And so are you," she said, reaching up to smooth the lapel of his black dinner jacket. "I'm the luckiest woman in the world to be spending this night with you."

For a few hours, she continued to bask in his attention. He was the perfect escort, the sexiest, most handsome man in the world, and he was all hers—until she happened to go to the ladies' room and disturb a conversation taking place among half a dozen women from last night's dinner party, among them Ortensia Costanza.

"…broke and besotted," she heard Ortensia sneer.

"She's ripe for the plucking, certainly," someone else agreed.

Then six pairs of eyes turned startled gazes Arlene's way as the door swung closed behind her. "Am I interrupting?" she asked hesitantly. A foolish question, since she obviously was. But five of them fell over themselves to deny it as they pretended to fix their already immaculate hairdos and touch up their already perfect lipstick.

"No, no, of course not! We were just talking about…"

"The grape harvest this year."

But they weren't. *She's* ripe for the picking is what Arlene had heard, and given their agitation at discovering her suddenly in their midst, who else could they have been referring to but her? Except what did she have that anyone would want?

"Really," she said steadily.

"Yes! But it's so nice to see you again, Arlene."

"Indeed yes. What a lovely gown!"

"Oh, absolutely! The color was created with you in mind."

"How are you enjoying the evening?" the oldest of the six, inquired, concern evident in her kind brown eyes. "Domenico's taking good care of you, is he?"

Arlene smiled. "He's being quite wonderful."

Ortensia stepped forward, five inches taller tonight in her spike-heeled shoes. Diamonds the size of sugar cubes dangled from her ears. Another even larger gem graced her right forefinger. Her well-endowed bosom swelled provocatively above the top of her strapless red satin gown. "And you don't have a clue why, do you, you poor little *micina*?"

"Ortensia, please!" one of the women begged.

She dismissed the warning with a toss of her head. "She deserves to know."

Do not dignify that remark by asking her to explain it, Arlene ordered herself, and promptly said, "Exactly what do you mean, Ortensia? Are you suggesting he's merely pretending to enjoy my company?"

"Oh, he enjoys it," she replied. "He enjoys it very much— for a couple of reasons. First, it makes him feel good to know he's saved another lost soul."

"Be quiet this instant, Ortensia!" the brown-eyed woman interrupted sharply. "You've gone far enough, and I refuse to stand by and watch you destroy another hapless woman whose only sin is that she's come between you and the man you've been trying to snare for more years than I care to count."

"Then feel free to leave, but I intend to set this poor creature straight. You," she continued, turning her inimical gaze on Arlene again, "assume he's showering you with attention because he finds you fascinating and irresistible. But the truth is, you don't really exist for him, not as a *person* or a *woman*."

"I haven't a clue what you're talking about," Arlene said flatly, even as the prickle of apprehension crawling over her skin told her she'd be better off not knowing.

A sigh gusted past Ortensia's pouty lips. "*Dio*, are you blind? Do you not see you're simply another stray he's taken on, just like those flea-bitten children from the slums of Paris that he lets run wild at his château every summer, and the orphans he sponsors in Bolivia, and Africa, and Romania?"

"I don't believe you," Arlene said numbly.

Ortensia snorted and threw out her hands to her frozen audience. "Explain it to her! Tell her she's not the first, and she won't be the last! That he's known as Signor Humanitarian in some circles because he's forever showering the rejects of this world with his largesse, no matter where he happens to find them."

Mutely Arlene turned to them, and saw how they couldn't meet her gaze.

"It's true, he does involve himself in many...worthy charities," one of them finally admitted. "He likes to help where he can, but, Arlene, that's not to say you're just another project to him. It's obvious to all of us that his interest in you is much more personal."

"*Dio*, you think? Is it possible I've misread the signs?" Ortensia clapped a hand to her bosom with dramatic flair and swung her gaze to Arlene again. "Am I indeed mistaken, *cara?* Could it be that the untouchable Domenico Silvaggio d'Avalos has abandoned his usual routine of merely opening his wallet, and has finally unlocked his heart, as well?"

Not about to let the woman know how rattled she was, Arlene traded stares with her. "I don't pretend to be his spokesperson. Why don't you ask him yourself, since you're so interested?"

Ortensia's eyes flashed with triumph. "I don't need to, Arlene!" she sneered. "I know a lame duck when I see one, almost as well as I know Domenico. He's the first to ride to the rescue in a crisis, and if it happens to involve a woman still young enough to have all her own teeth, well, so much the better. He is, after all, a red-blooded Sardinian of the first order. The only difference between you and dozens before you is that he's looking to be rewarded with more than just a roll in the hay."

"He's after my vast fortune, you mean? My goodness, he's in for a big disappointment!"

She spoke lightly, desperate to hide her growing dismay, but Ortensia wasn't deceived. *"Idiota!"* she spat with transparent contempt. "Your wealth is nothing more than pocket change to him. It's your land that he covets. Seducing you just happened to be the easiest way to get it, and if you haven't yet figured that out, you're not just naive, you're downright feeble-minded."

"All right, that's enough!" Snapping closed her evening bag, the brown-eyed woman manacled Ortensia by the wrist and frog-marched her to the door. "This ends now."

The four left behind looked at Arlene from shifty, sympathetic eyes. "Pay no attention," one finally muttered, edging toward the door. "Ortensia is a loose cannon at the best of times."

Perhaps so, but she'd scored a direct hit—and Arlene had only herself to blame. She was the one who'd confided everything about herself to Domenico, right down to the last details of her inheritance.

…broke and besotted!

She's ripe for the plucking….

At least she hadn't told him she loved him. And she never would.

Infuriated as much by her own foolishness as Ortensia's spitefully accurate portrayal, Arlene rallied her shredded pride. "No apologies, please, and no explanations. I'm well aware what kind of woman Ortensia is."

After all, hadn't Domenico pretty much spelled it out, just last night? *There's no telling what next might come out of her mouth….*

Well, how about the truth, Domenico? she thought bitterly.

CHAPTER NINE

PREPARED to do whatever it took to get through the remainder of that endless, agonizing evening, Arlene pinned a brilliant smile on her face, returned to the table where he sat waiting for her, and acted out the charade of a woman having the time of her life.

She'd rubbed shoulders with millionaires before, even if it had been only in her capacity as legal secretary to the law firm's senior partner, but she was smart, she was observant and she knew how they behaved. Consequently she acted witty and charming, looked suitably interested in whatever conversation happened to be taking place, laughed in all the right places and generally shimmered just like her dress. Domenico's last memory of her would not be the pathetic nobody he'd temporarily elevated to his rarified level, but a woman well able to hold her own, regardless of the society in which she found herself.

Still, she paid a terrible price. Every smile, every bright, amusing remark found its origin in the bitter taste of disillusionment.

There's nothing remarkable about lending a hand when it's needed, he'd said, not two days earlier. *What's money for, after all, if it can't be put to good use? A man's material wealth doesn't preclude his right to decency and compassion.*

Although he hadn't exactly lied to her, he'd deceived her anyway by not spelling out all that he'd meant by that, but what hurt the most was knowing that she was the architect of her own misery. She should have said "no" to him a long time ago. Instead she'd ignored the signs posted along the way and walked blindly into a fool's paradise.

She'd climbed into his bed, even though he'd never said a word to make her believe he was interested in anything more than a temporary distraction; a fling spiced with unforgettable sex. After all, he was, as Ortensia had pointed out with succinct venom, a normal, red-blooded man. He was kind, and he was generous—in Arlene's case, donating his body as well as his considerable expertise in other areas. And he'd asked nothing in return, most especially not that she fall in love with him. She'd done that all by herself.

But he would never know she was broken inside. If she couldn't have his love, she wasn't about to settle for his pity.

By the time the evening dragged to a close, her face ached from its perpetual smile. All she wanted was for the pain to end; to leave Paris behind and to forget there'd ever been a tall, dark Sardinian who'd broken her heart. But first, there was the night to get through, and Domenico made it very plain that, for him, it was far from over.

"You were magnificent tonight, *cara*," he murmured, sweeping her cape from her shoulders the very second they set foot in the suite, and sewing a seam of tiny, exquisite kisses along the curve of her shoulder. "I could barely contain my impatience to be alone with you."

"Nor I with you," she said, injecting just the right degree of regret into the words, "but I'm so worn out that all I really want is to sleep."

"And you shall," he said, gliding the zipper of her dress smoothly down her spine. "In my arms, where you belong."

"Domenico...!" she objected on a sigh, but her protestations were drowned out by the whisper of fabric sliding away from her body until only his hands lay next to her skin.

The beguiling mists of passion closed around her, robbing her of the will to resist. She lifted her face for his kiss. Let her arms steal around his neck.

"Still too tired?" he murmured, and when she shook her head, unable to deny him, he carried her to his bed and stripped off his own clothes. Aligning his body with hers, he buried himself inside her. And with each deep, slow thrust, he stole a little more of her soul.

She tried to remain detached; to protect her grieving heart by being an observer, not a participant. But he knew her weaknesses and exploited them without mercy. Just when she thought she would scream for the exquisite agony he inflicted, he made a sound in his throat, low and guttural, and in a lightning move, rolled onto his back and positioned her so that she sat astride him.

Cupping her bottom, he pinned her against him in an attempt to halt the tide threatening to sweep them both past the point of no return. "Be still, my love, and make this moment last," he begged, sweat beading his brow.

She wished it could be so, but she'd been taken prisoner by a demon within herself; become the victim of a need so unappeasable, it would settle for nothing but immediate and total surrender. Fight it as she might, the tension coiled tighter within her, became unbearable, until she shattered into a thousand glittering prisms. Into stardust. Into ecstasy.

He tensed beneath her. Muttered her name once, drawing it out like a plea. Her vision filmed with tears, she looked down at him and thought she had never seen such tortured beauty in a man.

She wished she dared say the unthinkable; wished she could tell him she loved him. But they weren't words he wanted to hear. All she could give him was release from his self-imposed prison. Which she did, leaning back and tilting her hips in a tiny, imperative thrust that sent him soaring into oblivion.

"Look what you do to me," he ground out on a labored breath, when at last he could compose himself. "You destroy me and make me come when I would hold back forever if I could, buried to the hilt in your sleek and willing flesh."

"Forever" wasn't part of the plan, though, and soon enough darkness gave way to the gray of a new dawn. Arlene had slept not a wink. Had used the passing hours to plan her farewell. There would be no tears, no clinging, no lamenting. Whatever the cost, she would hold herself together long enough to make a dignified exit.

Easing herself carefully from his bed, she stole to her own room, stopping in the salon just long enough to scoop up her evening gown and other items from last night. Stuffing them into her suitcase, she took the clothes she'd wear for traveling, and locked herself in her bathroom. Within the hour, she was bathed, dressed and looking amazingly self-possessed, considering she was falling apart inside.

He was already up and waiting for her when she left her bedroom for the last time. Freshly shaved, and with his dark hair brushed severely in place, he looked solemn as an undertaker in black trousers and black turtleneck sweater. "We have time for breakfast before we leave for the airport," he said.

But she'd anticipated this might be what he had in mind, and had her answer ready. "No need for you to do that," she said cheerfully, even as her heart began to splinter. "For a start, I arranged to meet Gail for breakfast."

"In that case, I'll call for my car and the three of us—"

"No, Domenico," she cut in, hanging on to her resolve with the desperation of a drowning woman. "No car, and no breakfast for three. I'm not big on lengthy farewells, so let's make it short, sweet and final, right here and right now."

"But, *cara*, what's the rush? I hoped we'd have time to talk about—"

"We've said everything there is to say. All that's left is for me to tell you again how deeply I appreciate all you've done for me."

Sounding baffled, hurt even, he said, "At least let me walk you down to the lobby."

And prolong the agony? "No."

He caught her hand. Inched her closer. "You really mean this to be goodbye?"

"Yes."

He framed her face between his hands. His breath winnowed over her hair. His beautiful blue eyes bored into hers. "It doesn't have to be."

"Yes, Domenico, it does," she said, because being near him, having him touch her, just intensified the agony. "We crossed paths for a little while, and although it was wonderful while it lasted, it was…"

She floundered, at a loss. To denigrate what they'd shared was more than she could bring herself to do. It had been too glorious. It had touched her too deeply.

"What was it, Arlene?" he inquired, the edge of steel in his voice echoed in the sudden winter chill of his eyes.

"Just a…an autumn fling." She shrugged. "It's over now. You have your life and I have mine, and we both know they're worlds apart, so let's not pretend otherwise."

He fixed her in a long, inscrutable gaze. "You're right," he finally said. "Long distance relationships have never appealed to me. Better to make a clean break now. Neither of us would be happy with an occasional weekend together."

"Exactly. What we've shared has been incredible. Perfect. Let's keep it that way." She tried to plaster on another of those phony smiles that were all teeth and no heart, but her face simply wouldn't cooperate. Eyes flooding, mouth trembling, she reached up and pressed a kiss to his cheek. "Thank you again. For everything."

His arms closed around her. She felt his chest heave, his mouth rest soft against her forehead, and knew she had to escape now, or break every promise she'd made to herself not to fall apart at the last minute. "Goodbye, Domenico," she whispered, and grabbing the handle on her suitcase, turned blindly to the door.

At the last minute, he spoke again, his voice a raspy shadow of its usual self. "Don't leave, Arlene."

She didn't look back. She couldn't. "I have to."

A heartbeat passed and she heard him sigh. "Then go if you must," he said, "but do it quickly."

A blessed numbness carried her through the next several hours. After one look at her face, Gail took over the business of checking them in, finding their departure gate, and settling her in her window seat. Not until they were well out across the Atlantic, and all but the champagne from lunch had been cleared away, did she say, "Okay, what gives? We're sitting here in the lap of luxury, courtesy of your man, but there was no sign of him at the airport and you look as if you're headed to your own funeral."

"He didn't come to the airport, and he's not mine."

"You had a falling out? A conflict of schedule?"

"Neither. Our time together ended, and we've gone our separate ways."

"Temporarily."

"Permanently."

"Don't be ridiculous!" Gail snorted. "A man doesn't go to all this trouble for a woman he doesn't care about."

"In this case, he does. He'd have done the same for anybody he decided could use a little help."

"I don't call flying the pair of us Executive Class from Paris to Toronto 'a little help,' especially since he wouldn't recognize me if he fell over me on the street."

"You're my friend."

"My point exactly. This is all about his feelings for you." Gail cleared her throat. "Not that it's any of my business, but you did sleep with him, didn't you?"

Arlene turned to the window, to the bright blue arc of sky beyond. As blue as his eyes. As empty as a future without him. The feeling seeped back into her body, and the pain that came with it was ferocious. Relentless. "Yes, but it didn't mean anything."

Gail choked on her glass of champagne. "He was a dud between the sheets? I don't believe it!"

"He was perfect. He *is* perfect. To everyone. All the time. He didn't single me out for attention."

"He said nothing about seeing you again?"

"He mentioned it."

"Aha!"

"He was being polite. Chivalrous."

"So no real expression of regret? No reluctance to let you go?"

...leave if you must, but do it quickly....

"A little, perhaps."

"And when you actually walked out the door?"

She felt again the soft touch of his mouth at her brow, the deep shudder of his chest. Heard the unwonted hoarseness in his voice, the sigh he hadn't been able to suppress. "I think we both found it…difficult."

"How about heartbreaking, Arlene? Or are you so afraid of the word 'love' that you can't find room for it in your image of what this relationship's really all about?"

But men like him didn't fall for women like her. She'd have done better to lock herself in a nunnery than go to bed with him. "It can't be love," she said wearily.

"I don't know about that," Gail replied, with characteristic bluntness. "In my experience, if it walks like a duck, and it quacks like a duck, it probably is a duck! So don't be too ready to turn your back on what might be the best thing that's ever happened to you."

The trouble was, Arlene knew the difference between pity and love, and between charity and love. Neither was an acceptable substitute. "Perhaps, but I can't think about it anymore," she said, reclining her seat and tucking a pillow behind her head. "I've hardly slept, the last two nights, and nothing's making much sense right now."

Originally he'd booked through from Paris to Santiago on a commercial flight after his Sunday meetings were concluded, but the emotional turmoil of the morning left Domenico in too foul a mood to be sociable with whoever happened to be sitting next to him. His own jet would get him where he had to go, but it involved three or more refueling stops and any number of delays. He was in no mood for that, either.

"Conspicuous consumption be damned," he muttered, and chartered a Gulfstream 450, scheduled to leave Le Bourget at nine that night. He'd be served an excellent dinner, do a little work and sleep comfortably during the flight which, even allowing for one refueling stop, shouldn't take more than fifteen hours. He'd be in Santiago by nine at the latest, Chile time, ready for the start of the business day. And far enough removed from anything to do with Arlene Russell that he shouldn't have any trouble putting her out of his mind.

All things considered, he ought to be glad she'd been so ready to move on. He'd accomplished what he set out to do, and done it well. She'd made useful contacts, impressed all the right people and he could go forward with a clear conscience.

Yet all through the long flight to South America, she was there inside his head. Worse, inside his heart. Her intelligence, her smile, her laugh, her impudent little shrug, her long, lovely legs and warm body...

Let me please you, she'd begged, just the other night, as if giving herself to him so sweetly, so generously, wasn't reward enough in itself. How had it happened that she'd so thoroughly invaded that part of him no other woman had managed to touch?

Groaning inwardly, he leaned his head against the back of the seat and closed his eyes, trying to shut her out. He'd be better off with someone like Ortensia Costanza, who never in a million years could turn his life upside-down.

Cold comfort, certainly, given his present state of mind, but he wasn't so far gone that he was willing to delude himself. *We're from different worlds,* Arlene had said—or words to that effect—and he could hardly deny the truth of that.

Sardinia was a land steeped in ancient customs, so culturally distinct from other regions of Europe that even mainland Italians felt like foreigners when they visited. But he was Sard through and through. Its emerald seas, untamed mountains and harsh sirocco winds were in his blood.

He might travel the world, own pieds-à-terre in Britain, France, the States and Australia. Yet only with the sandy clay and granite foundation of his island under his feet was he ever really at home, and he knew himself too well to think he could set up permanent residence anywhere else. But Arlene had made it clear her future was bound up in an inheritance that lay half a world away.

Even with reality staring him in the face, though, she continued to linger. *Nice legs*, he heard her whisper, when he went to taste the glass of wine the flight steward served him, an hour out of Paris. From there, it was a quantum leap of memory to *her* legs, long and luscious, wrapped around his waist, and the inarticulate little whimpers she made just before she came.

The idea of her responding to any other man like that filled him with black rage. She belonged to him.

Except, she didn't want him. And what kind of fool was he even to be thinking that four nights of unparalleled sex made for a sound and lasting relationship? He'd bedded enough women in his time to know better—more than one in Santiago where it was summertime and he could forget the chill, brisk winds of Paris, and Arlene Russell's sweet face and clear gray eyes, and warm, delicious body.

She spent her first night back in Canada at Gail's apartment, just long enough to return the things she'd borrowed and catch her breath before she boarded another jet, the next day, and headed west.

British Columbia's interior greeted her with a blast of Arctic air and snowflakes drifting down from a leaden sky. She'd phoned ahead, to alert Cal Sweeney, the caretaker, to her arrival. But her house, the first she'd ever lived in as an adult, let alone owned, was no more inviting than the weather. Gloomy and neglected, it begged for a woman's touch. Cal, though, whom she'd met only briefly the first time she'd visited, had little faith in women in general and her in particular, something he made abundantly clear, the minute he opened the front door to her.

"Reckon you'll last as long in these parts as a hothouse flower in winter," he declared sourly, eyeing the fancy suede boots and woollen cape she'd bought in Alghero, a small lifetime ago. "Well, since you're the boss now and you're here anyway, I suppose I have to let you in, though I'm danged if I know what use you'll be. Reckon old Frank lost what few marbles he had left, to be handing this place over to a city wench from down east."

"Lovely to see you again, too, Mr. Sweeney," she replied sweetly, marching past him and surveying her domain.

Like the one at Domenico's parents' home, the entrance hall was large and lofty, with a staircase rising at one side. It even had a rather grand old library table centered under a wrought-iron chandelier. But there the resemblance ended. This table was piled high with yellowed newspapers, and half the bulbs were burned out in the chandelier. She supposed she should be grateful. More reminders of Domenico she did not need. He already filled her every waking thought.

Down in the cellar, a furnace clanked and groaned, blowing blasts of hot air through the heating vents and disturbing the dust balls nestled along the baseboards, which shouldn't have come as any great surprise. The first time she'd seen the house, she'd realized it needed work. But the sun had been shining that day, and she was filled with hope and excitement. In today's dim light, it looked infinitely worse than she remembered. Grim, depressed and totally devoid of optimism, it was, she thought, right in sync with the way she felt.

As if sensing her sadness, the greyhounds loped over and pushed their cold, damp noses against her leg. Bending down, she stroked their silky heads. "What are the dogs' names again? Sable—?"

"Sam and Sadie. And I'm tellin' you now, forget any ideas you might have about getting rid of 'em. They go, I go with 'em—and, missy, you'll be up the creek without paddle if I'm not around to steer you in the right direction."

"I have no intention of getting rid of them," she informed him. "Given your attitude, though, I might decide I can do very well without you."

His faded blue eyes almost disappearing in the network of weathered wrinkles that made up his face, he inspected her at further length, then crowed with sudden laughter. "Got a real mouth on you, haven't you, missy? Maybe you're Frank's kin, after all."

A dubious and decidedly backhanded compliment at best, she thought, but sensed she'd passed some sort of test. "Thank you—I think!"

He nodded and jerked his head to where the taxi driver had left her suitcases at the foot of the steps. "I'll give you a hand carting in your bags. You want 'em in the big room facing the lake?"

"I don't think so. I'd like to take another look around first." She glanced at the drab green paint adorning the walls. As she recalled, the same uninspired color scheme pretty much ran through the whole house, and she couldn't see the point of moving into the master bedroom until she'd fixed it up to her liking. "For now, leave them in the room at the top of the stairs—unless that's where you sleep."

He let fly with another cackle. "Not likely, missy! Me and the hounds live in the old maid's suite, the other side of the kitchen. You've got this end of the house all to yourself."

He hauled her suitcases inside and started up the stairs, leaving her to rediscover the main floor. Both the large living room and formal dining room had fireplaces which probably hadn't been used in years, judging by the cobwebs festooning their tarnished brass andirons. But the tiles surrounding them were hand painted and quite lovely, as she saw when she rubbed at the dust dulling their surface. And the fir floors, though in similarly sad shape, would be gorgeous when they were cleaned up, as would the tall windows.

It had been a beautiful house once, and it could be again, given a little elbow grease and a fresh coat of paint. "Just what I need to take my mind off *him*," she murmured to the dogs, who'd followed her on her tour. If she worked outside when the weather permitted, and tackled the interior of the house when it didn't, perhaps she'd end up exhausted enough to fall into bed at night and sleep, instead of lying awake pining for a man who, despite his apparent reluctance to let her go, had done so anyway.

A big country kitchen, a small room that might serve as an office, and a powder room completed the downstairs, except for Cal Sweeney's quarters, which were quite separate, situated as they were in their own wing. Upstairs were four bedrooms and two baths. An awful lot of house for one lovesick woman, two dogs and an ill-tempered old man, but even today, the view from the windows was stunning.

The bare branches of the gnarled old fruit trees in the garden rose black against the sky. If the cold weather continued overnight, by morning the tangle of unpruned shrubs and overgrown flower beds would be hidden under a blanket of snow. A thin skin of ice covered the surface of the lake and to the west, on the far shore, a ridge of hills cast dark shadows over the landscape. On a clear day, it would look like a Christmas card. Perhaps in this quiet place, which held no memories of Domenico, she would one day find peace again, and hope, and happiness.

"I made stew," Cal announced, coming upon her toward evening, as she inspected the contents of the refrigerator. "It's not fancy, but there's enough for you, if you don't mind eating in the kitchen."

Recognizing the invitation as an overture of sorts, she accepted and sat at the table, watching as he ladled chunks of meat and vegetables onto plates, filled two bowls for the dogs, and cut thick slices of bread.

"Got this at the bakery in town," he said, rapping the loaf with the knife. "There's a decent market there, as well. You don't need to drive thirty miles to the next stop down the highway, unless you're too posh to buy from the locals."

"I'm not too posh, Cal," she told him quietly. "I'm an ordinary working individual, just like you."

"Well, you've taken on a hell of a job by coming here, missy. This property's been dying on its feet for years. I can't remember the last time we brought in a decent harvest."

"I know. And I'm counting on you to help me bring it back to life."

"Got pots of money stashed in them suitcases, have you?"

"No. But I have an apartment I'm selling, and savings bonds I can use in the meantime—even a pension fund I can access, at a pinch."

He waved his fork at her. "And what do you know about growing grapes?"

"Next to nothing," she admitted, and winced inwardly at the poignant stab of memories suddenly crowding her mind. If only there was a way to retain everything she'd learned, but erase all thought of the man who'd taught her. "How much do you know?"

"Enough."

"Then I'll learn from you."

"Reckon you don't have much choice," he grumbled, but she heard the note of respect in his voice.

"We'll start tomorrow."

"Not much you can do in this weather."

"Unless we wake up to a foot of snow, we can take a look at the fields and talk about what has to be done when spring comes."

"Not if you plan to wear them silly boots," he said. "They'll be next to useless."

"Okay, we'll begin with a trip to town. You be my guide and show me where to shop and what to buy."

He dropped his fork with a clatter and stared at her, bug-eyed. "You kidding me, missy? I don't shop for women's things."

"How about a car, then? I didn't bother with one in Toronto, but I can see I'll need one here."

"That I can do," he said, and actually smiled at her. "Maybe you'll do, too, missy, with me around to keep you in line."

And so began their unlikely friendship. Cal Sweeney was no elegant, mannerly, silver-haired Emile. He was cantankerous, rough around the edges and unabashedly outspoken. But he was on her side, and he had a soft spot for the dogs.

Would it be enough, she wondered.

At first, it seemed it would, because she refused to leave herself enough time to look at the alternatives. She outfitted herself for winter in the country, and decided buying a truck made more sense than a car.

The furniture and other belongings she'd had shipped out from Toronto finally arrived. She stowed everything in the garage until she'd cleaned up the house. For the present, she was using only one bedroom, one bathroom and the kitchen. The other rooms she put on hold.

She walked over every inch of her land, taking comfort in the knowledge that it *was* her land, despite the ragged disrepair of its trellises, its outdated irrigation system and general air of desolate abandonment. She began the backbreaking task of clearing the near acre, hoping that, when spring came, at least some of it would be ready for planting.

After observing from a distance for several days, Cal eventually joined her. "Didn't reckon you'd stick with it," he declared, at the end of the second week, when she was so stiff and sore from the arduous pace she'd set herself, she could barely walk.

"I'm not giving up," she told him, massaging her aching back. "I don't know how I'll do it, but I'm going to make a success of this vineyard or die trying."

"And I ain't givin' up on you, missy," he said gruffly. "We're in this together."

When the snow returned at the beginning of December and put an end to working outside, she turned her attention to fixing up the house. She shoveled out years of rubbish, and scrubbed everything down until her hands were raw.

She found an old sewing machine in the attic, bought a bolt of heavy burgundy brocade at a fire sale and made drapes for all the windows. Some of the old furniture she'd inherited was good for nothing but firewood, but other pieces she brought back to life, removing years of grime with solvent, then rubbing them to a satin finish with lavender scented beeswax.

All this cost money, far more than she'd anticipated. She

was depleting her savings at an alarming rate, in a driven attempt to turn her lurking, ever-present misery into joy. Sorting through the debris and neglect to find contentment, and struggling to make ends meet until her apartment sold.

The withered vines, the house, the dogs and Cal—*these* were what her life was all about now. She had to make a success of it.

She prayed to forget Domenico, but her prayers went unanswered. In response to her letter of thanks to his parents, she'd received warm replies, not just from them but from his sisters, too.

"We hoped we'd see you again before you returned home," Renata had written. "Come back again and stay longer, the next time."

But there hadn't been a word from him. No doubt he'd moved on to another needy case. Yet he was everywhere that Arlene turned: in the gravelly soil when she climbed the slope of the land; in the bare rows of the vines, and the still moonlit night. She heard his voice as she painted the old house, buffed its floors and polished its windows. She saw his face in the frozen surface of the lake, in the wind-driven clouds racing across the sky.

The worst by far, though, was when she sat in bed at night, supposedly trying to formulate a plan of action that wouldn't strip away the last of her dwindling resources, but instead recalling in vivid, tactile detail the times she'd been in bed with him. How she'd cried out his name when he brought her to orgasm. How she'd bitten her knuckles to stifle the words she'd longed to utter: *I love you!*

Long distance relationships have never appealed to me, he'd said, that last day in Paris. *Better to make a clean break now. Neither of us would be happy with an occasional weekend....*

At the time, she'd convinced herself he was right, but knew

now that he'd been wrong. Anything was better than nothing—a weekend, a day, an hour. If he was to phone her...

Sam and Sadie watched her mournfully when she cried, and butted her anxiously with their soft muzzles. Cal scolded her for wearing herself to a shadow trying to restore the house.

"Rome wasn't built in a day, missy. This place's been falling apart for years, and you ain't gonna bring it back to glory overnight, no more than them withered old vines out there is gonna bear fruit next summer."

She'd given Domenico everything she was, everything she had: her body, her heart, her soul. But when their time together ended, she'd walked away and he'd let her go. Now, the only ones on earth who cared whether she lived or died were Cal and the greyhounds.

They had to be enough. They *had* to be!

But money was tight. The only offer she'd received on her apartment had fallen through when the prospective buyer had failed to qualify for a mortgage, and as the second week of December dragged to a close, she knew that her only hope of keeping her little family together left her with only one option.

CHAPTER TEN

"To SECURE our future," she'd told Cal the next day, when he'd asked where she was going, *all dressed up to the nines like some city wench.* "Break out the homemade wine. Tonight, we celebrate."

Two hours later, she drove out of town to a stretch of road that saw very little traffic. There she pulled over, switched off the engine and putting her head down on the steering wheel, she burst into tears.

Ralph McKinley, the bank manager, had refused her application for a loan. She had not, as she'd assumed, inherited her seven acres of vineyards outright. She had inherited the remaining ninety years of a ninety-nine-year lease on aboriginal land owned by the local First Nations Band. And what that meant, in terms of cold, hard cash, was that she had only her house and outbuildings to put up as collateral, which, according to McKinley, wasn't nearly enough.

According to him, the best she could hope was that a private investor would step forward and provide the financial resources she needed. "A slim chance, at best," he'd told her frankly, "and usually one that comes with a very high rate of interest, but such offers do happen occasionally if a company is looking for a tax shelter."

How had things come to such a pass? she wondered miserably. Three months ago, her life had been in perfect, albeit unexciting order. Now it was in a tailspin. Her savings were almost all gone, the money she hoped to make on the sale of her apartment hadn't yet materialized and she was worried sick, stressed out, heartbroken and completely exhausted. And if all that wasn't enough, Christmas lay just around the corner and it promised to be the bleakest she'd ever known—which, given her unhappy childhood, was saying a lot.

She had no one to blame but herself for her sorry situation. She'd rushed into accepting a legacy without reading the fine print in her great-uncle's will, and she'd rushed into an affair with a charismatic stranger without calculating the emotional price she'd have to pay. And the result was a meltdown of gigantic proportion, on a strip of deserted road in a remote corner of British Columbia held in the iron grip of winter.

"You're looking a bit green around the gills, missy," Cal announced, when she finally pulled herself together enough to make it home. "The future ain't looking as bright you thought it was, is it?"

Too worn down to put a brave face on the situation, she said, "I tried to borrow money from the bank, but they turned me down, and if my apartment doesn't sell soon, Cal, I don't know how I can keep this place going."

"What do you mean, 'you?' We're in this together, Arlene, and I've got a few dollars stashed away that you can have."

He almost never called her "Arlene." That he did so now, and with such rough affection, tipped her over the edge into another flood of tears. "I can't take your money," she wailed.

"Don't see why not. I've got no use for it," he said, practically pushing her into the living room where a fire blazed in the hearth. "As for that place you've got down east, somebody'll buy it, sooner or later, so stop your bawling. It's upsetting our dogs."

"Oh, Cal!" She smeared her hands over her face and managed a watery smile. "How will I ever repay you for sticking by me through all this?"

"I'll tell you how. Get yourself to the clinic in town and tell that half-assed young sprig that calls himself a doctor to give you the once-over. You're not the weepy kind, missy. It takes more than a bit of a setback to make you cry. Wouldn't surprise me if your battery's low, what with the way you've been knocking yourself out with this house, and you need a pick-me-up of some sort."

"You might be right," she admitted. "I *have* been feeling a bit run-down, lately. I'll book an appointment for next week."

"Right." He hooked his thumbs in his belt and looked around the room. "Now, where do you want the Christmas tree?"

"I wasn't planning on having one," she said, jarred out of her self-pity by the sudden change of subject.

"Too damn bad. I went out and cut one while you were gone this morning. So make up your mind where it goes, or I'll do it for you."

"I...suppose in the corner between the windows."

"Glad you think so because that's where it's going anyway. I'll get started on it while you make us something to eat. I'm so hungry, my stomach's beginning to think my throat's been cut."

At that she actually managed a laugh. "Let me change out of this suit," she said, heading for the stairs, "then I'll fix us some soup and a sandwich. But about the tree, Cal, you know we don't have any decorations or lights for it?"

"That don't matter as long as it smells right. Anyhow, the idea's what counts. Families put up Christmas trees, it's as simple as that."

He'd never know how his words affected her; how they lifted her spirits. She'd envied other people all her life for the families they took for granted, and learned to guard her heart against the hurt. But Domenico had managed to steal it in a matter of weeks—of days, even. He'd made her aware of all she'd missed, not just passion on a grand scale, but the warmth of belonging.

Well now, after nearly thirty years, she had Cal and she had the greyhounds. Not much by most people's standards, probably, but they gave her a sense of belonging she'd never before known. Even though the man she missed with an ache that never went away, wasn't part of the package, they helped make the pain just a little more bearable.

She set up an appointment at the clinic for the following Monday afternoon. Aware that Christmas was just three days away and she'd done nothing to make it special, she decided to dip into her meager savings and go shopping beforehand.

She was ready to leave the house just after eleven, when Ralph McKinley phoned and asked her to stop by his office. Frowning, she said, "I've got some time today, if that's convenient, but I hope it's not more bad news. I'm not overdrawn on my account, am I?"

"No, no," he said, sounding positively festive. "Nothing like that. What time's good for you?"

"I can be there in half an hour."

"Fine," he said. "See you then. Oh, and Ms. Russell? I think you're going to be very pleased with my news."

Had Great-Uncle Frank left a safe-deposit box full of hundred-dollar bills no one had remembered to tell her about? she wondered, slowing down at the intersection to Main Street and pulling into a parking slot right outside the bank.

"A little brisk out, isn't it?" Ralph McKinley remarked jovially, greeting her at the door and ushering her into his office. "May I get my assistant to bring you coffee to warm you up, Ms. Russell?"

"No, thank you," she said. She was off coffee, lately. Not only that, this office held no fond memories for her and she wasn't sure the butterflies in her stomach could tolerate extra company. Despite his earlier reassurances, she was as nervous now as she had been the first time she sat across the desk from him.

"Then I'll get straight to the point. You might recall, when you were here last, my mentioning that certain wealthy individuals occasionally choose to back ventures that fall outside the boundaries set by official lending institutions such as ours."

"Yes," she said, hard-pressed not to tell him to forget the jargon and cut to the chase. "Are you saying someone has expressed an interest in my situation?"

"In fact, yes." He pushed a single sheet of paper across the desk. "The fine print is all here, but what it essentially boils down to is that a private party has offered to finance the restoration of your vineyard far beyond anything the bank could offer, even if it were in a position to lend you the money you need."

"You also told me that this kind of offer comes at a much higher cost than that charged by the bank."

"Not in this case, as it happens. The agreement calls for you to do the work, and the investor to provide the funding, in effect becoming a silent partner."

"Who'll take my property if I default on repayment."

"No. The terms of the agreement stipulate two conditions only—an equal share of future profits, and first option to buy out your half of the business at fair market value, should you decide to sell."

"Why would anyone want it, if the land isn't part of the deal?"

"Because your lease is good for another ninety years. With the right backing and proper management, there's a fortune to be made in a tenth of that time. From a purely practical standpoint, the return on a fifty percent share of profits over the long-term far outstrips what an investor could normally expect to make on a standard loan, even allowing for a higher than normal interest rate."

"It sounds too good to be true. Who is this angel of mercy?"

"No name that would mean anything to you. It's a numbered company, WMS830090. But I can tell you that the offer is entirely legitimate and aboveboard. Take a moment to look over the contract, Ms. Russell. It's very straightforward and will, I think, put your mind at ease. Then, if you're satisfied with what you see and are agreeable, I'll witness your signature and the money will be transferred into your account immediately."

"And if I have questions?"

"I'm authorized to answer them. Now if you'll excuse me, I need to have a word with one of my tellers."

Left alone, Arlene took a deep breath and tried to control her trembling hands. If this was a genuine offer, it was also a godsend. But it was Christmas, the season of miracles, and maybe she should be thankful one had come her way, instead of sniffing around like a suspicious bloodhound.

But, *Don't be hasty this time,* her common sense cautioned. *Read every word twice—on the lines and between them, too.* As contracts went, this one might be simple as ABC, but she'd sign nothing until a lawyer had gone over it with a fine-tooth comb.

"I'll give Greg Lawson a call," McKinley offered, when she told him her decision. "His office is just across the street. You could go over there right away, if he's free."

As it happened, the lawyer was just leaving for lunch and, agreeing to stop by the bank on his way out, showed up within minutes. "I have no problem advising you to accept any of this, Arlene," he said, after examining the document thoroughly. "My only question is, who signs on behalf of the investor company?"

"I do," Ralph McKinley said. "I have power of attorney to represent the client."

The lawyer shrugged. "Then grab a pen and Merry Christmas, Arlene!"

People really couldn't walk on air. They put one foot in front of the other and very carefully made their way along the icy sidewalk. But Arlene's spirits soared sky high as she headed home just after four o'clock, with a clean bill of health and a truck full of goodies.

"You had a complete physical less than six months ago, so I don't see the need for another at this time," the doctor had said, after checking her heart, her lungs and her blood pressure. "I'll send blood samples to the lab, just to be on the safe side, but as far as I can tell, there's not much wrong with you that a restful, relaxed Christmas won't fix."

From there, she'd driven to the shopping mall in another, larger town, several miles farther down the highway. Tonight, there'd be wrapped gifts for Cal and the greyhounds, under a tree decorated with strings of colored lights and shiny glass balls.

That evening, when he came in from stacking more firewood on the back porch, she had Cal's favorite dinner waiting: roast prime rib of beef, mashed potatoes, carrots and gravy, and a bottle of good red wine, with hot apple pie and ice cream for dessert. Plain, honest food, just like him, served in the dining room instead of the kitchen, with candles on the table, and festive paper napkins.

"Pretty fancy," he declared, eyeing his plate. "We come into money, did we?"

"As a matter of fact, we did," she replied, and told him about her meeting at the bank.

"Something fishy about this deal, if you ask me," he rumbled. "Folk don't give somethin' without expecting something in return—especially not rich folk! That's how they made their money in the first place. Mark my words, missy, there's a catch somewhere. You just ain't bumped into it yet."

"If there is, it sneaked past a bank manager and a lawyer. Both Ralph McKinley and Greg Lawson gave their stamp of approval."

"McKinley's a sharp cookie," he admitted grudgingly. "Not much gets by him. And young Lawson's not so bad, either, considerin' he a lawyer."

"Exactly! And it's not as if I've signed away my inheritance."

"You've given some stranger first dibs at buying this place if you decide to sell," he said darkly.

"I have no intention of selling, if that's what's worrying you." She looked around at the walls newly painted a soft butter-cream; at the sparkling moldings, the gleaming floor. Logs crackled in the fireplace, while outside, fat snowflakes drifted down and batted against the windows like blind white moths. Across the hall, the lights from the Christmas tree threw muted shades of color across the living room. "I love this place, Cal. It's become my home—and you're my family."

He cleared his throat and made a big production of piling potatoes on his fork. "Some family!" he muttered hoarsely. "A wench like you should have a husband and kids, not be making do with a couple of aging dogs and an old fart like me."

"Not even if I happen to be rather fond of aging dogs and old farts?"

He let out one of his famous cackles. "Watch your mouth, missy, unless you want it washed out with soap."

Smiling, she sat in silence a while, more at peace than she'd been in weeks. She didn't delude herself. She knew the road ahead would be hard, that money alone wasn't enough to bring her vineyard back to life; that it required dedication and commitment and patience.

She knew, too, that the perennial ache of missing Domenico would continue to haunt her in the middle of the night, or make a sneak attack during the day, and that when it did, the pain it brought would leave her breathless. Which was why she was so grateful for times like this, when contentment reigned supreme, even if it was only for a little while.

"We've never talked about this before, Cal," she said, after the meal was cleared away and they sat by the fire in the living room, with the dogs snoozing at their feet, "but how did this place fall into such disrepair?"

"Liquor," he said bluntly. "Frank always liked his booze, but he really started hitting the bottle about seven years back, when we lost most of the harvest two seasons in a row. Drank himself to death in the end. I love everything to do with growin' wine grapes, and tried to keep things going, but it's more than a one-man job and I ain't as young as I used to be. You want to make a go of it here, Arlene, you're gonna have to hire extra labor, come spring."

"I'll be relying on you to do that. As far as I'm concerned, you're the man in charge of the vineyard and what you say, goes."

He shuffled to his feet. "Reckon I can live with that, missy," he said. "You okay here by yourself for a spell?"

"Of course. It's been a long day, so I'm going to put my feet up and enjoy the fire and the Christmas tree, and maybe watch a little TV."

"Then I'll throw a couple more logs on the fire, and take the dogs for a run before I turn in myself."

After he'd gone, she went upstairs, took a quick shower and put on a long white nightgown embroidered with rosebuds and forget-me-nots, her warm rose-pink chenille dressing gown and matching slippers. So what if she looked like somebody's granny? It wasn't as if she was expecting company.

Scooping up the contract she'd left on the hall table, she returned to the living room and had just settled down in her favorite armchair when the doorbell rang.

Thinking Cal must have accidentally locked himself out at the back, she trudged through the hall and opened the front door.

Sure enough, Cal stood there with the dogs, but they weren't alone. "Caught this guy snooping around the place," he said. "Drivin' the same car as I saw creeping around here yesterday like a fox circling the henhouse. Claims you know him. That so?"

"Yes, I know him," she said dully. And she knew, too, in a flash of insight as blinding as it was devastating, exactly who her anonymous benefactor was.

"Arlene," Domenico said, wrapping her in the unforgettable, sexy timbre of his voice. "It's wonderful to see you again. May I come in?"

CHAPTER ELEVEN

FROM her expression, he was obviously about as welcome as the bubonic plague, and given the way she'd walked away from him in Paris, he supposed he shouldn't have expected anything else. But she'd haunted him for weeks now, and he was tired of being on the losing end of a battle he hadn't a hope of winning. Like it or not, she was in his blood. The time had come to win her over, or exorcise her from his mind *and* his heart, once and for all.

"May I come in?" he asked again, locking gazes with her.

She gave the merest nod and moved well back, as if afraid that if he touched her, he might contaminate her. She'd lost weight, he noticed. Although the loose robe she wore camouflaged her body, the hollows beneath her cheekbones were more pronounced, her jaw more sharply defined. She looked drained, exhausted, and he had an overpowering impulse to gather her in his arms and never let her go.

Why hadn't she taken better care of herself? And why had he waited so long to come to her rescue?

Stamping the snow from his shoes, he stepped inside.

The old man slammed the door shut. "You want me to stick around, missy?" he asked, fixing Domenico in an evil glare.

"It's not necessary," she said. "Our visitor won't be staying long."

"I'll be in the kitchen, if you change your mind."

"Thanks, Cal."

She waited until he'd disappeared before turning her attention to Domenico again. "Why are you here?"

"Because I couldn't stay away."

She curled her lip. "Of course not. What satisfaction is there in conferring favors on someone, if you're not on hand to wallow in their gratitude? The only surprise is that you waited this long to show up."

He'd bent down to stroke the dogs who were winding around his legs, begging for affection, but at her words, he abruptly straightened again. *"What?"*

"Oh, please!" she said scornfully, heading for a room to the right of the front door. "I know you're my anonymous investor, Domenico. The pity of it is that I didn't figure it out sooner. It's not as if your friend Ortensia didn't warn me."

He followed her and found himself in a handsome salon illuminated only by the lights on a fragrant Christmas tree and the flames in the tiled hearth leaping up the chimney. "What has Ortensia Costanza to do with any of this?"

"She told me you coveted my land. I didn't believe her." Her lovely mouth curved in a bitter smile. "Silly me! I should have remembered you were the one who told me you don't let anything stand in the way of your going after the things you want."

"Did it ever occur to you that I might want you?"

"You had me, Domenico. In Paris."

A flicker of anger ruffled his composure. "Disdain me if you must, Arlene, but do not try to cheapen what we shared in Paris. I will not allow it."

"And I will not allow you to manipulate me. I am not a plaything you may pick up or leave at whim."

She darted to a table next to an armchair by the fire, grabbed what he at once recognized as the contract he'd had drawn up, and flung it at him. Catching it in one hand, he said, "I've never treated you as such. Where you're concerned, I have always acted in good faith."

"You have tried to buy me, and I'm not for sale."

"I have tried to help you because I care about you."

"I don't want you to *care* about me, and I don't need your help. So if you came all the way from Sardinia to dig me out of the hole you think I'm in, you've wasted your time."

"I was already in North America, and decided to stop by to see you, on my way home."

She shot him a look of pure disbelief. "Where in North America?"

"My alma mater in Fresno, California."

"California?" She gave a hoot of laughter but it was belied by the desolation in her gray eyes. "I suggest you took a wrong turn somewhere south of the border!"

He unbuttoned his overcoat. "That's one of the perks of owning my own jet, Arlene," he drawled. "Within reason, I get to choose in which direction it flies and where it lands. In this case, I chose here, because from everything I've heard—"

"What have you heard?" she flared. "Who's been talking about me behind my back? If it was Ralph McKinley at the bank—"

"It wasn't Ralph McKinley," he said. "*Dio*, Arlene, I've got business contacts all over the world, including this little corner of it. A couple of phone calls were enough to confirm what I'd suspected all along. You've inherited serious trouble with this property and need a hefty infusion of cash to get you out of it."

"So you rushed in to save the day?" She shot the question at him, loaded with sarcasm.

Steeling himself to patience, he said, "Somebody had to, and I didn't see anyone else volunteering for the job. I wasn't about to stand idly by and do nothing. That's not how I operate, Arlene."

"I know exactly how you operate," she said, her eyes suddenly bright with tears. "You use money to buy whatever you want, whether it happens to be things or people. You bought a château in France because, to quote you, it took your fancy. Then you bought a family to run it for you. You don't live there, so to give the staff something to do besides rattle around in a place large enough to be a hotel, you sponsor underprivileged children to spend their summers there."

"Not just their summers," he interrupted curtly. "They come at Christmas and Easter, too. They fill the rooms with their laughter, and they spill milk and cookie crumbs on the furniture. They race over the grounds, sail little wooden boats on the lake, climb trees and learn to swim in the pool. If you're going to run an inventory of my perceived failings, at least do me the courtesy of getting all the facts before you condemn me."

She grimaced, disgust plain on her face. "The point is, you're a collector, Domenico, and you particularly like collecting needy people because it makes you feel good. And if the flavor of the month happens also to hold a lease on a prime chunk of land, well, why not acquire the rights to that, too, while you're at it? Not because it once belonged to royalty like your château. Not because its vineyards are flourishing. Not for any reason at all but because you *fancy* it."

Breasts heaving, she stopped just long enough to draw in an irate breath before firing a last shot. "But I'll see you in hell before I let you have it!"

Astounded by her outburst, he shook his head. "Do you hear yourself, woman? To suggest I'm after your land is ludicrous. Tell me what possible use I have for seven paltry acres when I have hundreds at my disposal all over the world, and every one of them doing what yours are not—namely producing quality wine grapes."

"Exactly!" she burst out, the tears slipping down her cheeks. "You have no use for them at all. You're not driven by *need*. You just enjoy *managing* people's lives. Well, you're not managing mine, so take your money and take yourself out of here!"

Her distress moved him more than he cared to admit. He had to hold himself back from cradling her body next to his and kissing away her anger, her suspicions and everything else that troubled her, along with her tears. But shocked by her lack of trust in his motives, he remained motionless. "If that's how you see me—as some paternalistic figure using you to boost his own ego—then there's nothing more to be said."

"Finally we agree on something!"

"Except this." He pulled his own copy of the contract from the inside pocket of his overcoat and, together with hers, ripped the papers in half and flung them on the fire. "There! You're off the hook. No silent partner trying to control your fate. No first option clause to buy you out if you ever decide to sell. Your precious land is safe, and so are you. I'm out of your life, as of now."

"Good!" she quavered. "Take your money with you when you go."

"I'm afraid I can no longer do that. It's deposited to your account and even I, world-class manipulator that I am, can't access it."

"Well, I certainly don't want it."

"Then give it to someone who does, burn it, do what the

devil you like with it." He swept his glance over the aging dogs snoozing by the fire; over the elderly caretaker who, obviously having heard the raised voices, had reappeared and stood now in the doorway, watching the final act of a fiasco the old Domenico would never have allowed to take place. "But if I had others depending on me, as you do, I'd put my pride aside and think about what's best for them before I threw away the chance to make their days more comfortable."

She started to reply, but choked on the words and buried her face in hands no longer smooth and white, but red and chapped, with the nails clipped short. A working woman's hands which it pained him to see.

Finally, in a muffled voice, she said, "Why did you have to come back into my life? Why couldn't you just leave me well enough alone?"

"It's called taking care of the people you love, Arlene, whether or not they care enough to love you back," he said, the words torn so harshly from him that his throat burned. "And if that offends your sensibilities, as well as my many other transgressions, then sue me!"

The force with which he slammed the front door as he stormed out made the dogs jump and the whole house shudder. "Pleased with yourself, are you?" Cal inquired calmly, into the ensuing silence.

Arlene lifted her head and looked at him through streaming eyes. "Don't tell me you're on his side," she wailed.

"Can't say as I see he's done anythin' so wrong—except take a load of abuse from you, that is. You pushed that man's patience too far, missy. I'm surprised he didn't walk out on you sooner. Reckon he's just a fool for love under them slick city duds he wears."

"He only said that to justify his actions. He doesn't really love me."

"Gave a dang good imitation of it then, is all I've got to say. In his place, I'd've hightailed it outta here the minute you got on your high horse and started accusing him of being the devil bent on making your life a misery. Which when I come to think of it, don't make much sense, seein' as how, most of the time, you've been plagued with misery anyway, mooning around the place like a lost lamb practically from the day you got here."

He crossed to the hearth and threw another log on the fire. "Reckon I know why now. What beats me is you lettin' him get away when it's as plain as the noses on them greyhounds that he's the man you want. But then, I never did pretend to understand what makes a woman tick. Saved myself a load of grief by never trying, too."

Taken aback by his words, she plucked a tissue from her pocket and mopped her eyes, then paced to the window and stared out at the thickly falling snow. The roads would be treacherous, especially out here in the country. "He's not used to weather like this," she said quietly. "I hope he drives carefully."

"He don't strike me as the type to let a bit of weather get the better of him."

"Out here, he might. I don't think it ever snows in Sardinia—at least, not the part where he lives. What if he has an accident, Cal?"

Anxiety nibbled at her, eroding her indignation. She'd said harsh, unforgivable things. Things meant to wound, to inflame. She'd stirred the man she loved more than life to an anger even greater than her own. His mouth, which once had seduced her with its heat, had grown hard and cold; his eyes, stony. He'd driven away in a rage.

Just two days earlier, a stranger traveling through the area had rounded a curve in the road too fast and ended up lying injured and half-frozen in the ditch, before someone came along and found him.

If Domenico had an accident, it would be her fault. How would she live with herself then, knowing she'd acted not out of righteous indignation at all, but out of irrational disappointment that, despite everything he'd been willing to give, for her it still hadn't been enough?

She clutched the collar of her dressing gown tight around her neck, as if by doing so, she could chase away the cold finger of dread stealing up her spine. Domenico Silvaggio d'Avalos was impossible. Controlling. Devious.

And if anything happened to him, she'd die.

Why had she sent him away, when what she most wanted was to run into his arms and beg him to forget everything she'd said, that last day in Paris? He'd hinted then that he didn't want their relationship to end, but even though he'd accepted her rejection gracefully enough at the time, she realized now that he'd never really given up on her.

If all he'd wanted was to be her benefactor, he could have arranged it from anywhere in the world. He didn't have to detour through Canada from California on his way back to Sardinia. He didn't have to risk his life driving on snow-clogged, unfamiliar roads.

"We miss you," Renata had written in her Christmas card. "*All* of us."

Belatedly Arlene recognized the message for what it truly implied.

A blast of cold air snaked around Arlene's ankles. The dogs stirred, stretched and wagged their tails. Cal must have opened the door to let them out for a last run before turning in.

"If he really loved me," Arlene said, "why couldn't he just say so, Cal, instead of trying to buy me off?"

"Because you're right," a deep, familiar, beloved voice replied. "I *am* very good at managing other people's lives—and just plain lousy at managing my own."

She spun around, her heart in her throat. He filled the doorway to the living room. Snowflakes glinted in his black hair, sprinkled his broad, black-clad shoulders. The light of battle shone in his eyes. He looked formidable. Dangerous.

"You came back!" she whispered.

"Just as well," Cal drawled. "Saves me having to go out looking for him." He squinted at them from beneath his bushy gray brows and brushed one hand against the other. "Reckon I'd better take the dogs and make myself scarce, five being a crowd and all that. The rest is up to the two of you."

Desperate to fill the silence he left behind, Arlene said, "It's a good thing you turned back. It really isn't a good night to be on the road. I have four bedrooms, not counting Cal's, so there's plenty of room for you to stay over, and—"

"I didn't come back because of the weather, Arlene."

She hardly dared phrase the question. "Why did you, then?"

"The same reason I gave, the last time you asked. Because I can't stay away, and heaven knows I've tried. When it came to recognizing what I needed to give my life true meaning, my fabled objectivity let me down badly."

He stepped closer. Trapped her against the window. Tilted her chin with his thumb so that she had to meet his gaze. "In the last two months, I've traveled to three continents and more than five countries, and you've followed me to every one. I'm here now because I've finally accepted that you're with me, no matter how far or fast I run. I can't live without you, Arlene. So unless you tell me to my face that you don't want me, ever, for any reason at all, I'm here to stay—and not in a guest bed-room, either!"

She stared at him, drowning in his summer-blue eyes. She'd been frozen inside. Gripped by hopelessness and fear. But with every word, every glance, every touch, he thawed a little more of the ice encasing her.

"Well?" he murmured. "What's your answer, *cara mia*? Am I wasting my time and yours, or do you care for me at least a little?"

"You know I do," she said on a trembling sigh.

"Enough to make a life with me?"

"How can I? Your home is in Sardinia."

"Yours could be, too." He closed in on her. Touched her jaw, traced a path over her throat, his fingers cool and sure.

"I can't just walk away from here," she protested. "When I accepted my inheritance, I made a commitment, to Cal and to the dogs. That might sound odd to you, but—"

"It sounds like the woman I know," he said. "The one who stands by her promises and who taught me that sharing ev-erything but his heart makes a pauper of a man."

"What are you saying?" she breathed, afraid to read more into his words than he meant.

"That I'm not asking you to break your word, or to give up this place. I understand how much it means to you."

"Not just to me. It's the only home Cal knows. He loves it here. He understands the land, and knows more about growing grapes here than I ever will. It's not his fault everything's so run-down. He wants nothing more than to see the vineyard brought back to how it used to be, before my great-uncle let it slip away, but he's too old to take on the job by himself."

"We'll find him the help he needs. It can be done, *tesoro*. We can spend part of the year here, if that's what you want.

I see how beautiful your country is, and I understand the roots we all have for our native land. But I meant it when I said that long distance relationships don't work for me. I need you by my side, Arlene, wherever home happens to be."

Take what he's offering and make it be enough, because a little with him is better than nothing at all. "As what?" she said, clinging by a thread to the edge of the precipice of reason. Desperately wanting to fling herself over and listen only to the urgent pleading of her heart.

"As my wife, of course!"

"Why?"

"Dio! That question again! Why do you think?"

"If I knew, I wouldn't ask."

"I love you. I already told you that."

"Not really. You threw the words at me, a little while ago, but they sounded more like a curse than a blessing."

"Then let me say them again now. *I love you!* I know that's not a magic formula, that there are problems we have to iron out. And I'd take them all away, if I could—"

She placed her hand against his mouth, hushing him. "No, Domenico! That's how we went off track in the first place. I'm not a child. You don't have to shield me from reality. Life comes with problems. That's just the way it is. But a couple learns to solve them together."

He smiled and slid his hand around her neck. "That poses some very interesting possibilities," he said, inching his mouth closer to hers.

She pulled back, knowing that if he kissed her, she'd agree to anything. "You make it all sound so simple, and it's not."

"Yes, it is," he said flatly. "The lesson I've learned is that finding the right one to love is difficult. The rest is very simple indeed." He drew her close a second time. "Must I beg?" he whispered against her hair. "Is it not enough that I offer you all that I am? That what I most want in this world is to make you happy? Can you not understand how it destroys me that you keep me at such a distance, that you refuse to let me show you, in every way, how much I treasure you?"

"Don't!" she begged, the last of her resistance washed away in a flood of scalding tears. "Please, please don't talk like that! You make me so ashamed."

"Of what? Your moral integrity? Your loyalty to those relying on you? Arlene, *mia innamorata*, these are among the reasons I fell in love with you. You are the woman I've been searching for almost half my life. Don't ask me to let you go, now that I've found you. Make my life complete. Say you'll marry me."

"Yes," she said, the last shard of ice in her heart melting under the impassioned heat of his gaze. "Oh, yes please!"

CHAPTER TWELVE

THE pain of remembering those Paris nights had been so acute that she'd willed them to die. Gradually, painstakingly, she'd buried them under the cumbersome, everyday concerns needing her attention at her new home, even likening the pang of regret that sometimes attacked, to the ghost of an amputated limb seeking to reconnect itself to its host. She'd told herself that what she'd had with Domenico was over. Nothing could bring it back again.

How quickly he taught her the error of her beliefs! In the shadowed warmth of her bedroom, with only the snowflakes nudging at the window to witness the miracle, he sealed their reconciliation, reacquainting himself with her body, and stoking the embers of buried desire with such finesse that they roared back to new life, all the wilder for their enforced hibernation.

Not an inch of her escaped his attention. "I have missed your silken skin, your scent," he murmured, and pinning her hands above her head, took first one, then the other nipple in his mouth.

Sensation streaked through her, wild and hot; lightning that ignited every cell in her body and left her throbbing and pooling in liquid fire. "Please, Domenico," she moaned, reaching for him. "Don't make me wait...it's been so long...please...!"

He was big and hard and ready. But he would not let his hunger dominate. "I have missed how you taste," he whispered. "The memory has haunted me through every long night, and I have woken up starving for you." And running his palms down her flanks, he buried his face between her thighs. Stroked his tongue over her slick and eager flesh.

It was more torture, more ecstasy than she could withstand. Lacking his self-discipline, she exploded in a million dazzling sparks that left her begging him please, please, to fill the terrible void she'd lived with for so long.

He entered her with an urgency that belied his formidable control. Thrust himself so deep that he touched her soul. "I have dreamed of the way you sigh, as you do now, to let me know I please you," he rasped at her ear. "And I have longed to feel you close around me and drain me of my strength…" He faltered, drew in a deep, agonized breath. "As you are about to do now…Arlene, *mia innamorata…*!"

He tensed, shuddered and spilled hot and free inside her. Caught in his frenzied rhythm, she climaxed again, her flesh contracting around his so fiercely that he groaned aloud with pleasure.

It should have been enough to satisfy them, but it wasn't.

Insatiable, inexhaustible, thrilling, the passion swept them through the quiet hours of the night until, with dawn still too distant to touch the horizon, she finally slept in his arms again, truly at peace for the first time in months.

Cal had the fire blazing in the dining room and the table laid for three when she and Domenico came downstairs, the next morning. "Reckon I don't need to ask if you got any rest last night," he commented snidely, dishing out crisp bacon and farm fresh eggs. "The pair of you look plumb wore out."

Arlene blushed, but Domenico laughed out loud. "I like a

man who doesn't mince his words. In the absence of her biological father, should I ask you for your blessing, Cal? Arlene has agreed to become my wife."

"Figured somethin' of the sort must've happened. Ain't never seen her so chipper and rosy," he said gruffly. "You aim to treat her right, do you?"

"In every way, every day."

"Glad to hear it. Wouldn't want to have to take you out behind the woodshed and lay a lickin' on you."

Since Domenico stood at least six inches taller, the odds of Cal's being able to carry out his threat were about as slim as his ever needing to try, Arlene thought, burying a smile. Yet despite his apparent satisfaction with the way things had turned out, something wasn't quite right with her old friend.

"So when's the wedding?" he inquired, concentrating on his eggs.

"We haven't set a firm date," she said, "but we're thinking early in the new year."

"Reckon you'll soon be gone from here, then. Ain't no reason for you to hang around a dump like this."

"It's not a dump!" she exclaimed. "It's just…a little tired."

But Domenico, picking up on the real problem, said, "My home's in Sardinia, Cal, and yes, we'll live there some of the time, but this is Arlene's home and marrying me doesn't mean she has to give it up."

"We've talked about it, and we're hoping you'll take charge of things here when we're away," Arlene added.

"We understand you'll need help getting the land back into shape, and exactly who you hire is your choice," Domenico continued, "but you're experienced enough to know you're facing a mammoth task if you want to plant in the spring."

"And since you can't be in two places at once, we think it

might be a good idea if you hire someone to take care of the household chores." Arlene looked at him questioningly. "A couple, perhaps? A woman who'll do the cooking and cleaning, and a man to tend the garden in summer, shovel snow and chop wood in winter. That kind of thing."

"I'm pretty set in my ways. Don't know as I'd want strangers underfoot all the time." Cal scratched his chin thoughtfully. "I could ask my sister, though. She still lives on the Niagara Peninsula where we grew up, but she's a widow and it's been pretty lonely for her, the last few years, seein' as she never had kids and there's no one left in the family but me."

"Do you think she'd move out here?"

"Don't see why not. Ain't nothin' keeping her there. And it'd be a shame to let the house go, after all the work you've done to make it look nice."

"We'd cover the cost of the move, of course," Domenico said, "and pay her a decent salary, just as we will you."

Cal shuffled uncomfortably in his seat. "It ain't got nothing to do with money. That's not why I stuck around here all this time."

"I know that," Domenico said, "But a man deserves recognition for his loyalty, and Arlene is trusting you to look after her interests while she's away."

"But you're more than an employee to me, Cal," Arlene was quick to add. "You're my family, and that brings me to something else I wanted to ask you. Will you walk me down the aisle on my wedding day?"

He stared at her a moment. "You don't want me, missy. I'm not posh like you. Never have been, never will be."

"It's you or nobody—and I'm going to need a strong arm to lean on."

He pulled a red checkered handkerchief out of his jeans

pocket and blew his nose. "You'll be wantin' them dogs to be bridesmaids, next."

"That hadn't occurred to me," she said, laughing. "But now that you mention it…! So what do you say, Cal? Can I count on you to be there for me?"

"Have I ever let you down?"

"Not once. I'd never have made it this far, if it hadn't been for you."

"Do I have to wear a monkey suit?"

"If I do, you do," Domenico said, with a grin.

"Where's this shindig taking place?"

Arlene was about to say they hadn't decided, but Domenico jumped in before she could speak. "Here. A bride should always be married from her own home."

"Goin' to be a pretty small wedding, then. She don't know anybody in these parts, except me."

"Well, we haven't drawn up a guest list, but my family will certainly attend, and there were twenty-three of them at the last count, although it'll probably be twenty-four by the new year."

"Spend a lot of time making babies, do they?"

"Among other things, yes."

"You plan on doing the same?"

Domenico looked at her, his glance so warm and intimate that she blushed again. "As many as Arlene wants."

"At least two," she said. "As for guests, I *do* have friends, Cal. They just happen to live too far away to visit, but I'm sure they'll come for my wedding. I hope your sister will, too. In fact, why don't you phone her this morning and sound her out on the idea of moving here?"

"Invite her for Christmas," Domenico suggested. "Give her the chance to look around the place and see what she'd be letting herself in for."

Arlene shook her head. "It's December 23. She'll never get a flight at such short notice."

"My jet's sitting on the runway, not forty kilometres away, *cara*. My pilot will have her here in time for Christmas Eve, if she chooses."

"But won't you be using the jet yourself?"

"Today. For a little while."

"More than just a little while, surely?" she said, stifling the disappointment welling up at the thought of his leaving again so soon. "It's a long way from here to Sardinia."

He raised her hand to his lips. "Who said anything about Sardinia? I'm spending Christmas with you, my love. And if it weren't that they've already made plans, I'd have my family join us. They're not used to this kind of weather, and the children would so much enjoy the snow. But there's always next year." He turned again to Cal. "Make that phone call, Cal."

"Thank you, Domenico," Arlene murmured, after Cal left the room. "I hadn't realized the impact our news would have on him—that he'd feel so…displaced. Thank you for putting his mind at ease."

"He's a good man, and I'll always be grateful to him for being here when you needed him." He pushed back his chair and dropped a kiss on her mouth. "Much though I'd rather spend the rest of the morning with you, I have to head out to the airport to take care of a little business, but I should be back no later than two or three o'clock."

"Drive carefully."

"Always," he said, and kissed her again. "I have far too much to lose, to do otherwise."

During the hours he was gone, Arlene first phoned Gail with her news and asked her to be her maid of honor, to which her friend gleefully agreed. Then, with Cal's sister, Thelma, having reluctantly agreed to spend the holiday with them, but only after much persuasion and her insistence on supplying homemade plum pudding, fruitcake and shortbread, Arlene made a run into town.

Overnight, her solitary Christmas for two had doubled to a festive four, and the roasting chicken she'd originally planned to serve wouldn't be enough. She stocked up on steaks for that night's dinner, as well as a ham, a turkey and a few other essentials to see them through the next few days.

Then, with time still hanging heavy on her hands, she went in search of a gift for her guests. She bought a lambswool scarf and bath oil for Thelma, but finding something for Domenico, the man who had everything, proved more difficult. Finally, she settled on a pair of fur-lined leather gloves, and promised herself she'd do better next year.

After lunch, she prepared a guest room for Thelma, making up the bed with freshly ironed sheets, and leaving a couple of magazines on the night table. She hung thick towels in the second bathroom, and put a basket of toiletries on the vanity.

When two o'clock came and still no sign of Domenico, she kept anxiety at bay by baking an apple pie, and preparing stuffed mushrooms and a salad to go with the steaks. She polished a pair of glass candlesticks until they sparkled like crystal, and centered them on the dining table with white candles and the scarlet poinsettia she'd bought in town.

At three-thirty, Domenico finally returned. "I was worried," she said, flying into his arms. "I thought you'd changed your mind about coming back."

"Not a chance," he assured her. "No matter where you happen to be, *tesoro*, I will always find my way back to you.

Now put on a warm jacket and a pair of winter boots, and show me your garden. It is a picture such as I'm not accustomed to seeing."

They took the dogs and walked down by the lake. The air was crisp and scented with woodsmoke; a Christmas card scene, with the water frozen to a sheen, the sky a pale, cloudless winter blue and the trees draped in snow.

"I'll miss them," Arlene said, watching as Sam and Sadie raced along the shore, sleek and swift under their faded plaid coats. "They've been such a comfort to me."

"Would you like to take them to Sardinia?"

"No, they're Cal's dogs. They belong here with him."

"You'll come back and see them often," he said, pulling her to a stop near an outcropping of rock. "In the meantime, I have something for you that might take your mind off leaving them. Consider it a promise for the future. Take off your gloves, my love."

He withdrew from his pocket a watered silk jeweler's box and opened it to reveal a solitaire diamond ring set in platinum. The fire of its many facets dazzled her. Magnificent in its classic simplicity, it left her breathless. "Where did you get it?" she gasped.

"In Vancouver. I phoned ahead to a jeweler I know of, and flew there this morning to select exactly the right engagement ring. I chose a round brilliant," he continued, slipping it on her finger, "because I knew it would look perfect on your hand. What do you think?"

She shook her head, at a loss. Where were the words to describe not just the style and quality of the gem, but the man who'd gone to so much trouble to buy it for her? "It's the most beautiful thing I've ever seen and gives me a reason to take better care of my nails from now on. You overwhelm me,

Domenico." Then, thinking of the leather gloves she'd bought for him, she grimaced. "But I don't have anything to give you that comes close to matching it."

"Are you happy?"

She drew his head down and brought her mouth to his. "Perfectly!"

"That's all the gift I need."

"So happy, I'm almost afraid."

"Don't be," he said, feathering kisses along over her eyelids and down her nose. "We deserve this, Arlene, my love."

A shout from the house intruded on the moment and, looking up, they saw Cal waving and gesturing from the back door. "Something about a phone call for you, I think," Domenico said, straining to hear. "It must be important that he's calling out like that. Go ahead and see what's the matter, *cara*, and I'll get the dogs."

Slipping and sliding up the steep path, she hurried back. "What is it?" she panted, when she reached the house.

"That doctor you saw the other day just phoned," Cal said soberly. "Claims it's important you call him back before the clinic closes, seeing as how today's the last day it's open until after Christmas."

A sliver of fear pierced her bliss. Spread like poison through her body, erasing all the light and joy and leaving nothing but darkness behind. She'd been too happy. Taken too much for granted. And this was her punishment. "Oh, Cal!"

He pressed a scrap of paper into her hand. "This here's the number, missy. Better get to it and find out what's going on."

Peeling off her coat, she closeted herself in the little office off the hall and almost fell into the chair behind the desk. Her hand trembled so badly, she had to punch in the numbers twice before she made the connection, then waited an interminable thirty seconds before the nurse-receptionist put her call through.

Finally the doctor came on the line. "Your blood tests came back, Arlene," he said.

"I see." Her voice sounded high, unnatural, almost shrill. "Is there something wrong?"

"That depends."

Her heart plummeted in her chest, so close to losing its moorings that she felt sick to her stomach. Just when paradise was within her grasp, fate was stepping in to snatch it away again. "I don't know what that means."

"Among others, the lab ran a quantitative pregnancy blood test. Your results show a high hCG count—Human Chorionic Gonadotropin. The pregnancy hormone, in layman's terms."

She dropped the phone. It hit the desk with a clatter and slithered onto her lap. Fumbling, she picked it up again. "Are you still there?" she heard him ask.

"Yes." She drew in a steadying breath. "Doctor, are you telling me I'm pregnant?"

"According to what I'm looking at here, very definitely. Didn't you suspect?"

"No," she said. "Not for a moment."

"When was your last menstrual period?"

She thought back, trying to remember. So much had happened in the last two months. "I'm not sure, although now that I think about it, I guess it must have been at the beginning of November."

"About eight weeks, then. That sounds about right. And you've shown no symptoms? No nausea, nothing like that?"

"Not really, no. As I mentioned when I came to see you, I've felt more tired than usual lately, but I put that down to overwork."

"Then I suggest you delegate for the next few months and

start taking it easy. You're showing a nice healthy level of hCG, but it doesn't pay to take unnecessary chances, especially during the first trimester." He paused, then asked, "Should I be congratulating you, Arlene, or is this not good news?"

"Its...*amazing* news! Congratulations are definitely in order. But I don't understand why it was so urgent that I return your call this quickly. Are you quite certain there's nothing wrong?"

"Well, we'll schedule you for a complete checkup after the holidays, just to be sure, although I'm pretty confident everything's in order. But the party season's upon us and I wanted to give you a heads-up on alcohol. It doesn't mix well with pregnancy."

"Oh!" she said. "No, of course not."

"That's it, then. Nothing else to worry about. I'll see you next week. In the meantime, Merry Christmas!"

"You, too," she replied and, hanging up the phone, sat a moment, catching her breath and trying to wrap her mind around the news.

She was expecting a baby. Domenico's baby. And she knew exactly when she'd conceived. The only time they hadn't used protection had been in Paris on the Friday, when she'd lured Domenico back to bed in the middle of the night.

She cupped her hands over her abdomen. His baby was growing in there. All the time she'd been crying over him, reviling him, missing him, his baby had grown limbs and fingers and toes. It had ears and a dot of a nose, and if it mattered at all, a test could probably determine whether it was a girl or a boy. How could she not have known?

Still trembling, she pushed away from the desk and went to the door. Opening it, she found Domenico and Cal stationed in the hall, waiting for her. Cal appeared haggard. Domenico's blue eyes had a bruised and hurting look to them.

He rushed forward. Gripped her arm and led her into the living room, with Cal shuffling along behind. "Tell us," he said, wrapping his arms around her. "We'll deal with it together, Arlene. The best doctors, the best treatment—whatever it takes, it's yours."

Oh, she was cruel! "Well," she said, drawing out the word until she thought Cal might smack her, "there's really not much that anyone can do to change the way things are. But I do have a Christmas gift for you, Domenico, that more or less puts your lovely diamond in the shade. But it won't be ready for a few months yet."

She stopped and smiled sweetly at both of them. "I'm pregnant."

"The hell you are!" Cal exploded, and fell into an armchair.

Domenico turned positively glassy-eyed. "Pregnant?"

"Yes," she said. "That means I'm having your baby. Sometime in August, I believe. I'll be able to give you a more accurate date after I see the doctor, next week."

Then, because she was brimming over with more happiness than any one body could hope to contain, she started to laugh. "We're having a baby, Domenico!" she chortled. "And you, Cal, you're going to be a granddaddy!"

The next minute she was sobbing in Domenico's arms and he was whispering in her ear, thanking her, and telling her that he loved her and treasured her more than anything on earth.

The dogs picked up on the excitement and started barking. And Cal began to cry.

It took about ten minutes for everyone to settle down, although, Arlene thought, things would never be the same again, and nor would she want them to be. From that point on, they could only get better.

Domenico produced a magnum of champagne he'd brought

back from Vancouver and poured a glass for Cal and himself. Cal found a bottle of sparkling grapefruit juice for Arlene. The lights on the Christmas tree sparkled in the dusk. The flames burned yellow and orange in the hearth. Outside, the snow began to fall again.

Domenico pulled Arlene close and curved a possessive arm around her waist. "To the future," he said, raising his glass. "To a new year, a wedding, and most of all to the woman who's given my life new and very real meaning. To you, Arlene, my darling one. I thank you from the bottom of my heart for trusting me to become the husband you deserve. I love you and I promise you now, with Cal as my witness, that I will treasure you for the rest of my life."

Her heart overflowing, Arlene lifted her face for his kiss. She was home at last, with the only man in the world she'd ever love.

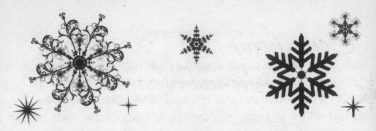

Wrap up warm this winter with Sarah Morgan...

Sleigh Bells in the Snow

Kayla Green loves business and hates Christmas.

So when Jackson O'Neil invites her to Snow Crystal Resort to discuss their business proposal... the last thing she's expecting is to stay for Christmas dinner. As the snowflakes continue to fall, will the woman who doesn't believe in the magic of Christmas finally fall under its spell...?

4th October

www.millsandboon.co.uk/sarahmorgan

Come home this Christmas to Fiona Harper

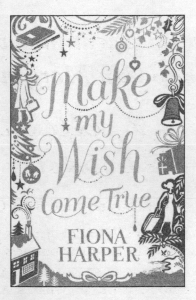

From the author of *Kiss Me Under the Mistletoe* comes a
Christmas tale of family and fun. Two sisters are ready
to swap their Christmases—the busy super-mum, Juliet,
getting the chance to escape it all on an exotic Christmas
getaway, whilst her glamorous work-obsessed sister,
Gemma, is plunged headfirst into the family Christmas
she always thought she'd hate.

www.millsandboon.co.uk